The Milky Way

{Bel Tra Chart Pack XVII}

Drenard

☆ ?

Lok

Palan

Glemot   ☆ ?   Dakura

Darrin

Canopus   Menkar

Sol

20K LY

100,000 Light Years

molly fyde

fyde

and the fight for peace

THE

BERN SAGA:

BOOK 4

by hugh howey

Molly Fyde
and the fight for peace

Copyright © 2013 by Hugh Howey

ISBN: 1481222953
ISBN-13: 9781481222952
www.hughhowey.com
Give feedback on the book at:
hughhowey@hotmail.com
Second Edition

Cover art by Jasper Schreurs

Printed in the U.S.A.

A Poem of Madness

Five links stand out in the chain that binds our will.
There are the primal urges, wound tight in nucleotidal strands.
There's the faith that surges through our clasped and supersti-
tious hands.
There are the politics of kings and queens, and their many rules.
There's culture, which forms mobs of motley fools.
Last come our decisions, stacked
up in piles of regret
that we long
to forget.
These five links stand out in the chain that binds our will.
They hold us, guide us, coerce us—
And we rattle them still.

~The Bern Seer~

0

**THE RAPE OF THE
CANYON QUEEN**

The cave hollows thundered with the Wadi's coming.
The great pads of her feet shuddered the rock as
claws the size of a lesser Wadi's tail met the walls
of her cave with the crack of shattered stone. When the
Canyon Queen moved, the world knew. For in her old
age, the great Wadi had done more than forget how
to scamper soft and slow—she had outgrown the *need*.

She came to a stop before one of the great watering
shafts, the circumference of the black well wider than
the span of her old birth canyon. The Canyon Queen
bent her thick neck and drank from the condensation

rushing out of side holes and gurgling down the deep shaft. She drank her fill, leaped across the gaping void, and continued her loud passage through the rock. As she bounded forward, her scent tongue picked up the vaporous trails of fear and haste from those scattering before her. None had ever grown to the Canyon Queen's size, not that any alive could remember. And nobody knew what to do about it but stay out of her way.

The massive Wadi took the last turn in her vast warren, and the round maw of light at its termination came into view. She loped toward it, reaching out with powerful limbs, gripping marble with her claws, pulling herself along in an ecstatic release of energy. She ran with the dizzying might of a thing unopposed and for the pure thrill of it.

At the end of the shaft, she paused to read the air beyond. The wind outside was, as always, a turbulent mess. Her home was situated on the brightest point of them all, where the two great lights stood directly overhead and rarely cast a shadow. It was a very long way from where the Canyon Queen was born—way around where the canyons squeezed tight, where the Wadi holes dwindled to the size of her claw, and where the winds blew strong and steady in the same direction.

Far enough around that way, just past her birth canyon, a Wadi could escape the light altogether, reaching a flat land of complete shade. The Canyon Queen knew. She knew a Wadi could scamper out into a world of solid cave-dark spoiled only by the shimmering glimmer caused by the two lights over the horizon. She knew such a place existed, where there were no canyons and no watering shafts, and Wadi would freeze if they stayed too long. She knew of such a place but now lived as far from there as possible. So far—so very far into the light—that she frequently struggled to remember how she had arrived.

The great Wadi tasted the swirling, raucous air outside her warren and tried to sink claws into that long-ago past, remembering.

oooo

Where have you been?

The young Wadi flew in agitated circles around the small cave. Dust drifted from the roof, caught in the light from the tunnel's entrance like a veil of worry. She exuded the same mixture of scents over and over: *Where have you been? Wherehaveyoubeen?*

Her mate-pair staggered into the cave to join her, his body finally catching up to the scent of his arrival. He rubbed against her, scales scratching scales, but the young Wadi pulled back, leaving room for an answer. *Where have you been? Wherehaveyoubeen?*

Her mate-pair had been missing for three sleeps, his scents trailing off to a sad nothing. Now he was back, but his smells were agitated and impossible to read. *Wherehaveyoubeen?*

Water.

That single concept pierced the noisy smells, making itself clear in the young Wadi's mind. She danced back and followed the cave's turns to their shaft of meager drippings, leading the way. She tasted her mate-pair following close behind. Her brain reeled with the days of sadness mixed with the new joy of his return, all of it jumbled with the confusion of why he'd left and where he'd been. She reached their craggy hole of condensation and rushed to the far side. Her mate-pair leaped eagerly to the drippings. He drank and exuded his story:

Dark, he scented. *Dark and cold. A walk so far the two lights burrow into the rock itself and the land erupts with color.*

Her mate-pair seemed to have lost his mind. The young Wadi licked the air, making sure she tasted it properly, wondering if perhaps he had spent three days chin-up to the two lights, roasting his brain.

Where did you go? She couldn't stop exuding it.

Her mate-pair continued to drink what little water was there. The young Wadi looked over her shoulder, wondering if they would have to break a truce and fight for a bigger stream—

The blue hunters.

The image of large beasts on two legs flashed through her mind, scattering the rest.

The blue hunters came while you slept, a long file of them wrapped in their single silver scale covering all but their faces.

The young Wadi silenced her own worries and latched on to the stream of smells. She bent her head close to her mate-pair's and breathed in every molecule lest some drift off to waste.

They took eggs from the shafts across the canyon. I followed even bigger hunters deeper while you slept. They took one of the mate-pairs we fought with last season—

Took?

The Wadi couldn't help the interruption. Her body felt full to bursting with a thousand smells to release. Her mate-pair stopped his futile licking on the now-dry rock. He gazed at her, the blacks of his eyes wide in order to see in the dark. Or wider than even that, she saw. They were wide with fear.

They came with silver claws as long as their bodies, claws that could reach in warrens and pull out Wadi and their eggs. I watched them from an abandoned shaft as they crept along in the shadows. One blue hunter came and looked in after me. I could see his long claw, but it was no longer shiny. Wadi blood covered it, and a body hung there, pierced through its belly.

The young Wadi bobbed her head, trying to make sense of the images. Smells of the blue hunters had drifted through the canyons before, and some of the older Wadi—those who came back to lay their eggs—would leak such thoughts at times, but they were always like ghost memories, nothing as vibrant and real and immediate as this.

What did you do?

I ran. I went deep in the caves, treading all over rock scented as someone else's. I didn't care. For all I knew, that someone else was gone, their body hanging on a claw. I ran until my brain cleared and I remembered you.

I was still sleeping?

It happened so fast. I came back through the fought-for interior, but no one was fighting. All were running. All were agitated. I ran past watering holes like we'd dreamed of, past eggs left abandoned, past Wadi twice my size and just as full of fear. I picked up your sleeping scent and came back to warn you. I was just around the bend when I heard the claw call.

Claw call? The young Wadi weaved her head around the scent, trying to make sense of its newness.

An urge to defend. To fight as one. I didn't know it either, but it seized me. It was one of the elder females, one of the dwindling come back to lay her eggs.

She wasn't dead yet?

Her mate-pair tapped his claws on the rock. *Close,* he scented. *Very close. She had just laid her eggs and was feeding them. She told us. She commanded us to save them. My head was full of pictures of small blue hunters clutching her unborn babies. Her rage became mine, her scents my inner thoughts. I had no defenses—*

A flood of *sorry* drowned out what her mate-pair was saying. He exuded a week's supply of begging forgiveness, of shame and self-pity. It hung like a black fog in the tunnel, obscuring all else. The young Wadi scampered up the wall and around the watering hole; she nestled against her mate-pair, oozing all the acceptance and soothing she could. Her bright cloud of scent soon dispelled his darker other, and she remembered why this was her mate-pair. He and no other.

I had no defenses, he oozed again. *I joined with the bigger Wadi, and we gave chase. We followed the blue hunters into the winds and away from the twin lights. There were attacks, which brought bigger hunters with claws that shot lightning a million paces and with such precision—*

Images of charred Wadi, of twitching limbs, of fighting and the dead—they flitted through the young Wadi's mind. She saw elder blue hunters coming to the rescue of the younger ones. She saw that this was some sick ritual, something they did often and in different places. This new danger danced in her vision, scaring her and mocking her at once.

My cowardliness saved me, her mate-pair scented.

The thought wafted away during a lull in the smells.

My cowardliness saved me. It had more might than the rage driving me along, the rage from this old female and her stolen eggs. Or maybe the two had the same might, because I couldn't return to you either. I was left following the eggs, wanting to retrieve them, but not knowing how. I had dreams of bringing them back and hatching them as my own. As if they were yours—

The young Wadi nestled closer to her mate-pair. *We'll have eggs enough*, she wanted to scent him, but didn't.

I followed them until the two lights sank beneath the rock and all became one great shadow. I followed them until the borrowed rage of the claw call melted from my bones and I felt, at last, how impossibly weary they were. I collapsed. I watched the blue hunters shrink across the black flatness, merging with so many other hunters in a bright, shiny warren that sat high on the ground. I lay on the cold rock and smelled nothing but death carried on the winds between me and these hunters. Death and alien excitement, our misery laced with their hope. It was awful. It was—

She pressed her scales close to her mate-pair and exuded calm and peace. The horror of his ordeal was so clear in her mind. Of all the terrible dreams of where her mate-pair had been for the last three sleeps, none compared to this.

I went in and out of sleeps so often, I lost track of time. My dreams were punctuated by alien scents, my mind filled with their jubilation and celebrations. The scents dissipated for some time, and then new ones returned. Images of more blue hunters filled me, tormenting me as I lay dying. I wanted them to come and take me, to put an end to it, but then I kept thinking of you, back here and all alone.

The young Wadi tensed; she looked through the darkness and searched for some sign of the hunters, of their coming. Her mate-pair picked up on the thoughts.

No, he scented her, *I staggered back to our canyon, their smells and the wind pushing me along, but they were not to follow. There are far more canyons than you can dream of. These new hunters chose to go down another—*

But for how long? she wanted to know. *How long before they return?*

Many sleeps, I hope.

We need to move away from this black place, she scented him.

When we're bigger, we will.

The Wadi slapped at the dry watering hole, her claws clicking with a hollow, fragile sound. *Grow bigger on this?*

She hated herself for scenting it. She hated the still air it brought between them. She scratched her mate-pair's scales and added to his fog of sorry.

He nuzzled her back, then scented: *When we're bigger, the eggs will come.*

What? What did he mean?

The female who lost her eggs, the dwindling elder, our minds became as one when her rage flooded inside me. I saw the story of her eggs—she showed us why they were worth saving. She had journeyed deep along the winds many thousands of sleeps ago, growing bigger as the caves grew. There were visions of her mate-pair, of her with eggs in her belly, of her body shrinking as she fed them, of a dangerous journey back to the cool hatching rocks where we were born, of her mate-pair dead from defending her—

Dead? The young Wadi nuzzled closer, her brain reeling from the shared experiences flashing through her mind.

Dead, but ready to live on in those eggs, to pass along all her scents and memories. Oh, but if not for my cowardice—

I'm glad of it, the young Wadi scented. *I don't want you dead.*

It's the way of the eggs, he scented her.

Then it's good we aren't having any.

We'll have them when we get bigger. Twice or triple our size now, and we'll be having them and fighting our way back here for the hatching.

Then we won't get bigger, the young Wadi said.

But if the hunters come again—?

She rubbed her scales against his, could feel his trembling weakness still skittering through his bones, his heart racing and light from his ordeal.

We'll claw through that canyon when we get to it, she scented. *For now, relax. Relax, and then we'll move from this darkness and claim a better watering shaft.*

Better shafts quickly became bigger shafts, and the two Wadi grew right along with them. It had been difficult to spot the changes at the time, since everything had enlarged together. Neighboring Wadi, their own claws, each other, the sizes of their ever-changing warrens, everything had grown as they made their way along the winds.

Suddenly, the Canyon Queen could remember it well. Her scent tongue probed the recesses of her mouth and tasted the myriad molecules lodged there over thousands of sleeps of forgetting. She looked down at her massive claws, each of them as big now as her entire *body* had been when she'd lost him.

She pressed one of her claws into the solid rock and watched the marble crack and splinter under the pressure. She had a sudden impulse to smash the weakened marble with her balled hand, breaking stone, or self, or both. She gripped the tunnel's edge instead and tasted the winds of the past for more memories.

She wasn't sure why she needed to dwell on it. Why now, with the tunnels not able to get bigger, would she think on smaller times? Perhaps she longed for a return to that far-gone ago. Perhaps her reign as the Canyon Queen had lasted longer than a mind could take. Or maybe it was her way of avoiding the conspiracy swirling on the winds around her—the quiet scheming of the large pack of male Wadi banding together to do at once what no single male had done for thousands and thousands of sleeps . . .

o o o o

Not here.

Why? The male Wadi craned his neck around and looked to the circle of light at the tunnel's entrance. The drippings from no less than three watering holes could be heard simultaneously, and the echoes of several deep interconnected passages swallowed his claw clicks with ease.

Is it not perfect? he scented.

The young Wadi flicked her scent tongue out. *It reeks of death*, she complained.

All these canyons reek of death.

But this is recent. Bad things happened here. I can almost see them.

The male Wadi tried his best to smell these things, but his mate-pair's tongue must've been a thousand times keener than his own. He noted the tinge of spilled blood, but he felt certain he could tease that odor out of any of the rock they'd covered for the past hundreds of sleeps. It was everywhere, which surely made this warren as good as any.

At least for the night, he scented softly. *Let's drink and stay one night.*

He meant to suggest *other* things as well, but it was hard to know if those yearnings drifted on the winds or stayed welled up inside him.

The one night, his mate-pair relented, and there was the smell of some exotic sweetness wrapped up in her thoughts that seemed to suggest other sorts of relenting. The male Wadi soaked his tongue in the hints, his body tingling with a love and joy made weary during their long jaunt to wider canyons. Made weary, but somehow made much deeper.

Rest here, he scented. *I'll get water for us both.*

Water and a secret surprise, he added to himself.

He ran back through their new warren to the largest of the three shafts, the one that held a steady drip. In this place, cooler air rising up from the bowels of the earth collected as beads of water on the rock above. It ran down, chill and clear, rubbing indentions into the wall of the shaft. The Wadi stuck his snout below the lip and sniffed deep. The solid food-treats of rock sliders could be smelled below. The Wadi tested his claws on the edge of the watering shaft, found they bit deep enough, and so he scampered over the edge and down.

A cold upwell of air surrounded him, the moist walls reflecting the chill deep into his bones. The Wadi dove farther, crossing another tunnel that smelled occupied, and then another under dispute, and suddenly he was below the canyon floor, deep enough to escape the comforting warmth of the sunlit rock above.

He had been down past the Wadi warrens only once before, and quite by accident. The treats he had discovered and brought back had pleased his mate-pair to no end, but she had never let him risk a return trip. Now, though, with the potential of making her with eggs, he thought the gesture was worth the cold. Especially for the nourishment it might bring their brood.

The sudden slip of a claw returned the Wadi's focus on the climb. He was far enough from the light for his eyes to be blinded, leaving just his wagging tongue to show him the way. The cold already made his joints stiff, and his heart raced to keep his insides warm and moving. He knew from that long-ago day of giving the blue hunters chase—and also from his near-dying fall below the canyon floor—that the cold was a danger. The key was to move fast and full of purpose, to *know* he was going to survive the ordeal. He had never known that before and had gotten lucky. *This* time, he would be swift and knowing. He would grab just a few.

The shaft twisted near the bottom, curving flat before jogging to one side. The Wadi kept to the roof of the tunnel, keeping out of the flow of gathering water. He released a soft trail of scent behind to mark the way out.

The crackle of rock sliders could be heard ahead of him. He tasted the air, took a turn, and then dove back down as the shaft deepened. There were more sliders farther in the shaft, but he wouldn't be greedy. He flexed his fingers, shaking the cold out of his joints. The numbness was already in the tip of his tail and growing toward his legs. He hoped his mate-pair wouldn't worry—

There! Two sliders, maybe three, clacking back and forth.

The dead husks of the small, black creatures were often found in the lowest warrens. The male Wadi had sniffed from neighbors that they were known to clean the skeletons of dead Wadi. They had certainly seemed intent on doing something like that when he had fallen into their midst many sleeps ago. The eating, however, had eventually gone the *other* way around, as the rock sliders proved to be tasty morsels once their teeth had been removed from his hide.

The Wadi crept forward, balancing haste with the need to be silent. He clung to the ceiling and crawled out over the gathered bugs, homing in on their scents and persistent clicks. He readied himself with courage smells, ignoring the cold swelling in his bones. Before he could reconsider, he released his grip, spun in the air, and fell claws-down across the small creatures.

The rock sliders erupted in a mix of hiss and clack, their little teeth buzzing within their hard, shiny shells. Two of them bit into the Wadi's belly and held tight. A third attempted to flee, but the Wadi slapped it with his hand and brought it close. He moved it near his soft belly until the rock slider's teeth sank deep.

He had them. Or *they* had *him*. Either way, it didn't matter—he knew from experience that the buggers wouldn't let go. With claws he could barely feel and muscles stiff with chill, he turned and ran back through the deep tunnel, following his scent trail around and up, running and scampering until the smell of his mate-pair began to intermingle with his own harried scents.

○ ○ ○ ○

Where did you go?

The young Wadi forced herself to scent the question calmly. Her mate-pair had dashed off amid a dizzying cloud of fondness and returned cold and trembling. He responded to her question by rolling to his back and reaching for the black critters—each one as big as his fist and attached to his belly.

Why? Whywhywhy?

She reached for one of the rock sliders and wrapped two sets of claws around it; her mate pair was leaking a bit of blood around the creature's bite. With a loud crunch, she broke the shell of the thing, forcing it to let go. She reached for another while her mate-pair worked to extricate the third.

For you, he was scenting.

Silly, silly Wadi.

She couldn't help but release the thought. The last two bugs came free with the pop of their shells. In the dim light of the tunnel entrance, she could see the rows of tiny holes in her mate-pair's flesh, all leaking the barest amounts of blood. It was all too often that his behavior confused her, and just as often that she found herself drawn closer to something she couldn't understand.

They're for tonight, he scented. *They're for our eggs.*

The young Wadi shivered as soon as the thoughts tickled her tongue. She forgot the dying rock sliders and pressed herself against her mate-pair. She forgot the scent of death hanging in their temporary home and rubbed her scales against his. She forgot the blood on him, the need for water, the need to remain aware, and just lost herself in the yielding. In the pleasure—

What was that?

She froze. The shivering cold in her mate-pair had subsided, but she could still feel the chill in his bones. She sniffed the air, but didn't quite smell—

There!

What is it? she scented, masking the ire at the moment's interruption.

Something is coming, her mate-pair scented. *Something—*

But he didn't finish the smell. The thought remained, half-formed and drifting, masked by the terrible odor of death come among them, the ripe and powerful stench of their warren's owner preceded by a whiff of his foul thirst for blood. Both odor and Wadi were heading their way, blazing down the freshly scented trail her mate-pair had left in tiny, wet, crimson paw prints.

Run!

They both scented out a cloud of it. A cloud of scampering to safety so thick, it was hard to tell where one of their thoughts ended and the other's began. The ideas swirled into one nasty vision of darting ever deeper into the growing and more dangerous canyons.

A surge of pure fright coursed up the young Wadi's back from the tip of her tail to the base of her neck. The scent of death and aggression that billowed up after them was not new. Twice before they had taken up residence in another's warren, and twice they had escaped by the width of a claw.

She ran, legs stretching to their fullest. She reached ahead for the rock, dug in her claws, and pulled herself along. She took turns at random, as her fear and racing mind dictated. She passed watering holes and occupancy smells and dreams of someone else's eggs. She flew through all the scents, chased as she was by an explosion of rage, of black thoughts so frightening and thick, they threatened to drown out all else.

They even smothered the fact that she was now running *alone*.

The Wadi stopped. She peered through the darkness behind her, searching for her love, for his moving dull brightness amid the black. She sniffed the air for her mate-pair, but his trail had thinned to nothing.

A new fear grew inside: a hollow powerfulness that threatened to consume her, an untarnished dread as bright and vivid as any emotion she'd ever scented. She teased apart the constituent molecules, trying to understand this novel horror—

It was the potential of being alone in the world, she realized.

The young Wadi turned and raced back along her route, following her trail of fear and sniffing for her mate-pair. She scrambled back through the egg-dreams and occupancy odors and over the watering holes. She hurried back toward the smell of death, a smell that had—

The Wadi came to a stop. She shivered uncontrollably.

A smell that had—

She opened her mouth and wailed into the dark tunnel, emitting a scream to outrace her thoughts. She dug her claws into the rock and threw her chest into the mad cry, allowing it to echo through the stone and race down the tunnel. She yelled and yelled to drown out the smell, a smell of death that had grown *stronger*. More vivid.

And more achingly familiar.

The Canyon Queen stood frozen by the mouth of her warren, her eyes moistened with old memories. There were some days when the long-ago seemed but a sleep or two away, when her scent tongue could probe her memory sacks and conjure visions as fresh and bright as the view of the suns-lit canyon before her. There were other times when the noise of so many smells from other Wadi made it hard to tease out what had happened in *her* lifetime and what were the latent memories of all those around her.

She forced her great muscles to relax as she sniffed the cloud of nostalgia for the brighter trails: trails of companionship, of longing and loving, of egg-dreams and playful scampering. It was these recollections, drawn out every so often, that had kept her going through the thousands and thousands of sleeps after his death. They had kept her wary of taking a new mate-pair. They had given her the strength to push ever deeper into the canyons, bringing those twin lights higher and higher, the shadows shallower and shallower. Those good memories had done much over the sleeps. They had even helped her do bad things. Helped her kill. Helped her survive. Helped her grow bigger and stronger than any Wadi in all the memories stirring on the winds.

And she would keep growing, she knew, as long as she never took a mate-pair. As long as she stayed eggless, with nothing to feed, nothing to grow outside of her, she would grow and grow until—

But even she didn't know.

She sniffed the air, hoping for answers, but the bright fog of her past still lingered and occluded the thoughts beyond. Her warren, situated as it was directly below the twin lights, was an area to which answers tended to drift. It placed her at the center of what she now knew to be a half-lit sphere, a world that went all the way around. That was one of the many answers that had drifted to her on the breeze. Another was where the wind came from—or more precisely, where it went. The hot air directly over her warren was always surging up, taking her thoughts and the thoughts of a billion Wadi with it. The wind rushed from all around her egg-shaped world, pushing toward her warren and away from the cold and dark before rising up toward the great twin lights. Somehow, those lights sucked and sucked at the air and never breathed it out. They pulled the winds up with the heat, dragging the scents of billions with them as they passed.

And the Canyon Queen lived at the heart of it all. She had lived there for thousands and thousands of sleeps, sniffing the air with every spare moment, looking amid all the countless answers for the one that wouldn't show itself. The answer to her great and sorrowful: *Why?*

It was this vigilance that had kept her sane, had filled her with many *other* answers, and had kept her alive.

But it would be her current fog of deep rememberings, her thoughts of long ago, that would doom the great Wadi. For it was then, with her senses numbed by a cloud of recollections, that the band of males came with their schemings.

It was then that they came to rape their Queen.

○ ○ ○ ○

They arrived in a number higher than counting, a number not needed for any Wadi purposes and therefore a number without name. It was more than the biggest number the Canyon Queen had in her head—two or three or ten *times* that number. When the first rows stormed her warren, they brought with them the awful smell of their mad plans. They reeked of the many closing in behind. Gone were their odors of occupancy and territory. Gone was the male competition. They had banded together, their thoughts intermingling. They had become something new and terrible and fully worthy of her fear.

The Canyon Queen snapped the necks of a few, their male bodies as big as males got, no more than the size of her arm from elbow to claw. She could kill two or three at a time, one in each paw. A sharp squeeze, a snapping like brittle rock, a flood of death smells. But the waves of the living kept coming after.

Claws sank into her back. Teeth wrapped around one of her great ribs. The Canyon Queen shrieked, her skull ringing with the sound of her own voice, and everything seemed to pause for a moment, taken aback by the mighty roar.

And then it resumed.

The Queen threw her body into the rock, crunching the male on her ribs. She swiped her tail in the darkening confines of her warren, swishing a Wadi off her back, his claws raking her flesh as he went.

One of the Wadi moved to fill her with eggs. She felt a cold sensation, felt her thighs buckle, her knees clench to her chest, her tail tuck protectively. She roared again and spun around, meeting the wave of Wadi pouring in through the back of her warren. She kicked the male off her flank, her body convulsing as his egg-dreams invaded her nostrils. Her scent-tongue became useless for any other danger. It remained in its pouch, sullied and hidden, as the lights from the canyons were finally extinguished by the writhing masses pressing their way inside.

The Canyon Queen began to kill full-grown males with wild abandon, cracking them like so many rock sliders. She crushed them, and more appeared. Their bodies soon packed all around her, each victory bringing more confinement. No matter which direction she faced, there were those with egg-dreams attacking her flank, hoping to dwindle her with their insemination, hoping to drive her off to the shallow canyons where she'd grow her eggs and die.

Tiny claw after tiny claw bit into her flesh, the thousand small nicks merging into a web of fierce wounds. The queen slipped in her own blood. One of her legs became pinned beneath her. More Wadi pressed in—the Wadi of a thousand warrens, drawn together by some scent of desperation. They crowded her. They sank their claws and teeth and worse into her. They packed themselves between the walls and her cut and leaking body. They stirred and slithered through the jumbled mess of dead and dying, and they took their turns with her. They were violent and rough. Feral. Mad with their victory and with the stench of the dead all around them.

The great Wadi's head became buried under those she had killed. She was no longer able to unclench her paws to add to their number. She whimpered, barely able to breathe. Tears of pain squeezed out her eyes. She choked on the horrid stench of it all as the males filled her with their egg-dreams.

They filled her, and they clawed her.

And she was the Canyon Queen no more.

It's her.

Let her pass.

We should help.

Don't go near her.

The thoughts stirred through the canyon hollows and swirled around the Wadi, her body still laced with scars. She ignored them and drank from the watering hole. She drank until the rivulet ran dry, her powerful thirst refusing to step aside like all the thousands of Wadi she'd run past on her dwindling, egg-filled journey. Rumors of her coming and of her past ran upwind faster than she could travel. Legends were growing of the eggs she would lay. Legends she aimed to prove false.

That way. Take this turn.
Use my home, I beg.
My birth warren is best.

The directions and pleadings were scented in feeble tendrils, choked back by the shared and ancient fear of her. She ignored them all. Her body was dwindling, returning to its birth-state as it prepared to give new life, but she had no intention of seeing it through. Her physical self could waste away, but nothing would take the memories lodged in her mind—the trillions and trillions of scent molecules saved up over thousands of sleeps of looking for answers. There was one there—one answer stolen from the winds—that she had never appreciated until now. It was the tale of an eggless canyon, where something in the rock made females sterile, where few Wadi dared to live but many went to die.

And that's where the worn-out Wadi would go: to the canyon where the blue hunters never came, to the land of the crazed females who arrested their dwindling to live in solitude and sorrow. She would travel there before the eggs came. She would go mad there before her brood could come and take her awful memories as their own. That would be her revenge against the males who had raped her, who had done so many awful things, none of which were more hideous than allowing her to live.

The Wadi drank her fill, practically feeling herself shrink as she did so. She cursed the need to pack away energy, to store it in parasitic eggs that would one day hatch as she lay dying. She drank her fill and moved on, ignoring the whispered scents of those around her who pleaded with her to reconsider her plans even as they scurried out of her way.

○ ○ ○ ○

Many sleeps went by. The periods of walking between each sleep were just as dreamlike and hazy. The Wadi had lived two lifetimes before; this was her third. There was a lifetime of loving and growing, a lifetime of powerful surety and haunting questions and thin shadows, and now a lifetime of wasting away. It seemed to her that many of the things that had happened in the past must have happened to some Wadi else. The fresh pain had long ago become dull aches. The dull aches had long ago become stiffness in her bones. Her bones had long ago begun to feel brittle and weak, not capable of holding such aches and pains. She could remember bad things happening to her.

She tried to pretend they had happened to some Wadi else.

○ ○ ○ ○

When she arrived, the Wadi found the eggless canyon a stagnant place, a near-odorless place. She had to strain herself to scent the life in the adjoining canyons, as it was feeble even there. Occasionally, a whiff of normalcy would invade, of eggs laid and Wadi living, but the winds would carry them off just as quickly, leaving behind the nothingness she had traveled so far to find.

She was vastly smaller than her former queen-self. She knew this despite the matching warrens and canyons, which had shrunk along with her. She could feel it in the tightness of her being, in the sensation of an entire form packed into the size and hardness of a single claw.

Bending close to the rocks, she sniffed deep. The stone revealed traces of those who had come before her. Their old smells lingered longer than she thought possible, untrampled by the scents of the boisterous living.

She spent her first few sleeps teasing out stories from the past. Stories of hunters—not blue for some reason—stalking the lifeless canyon once an eon or so. She scented stories of sadness similar to her own, of Wadi without hope coming to a place where they could wither in peace. She sniffed deep from the cool rock, finding answers in the small, eggless place that had eluded her when she ruled all. She found more truth in that quiet sadness than she had uncovered in her days at the apex beneath the full glory of the twin lights. She found more in common with these *other* Wadi, her sisters in time, who had lost everything but their desire to remember and *be* remembered. Here was the land of the pair-less, of those whose bonds had grown so strong that when broken they could not be mended.

The answers finally came, and the Wadi knew she was home.

The poison in the rock soaked deep, slowing her descent into nothing.

They soaked deep, antidotes to the egg-dream poisons within her.

○ ○ ○ ○

It felt like many sleeps later that the hunters came, the ones of the occasional eons. They were not blue, like the tales of so many. Not blue like the story her mate-pair had told her. They were pungent with different smells: odors of confusion and fear.

She sniffed one hunter's progress as he went deep down the winds, his mind leaking thoughts of large Wadi dead, but leaking them with a thirst the old Wadi found sweet on her tongue. There were thoughts of a mate-pair in this hunter's mind. She sniffed him go deep into the canyons until his scent was gone. She did not welcome this intrusion of questions into her realm of answers.

More of the alien hunters came not long after. One smelled foul, his desires leaking like black smoke full of pilfered eggs. His trail came feeble but stark as it worked its way over from a neighboring canyon. The Wadi marveled at the lack of response from her brethren. Could they not smell this?

By the time they did, it was too late. Many canyons away, an egg was stolen. The black thoughts swirled with joy and ire.

The Wadi stirred, this intrusion shattering the sameness and ageless sleeps. She was moving to rouse those in her adjoining warrens when one of the not-blue hunters entered the eggless canyon. Columns of multi-hued thoughts snaked down the winds ahead of her, ahead of this frightened and weary hunter. The old Wadi scented them deep, confused not by the alien nature of the mind leaking them, but by the *familiarity*.

She left her watering hole and followed the smells of this hunter, tracing them through the porous rock. There was something in them that matched her long-ago life. Her *first* life. Something of hope and happy not-knowing. Something of excited fear, rather than the fear of dread. Something of passion, even if the molecules didn't quite fit her tongue's receptors. And then she knew what it was: it was the hunter's thoughts of a mate-pair that had the Wadi scampering from disused warren to disused warren. There was something in this alien's emanations that reminded the Wadi of *herself*. A long-ago self the males hadn't killed, had barely even clawed. A younger Wadi with an aching, hopeful heart.

She paused to drink from another hole, and that was when the odors changed. There was a fight. Wadi and alien fear mixed in the air as the two clashed. One of her mad, egg-less neighbors had been attracted to the same scent, that odor of hope and pure new bonding like an antidote to their poison. The hunter with the mate-pair thoughts became injured. Injured and running, the fear no longer excitement, but dread. The old Wadi ran through the tunnels as well, chasing that previous scent, that *good* scent, and trying to win it back.

She ran through warren after warren, her claws clacking the rock, her arms and legs growing weary. Thirst consumed her, but still she ran. She followed the mad dash of the hunter with the pure smells, now tinged with fright. She tried telling the creature to stop, to give up more of the memories, more of the long-ago.

And the hunter *did* stop, seeming to hear her pleas.

The hunter stopped and rested against the rock. There were pure thoughts again—the hunter was dripping with them. The Wadi crept closer, sniffing the thick emotions. She rounded a bend to find light filtering into the mouth of a tunnel. The canyon beyond was bright with the glow of the low twins and groaning with the wind passing through. The Wadi moved closer, and then something moved into the mouth of the tunnel. A white something, still and lifeless. The Wadi sniffed the air. She could smell the moisture in the thing, this ball of crumpled white, but more than that: she could smell the hunter's delicious thoughts. The white thing was laden with them. *Dripping* with them. Tempting and tasty and dangerously full of hope.

The Wadi laid out on the cool rock, her belly warm and quivering from the long run. She lay there and watched the white temptation, wondering what it would do.

Wondering what *she* would do.

PART XVII

ESCAPE

*"What good is the running,
with nothing to run to?"*

~The Bern Seer~

I
=
LOK

Three sets of landing struts settled to the packed soil of the Lokian forest, one of them squeaking slightly, in need of oil. Molly looked out through the carboglass where large shadows danced at the edge of a wooded clearing, the black puppets thrown high and wavering from the light of so many campfires. Her mother's voice continued to drone in her helmet's speakers, complaining and asking questions about Molly's refusal to jump to hyperspace. Molly pulled her helmet off and closed its visor, trapping her mom's voice inside the dented shell.

"I'm sorry," she whispered, apologizing for disappointing her mom and for not being able to explain herself. She placed her helmet on its rack and patted her Wadi as the colorful lizard settled across her shoulders.

Walter turned and faced her general direction from the nav chair. He still had his modified welding goggles on for the jump to hyperspace, which meant he was practically blind.

"But we're gonna go ssoon, right?" He waved his hands out at Molly, the black goggles contrasting with his silvery skin and making him look comical.

"As soon as we can," Molly said. "I promise." She laughed. "Until then, you can take those off."

Walter hissed his annoyance but reluctantly removed the goggles. Molly wasn't sure why he had been so eager to dash off to hyperspace to rescue Cole and her father, but he seemed nearly as miffed as her mom about the sudden change in plans.

Even with the visor closed and the volume down, Molly could still hear her mother's muffled questions raining down from the rack behind her. She felt horrible for not explaining herself better. She felt even worse for not fully understanding the decision herself. As much as she longed to rush off to Cole, as hard as she'd struggled the past weeks to secure the fusion fuel necessary, when the moment had arrived with her finger on the button . . . she just couldn't do it. She couldn't leave the Callites, who had lost so many family members to Bekkie's blood-draining operation. She couldn't abandon Saunders and his crewmen, who had survived a shipwreck that had spared so few. Molly tried not to think she was throwing her life away in a futile gesture of heroism, some primal urge to strike out at the Bern ships that had tormented her home planet from orbit, but given the odds that her return could do any good, there were few other interpretations.

Her Wadi licked the air contentedly as Molly powered the ship down and shut off the flight systems. The colorful lizard from Drenard seemed to be the only crew member left who wasn't upset at Molly's decision. She patted the animal on the head and moved to step over the control console, leaving Walter to fumble with his harness. As she hurried back through the cargo bay, Molly began working on an explanation for Saunders and the others as to why she had chosen to stay.

The cargo ramp creaked out into the Lokian night and then lowered toward the dew-soaked grass beyond. Molly watched as a clearing full of curious faces was revealed by the descending plate of steel. Cat was the first person to come inside. She jumped to the ramp before its lip even reached the ground.

"You forget something?" the Callite asked, a wide smile across her dark, scaly face.

Molly ran down the ramp to meet her, and the two women squeezed each other's arms. "I just couldn't leave," she said, the simple truth slicing through a hundred half-forged excuses. Molly looked over Cat's shoulder to see Scottie and Saunders stomping up the ramp behind her, their faces scrunched up in confused smiles.

"Besides," Molly said, "I think I have an idea."

"What kind of idea?" Saunders asked, stepping up to join them.

Molly looked from the navy admiral—her former superior at the Academy—to Scottie, the old illicit fuser and new friend. The two men represented opposite ends on as wide a chasm as law could allow. Molly wondered how best to speak in front of both of them, how to explain her plan without divulging any secrets about *Parsona's* illegal hyperdrive—a drive that could move things across the galaxy without a care for what got in the way. Saunders wouldn't enjoy hearing those details, and Scottie would probably be miffed to hear how much her plan relied on navy skills and tactics. Molly looked from one of them to the other, not knowing where to start.

"Does this mean you're not rushing off to hyperspace?" Scottie asked.

Molly shook her head. "I'm staying. For now."

Saunders pointed up. "Does this plan involve attacking those bastards up there?"

Molly nodded.

"This is gonna be like one of your crazy simulator stunts, isn't it?" Saunders smiled and crossed his arms. "Well c'mon, let's hear it."

Molly held out her hands, trying to slow both of them down. The risk of revealing her hyperdrive to Saunders had won out in her mind—she couldn't do it, so she needed a cover story of some sort.

"I have a few details I need to hammer out with these guys first," she said, nodding to Cat and Scottie. She looked over her shoulder as Walter padded out into the cargo bay, his goggles down around his neck. "Besides, it's already late, and it looks like you still need help distributing the food and water. Let's tend to the Callites. I'll talk to my friends later tonight, and we'll meet with you in the morning."

Saunders frowned. "I don't like being left out of the discussion," he said.

Molly stepped closer, wary of the crowd gathering around the ship, eyes and ears wide. "I know," she said softly. She felt sorry for the admiral, imagining how helpless he must feel with nothing to do for the paltry few survivors of his once-powerful fleet. He couldn't even speak freely among his staff now that she'd told him of the Bern threat and the stark physical similarities between them and humans.

"Look," she told him, "I really need you to trust me on this."

Saunders seemed about to argue, but his frown cracked into a wan smile, his fat jowls lifting just a little. He squeezed Molly's shoulder and looked out over the two groups of haggard survivors in the clearing.

"I suppose I owe you a little trust," Saunders said, referring perhaps to having doubted her before and having thrown her in jail. The old man turned back to face her, his eyes wet and reflecting *Parsona's* interior lights. "And I'm glad you decided to stick around," he said, forcing a smile.

Molly nodded and smiled back. She suddenly sensed just how much he meant it, this man who had once expelled her. And for the first time, her decision to stay resonated within her as the right choice.

oooo

There was no sleep that night as Molly and her friends stayed up and discussed her germ of a plan for dealing with the Bern fleet. They huddled together around a campfire built under *Parsona's* starboard wing and nurtured the idea, watching it sprout and grow as they each offered suggestions and pointed out various flaws. They spoke in hushed whispers, and even by the standards of Bekkie's short days, dawn seemed to arrive in a rush.

Morning was heralded by the popping of rekindled fires within the woods as early risers awoke to stoke dying embers. Gradually, the first smattering of humans and Callites emerged from their scattered camps; they crossed the clearing on weary legs, looking to *Parsona* for some odd supply item or just for the use of its bathrooms. Molly greeted them and made them feel welcome even as Walter cast suspicious glances their way.

When one of the navy crewmen exited *Parsona* with a load of fresh laundry, Molly asked him to send for Saunders, and the crewman agreed.

"Are we sure we've got our story straight?" Molly asked. She rubbed her weary eyes and looked to her friends around the fire, each of them nodding with as much enthusiasm as they could muster despite their lack of sleep. Leaning forward, she grabbed a pot of coffee from a flat stone near the fire and topped up her mug. She hoped the jolt of caffeine would help her regain some energy before the day's plan was spelled out and acted upon.

After a few minutes, Saunders arrived alone, his sagging jowls and dark-rimmed eyes signifying a similarly restless night. He lowered his considerable bulk to one of the blankets and eagerly accepted a cup of coffee, wrapping both meaty hands around the steaming mug. Cat said hello while Scottie greeted the old navy veteran with the sheepishness of an outlaw waving to a passing sheriff. Walter didn't even acknowledge Saunders's arrival; the Palan boy sat across the fire from Molly, continually poking the logs with a stick to send out showers of rising embers.

"You ready to tell me about this plan of yours?" Saunders asked. He blew across the surface of his coffee, sending a wisp of heat toward the fire.

"Yeah." Molly took a sip of her own coffee and thought about where best to start.

"And what is this plan for, exactly?" Saunders asked. "Will it help stop the Drenard attack? Or is it just for the bastards who shot down my fleet?"

Molly raised her eyebrows. "It's for all of it. Hopefully."

Saunders smiled. He took another loud sip from his coffee and waved one hand in a small circle, pleading for her to get on with it.

"My friends here," she indicated Scottie and Cat. "They know something about these rifts, these tears in space like the one the Bern fleet is coming out of."

Molly took another sip of coffee, steeling herself for the half-truths that were to follow. "These rifts are everywhere," she lied. "There's even one very close to us, right here in these woods, and my friends know how to control it." Molly chose her words carefully, using the language she and the others had decided upon in order to not reveal the special properties of *Parsona's* hyperdrive.

Saunders glanced across the fire at Cat and Scottie. He raised his eyebrows. "*Control* it?"

Molly nodded. "We can send people through this rift to wherever we like."

"Wherever? You mean like through hyperspace?"

"Yeah. It's similar, but without the limitations." Molly felt a wave of nausea as the lies piled up. Creating a fairytale to keep her hyperdrive secret was going to become burdensome, and fast.

"The thing is, traveling through this rift is a one-way trip," she said, which *wasn't* a lie. She forced herself to meet Saunders's gaze "We've got a plan for how we can make life miserable for the Bern." She waved her arm toward the edge of the woods where the surviving members of *Gloria's* crew were mingling and working to improve the encampment. "We have enough pilots," she said. "We just need a fleet, right?"

Saunders shook his head, his jowls jiggling back and forth. "Are you crazy? Did you see what happened yesterday? This is not the Tchung we're dealing with. An entire naval fleet is scattered across this planet in utter ruin—" Saunders held his mouth open as if to say more, but Molly could see his cheeks twitching, the tears welling up at the bottoms of his eyes.

"I know, sir, just hear me out. The fleet I'm thinking of will give *anything* a run for its money. It's the most battle-tested fleet in the entire galaxy."

Saunders frowned. "More powerful than Zebra, the most advanced fleet in the navy's arsenal?" He waved his mug in the air, sending a dark wave of coffee over the edge. "Such a fleet doesn't exist!"

"It does at Darrin," Molly said, keeping her cool. "It's the one place in GN-controlled space that even the navy can't go."

Saunders laughed. He set his coffee in the dirt and wiped his palm on his too-small flight suit. "*Darrin?* And what fleet do you suppose we'll use to get *that* one? They would make even quicker work of us than the Bern did!"

Molly shook her head. "No, we don't use a fleet. We use the *rift*. Don't you see? We send people *straight* to the ships. We can place teams inside Darrin garages and nab a fleet right out from underneath them!"

Saunders chewed his lip. "Too many problems. For one, even my StarCarrier doesn't have chart data for Darrin that accurate, so you'd be lucky to end up anywhere near one of their hideouts. I mean, nobody legit has been there since their civil war, and besides—"

"My nav computer has the entire system scanned from just a month ago," Molly interrupted. She jabbed a thumb back toward *Parsona*.

Saunders shot her a look that suggested this wasn't something to brag about.

"Then there's the pilot codes to consider," he said. "Nobody leaves their ships unlocked—"

"These guys do. They trust their force fields way too much. I—well, I kinda flew one of their ships back to Earth the day that . . . you know, with Lucin—"

"Are you *kidding?*"

Molly raised her hands. "I swear on my father, I did these things with the best of intentions."

Scottie leaned over to Cat and whispered loudly: "She sounds like one of us, now."

The two of them snickered. Molly was so tired, she nearly joined them.

"We would need weapons," Saunders said, ignoring the others. "The ban on Lok is going to make that difficult—"

"Covered, and it'll actually be the most unpleasant part of our plan."

Saunders reached again for his coffee. "Which is?"

"We raid the StarCarrier, sir. We send in a team with climbing gear to rappel down to the armory. You've got the access codes, and we need to grab enough flight suits for the pilots, anyway. I'll take a small group in my ship to do this while you brief and prepare the others. Some of them might not feel ready for this kind of raid, but we're gonna need everyone. You'll have to make them believe this'll work."

"But *will* it work?" Saunders looked into his mug, staring down at it like an oracle searching a muddy well. "Lok and Darrin are on opposite sides of the galaxy," he whispered. "If this rift of yours can get them there like you say, it's still, what, five days' flight time to get them back?"

"Actually, sir, I think it can be done in three days. We plotted it out last night on our charts. It requires skirting the galactic center and quick-cycling the hyperdrives each time, but—"

"The hyperdrives will be toast if you quick-cycle them three jumps in a row," Saunders said.

Molly nodded. "I agree, that's why—"

"It's gonna be a one-way trip in *both* directions, Admiral," Cat said.

Saunders mulled this over. He looked out toward the edge of the clearing, where his people and the Callites were making breakfast and consoling one another for their losses.

"Most of my people haven't flown a real mission their entire careers," he finally said. "I've got maybe twelve decent pilots over there."

"Thirteen, including you," Molly said. "And several of the Callites can fly. The rest will be needed for adequate crew on each ship, and to help during the raids on the Darrin asteroids. Besides, they should be more comfortable behind the stick by the time they get back here. We'll have them drill some maneuvers on the way."

Saunders shook his head. "I don't know. And what's all this *you* nonsense? You're coming with us if we do this. We'll need you most of all."

Molly shook her head. "No can do. I'm gonna be busy while you guys are gone."

"Doing *what?*" Saunders asked.

"Taking out that big ship," Molly said, glancing up.

"That small moon up there?" Saunders's eyes widened.

"Yeah. We think it's what knocked you guys out of orbit." Molly nodded to Scottie. "The Callite shuttles from Bekkie didn't start going down until after it arrived. We think it can control gravity fields in a localized manner. We'll need to destroy it before you guys come back from Darrin; otherwise, you won't stand a chance."

"And how in the galaxy are you planning on taking it out with just your one ship?"

"Well—" Molly took another sip of her coffee. "After we send you guys out to Darrin, we're gonna go back to the StarCarrier."

"What for?"

"For all the Firehawk missiles my ship can hold."

"And you're going to fire them, how?" Saunders frowned. "Have you got any Firehawks I don't know about?"

Molly shook her head. "We use the rifts," she said, stretching the truth once again to protect *Parsona's* hyperdrive. In reality, she didn't plan on carrying the missiles out at all. Instead, they would send them up from within the StarCarrier, where she and her friends would be safe and out of sight.

Saunders crossed his arms. "And I suppose these rifts are going to arm them for you as well? Or do you have some magical ability to remotely detonate navy missiles?"

Molly smiled. She looked across the fire and gave Walter a wink.

"We've got it covered," she said. "And it's probably best you don't know."

2

HYPERSPACE

The ready room of the Drenard Headquarters buzzed with the accented whispers of a dozen alien races. They stood in five lines and prepared themselves for one final raid across hyperspace. Cole Mendonça stood among them, wearing the same sort of white combat suit as the others and nervously gripping his buckblade. He stared down at his feet, at the dull path worn into the steel beneath them, the sign of many thousands of boots shuffling forward on previous raids.

"Good luck," someone behind him said.

Cole turned and nodded mutely to Larken, his group's translator. Larken squeezed Cole's shoulder and then patted it twice.

Cole glanced over at Mortimor, who had just given a last series of instructions to the five squads before joining the group lined up beside his.

"I didn't know you were going," Cole said.

"Ran out of people who speak Bern." Mortimor nodded toward the row of hyperdrive platforms in front of them where the five pilots sat, their arms wrapped around their shins. "Now pay attention," Mortimor said.

Cole nodded and focused on the platforms. A moment later, the light over each pilot switched from red to green. There was a loud beeping sound from the row of control consoles followed by a pop as the five large cages in the back of the room—cages Cole had designed and helped build—vanished.

A moment later, the pilots followed, winking out of existence with a muted pop, as air from the room crashed together to fill the void they had left behind. The row of navigators jumped up to take their place on the platforms. They turned, fell to their butts and tucked their chins, only having three seconds between jumps to prepare themselves.

Cole glanced over at the navigator in Mortimor's line. A lock of bright red hair spilled out of Penny's hood as she settled into place. Her eyes met Cole's for a brief moment just before her head went down. There was a soft pop, and she too disappeared from the room, leaving Cole awash in a tremble of nerves.

It was all happening so fast.

Cole's heart missed a beat as he took a step forward, shuffling the steel decking ever duller. He chanced a glance to the side at the neighboring line. Mortimor was looking straight ahead, the man's beard and combat hood hiding whatever he was thinking. Cole wished he'd known Molly's old man was going on the raid. He would've switched places with someone to be in Mortimor's group and been able to keep an eye on him—

The lines surged forward again. Cole felt Larken's hand on his back, pushing him along. Suddenly, Cole found himself beside the console operator, right in front of the jump platform. Marx, the Callite swordsman who would help Cole clear the Bern ship's corridors, plopped down on the platform. The alien looked up, and time slowed down to a crawl. Cole watched Marx's arms wrap around his shins, saw the man's scaly chin tuck against his knees—and then the alien was gone. More air crashed together so close, Cole felt the sucking breeze on his cheeks. He jumped up to the platform and sat down as quickly as he could, then spun around to face what he hoped would be an exit once he popped inside the steel cage. In the back of his mind, he counted:

Three.

He grabbed his shins and tucked his head, squeezing his buckblade as tightly as he dared without crushing it. A thousand sword fighting tips from his practice sessions with Penny flashed through his mind.

Two.

A sickening sensation clawed at Cole's stomach as he wondered if the raid was a mistake. He tried to remember what the Seer had said about free will, but then the silent counting in his mind clicked down to—

One.

•• 2 ••

The ready room of the Underground headquarters disappeared. One moment Larken was standing before him, looking down at his sword and waiting his turn. The next, Cole was seeing the interior of a metal box. He fell half a meter out of the air and landed on his ass, smacking solid steel. Cole felt a rush of adrenaline—the raid had really begun! He sprang forward and launched himself through the clean hole the pilot had cut in the side of the cage. It was a couple meters to the ship's deck below. Cole hit the plating in a roll and looked around.

Marx stood off to starboard, his buckblade drawn. The Callite turned and glanced over his shoulder at Cole.

"Go," the alien said. Marx spun and ran down the corridor, looking for Bern crewmen to kill. Up ahead, Cole could hear the pilot and navigator stomping forward to secure the cockpit. Cole felt a sick lurch in his stomach as he imagined where they were: his squad had just jumped across hyperspace and into the belly of an enemy ship flying in formation with thousands of other enemy ships. He looked once more to Marx, but the Callite was already out of sight, disappearing around a bend in the corridor. Cole remembered his duty: he should be running in the opposite direction. He spun and headed off, catching a glimpse of Larken as the translator leaped out of the suspended cage.

The image of the metal box stuck with Cole as he ran aft. Protruding from a solid bulkhead—twisted sheets of metal peeled back from the expanding grav plates—it had worked exactly as he'd imagined. No matter where the box had ended up in hyperspace, those expanding sheets of steel in its center would've provided a safe pocket of emptiness for them to arrive inside of. The first part of his plan had worked flaw-lessly. Cole felt a surge of hope wash away some of his anxiety. He was that much closer to Molly.

As he ran down the ship's corridor—his thoughts straying from his duty—Cole finally remembered to flick off the safety on his buckblade. He reminded himself of the grisly task that lay before him: he would need to kill without hesitation.

He ducked through a passageway, the thick, airtight door left open and secured to the bulkhead. There was a funny script of writing above the hatch in neat red ink, the shape and style of the language resembling nothing Cole had ever seen. The peculiar writing stood in stark contrast to the rest of his sur-roundings. Otherwise, Cole could've been running through a navy ship. The size of the passageways, the spacing from ceiling to floor, even the height and ergonomics of the control pods on the walls—they were all identical to a human craft.

Cole turned a corner and was reminded why this was so. The figure strolling down the hallway in his direction looked perfectly human. Even the confusion and shock on the Bern's face were familiar—and much easier to read than the red script had been.

The Bern crewman fumbled at his belt—whether for gun or radio or what else, Cole didn't wait to find out. He flicked on his buckblade and swung up in an angle four as the Bern pulled something from his hip—

The Bern's head fell sideways, removed from his torso in a slanted wound from neck to ear. Cole danced out of the way, cursing himself for being so sloppy, and not just for the fountain of gore erupting from the Bern's neck and splattering the wall, but the poor reflex of going for a soft spot. He needed to remember the power of the weapon he was holding. The goal was to aim for the torso or anything difficult to miss, or to make it hard for the enemy to pull out of the way. There was no such thing as a "soft spot" for the buckblade. There were just *spots*. Any spot would do.

As the Bern's body hit the floor, Cole gathered himself together. He took one look at his artificial arm, remembering the stakes. He then turned and ran deeper into the ship, stopping to check every turn, nook, and corridor.

He took his next two victims by surprise. Both deaths were uniquely horrific, but neither felt as personal as he'd feared they would. The blade slid through their bodies, and even some of the ship's equipment that was in the way, without an ounce of resistance. It felt more like casting a spell on someone from a distance than a physical strike. All he did was wave a wand—and a body was split in two.

Cole took every right turn as he headed aft to make sure he covered the entire deck. He went through a dozen Bern in the process. He tried to remember Mortimor's warning to do minimal damage to the ship with follow-throughs, a real concern when fighting in close quarters with buckblades. An accidental swipe could easily destroy something crucial in a ship they needed in order to escape hyperspace.

Rounding another corner, Cole nearly collided with Marx, who was jogging the other direction. Both swordsmen flinched, readying to strike—but they were able to restrain themselves. They stood in the passageway panting, splattered with alien blood, holding their invisible swords and smiling grimly at each other.

"Any stairs or lifts?" Cole asked, out of breath more from the adrenaline dump than the long run.

"No," Marx said, his English accented with the coughing sound of a Callite. "Looks like a single-deck design. Lucky we didn't end up in mechanical spaces." Marx nodded the direction Cole had come from. "Let's get to the cockpit. Sweep your side again."

Cole gave Marx a thumbs-up and then wondered if the Callite even knew how to interpret the gesture. "Gotcha," he said, and ran off the same way he'd arrived. Once again, he couldn't believe how well the raid was going.

•• 1 ••

The last thing Penny saw of the ready room was Cole, the poor boy's face drenched in nerves. Then she closed her eyes and waited for the drop in her stomach, followed by the crashing down to the deck.

As soon as her butt hit cold steel, she launched forward, expecting to find a clean hole cut in the side of the cage. What she found instead was Jym, her pilot, pressed up against one wall and cursing at his clearly malfunctioning buckblade.

Penny felt a wave of panic; she barely remembered to jump to the side and get out of the way of her next squad mate, but self-preservation moved her just in time. She powered up her own blade and pushed it through the cage wall. As she began making a wide circle through the solid steel, she heard a pop of air behind her, followed by the sound of Stella gasping with alarm at the sight of the cramped cube, a cube that should've been empty.

Penny turned to warn her, to drag her out of the way, but it was too late. A few heartbeats later, Gregury jumped in and fused with Stella. The squad mates became a sickening, two-headed monster— half Serral and half human. Screams of raw agony blared out of them both—fading to gruesome moans as intertwined organs ceased to function.

Jym threw down his sword and grabbed Stella's boots. He threw his hands up, flipping the tangled mass of limbs backward and out of the way. Penny pressed herself to the wall as Mortimor fell out of the air in a tight ball, missing by inches having some part of him fused with one of the others.

The screaming from Stella and Gregury fell silent. Penny thought about putting them out of their misery with her blade, but they were already dead before she could steel herself. Jym, the group's pilot and therefore the one who was responsible for cutting an exit out of the box, cursed and kicked his dead buck-blade in disgust.

Mortimor scanned the tight confines of the box and seemed to take it all in. He reached down and picked up one of the dropped swords from the two dead squad mates. "Jym, you go forward alone and clear the cockpit." He handed him the retrieved sword. "Penny, you take starboard. I'll clear port. Go!"

Penny nodded. Translator and navigator had instantly become swordsmen, she and Mortimor reverting to older, more comfortable roles. She finished her cut in the wall and kicked the center of the crude circle. The heavy steel fell away, exposing the Bern ship's decking half a meter above the floor of the box. Two sets of legs stood there—Bern crewmen studying the strange cube that had appeared inside their starship. Penny swiped through all four limbs with a wave of her hand. She jumped out to the deck and silenced the screaming forms before they hit the ground.

It was a messy start, blood slicking the deck around the box, but Penny didn't pause to help the others. She ran aft along the port side, thinking of the look on Stella's face before Gregury had jumped in, and how different she had looked just moments later with her wide, lifeless eyes. The horrific sight— the suddenness of the switch from life to death—gave Penny fuel for moving swiftly through the craft, slicing down all the bewildered Bern who stood in her way.

•• 5 ••

The windshield of the impounded Bern craft was dusted in a never-ending torrent of snowflakes. The flurries impacted right in front of her and slid to the side, gathering in miniature drifts. The sight of the stuff, coupled with the harsh whiteness beyond, made it easier to fly by the instruments than stare into the mesmerizing sameness.

And so Anlyn Hooo—Drenard princess, member of the Great Circle— kept her head down as she piloted the Bern craft through hyperspace. It had been two weeks to the day. Two weeks of exhausting one-hour shifts, causing her to develop a powerful antipathy to the sight of the relentless snow outside. She preferred to rest her chin on her chest and monitor beneath drooping eyelids their ship's position within the vast invasion fleet, following everything from the instrument readouts.

Edison snored beside her in his gruff and intermittent way. The massive Glemot, her copilot and fiancé, was fast asleep with the radio mic clutched in his paws. Anlyn checked the ship's clock, dreading the answer to her weary and eternal question: *How much time left on my shift?*

Forty minutes.

It filled Anlyn with guilt and dread. Dread for the perceived hours and days it would take for those forty minutes to tick down and guilt for knowing that Edison would have to take over for her once they did.

Another ship passed through the open rift ahead, and the fleet adjusted accordingly. Anlyn felt a rush of adrenaline as she leaned forward, gripped the control stick, and matched the precise movements of the Bern. It took every ounce of her will to fly like a fresh pilot, alert and ready, rather than the half-dead thing she had become. A thousand times over the past weeks, Anlyn had foreseen the end to her and Edison's endurance: There would be a wobble and a gradual falling out of formation. Barked orders full of suspicion would follow, and Edison's sleep-deprived lies would not wash them away. The final stage would be missiles and plasma bolts to end their fitful ruse—

A loud bang in the rear of their ship interrupted Anlyn's thoughts. Edison bolted upright, the radio coming to his mouth in reflex. He scanned the dash before looking to Anlyn in confusion.

"Diagnose!" he said in his native English.

Anlyn shook her head. "I don't know," she said. She tried to force the cobwebs aside and think clearly. "It sounded mechanical, but none of the gauges have so much as twitched." She looked to the SADAR, but it was nearly useless in the driving snow. "The fleet is moving again. Maybe it was a collision?"

Edison began to rise from his seat to go inspect the cause of the noise, but Anlyn placed a hand on his chest and attempted to push him back.

"I can't speak Bern," she reminded him. She glanced at the mic in his hand. "Stay here in case the fleet calls. I'll go see what it was."

She unbuckled her harness while Edison yawned, his long, furry arms running out of room for a decent stretch. She ducked under his elbow and padded out of the cockpit on wobbly legs, heading aft. In her sleepy pilot brain, she went over all the possible causes for the loud, metallic sound. A ceiling panel could've fallen loose and slammed into the decking. A storage cabinet could've vibrated off its rivets. One of the generators could've thrown a rod.

But then she heard something else, something easier to recognize. It was a thumping sound, rhythmic, just like the footfalls of someone running.

And it was getting *louder*.

•• 2 ••

Cole finished his second sweep of the port side, seeing nothing more than the messes he had left behind the first time. He reached the cockpit after Marx and helped the large Callite drag Bern bodies out of the way. It looked as if the pilot and copilot had cut down several Bern in taking over control of the ship.

Despite the design of his Underground boots, made to grip through blood and ice, Cole found himself slipping and sliding as he dragged a Bern's torso out of the cockpit's narrow hallway. There was a gruesome normalcy to the task, like arranging furniture, that nearly made Cole gag. He forced himself to not look the dead man in the eye as he added him to a pile Marx had already started. The Callite threw a plastic tarp over the figures while Cole looked for something to mop up the blood. There was no way they could work with such a thick pool of it right in the cockpit. He pulled a jacket off one of the Bern crewmen, looking away from the human-like face as he did so. He threw the jacket down into the spilled gore and pushed it around with his boot, trying to mop a path through the mess.

"Ryke was right about the windshields," Cole heard the navigator say. "They're already darkened, so we won't be needing our goggles."

"Keep 'em around your necks anyway," someone else in the cockpit barked.

A third voice burst out in a strange language, causing Cole to pause from his dirty work and scramble for his buckblade. The cadence and inflection of the words sounded similar to what several Bern crewmen had been shouting before Cole had cut them down.

"Shhh!" somebody hissed. "Complete silence!"

Cole left the soiled jacket wadded up against the bulkhead and stuck his head in the cockpit. He watched as Larken, the squad translator, leaned forward from one of the seats and spoke foreign words—the same *type* of words—into the mic. Everyone froze, anxious and tense.

When he stopped speaking, a voice came through the radio again. Larken held his eyes closed and turned to face the pilot. He nodded now and then as the rapid Bern continued.

"What was *that* about?" the pilot asked as soon as the voice fell silent.

"They want us to check for any problems. One of the other ships called something in, and now they won't respond."

"You want me to go check?" the navigator asked, jabbing a thumb over his shoulder.

"Moron," the pilot said. "*We're* the problem."

"One of the other squads must be in trouble," Cole said.

"That's why we sent five groups," the pilot muttered. He turned to the navigator. "Call HQ on the carrier frequency, but keep it short. Just give them our velocity and the coordinates for our cargo bay, one meter off the deck. Tell them we're secure and can hold as much as they can send."

The navigator nodded and pulled his long-wave radio from his pack.

The pilot looked over his shoulder. "Marx, you and Cole head back to the cargo bay and coordinate our arrivals. Let's pack as much as we can into this puppy, just in case we're the only ones who make it through to the other side."

"Yes, sir," Marx said from behind Cole. The Callite stomped aft through the thin skim of drying blood.

Cole took off after him, his thoughts divided between how well his squad had done on their portion of the raid—and on which of the other groups had run into trouble.

•• 1 ••

Penny raced through the ship's corridors, the dying screams of the last Bern crewman echoing in her ears. She slowed to round a bend in the passageway and found herself in the aftermost section, the rumble of powerful thrusters audible through the thick bulkhead.

The sound intensified as a door opened. A Bern engineer stepped out, his gray coveralls spotted with grease stains. Penny sliced him in half before he could even register her presence. She watched the two pieces of meat fall to the deck, strings of interior organs spilling out in a thick soup. She studied the odd arrangement, the fleshy interior, and felt more curiosity than horror.

A rhythmic clanging rang out over the roar from the open thruster room. Penny kicked the door shut to hear better. It was footsteps. Someone running. She prepared her blade just as Mortimor jogged around the corner and came to a panting stop.

"You okay?" he asked. He pulled his bloodspecked hood back and ran his fingers through his graying hair.

Penny nodded and lowered her sword. "I think this is the last—"

Before she could finish the sentence, Penny flew into the air and slammed into the rear bulkhead. Mortimor followed, his limbs flying out for balance.

Gravity returned, and they both fell to the deck. Penny felt her weight lessen again, as if the ship was dropping altitude, but the grav panels should've more than compensated for any maneuvering. She looked across at Mortimor, her hands splayed wide and her fingers digging into the grating on the floor.

"The cockpit!" Mortimor yelled.

Penny pushed herself to her feet. The whine of the thrusters in the next room suddenly lowered in pitch—and then the engines began screaming higher and harder than before. Something was wrong. She took off, churning up the meters back to the cockpit, her legs hammering away at the artificial gravity, her mind willing it to last.

•• 5 ••

The pounding of the approaching footsteps came faster than Anlyn could retreat. She stood, frozen in place, comprehending the noise but not understanding how it was possible. When the Bern rounded the corner, dressed in a suit of all white, she collapsed in stark horror, her already fatigued legs turning to soup. Her brain boiled with confusion and fear. She scrambled back from the figure and tried to scream for Edison, but her voice wouldn't heed her. In the back of her muddy mind, she finally matched up the banging sound she had heard with a ship locking to theirs. She imagined a squad of Bern troopers boarding their craft. She wondered what mistake she'd made to end their ruse.

We're doomed, Anlyn thought. The figure approached, his eyes wide and his hands clenched together high over his head. Someone else ran up behind the Bern—some unknown race—also with his hands double-gripping an unseen device.

"What are you waiting on?" the alien in the back yelled.

In some fuzzy corner of Anlyn's mind, she realized he had yelled it in *English*. This alien, also in all white, tried to get around the Bern, pushing him to the side.

"It's a Drenard, man!" The Bern held the alien back and looked toward Anlyn. "Maybe she's like a sex slave or something."

"Sex slave? You stay away!" Anlyn yelled. She kicked at the decking in an attempt to scramble toward the cockpit.

"Stop moving," the Bern said. He leveled some sort of object at her.

"Wait!" The unknown alien reached for the Bern ahead of him. "She speaks *English*?"

Another Bern ran up behind the other two, his uniform identical.

"What the hell is going on here?" he asked. He spotted Anlyn. "What the *flank*?" He spoke some Bern to her as he reached for something on his belt.

"She speaks English," the other Bern said over his shoulder. He looked again to Anlyn, his eyes narrowed warily as he stepped forward. "Where's the rest of your crew?" he asked her.

"Screw this diplomacy," the other Bern said. "We need to secure the cockpit!"

All three figures moved closer—and then the faces of the two Bern turned as white as their suits. Their eyes bulged as they gaped high over Anlyn's head.

"Desist!" Edison roared from behind her. He followed with something equally terse and forceful in Bern.

Anlyn turned to see her fiancé reared up, the fur along his arms waving as if in a stiff breeze. She scrambled away from the three figures and tried to get to the other side of Edison, eager to put his imposing bulk between herself and this strange threat that had invaded their ship.

•• 1 ••

Penny sprinted toward the cockpit, fearful of the mechanical failure that had lifted her and Mortimor off their feet before slamming them to the deck. When she reached the ship's cargo bay, she noticed a bright light flooding down the corridor from the cockpit: it was the telltale flash of hyperspace's unshielded and blinding photons.

Penny pulled her goggles out of her collar and forced them in place with one hand. She heard the drone of a steady wind and felt the air in the ship grow colder as she got closer. She stepped over two dead Bern, their guts spilled and dripping through the deck grating. The ship's grav panels lurched again, sending her sideways into another bulkhead. Penny bounced off and staggered forward, calling for Jym. A flurry of snow swirled around her, melting in the air.

"Up here!" Jym yelled. Penny ducked into the cockpit and saw the Pheron pilot peering back from one of the flight seats. Beyond him, the ship's canopy had been blown wide open, letting in the snow and light. The fur on Jym's face whipped around in the breeze, but even that, coupled with his black goggles, couldn't hide all the alien's panic.

Penny ran toward the nav seat to help with the flight controls and then saw the spot was already occupied. A beheaded Bern, his arms still twitching, sat behind a collection of smashed instrument panels.

"What happened?" Penny asked. She attempted to pull the body out of the seat, but it must've weighed a ton.

"No flankin clue!" Jym yelled. "And that thing ain't flesh." He let go of the controls and waved a hand at the Bern. "Took its head off from behind, and the flanker went ballistic, smashing the dash and the canopy. I think the grav systems are toast. I'm not gonna be able to keep us airborne!"

Penny peered through the hole in the canopy, past the snow billowing in to dust the controls and ice everything over. Beyond the craggy hole lay the endless white of hyperspace and the flurries she hated so much. Looking down at the beheaded Bern, she didn't see any organs inside the neck, just the sheen of metal. It made her feel nauseous, looking at it. She pulled out her sword and gritted her teeth. Carefully, using slow motions, she carved the mechanical Bern and his chair in half, right down the middle. Another clean sweep sideways—careful as the ship lurched again—and she had pieces small enough to carry out of the cockpit. Again, no blood and hardly any oil or grease.

After the body parts were removed, Penny crouched behind the nav controls and tried to help Jym pull the ship's nose up. The SADAR screen ahead of her was demolished, giving her little to go by, so she looked to Jym's instruments as a guide. A voice crackled through the radio, barely audible over the whipping wind. It said something in Bern right as Mortimor staggered into the cockpit, breathing hard.

"Did you catch that?" Penny yelled back to Mortimor.

He reached for the mic. "Yeah," he said. He surveyed the damage to the dash and sucked in a deep breath. "Both of you keep quiet."

"What're you gonna say?" Jym asked.

Mortimor shot him a look. His chest heaved with another deep gulp of air, his beard catching the snow. "I'm going to tell the rest of the Bern fleet that we've suffered a mechanical failure so they won't think anything's amiss." He looked to Jym's instruments as he brought the mic up to his mouth. "And then I'm gonna inform them that we're going down," Mortimor said grimly.

•• 2 ••

Cole and Marx coordinated arrivals as the Underground kept their jump platforms busy evacuating the base of its personnel and essentials. Anyone assigned to support crew, they directed aft. As members of the evac crew appeared in the cargo bay, they assigned them duties and loaded them up with the gear also coming through every five seconds or so. Cole marveled at the military precision of it all. An absolute flood of people and supplies were washing aboard the ship.

Up in the cockpit, the flight crew did an incredible job of holding the Bern craft steady while updating HQ with coordinates. Each arrival appeared in the exact same spot of empty air. The more that came aboard, the more Cole felt a step closer to getting out of that infernal place and tracking down Molly. He was so close he could practically remember what her hair smelled like, when just a few days ago he'd had difficulty picturing her face—

"We've got trouble!"

The shout from the cockpit shattered Cole's thoughts. He and Marx glanced at each other. Marx pulled a large sack of supplies out of the arrival point and handed it off to the alien who had jumped in just prior.

"I'll go," Cole said.

Marx nodded as another member of the Underground fell out of the air and landed in a neat crouch. "I'm gonna insist Arthur come with the next group," Marx said, reaching for his radio. "Protocol and seniority be damned, we need him here."

"Agreed." Cole slapped Marx on the shoulder and ran to the cockpit.

"What's going on?" he asked the flight crew.

Larken spun around. The mic was trembling in his hand. "First group's going down," he sputtered.

"Someone from the ship broadcasted a mechanical failure in Bern. I'm pretty sure it was Mortimor."

The pilot took one hand off the steering column and grabbed Larken's wrist; he pulled the mic away from the translator's mouth. "You're not gonna transmit anything to them, are you?"

"No, man! I'm just waiting for the Bern to get suspicious!"

"Calm down, both of you," Cole said. He stepped up behind the translator and checked the strange-looking SADAR, which was a beehive of blips and odd figures. "Where does it show their altitude?" He glanced over the shapes on the screen, not recognizing any of them as numbers.

"Right there." The pilot tapped the screen. "And that's Group One's ship." He indicated one of the blobs. "They're going down soft by the looks of it. Not far from the Luddite camp."

"Is that their camp there?" Cole reached over and tapped the screen.

"Only thing low enough," the pilot growled.

"Well then, they aren't going down *near* them," Cole said. "I think they're trying to land *on* them."

The radio squawked with more rapid Bern. Larken turned to the pilot, his knuckles white around the mic.

"I think he's right, sir."

•• 5 ••

The trio of white-clad warriors shuffled down the corridor toward Edison and Anlyn, their courage seeming to have rallied as they raised the strange cylinders in their hands.

"Desist!" Edison roared once more. He berated himself for leaving his lance in the cockpit as Anlyn scooted safely around him. "Stay where you are!" he tried in Bern.

One of the Bern stiffened and pulled back on the alien ahead of him. "We're taking over control of your ship," he returned in Bern. "On your knees!"

Edison took a step back and growled at Anlyn to return to the cockpit. As she ran off, the three attackers surged forward, the one in the front bringing his empty hands up high as if wielding an invisible club.

Edison threw his feet forward and fell flat on his back, sending a shiver through the deck. He brought his knees up to his chest as some unseen thing whizzed through the air above him. Kicking out, he caught the figure in the chest and sent him sprawling back into the other two.

Something clattered to the ground nearby. Reaching forward to grab it—a metal cylinder of some sort—Edison paused. The bulkhead to the side of the device was sparking. A thin line of destruction streaked across the solid steel as the cylinder rolled across the deck toward him. Edison's scientific thought processes kicked into high gear. He picked the thing up, keeping the laser end pointed away. He leveled the device at the three men.

Nothing happened.

Insufficient range, he figured.

He took a step forward, and the other two figures in white dropped their cylinders and raised their hands.

"We give up!" one of them said in English.

"Excellent maneuver." Edison aimed the strange cylinder at the one who had spoken in Bern and switched to that language himself:

"Now, who in hyperspace *are* you people?"

•• 2 ••

Cole watched the blip on the SADAR, the one showing Mortimor's ship descending toward the frozen wastelands of hyperspace. The pilot and translator were yelling back and forth, arguing about what to do for them, but it was mere background noise. All Cole could think about was what might have gone wrong with Mortimor's group and how *he* should've been there with them.

He snapped himself out of the unproductive thoughts and looked around at the bickering crew. The raid was going to fall apart over this, he realized. Mortimor's mythical status as leader of the Underground was now going to be a distraction rather than a motivating force.

Cole ran out of the cockpit and returned to the cargo bay. He tore open one metal cabinet and locker after another, looking through the ship's supplies for anything resembling a gravchute, or even an old-fashioned glider. Every five seconds or so, he heard a soft pop as more people and gear arrived from HQ. The finality and awfulness of the raid, of using up what remained of the fusion fuel, of abandoning the Underground's headquarters—it all dawned on him as a colossal mistake.

Someone grabbed him by the shoulder. Cole turned to find Arthur Dakura frowning at him.

"What's the emergency?" Arthur asked. He looked annoyed to have been brought aboard out of order.

"One group is going down," Cole said. He slammed a locker shut and flung open another. "And I'm going down after them."

Arthur grabbed Cole's shoulders. He pulled him away from the cabinet just as Cole started rummaging around inside it. "That's a negative," Arthur said. "Drawing any more attention will just threaten the other squads. Now, which group did you say is going down?"

Cole clenched and unclenched his teeth. "I told you," he said. "Group One."

Arthur's eyes darted back and forth, searching Cole's.

"Mortimor's group," Cole whispered.

•• 5 ••

Anlyn reached the cockpit and made sure the Bern ship was still holding position and that the fleet hadn't adjusted itself around them. She grabbed Edison's lance and ran back aft as the sounds of a struggle and a bout of yelling sent shivers of fear up her spine. She half expected to find dozens of Bern in the cargo bay by the time she returned, the illusion of another ship locked to theirs still lingering.

She entered the bay with the lance level, fully prepared to send its pyrotechnic fireworks into her enemy. What she found instead was Edison standing bold before the three figures, something in his hand aimed at them. Two of the figures held their arms in the air. The other clutched his stomach, in obvious pain but still attempting to speak. His efforts were interrupted by the arrival of two more white-suited aliens running up from the rear, neither of them Bern. Anlyn recognized one of them as a Pheral, the other a Callite. Her head swelled with confusion; the Bern were not known to ally themselves with other races.

The original three held the new arrivals back, telling them in English to be careful. Edison roared at the two in the back to drop their weapons, which they refused to do.

Anlyn stepped beside Edison with the lance level, hoping it looked suitably fierce. "Which of you speaks English?" she asked.

"We all do," the Pheral said. He pulled the white hood off his head, revealing his yellowish, mottled skin. "What's a Drenard doing working for the Bern?"

"We're not *with* the Bern," Anlyn said, beginning to sense that this group wasn't either. "This is Lord Campton, and I am Anlyn Hooo. We are members of the Drenard Circle and come as ambassad—"

Anlyn fell silent as the group of aliens sank to their knees, their eyes wide and mouths open. Weapons that had been held at the ready immediately moved into tucked positions of submission.

"Hooo of the royal line," one of the figures whispered.

The one clutching his stomach seemed to forget his pain, his grimace morphing into a wide smile as he looked up at her and Edison. "We are members of the Drenard Underground," the man said. "We are protectors of the rift, and we are honored to serve."

Softly, one of the five began saying something, chanting. Others joined in.

Anlyn stood, welded to the decking in abject shock, just barely able to make out the words. They were the words of the Bern Seer. The collection of aliens was chanting the *prophecy*.

Edison and Anlyn turned toward each other, neither of them able to speak.

Edison lowered his weapon.

And rolled his eyes.

3

GROUP TWO

The steady flow of gear and evacuees into Group Two's hijacked ship ceased for a moment. Marx and members of the Evac Crew stared at the empty space in the center of the cargo bay, their feet shuffling impatiently. Finally, the air popped, and a gravchute and set of jump gear appeared, seemingly out of nowhere, and fell to the deck in a jumbled heap. Cole rushed forward to his special delivery, ignoring the grumbles from the others as he passed. He pulled the chute and gear out of the rough circle of aliens to an empty corner of the cargo bay. He began shrugging the gravchute over his white combat uniform as Arthur hurried over and resumed his protestations.

"If Mortimor was here to tell you himself," Arthur told Cole, "even *he* would say you shouldn't go."

Cole nodded his agreement and shrugged the other strap on. "I'm sure you're right," he said. He could clearly remember Mortimor berating him for going it alone after two traitors in a hyperskimmer.

Arthur squeezed Cole's arm and pulled his hand away from the straps before Cole could cinch them tighter. "I really can't let you do this," Arthur said, finally going for all-out force.

Cole grabbed Arthur's wrist with his new mechanical hand and squeezed back even harder. "And I can't let you stop me," he said.

Arthur grimaced and let go. The old engineer and roboticist rubbed his wrist. "Ain't that the dog biting the hand—?"

"I'm sorry, Arthur, I really am, but I can't leave hyperspace without him."

"And how do you plan on getting him *back?*" Arthur asked. "There's no one at HQ to man a skimmer. Are you just gonna stay behind in hyperspace *with* him? Look, he's like a brother to me, so I get where you're coming from, but he specifically told me—he *ordered* me to keep an eye on you."

Cole glanced down at the chute's controls to check the battery levels and then looked up at Arthur. "I have to try *something*," Cole said. "I can't go back if we don't. Molly would never—I'd never forgive myself."

Arthur rested a hand on Cole's shoulder, but his grip no longer felt as if it were meant to fix him in place. It was a clasp of understanding, of finally getting where Cole was coming from. He looked around the bay at all the commotion, at the supplies and people pouring through. A crate of power cells for the buckblades arrived with a sharp crack of air. One of the crate's boards popped loose as it slammed into the deck, disgorging cells. A frantic swarm of activity ensued, attempting to clear the space before the next arrival. Arthur turned back to Cole.

"Listen to me, there's no point in going if you don't have a way back."

Cole pulled the harness points tight on the grav suit and slapped the battery pack for good luck. "I'm taking care of my half by going down there. You got any ideas for the other?"

Arthur nodded. "Yeah, damnit, I do. But if Mortimor asks, you have to tell him this was all your plan. I had *nothing* to do with it."

"Fine," Cole said, smiling. "What is it?"

•• 5 ••

Anlyn and Edison stood together in the rear half of the Bern craft's cockpit, leaning on each other, thankful to no longer be needed. Weeks of abject exhaustion had been peeled away by the adrenaline rush of being boarded by attackers, and then the relief of finding out who the strange men were. Anlyn knew of the Underground; she had heard whispers among her uncles of this distant band of rogues fighting for peace between her people and the humans. She never expected in her wildest dreams to meet any of them, much less for them to know who she was. And now they had arrived, seeming like Bern attackers, several of them looking like Bern in every way possible, but proving to be saviors with their piloting expertise and ability to translate Bern and operate the radio. She and Edison finally had a crew to take shifts and allow them to rest.

None of the Underground members had resting on their minds, however. While two of the crew manned the cockpit, the remaining three worked to clear the cargo bay. Anlyn wasn't sure how these people had arrived, but they were going to use the same trick to bring in even more of their comrades. The prospect of having someone take over for them, to go and sleep or shower or eat if she chose, made Anlyn's head swim with relief. She rested her head against

Edison while Len, the translator sitting in the nav seat, conferred with the rest of the Bern fleet. Anlyn looked up to Edison, sensitive to any sign of double-dealing, but he had his brow down and kept nodding, as if he agreed with what was being said. When the chatter ceased, Len hung up the radio and turned to the others, frowning.

"We're eighth in line," he said. "Our group commander is sending us the coordinates for the rift now."

The tension of the past weeks melted out of Anlyn's muscles. Not only did they now have extra crew to take shifts, there was actually an end in sight. An end to the snow, to the constant maneuvering, and an end to the stifling claustrophobia of being surrounded by a vast enemy fleet. Her skin positively shivered with the thought of leaving that place, but she had a difficult time reconciling her joy with the dour look on Len's face.

"But isn't that good?" she asked.

Len shook his head. "It doesn't give us much time to get our share of people and supplies out of HQ, which means an extra burden on the others. Especially since—" Len turned to Douglas, the pilot. "One of the squads didn't make it. It was Mortimor's group, so we're down to four ships."

Douglas cursed under his breath. He shook his head. "So who's in charge?"

"Over here? I don't know. Arthur isn't at HQ any-more—he jumped out of order. Everything's gone to hell. What I do know is that the first group through the rift is temporarily in charge on the other side, so we need to focus."

"All right." The pilot nodded. "Go tell the others, then. We need to get Ryke and his equipment up here. We'll take the lead on the other side, which means clos-ing this damn rift might fall to us."

"What's going on?" Anlyn asked. She stood aside as Len pushed his way past and disappeared aft. "You're trying to close the rift? Will that stop the invasion?"

Edison returned to his seat and adjusted one of the radio dials. The pilot turned to face Anlyn. "We're going to close the rift from the other side. Even if there wasn't a massive fleet guarding it over here, there's just no way to access it in this slop." He gestured toward the snow. "Honestly, though, this whole thing was thrown together in a few days. You're best off talking to Ryke about it when he gets here."

"That's not *the* Ryke, is it?" Anlyn asked. Among the whispers of the Underground, his legend, how the first messages sent to Drenard led to the group's formation, was less hushed talk and more of a can-yon's howl.

"The same," said Douglas. "He's gonna be pretty excited to meet a member of the Circle."

"It isn't an honor, I assure you. Especially not now. Haven't you heard of the invasion?"

"*This* one?" Douglas waved one hand at the windshield, his brows drooping. "Yeah, I'm aware of it."

"Negative," Edison said, settling back in his seat. "The one with Drenard as its originating locus."

"My empire has declared war on the humans," Anlyn explained.

"You've gotta be kidding," Douglas said. "Why would they do *that*?"

"I have no idea. Why am I defying the Circle's decree? Why did you join the Underground? Why are any of us doing anything?"

Len ran back into the cockpit. "Ryke's on his way, sir, but there's gonna be a delay. Some emergency shipment to Group Two has the timetables fouled."

"Emergency equipment? What for?"

"It wasn't clear. HQ said they were putting something together for a rescue attempt of Group One. It sounds as if that new guy is jumping down to help them."

The pilot turned, his eyes wide. "Cole? What do you mean, *jumping down*?"

"Gravchute, sir, but it's all rumors from what I can tell. Sounds as if the kid wants to bail out of Group

Two's ship, if you can believe that. If you ask me, there's way too much chatter about it on the carrier frequency. It's gonna get us spotted if they keep it up."

"Well, at least we'll be through the rift before the fool causes too much trouble and gets the rest exposed."

Edison grunted. "Uncanny similarity between label and behavior of a Cole I'm acquainted with." He rose from his seat and moved aside for Len to take his place.

Anlyn laughed.

The pilot jabbed a thumb at Edison. "What did he say?"

"Nothing," Anlyn said. "Just that the guy you're talking about reminds him of a friend of ours. Same name."

"Yeah? Yours a troublemaker, too?" The pilot shook his head. "This kid's been in camp for less than a week and he's got the brass to chase down infiltrators in a skimmer when he hasn't even been checked out to pilot the damn machines."

"Figured it out pretty quick," Len said as he adjusted something on the dash.

"Yeah?" The pilot turned to him. "Did those two hyperskimmers come back in one piece?"

"No, but neither did those two traitors," Len rejoined.

Douglas shrugged. "Still, that shouldn't give him license to dream up a raid like this." He laughed. "Then again, rumor has it he's dating the old man's daughter, and we all know where *that'll* get you . . ."

"He's dating Fyde's *daughter*?" Len asked. He reached back and slipped his arms into the flight harness. "Hyperspace, man, I didn't hear that rumor—"

"Wait," Anlyn said. She grabbed Len by the shoulder. "Fyde? *Mortimor* Fyde?"

Len smiled. "Perfect. Nothing can get out of hyperspace, except of course for Mortimor's reputation." He turned to Anlyn. "Whatever you've heard about the old man—"

"No," Anlyn said, shaking her head. "Your Cole and *our* Cole are the same person." She turned to Edison. "What in the *galaxy* is *he* doing here?"

Edison shrugged. A rare, confused look settled across his face. It was a look that gave Anlyn chills.

Farther aft, there was a loud pop of air.

The first in an eager line of people and supplies had boarded their ship.

•• 2 ••

Before stepping into the airlock, Cole let Arthur check his gravchute. After going over the straps and readouts, Arthur slapped Cole's helmet twice. Cole turned and raised his visor.

"Wish me luck!"

"What I wish is that I'd been able to talk you out of this."

"No way," Cole said. "I'm looking forward to it. Now get back; I wanna beat them down there."

Arthur pressed his lips together but nodded. "Okay," he said. "Good luck." He scanned Cole's jumpsuit one more time, his eyes flickering over the combat harness. "Better put those grenades in a pocket before you jump. The pins'll pop loose if you go down hard."

Cole nodded and unclipped the two precious grenades—gifts from the normally tight munitions officer. He backed into the lock, leaving Arthur just past the jamb, and then slapped the inner hatch shut and turned to the outer door. Spreading his feet wide, he grabbed one of the handles rimming the hatch and memorized the location of the door controls. He slid his black goggles into place and snapped his visor shut. Reaching out in the new and absolute darkness, he felt for the controls, lifted the protective cover, and pressed the red button. The outer door before him irised open, and a flood of hyperspace photons peeled his blindness away, the darkened goggles providing him with normal vision.

There was a little suction from the wind outside, but not much. Cole stuck his head out to see where the wings were on the Bern ship; he spotted them high and behind. He turned and saw Arthur smiling at him through the porthole, his own goggles down over his eyes. Cole gave the old trillionaire the thumbs-up and then jumped out sideways, stiffening his body to plummet faster as he angled down through the curtain of fluttering white snow.

Cole immediately felt the frigid air through the fabric of his flight suit, but his helmet blocked out most of the wind's noise. Just as in his Academy jump training, there was an odd sensation missing from leaping out of a moving ship. He expected his stomach to rise into his throat, but nothing of the sort took place. All he felt was the friction of a cold breeze as he plummeted like a dropped dart.

Cole checked the altimeter on his wrist to gauge his rate of descent. It was an older navy model, nearly an antique, but the controls had been easy enough to work out. He held the device in front of his visor and watched it tick down the meters of elevation on the several grids. One showed his falling rate, the other his distance to target—which was locked onto the coordinates of the Luddite camp. Cole altered course by twisting his torso as he switched the grav chute into reverse for maximum speed. If Group One was able to slow the descent of their Bern craft enough, he *just* might be able to beat them to the ground.

Cole looked back to the altimeter on his wrist and wondered what sort of ship had carried the outdated device to hyperspace. What ship had brought the gravchute, for that matter? An older model Firehawk? One of the ancient Sparrows? Definitely something navy and a few generations back, he thought. He moved his hand aside, satisfied with his rate of descent—just in time to see a Bern ship coalesce out of the snow directly below him.

"Flank!"

Cole threw his arms wide and cupped his gloved hands to catch the air. He slowed and veered to one side, missing the flying craft but coming close enough to create a wash effect, which sent him tumbling in a confused ball. He threw his arms and legs out again, fighting to stabilize himself, and then saw another ship go by in the distance. The tight formation of black shapes hung in the snow all around him, nearly invisible in the flurries until it was too late.

As soon as Cole regained control, he forced himself back into a dive and zipped down through the sideways snow, despite his trepidations. When he glanced at his altimeter again, he did so quickly, resuming his vigilance and hoping his near miss hadn't shown up on the Bern craft's SADAR.

He was a few thousand meters up and five hundred off target when he saw the dark mass of the Luddite camp below. The massive black village moved across a white backdrop of packed snow so solid, it made the spotted air seem suddenly gray. Cole angled his body to correct course, relief washing over him as he no longer needed to fear a midair collision. His comfort was brief, however. Orange flashes—naked fires—blazed across the rear portion of the Luddite village. The flames winked through the snow, delineating the outline of a ship-like form sprawled wide across the camp. It was Mortimor's ship. Cole was late for the party.

When the top of the village's tall mast zipped by just a few dozen meters away, Cole popped the chute's controls in the other direction. The grav nullifiers kicked upward, the straps wrenching the air out of Cole's chest, and still he continued to fall, his incredible velocity too much to quickly overcome. Even through his closed helmet, he could hear the gravchute screaming above the wind. Cole glanced at his altimeter. Fifty meters. Steering with his shoulders, he picked a clear piece of forward decking where Byrne's ship and a Firehawk had been parked during his last visit. He felt a sickening sensation as he saw how many fur-clad Luddites were running to and fro below him.

The deck swelled closer. Cole braced for impact.

The idea was to hit running, but he came in too fast. His knees buckled, and he went into a roll to dissipate the force. He felt his pack bang violently against the deck, and he ended up in an uncomfortable sprawl. Cole pushed himself up, quickly unbuckled his harness, and let the overworked chute drift to the ground. And then, out of nowhere, a Luddite came at him, screaming. Cole yanked his buckblade free and fumbled for the switch. The man swung at him with a sideways blow.

Cole immediately turned his blade vertical and locked his new arm in place. Pistons and rods stood firm where once muscle and sinew lay. His attacker's buckblade bounced back before it reached Cole's, repelled from the like gravitational field so fast, it simply flew out of the figure's hands. Cole stepped out of the way, allowing the man's momentum to carry him by, and then brought his own blade down on the man's shoulder and out his opposite hip.

The man's torso fell a few meters from his legs, his heart visible in its ribcage, still beating. Cole looked up from the two pieces toward the downed ship in the distance, far beyond the mast. All across the deck, dozens of figures moved toward the crash site—more than Cole thought he could fight through. He considered the plan Arthur had come up with and suddenly felt too exposed to pull it off. He was one idiot, alone and ill-prepared, against a legion of hardened maniacs. With the crash of the ship, the element of surprise was gone. Every able-bodied Luddite was now crawling across the camp, looking for trouble. And in his white suit, Cole stood out like an albino on a Mediterranean beach.

He looked off to the side, beyond the village's railings, at all the snow streaking by. He kept turning and faced the bow, where a massive wall, shaped in a tall vee, parted the sideways flurries.

The plan had been to meet up with Mortimor and the rest of his crew, and then wait for Arthur's special delivery to extract them. But first, Cole thought he should take a bit of a detour and do what he did best:

Improvise.

4

LUDDITE CAMP

Penny helped Jym up from the ground, the pilot having been thrown out of his seat when their hijacked craft crashed into the Luddite camp. Mortimor clung to the dash nearby; he peered through the busted canopy at the jumbled structures in the village below. It had been Penny's idea to try to land on the Luddite village, partly to do some damage, but mostly to keep from being buried in the snow and pushed back into the oblivion of hyperspace.

Jym clasped Penny's wrists and stood up with her assistance.

"Thanks," he said, gathering himself.

He seemed about to say something else, but Penny raised her hand to quiet him. She leaned toward the cockpit door. Somewhere aft, she could hear the hiss of plasma torches and the clanging of outer hull plating. "They're already cutting their way inside," she told the others. "I don't think they're happy with our parking job."

"We'll make our stand in the cargo bay," Mortimor told her. He patted Jym on the back, and both men reached for their blades.

Penny nodded her agreement, and the three of them made their way aft, leaning to one side to compensate for the tilt of the deck and the Bern craft's busted grav panels.

"If anyone gets caught and interrogated, this was the extent of the raid, okay?" Mortimor gave them both a serious look. "It was just us, and our goal was to bring down one of their ships and damage the village. No word of the other crews, no matter what they do to us."

They nodded, each of them well aware of the Luddite fondness for removing limbs.

Mortimor led them out of the cockpit. "Penny, you stay behind as backup in case one of us goes down. Jym, you cover the port side."

"Don't try to protect me," Penny said. "I'm the best here with a blade." She stepped ahead of the other two. "I'll take the starboard—"

"Watch out!" Jym yelled, raising his buckblade.

Penny turned and got hers up as well. Two Luds stormed into the bay, slowing up when they saw they were outnumbered. "Do this fast," Penny said. "We've got to take them in small bites."

Mortimor ran down the far side of the cargo bay, threatening to flank them. Penny pushed forward, forcing them to think about two dangers at once. One of the men seemed timid. Penny screamed and lunged at him, giving Mortimor time to get behind.

The attack took just a few seconds, and then there was more mess piled up in the ship, Human and Bern bits indistinguishable.

"Are we better off down on the village deck?" Jym asked. "It's gonna get awful crowded in here."

Penny looked to Mortimor and saw a grim seriousness in his furrowed brow and set lips. "It's just a numbers game, isn't it?" she asked him. "We're just seeing how many we can take with us?"

Mortimor nodded. "Hopefully this'll scare the Bern and speed up the invasion. Maybe we'll end up ushering the other groups through the rift quicker. I say we take out a few more Luds here. After that, they'll know what they're up against, that this isn't a friendly crash landing."

"And then what?" Jym asked.

Mortimor shrugged. "I don't suppose it'll be long before we find out."

o o o o

Cole sprinted away from the crashed ship toward the bow of the Luddite village. He angled to starboard, his improvised plan hatching as he went. He headed for the edge of the giant wedge that parted the horizontal snow of hyperspace and kept the flurries from settling on the deck. It was nothing more than a thick, vertical wall of steel in the shape of a V, creating a sideways roof over the mobile town. With his sword extended and held firmly by his waist, Cole jogged close to the wall, the handle of his blade held just centimeters away. He could only hope that the invisible buckblade was long enough to extend all the way through the metal plating. Looking back as he ran, he saw a jagged line being created—the rise and fall of his gait measured in a fine crack of destruction through the tall shield.

Cole paced himself, recognizing that he had a decent jog ahead. He settled into a rhythm and concentrated on his breathing, trying to ignore the increasing heft of his boots. He followed the tall V to the bow, checking now and then to ensure that his blade was still on. Then he traced his way down the port side.

Before he got through three quarters of the other side of the wall, Cole heard a satisfying groan of steel as the remaining section struggled to hold up the rest. He cut another dozen meters, running faster and waiting for the wails of distressed steel to increase their pitch, and then he sprinted down the rail directly aft, pumping his legs as fast as he could to outpace what he figured to be a toppling mountain of metal about thirty meters tall.

He looked back only once, which was all it took to make him run even faster. The wall was bending around the portion still connected, singing and shrieking as thick metal crumpled like tin. An avalanche of snow shivered from the wedge, and more than a meter of hard pack calved off like a fractured iceberg. The great white sheets crashed and exploded on the deck, followed soon after by the cliff of thick, welded plates that formerly made up the bow shield.

The force of the impact shot up through Cole's boots like an earthquake, throwing him to the ground. He rolled and slid, came to a graceless stop, and then spun around, gasping for breath as he surveyed the damage he'd wrought.

He had easily cleared the falling wall, even though it had felt a lot closer when it hit. The massive wave of packed snow had slid closer, but probably never posed a threat even if it had reached him. Hitting him in the face—spotting his dark goggles with blooms of moisture—came the only bombardment from his efforts: *Snow*. Flying sideways and already dusting the deck, the flakes spun and twirled around him, creating a thick mist of white as they coursed through the air unabated.

Looking aft toward the crash site, Cole watched the spreading veil twist its way toward the distant structures, swallowing everything in a sticky cloud. Dark shapes could be seen moving about, the ferocious slam of steel having created just the sort of panic he'd hoped for. The other part of his impromptu plan seemed to be working as well: he could now see the dark figures more clearly. Swaddled in their matted furs, they stood out stark against the new white land he had unleashed.

Cole jogged aft and stopped to retrieve his grav chute. He found it already dusted with snow. He slung it over his white uniform and then pulled his buckblade back out and flicked off the safety. Picking out the nearest Luddites, he stole their direction, his sword armed and at the ready. As he closed the distance—their beastly shapes standing out clear as day against the snow—he wondered just how well *they* would be able to see *him*.

o o o o

Penny and Mortimor stood over another pair of overanxious Luds, the pieces of them leaking fluids. She heard someone barking orders farther down the hull and knew the easy kills were done. The furballs were getting organized.

"We can't stay here," Mortimor said.

"What about the floor?" Jym asked. He traced an imaginary slash through the decking.

"No!" Penny said, holding out a hand. "There's no telling what you'd slice through. The forward thrusters might get their fuel from somewhere aft of here."

"Then how about around the portholes?" Jym asked. "Maybe there's a rooftop to jump to—"

"We're too high for that," Mortimor said. He pointed to the flakes of snow drifting through the busted canopy. "In fact, are we higher than the camp's bow shield?"

Penny powered down her sword and ran toward the cockpit, disappearing into the swirling flurries leaking through the hole in the canopy. "No way we're that high," she called back to them. "The main deck can't be more than twenty meters up." She looked out through the shattered glass at the rooftops below. The mast in the distance was just a hazy strand of black rising up through a sudden blizzard.

She turned back to the others. "I think the impact of our crash took out the bow shield—"

A loud bang cut her off, followed by a shudder that traveled through the deck. Penny stepped back into the cargo bay as several identical, calamitous sounds reverberated through the hull.

"What is *that*?" Jym asked. He turned side to side anxiously, his buckblade held out.

"Careful," Penny said, flipping on her own blade in case she needed to protect herself from his.

Another bang. Extremely close.

Mortimor looked up at the ceiling. "I think they're surrounding us, preparing to come in from the top." He motioned with his hands. "Everyone in the center of the bay, back to back. Watch your angles."

Jym and Mortimor lined up facing aft, and Penny formed the head of the triangle, watching the cockpit. Another bang rang out, and then Penny heard the dull pounding of footsteps on the roof of the ship. Someone whistled in the distance—the only warning they got before a dozen Luddites began cutting their way down through the ceiling. There was a horrible din of clanging metal as cut circles of steel clattered within the mechanical spaces over their heads. And then came the shrill fury of Luddite war-cries, paced by the stomping of their approaching boots from all directions—

o o o o

Cole skirted the tower's base, partly because of the small group guarding its perimeter, but mostly out of fear of its effects on time. The grav chute on his back made jogging uncomfortable; Cole cinched it tighter and steadied it with one hand while he held his blade in the other. He entered a small clearing he remembered from his last desperate run through the village. The only difference now was the looming hulk of a massive spaceship sprawled in the distance.

As Cole neared, he thought he could see figures running across the wings of the ship, far above the deck. He stopped near one of the sheds and watched more dark blobs scurry up what looked like steel beams dropped onto the fuselage, giving the Luddites a way up. He reached down and turned his chute to full lift but left the power off. He wondered if his idea would work, or if he'd have to scurry up the beams after them.

Putting his blade away, Cole took a few deep breaths as he picked out the first building. Visualizing each step—virtually running his muscles though the entire process—he dug one boot into the deck and pressed the other against the wall of the building behind him. Grimacing, Cole shoved off, running as fast as he could for the low structure he'd chosen.

The distances were complete guesswork, made on intuition and a feel for the chute's power on the way down. Cole jumped up about ten meters before reaching the wall and jammed the chute on. His stomach dropped and his throat constricted at the odd sensation of going up through the air higher than his legs had sent him. Even so, he'd been overly optimistic—he reached the top of his augmented leap and drifted back down much too far away, his forward momentum from the sprint taking him directly toward the building's steel wall.

Cole braced for impact and brought one hand up to protect his face, the other reaching for the roof's edge. He hit so hard, he nearly bounced off, but his right hand clutched the top of the wall with an iron grip, leaving him dangling.

Tensing his new arm, and with the aid of the grav chute set to max, Cole vaulted to the top of the roof with an eerie ease. The combined might of the two devices, chute and arm, made him feel giddy. *Powerful.*

He shut the chute back down so his feet would have enough traction to run and lined himself up with a taller building across a wide alley. Cole took off, planning in advance the next sequence of jumps on his way up to the Bern craft's cockpit.

○ ○ ○ ○

The Luddite battle cries came from all directions, nearly masking the thunder of rushing boots. Ceiling panels rained down, cut in rough circles, one of them nearly crashing on top of the defensive trio.

The clanging of so much steel just added to the confusion. Penny almost left one nearby attacker to Mortimor and then realized the Lud was in her zone. She feinted high, and he brought his blade up to counter. In a blur, she swooped for his ankles. The Lud's boots stayed planted in an expert attack base even as the rest of him collapsed to the deck, screaming. Penny finished him off with a slice across the torso and then turned to fend off a blow from a second Lud who had jumped down from above. In her peripheral, she saw Mortimor and Jym parrying their own attacks from behind.

The war cries mixed with agony wails as several Luds bled out. Penny checked over her shoulder after sending an attacker's arm flying and saw that Jym was among the screaming. He writhed on the deck, one of his legs off, but he continued lashing madly at the ankles of the men aft of him. Penny turned around as two more Luds jumped down. She dispatched one but left herself open to the second. She saw the attack while still following through with her own, but it came too fast. Her non-sword arm was left hanging out in space from the twisting momentum of her torso. It came off clean, just below her elbow, and a deep nick opened along her thigh as well.

She ducked the next blow and went for the knees with an angle two, taking away the fur-clad man's mobility.

"Cockpit!" she yelled to Mortimor. She dispatched the wounded attacker who had taken her arm and ran forward as more of the horde rained in around them. Penny turned to see if Mortimor was still with her. She ground her teeth when she saw blood streaming down one of his hands and running off in a tight rivulet. It splattered the deck as he performed unorthodox, desperate swings with his other hand.

There were at least a dozen Luds in the cargo bay. One of them silenced Jym as the group pressed forward, forcing her and Mortimor toward the cockpit. More banging rang out above, letting Penny know there was no safe exit. They were surrounded and critically outnumbered.

One began barking orders to the others, planning the last surge, when Penny realized the encirclement was complete. With a loud bang, a large portion of the cockpit canopy fell in just as she and Mortimor were squeezing through the passageway. She barely had room to defend herself as two Luds crashed through the opening, their swords held on opposite sides and poised for a deadly pincer attack.

Penny picked one of them to counter, the other side of her body bracing for a killing blow. Tensing up, she swung her blade into position, and both men froze. Their arms went slack, the pincer attack falling into limp impotence. Both their torsos opened with an avalanche of intestines, bright joints of spine sticking up through the mess as the tops of the men fell away.

As the lifeless, gory heaps crashed to the deck, they revealed behind them the hazy outline of someone in white—someone framed fuzzily against the torrent of snow. Penny couldn't make out much of their savior, but she did note the barest hint of a classical fencer's stance—a stance normally guaranteed to get buckbladers killed.

o o o o

Cole put his blade away. He held on to the edge of the canopy with one hand and fumbled inside a combat pouch with the other. He pulled out one of two blast grenades and clipped the pin to a snap on the front of his suit. Ahead of him, Penny and Mortimor were backing into the tight cockpit, slipping on the mess he'd created on the floor. Without adequate room for defensive posturing, their repelling blades threatened themselves and each other as much as they promised to protect them. Beyond his two wounded friends, Cole saw a file of attackers lining up for their chance at a killing blow.

"Grab on!" Cole yelled into the cockpit. His boots tenuously gripped the ship's icy hull as he held out a hand toward Penny.

Penny screamed over her shoulder at Mortimor, who relented, turned, and put away his blade. He stepped onto the pilot's seat and reached for Cole.

With a loud cry, Penny lunged and swung at the first Luddite to enter the cockpit. Their blades flew away from each other and did damage to the ship. Mortimor scampered up onto the dash and out into the snow-streaked air, yelling for Penny to follow. Her attacker pressed forward, threatening them all with any rebound from Penny's blade.

Cole watched as she dove forward, below the attack, swinging upward at her foe's elbow as she flew inside his range.

Both of them crashed to the ground, slipping in the guts on the decking. Penny pushed herself up as the next guy came storming in. She turned, sliding, and scampered toward the others as an invisible blade whisked back and forth behind her, eager to cut her in two.

Cole let go of the jagged canopy and ripped the grenade from his suit. He tossed it over Penny's head and yelled: "Jump!"

One of Cole's arms held Mortimor with an iron grip—the other reached out for her.

Penny came through the hole in the canopy, crashing into both men. They all clutched at one another, falling backward onto the icy nose of the great Bern ship. Cole fumbled along the side of the grav chute, struggling to find the damned power button and trying not to lose his grip on the others as they slid across the slick steel.

He was still fumbling for the switch when they reached the edge of the gracefully curved nose, and then all three went tumbling over and out into the great quiet and snow-filled air.

5

LUDDITE CAMP

Just as the three of them slid off the nose of the Bern craft, Cole heard a satisfying thump from the grenade he'd left behind. The trio tumbled into the air, the snow below and all around them brightening for a moment as the flash of the explosion reflected off a million flecks of floating ice.

Cole didn't have time to enjoy the effects of the blast. They plummeted through nothingness, spiraling down toward the metal decking far below, while someone screamed in his ear—

It was the *gravchute*, Cole realized.

He held Mortimor—his new arm clinched tight around the man's waist—and Penny latched onto him

117

with an iron grip of her own. The chute trilled with a dying might, pushing up with every ounce of engineering left in it. Still, they hit the deck as if they'd fallen from a story up, all three of them flying apart with grunts and sickening thuds.

The gravchute felt fit to explode, the heat of the thing scorching Cole's back through his combat suit. He sat up and cut it loose, watching as it shot up from the deck before falling silent and crashing back down a stone's throw away.

Mortimor seemed slow to get up, one of his arms pressed tight to his stomach. Cole stood to help him and then felt a jolt of electricity in his ankle, tendons crying out for him to go prone and remain there. He ignored them and limped to Mortimor, hoping it was just a sprain.

Helping the older man up, Cole noticed the deep gash in his outfit, right across his abdomen; Mortimor's white suit was splattered with streams of red, his arm cut as well.

Mortimor must've seen the look on Cole's face.

"It's not that bad," Mortimer said, grunting as he got to his feet. "What's bad is you jumping down here to die with us."

"I've got a plan," Cole said, grimacing. Penny limped over, her buckblade already out as she looked to the sky for pursuers. Cole saw for the first time that one of her hands was missing, almost up to the elbow. He nearly gagged at the sight of fluid leaking out of the stump—until he realized it wasn't blood.

"You okay?" Mortimor asked her.

She held up her arm. Her eyes narrowed as she peered at it through the snow. "The problem might be my leg," she said, indicating a deep gash in her thigh. "Actuator cable got severed."

Cole wanted to ask just how much of her was human, but the look on her face reminded him that they were out of the pan, and now they needed to escape the fire. He unzipped another pocket and fumbled for his radio, looking around the wreckage as he did so to get his bearings.

"We've got to get away from the ship," he said, nodding forward and toward the village's mast. "Can everyone move?"

Mortimor and Penny both nodded and scampered uneasily toward the camp's bow. Cole took one step and collapsed to his knees, the pain in his ankle overpowering his adrenaline.

Penny saw him go down and limped back to him. She put her blade away and wrapped her arm around his back.

"Guess you just answered your own question," she said.

Cole grunted, adjusted his goggles, and let her carry the weight from his bad foot. The three of them labored forward into the snow, leaving a trail of blood and hydraulic fluid behind.

"What's this about a plan?" Penny asked. "Is it better than your last one?"

Cole grimaced and nodded. He pointed with the radio's antenna, gesturing to an alley through the line of buildings ahead, the same ones he'd used to leap-frog up to the cockpit.

"There's a small clearing through there. We need to get to it as quick as we can." He squeezed the transmit button on the radio as Mortimor led them through the flurries. "Thrower, this is Relay," he said. "Limber up for the toss."

He and Penny ducked into the alley after Mortimor. Cole looked over his shoulder and checked for signs of pursuit.

"I don't like the sound of your code," Penny said.

Cole ignored her and flicked on the radio's locator. They exited the crack between the two buildings and found Mortimor standing over two halves of a man, his buckblade out, his wounded arm leaking a steady stream of blood. Cole reached for his own blade and looked around for signs of danger, but there was nothing through the thick veil of snow that he could see. He hobbled past Mortimor, toward the center of the clearing, and was amazed to see how quickly the drifts were forming around the bases of the buildings. Then he recalled how swiftly Riggs's Firehawk had been buried. He spoke into the radio again, wincing as he did so at the thought of his dead friend.

"Thrower, Relay here. Toss away. Miss to any side by a few meters."

"What's going on?" Mortimor asked. He tucked his blade away and clutched his arm to slow the bleeding. His neat, brown beard was covered in flecks of melting snow, giving him the look of a mountaineer. The blood splattered all across his white suit, however, made him appear more like an emergency room surgeon.

"Huddle together," Cole said. He pulled Mortimor close, realizing suddenly how much he had come to like the old man. It was almost impossible to imagine surviving this, actually being someplace safe and warm where nobody was bleeding, but he still felt an overpowering urge to get there, that mystical sanctuary, and to do his best to impress this man who felt more like a father than anyone ever had.

He pulled Penny closer and fumbled for the other grenade. He clipped it to his suit as a loud popping sound preceded the nearby clang of metal on metal.

Cole glanced around and spotted the jump platform that had popped out of thin air, sent by one of the larger cage platforms at HQ. It was a big sacrifice, slowing the evacuation. The fact that they sent it at all reminded Cole how much others must also feel for the old man. He let go of Mortimor and limped toward it.

"Is that what I think it is?" Penny asked.

Cole nodded and pushed the control console off the platform's base. He used his strong arm to drag the battery Arthur had wired up, tucking it in the lee of the console to keep the snow off the contacts.

"What's to stop them from following us?" Mortimor asked.

Cole pulled out his radio; he turned and patted the grenade on his chest. With a smile, he squeezed the transmit button. "Catcher, this is Relay. Feed the numbers."

"Oh, *flank!*" said Penny. She pointed over his shoulder.

Cole turned as the first dark form exited the narrow alley and charged through the snow toward them.

"You first!" Cole shouted to Mortimor. He shoved the older man toward the small platform and drew his blade. Mortimor seemed on the verge of arguing, and then he glanced down at his blood-soaked uniform. He nodded weakly and took a step back. Cole turned as Penny sliced through the first attacker, her handless arm swinging for counterbalance and sending out a gray stream of fluids among the white flakes.

Yet another surge of adrenaline coursed through Cole's body, numbing the pain in his ankle and staving off exhaustion. He thanked his overworked gland, wondering if the last month had somehow tripled its reserve, and shuffled through the slick film of snow to pull Penny back. Behind him, half a shout from Mortimor was cut short by a pop of air. Cole didn't turn to make sure he was gone—he just urged Penny to get in place as two more men came forward, the snow swirling around them and coating their fur. The cluster of Luddites approached slowly now, wary like a pack of beasts stalking a wounded prey.

Penny moved to flank them, but Cole yanked her back and shoved her toward the platform. He kept his eyes on the men as he shouted over his shoulder: "Go! Before more come."

One of the men lunged, his arms spinning with a powerful attack. Cole raised his blade, trying to visualize the angles of deflection, when Penny's arm flashed beside him, throwing something.

The man went down in a heap, the front of his fur wrappings split open, a buckblade hilt lodged in his sternum.

The other men took a step back, moving their blades to a defensive position as they watched their friend writhe on the ground. Cole heard another statement half-said, this time by Penny, followed by a pop of air. He backed up slowly and glanced down at the grenade dangling from his chest. Several more men entered the clearing. Cole was alone but preparing to jump out after the others.

"He's mine!" someone roared.

A figure stepped forward from the rest, pulling the other beasts away by their shoulders. Cole felt the edge of the platform behind him with one boot. He reached up and wrapped his hand around the grenade, preparing to drop it near the pedestal, to count to three, and then to jump out. His wild plan was coming off without a hitch.

He looked up as the approaching figure began unwrapping his face, revealing blond hair so bright it made the snow seem dingy and gray.

Too late, thought Cole, as he began to tug the grenade loose. He looked down to make sure the pin was going to come free, then caught sight of a different glint of metal: a scratch in his new hand, the pink flesh peeled back to reveal a small hydraulic rod lined up with one of his knuckles.

Cole loosened his iron grip on the grenade and watched as the piston responded. He remembered how he had come to possess the hand. He remembered what the Luddites had done to Riggs. He remembered what *he* had done to Riggs.

Cole let go of the grenade completely, dropping his arm away from his chest. He reached instead for his buckblade, metal wrapping around metal. He peered up at Joshua, the man who had taken his arm, and forgot for a moment the need for his own escape . . .

o o o o

Penny fell out of the air with a thud. The second half of her scream, a warning to Cole, remained caught in her throat, cut short by her skip across hyperspace. Several pairs of hands clasped her, dragging her out of the way before they began searching her for damage.

"Send the numbers!" someone yelled.

Penny looked toward the voice. It was Arthur, who stood at the inner edge of a circle formed around the spot she had just fallen through. A group of aliens stood there, waiting for another arrival.

A bright flash of a welding torch blossomed in Penny's peripheral. She noted the stench of burning metal as some mechanic worked to staunch her loss of fluids.

"Not now," she told him. She pushed the various worried hands away, the amount of stimulation buzzing on all sides driving her over the brink. She looked around for Mortimor, only to find his legs sticking out from a clustered mob of soldiers pretending to be medics. Scanning the sparse assemblage, Penny realized she wasn't on a lifeboat full of hope. Whatever group had received them, it wasn't the basket getting all the best eggs from HQ.

She grabbed the sleeve of one of the men inspecting her various gashes. "Where is everyone?" she asked.

"Three groups are through the rift," the man said. "We got a bum slot in the queue."

The man started to say more, but Penny's mind was already elsewhere. It felt as if it had been an hour since she'd vanished from the Luddite village and spilled out across the deck. Surely it had been long enough for the platform to recharge. Where was Cole?

She looked back to the center of the empty circle, her gaze joining dozens of others as they waited for another pop of air.

"Where the hell are you?" Penny asked no one.

o o o o

Cole could see in his peripheral that he was being surrounded. He could also tell that Joshua would strike down any of his own men who dared attack him first. He put the crowd out of mind, which had him forgetting the danger inherent in the jump platform—the ease with which Ryke's magical device could be used against the ongoing raid above.

He forgot these things and took a step forward, raising his sword and trying his best to not limp on his busted ankle. Cole remembered what Penny had told him during their first buckblade lesson: There was nothing heroic about these fights. There were no speeches. It was one slash, and then it was over.

Keeping his feet in an orthodox fencer's stance, he swung his blade like a traditional sword, which elicited chuckles from the tightening circle and forced a smile across Joshua's face.

The Luddite leader darted into range, swinging one of the power angles Cole had hoped for. Cole locked up his new wrist, his elbow, and his shoulder. He transferred his weight to the ball of his good foot and brought his blade around to block the attack.

The rebound should have thrown his own blade into his knees, taking off both limbs in a gory recreation of his first sparring mistake. Instead, with his stance soft and with all his weight on the ball of one boot, the force of the magnetic repulsion spun him completely around, his elbow, wrist, and shoulder locked solid.

Cole went full circle, twirling like a child's top. He raised his blade, for a brief moment facing away from Joshua and his men, watching his hand as it steered the invisible sword in a great circle.

When he came around expecting to slice Joshua in half, Cole felt his buckblade rebound off Joshua's sword once again.

But the rebound was milder this time.

As the world fell back into focus, Cole saw why: his sword had passed through Joshua's waist to meet the man's still-frozen attack on the other side of his body, bounced off, and slid back through the man's chest once more.

Cole threw both arms out and regained his balance as Joshua fell in pieces.

The wide arc of fur-clad warriors lit up with furious shouts, screams of disbelief, and outrage. Cole took a step toward the platform, counting. Several of the men ran forward, their full-throated fury befitting their animalistic garb, their arms high with attacks meant to kill.

When Cole got to "three," he took a last step back, activating the platform with his weight and dropping a small metal pin before he went.

He left the howling men with a gentle pop of air.

Followed by a very loud bang.

oooo

Cole fell out of the air and slammed into the metal decking of the Bern ship. A scattering of snowflakes—caught up in the platform's energistic bubble—drifted down around him. An alien rushed to his side and began probing for wounds. Beyond, a cacophony of shouts and worried conversations merged into a nervous, indecipherable patter.

The Underground member tending to him said something in a foreign tongue. Cole shook his head. He looked around for Penny and Mortimor as the leg of his combat suit was cut back to expose his injured ankle. In a cluster of confused, trembling bodies to one side, Cole saw Penny's bright-red mane. She was in the same pose in which he'd first seen her: leaning over a patient, splattered with blood, a mask of rigid worry on her face.

"Penny!"

She looked up, and Cole read the news in her set jaw. One of Mortimor's hands clutched the folds of her combat suit just below her shoulder. Cole tried to swallow the lump in his throat; he attempted to stand, but the alien medic forced him back down. The figure held Cole in place while a needle went into his ankle, deep as the bone. Cole clenched his teeth at the pinch and metallic sting. A surge of icy numbness spread through his foot. The alien stood back, still chattering in a foreign tongue.

Cole rose and hobbled over to Penny and Mortimor, practically hopping on one foot. A corner of the hijacked Bern ship's cargo bay had been transformed into a disorganized operating room. A Pheron knelt on the other side of Mortimor and was just finishing sewing up a wound on his exposed abdomen. The skin all around it was smeared pink from being wiped free of blood.

Cole collapsed by Penny. "What're we waiting on?" he asked. He glanced toward the cockpit. "We need to get him help. We need to get back to HQ—"

"There's nothing there," Penny said, shaking her head. "These are the last of the technicians. Everyone's out."

"We need to get through the rift, then."

Penny nodded toward one of the crewmen. "They say we've got about a day of waiting."

Cole looked around. Most of the gathered figures were peering back. They were looking to Mortimor, who lay perfectly still, his head in Penny's lap.

One more glance at the man's wounds, and Cole saw quite clearly that they might have a day of waiting ahead of them, but Mortimor's body didn't have a day of life left in it. The old man's eyes fluttered.

He looked up at Penny as she stroked his brown hair streaked with gray.

Mortimor coughed. A shaking hand came up to cover his mouth much too late. Cole reached for a pad of gauze in the medical kit and dabbed at the fresh blood on Mortimor's beard, unable to stand the sight of it there.

Mortimor closed his eyes.

"I need you to stay with us," Cole demanded.

"A little rest," Mortimor whispered, his voice a quiet rasp. "A little rest, and I'll be just fine."

"No," Penny said, gently shaking his shoulders. "You need to stay awake. I need you to keep talking."

Mortimor shook his head, just barely. He started to say something, and then another coughing fit seized him. Flecks of foamy red flew past his shaking fist. Some of it spotted his beard.

"Can't," he croaked. His lids fell shut slowly and then reopened. "Hurts to talk," he whispered.

Cole rested a hand on the old man's chest and tried to think of what to say to keep him engaged. Mortimor turned to him, his eyes half shut.

"Talk to me," he said, as if sensing Cole's thoughts.

"Everything's gonna be okay," Cole told him feebly. "We're queued up for the rift. Once we get through, we're gonna get you some better help."

Mortimor closed his eyes and shook his head. "I don't wanna be lied to," he whispered, his voice barely audible.

What he said next was even closer to silence—his lips moved, but Cole couldn't understand a word.

"What?" Cole leaned closer. "What did you say?"

"Tell me . . ." Mortimor grimaced, his hand moving to his pink-stained stomach. "I want to know about her," he whispered, "before I go."

"Who?" Cole asked. "And you're not going anywhere. You just hang in there."

Mortimor coughed, sending up another crimson shower. He shook his head feebly. "No more lies," he whispered. "I don't have time for them."

"What do you want me to say?" Cole asked. He looked to Penny for help, but her attention was fixed on Mortimor. "What am I supposed to do?"

"Mollie," Mortimor croaked. He said her name again: "Mollie. Tell me about my daughter. Talk to me about what she's like while I rest my eyes just a little . . ."

PART XVIII

COLE

*"To those who make them,
everything's conspiracy."*

~The Bern Seer~

6

PORTUGAL,

EARTH · SIX YEARS EARLIER

"Do you swear to tell the truth, the whole truth, and nothing but the truth, so help you Gods?"

The words startled Cole, that last one especially. He glanced from the bailiff to the judge sitting in the elevated dais to his side. The judge nodded at him, urging Cole along.

Cole looked down at his hand, which felt heavy on the black Bible. He could feel the bumps and ridges on the book's cover, like the skin of something that might bite him. He was suddenly aware of the hundreds of gazes and cameras aimed his way, all the judgment pouring out of them. It was the book, he realized. It all came back to that scaly book.

"Do you swear to tell the whole truth?" the bailiff asked again.

A lawyer turned to the judge and let out an exasperated sigh.

It was a simple question, Cole knew. Probably the simplest anyone would ask of him. If he couldn't answer this one, how was he going to survive the rest? He swept his gaze out over the sea of faces in all those rows of benches and up to the packed balcony. Spectators were even pressed tight along the back wall, jostling with one another to see. The double doors at the end of the center aisle opened, and Cole watched a uniformed officer wave off whoever was attempting to enter.

"Do you swear to tell the truth?" the bailiff demanded, his impatience laced with venom.

Cole nodded.

"We need to hear you say it, son," the judge told him.

"I swear," Cole said. He lifted his hand from the Bible and rubbed the pads of his fingers together. They were warm, or maybe he was just imagining it.

"Please be seated."

Cole sat. There was something comforting in being told to sit or stand, and when. He looked down at his feet, wondering if there was a place to kneel as well.

"I'd like to start with the . . . *event*," the lawyer said. He stressed the last word, his voice regaining its honeyed quality as it was projected out more for the audience than for Cole. "Can you tell us where you were on the day the research institute was destroyed?"

Cole swallowed. He ran the question back in his mind a few times, wary of making any mistakes.

"I was in the barrio," he finally said.

Laughter rolled through the crowd, perhaps at the outlandish idea that a slum rat such as him would be anywhere *else*.

"Where were you *exactly*?" the lawyer demanded. He crossed his arms and turned to the benches, which Cole suddenly realized were arranged very much like church pews. Everyone was facing him, rapt and expectant, with wide grins still pinned to the faces of those who had been laughing. He was practically on an altar, Cole realized. One of the altars of old, where defenseless things were sacrificed to higher powers. That's where he was—not in a courtroom.

"Answer the question," the judge intoned.

I was in the barrio, Cole repeated to himself. He wasn't sure what to say, but the people in the pews had laughed because they knew he couldn't have been anywhere else. They had laughed because *in the barrio* meant nothing to them. It was an imprecise sprawl, and yet it was Cole's entire universe. He thought the question over again, wondering what the lawyer wanted, wondering how not to give it to him. He looked out over the congregation, their eyes and mocking smiles wide.

"I was up on the water tower," he blurted out, the truth spilling from him before he could contain it.

•• TWO WEEKS EARLIER ••

Cole gripped rungs still wet with the morning's dew and began his long and routine climb up the metal ladder. Chipping paint uncoiled from the old steel beneath his hands, revealing muddy, gold rust beneath. He climbed quickly, and the water tower above rang with his movement, almost as if sensing his arrival.

When he finally reached the grated platform high above, Cole saw that the sun had not yet risen to light up his small patch of Portugal. Its first rays barely leaked over the horizon to give the swollen belly of the water tower a pale glow. He ran his hands along the curved and riveted panels as he circled the giant container. There was no need to rap it with his knuckles; his footfalls made the entire structure rattle with an obvious, tinny emptiness.

When Cole reached the east side, he plopped down on the metal grating, the cold and wet steel pressing up through the seat of his blue shorts. He dangled his thin legs out over the edge, wiped the moisture from the rail ahead of him, and leaned forward to gaze out over his unlucky home.

The barrio.

Land of filth and muck and muddy sorrow. A slum crowded with people bustling and jostling to be anywhere else.

Cole's eyes wandered up twisted alleys barely visible in the pre-dawn darkness. The tight streets appeared as black cracks among the dull gray of wooden and metal shacks, all of it a maze of winding anarchy. Twinkling everywhere above this maze was a wet web of electrical and telephone lines entangling the rooftops in a confused snare. It was like a net cast from the heavens to trap any of the floundering, flapping, filthy poor who happened to worm their way out of the labyrinth below.

Cole looked farther up Angústia Hill, where the sides of leaning shacks caught some of the looming day's light. Twisted planes of steel glowed as if still molten. They brought into clear relief the jumbled nature of the ad-hoc town: the shared walls and overlapping corrugated roofs; the rebar bones poking up through abandoned second-story dreams; the wisps of smoke from cooking fires that cascaded from under eaves instead of traveling up proper stovepipes. For as far as his twelve-year-old eyes could see, the surface of his cursed Portugal was covered with slipshod shanties. It was a landscape of jumbled cubes, like a sack of individual little dice poured into the mud by gods playing some crooked game, a game where all the pips came up craps every time.

Cole rested his arms on the railing and swung his feet out over it all.

"This world doesn't suck—it's just *stuck*."

He chanted the singsong phrase to himself, trying to sound as convincing as the sisters.

"All that's due is a miracle or two—"

The rest of the rhyme's hopeless optimism was interrupted by the soft clang of hands and feet slapping steel rungs far below. The tower swayed slightly as someone else reached the platform and came to take away his solitude and depressing vista. Cole turned and gazed down the curving walkway as light footsteps rang his way.

"Holá, brother," someone out of sight called too loudly. "It's just me."

Cole's heart practically pounded straight through his ribcage when Joanna, his sister in name only, came into view. She rounded the belly of the water tower, squeezing her way along the narrow walkway just as the sun broached the horizon with the sudden intensity only a valley could know.

A warm glow bathed Joanna's walnut skin and gave her straight black hair an obsidian sheen. The timing of the day's dawn and her arrival were spectacular. It was a combination nearly as potent as it was torturous. Cole's new awareness of the opposite sex had coincided perfectly with his adoption into the religious order of Miracle Makers. For obvious hormonal reasons, joining a sect that promoted abstinence had seemed a pain-less no-brainer just six months ago. Now, it was excruciating.

"Holá, Sister Joanna," Cole said, stressing her name more than the cursed honorific. "What are *you* doing here?"

The smile on Joanna's face melted, and Cole swore the sun itself dimmed. He felt like an ass for the way his question sounded, even to his own ears.

"Am I not welcome?" Joanna asked.

"No," Cole said. "It's not that. I'm sorry, it's just that I'm surprised. I never knew you came up here."

"I never have," Joanna said. She took a few more steps toward Cole, her hand brushing the wet railing as she went. The action sent a cascade of dewdrops plummeting and twinkling from the rail and down through the rays of new sunshine.

Cole swallowed and went to stand up, but then Joanna's hand was on his shoulder, fixing him in place. His head swam with confusion and nubile hormones, his mouth about to leak shameful admissions—

And then Joanna simply sat down beside him, having used his shoulder to steady herself on the narrow walkway. She scooted side to side a little and then wiped at the back of her shorts, the same shade of blue as his.

"It's wet."

"The dew," Cole pointed out like an idiot. He leaned away from her and felt his own wet shorts, as if confirming it, or maybe highlighting something they had in common. He wasn't sure.

"It's pretty up here."

Cole watched as Joanna brushed more wetness from the lower railing ahead of them, sending another straight line of dewdrops raining down, some of them splashing wide against her bare thighs. She leaned forward and rested her arms on top of the cleared surface and gazed out over the barrio.

"You think this is *pretty*?" Cole whispered. He had to fight from telling her what *he* thought was pretty. It sure wasn't the barrio.

Joanna turned to him and smiled, and surely the sun crept higher over Angústia Hill, soaking the older girl in extra honeyed light and Cole in more heat. "Of course," she said. "Just look at all the people starting a new day." She swept a perfect arm out over the slums. "Smell all that fresh food and that crisp air."

Cole begrudgingly tore his eyes off her arm and looked beyond it to the rolling hills soaked in shacks. He focused on the people this time, not remembering if they were even out and about before, though he was sure they must've been. He matched the rhythmic hissing sound of a straw broom with a shopkeeper sending horizontal wisps of dust into the street. The distant clatter of a screen door was followed by a barely audible call for some animal or child to come inside. The scent of fried plantains stirred weakly in a morning air that Cole had to admit was crisp and cool. As the light of the rising sun spilled down alleys he knew like the lines of his own knuckles, Cole saw how much activity there was up and down them. He looked out over the vista through *Joanna's* eyes, or perhaps through the eyes of a young boy, newly smitten.

"I've always come up here to look down on this place," Cole admitted shamefully.

"It *is* a nice spot," Joanna said, obviously missing Cole's point and taking the "down" as literal instead of figurative. "I'm glad Marco told me about it."

Cole peeled his eyes away from two kids chasing each other through the streets, laughing and screaming, and turned to Joanna. "*Marco* told you about this spot?"

Joanna nodded. "He said the sunrise up here was magical. Said I should come up today because it was gonna be a good one." She turned her head to the side and rested her high cheeks on her smooth forearm. "He was right."

Cole blushed. He ran his finger along the underside of the railing, knocking the hanging dew loose. He knew for a fact that Marco never got up early enough for a sunrise in his life, but he'd have to thank the old bastard for divulging Cole's secret spot. Maybe his group leader wasn't such a bad guy after all.

"Hey, Cole?"

Cole saw that he was idly peeling paint from the railing. He stopped and looked to Joanna.

"Yeah?"

"I've got something I want to ask you."

Cole lost himself in Joanna's eyes, which somehow looked so much younger than her fourteen years, and so much older as well. They were the eyes of a girl who had survived a bunch of days without seeing anything bad enough to scar them. They were a woman's eyes untouched. In the back of Cole's boy-brain, he knew she was waiting on a response from him, but he lost himself in the black and brown ridges around her pupils. He felt as if he could dive straight into them, cleansing himself of the filth and muck of the barrio, escaping away to some more beautiful place—

And then a twinkle burst in Joanna's eye.

It grew into a flash, a shattering of brightness, a yellow starburst spreading out through the brown. Her eyes twitched to the side and focused on something in the distance, and Cole realized he was seeing not some internal twinkle, but the reflection of some bright light. He turned just as a great rumble arrived, followed soon after by a too-warm breeze. Out in the center of the barrio, right in the middle of the new government district, a terrible ball of orange was dissipating in the sky.

Cole watched, stunned senseless, as the fire morphed into a cloud of black smoke. It churned up into the sky, flattening and growing dirty white as it did so.

The rumble grew, and soon the water tower was trembling in harmony. Cole felt Joanna's hands settle on the back of his, squeezing. He in turn gripped the rail in raw terror as the empty tower swayed in an unnatural breeze.

"What in the Almighty's name?" Joanna breathed.

The cloud slid through all the hues of gray to the color of ash and then rose up and blended with the natural puffs high in the sky. Sirens called out like startled birds, wailing in the far distance where wealthy people paid to be protected from whatever had just happened.

"Was that a bomb?" Joanna asked.

Her hands were still on Cole's, even as the tower settled back to stillness.

"It didn't *sound* like a bomb," Cole sputtered.

Joanna finally pulled her hands away, creating a fathomless distance between her and Cole measured in mere centimeters.

"Have you heard bombs *before?*"

Cole shook his head slowly. He noted the odd way the shacks along the hillside all around the blast were pushed flat in concentric circles. Something about that was screaming at him to be understood. To be recognized as familiar.

"Just in a few movies," Cole admitted, not taking his eyes off the scene. The crying and shouting of people added to the screaming din of the sirens.

"Are we safe up here?" Joanna asked. She gripped the rail and stuck her chin out over her knuckles, peering down. "Maybe we should go see if we can help. I bet the Miracle Makers need us right now. They'll be worried and looking for volunteers—"

Cole nodded. He could see tiny silhouettes creeping up the alleys toward the blast, picking their way through rubble, hands on stunned heads with elbows sharp to either side, some of them doubtlessly adding to the cacophony of mad sounds screeching over the barrio.

"C'mon," Joanna said. She scrambled to her feet and shook Cole's shoulder. Her voice was full of fear and anxiety, and yet she seemed to have more wits about herself than Cole. "Let's go find Marco," she said. "He'll know what to do."

"Marco," Cole repeated. He bit his lip, remembering vaguely some conversation he'd had with his fellow Miracle Maker a few months ago. "Yeah," he said, tearing his eyes away from the horrific scene, the smoky aftermath of a blast that must've claimed so many. "Let's go find Marco," he said.

7

THE COURTROOM

The lawyer smiled at Cole's answer. "And wouldn't you say that the water tower provided a most excellent vantage of the day's events?" He continued to smile, but Cole saw the lawyer's teeth as more for biting and gnashing and tearing out flesh than for evincing pleasure.

He nodded. Cole knew there was danger in the question, but his mind was a fog, the truth billowing in him like a suffocating smoke.

"Speak up."

"I could see everything," Cole said. He looked to his own lawyer behind her table and wondered when he could start answering *her* questions. Each step felt like a trap with this guy.

"And at this time you were already an initiate in the . . . " The lawyer shook a piece of paper stiff and seemed to read the next, as if anyone could now get it wrong. "The Holy Order of God's Miracle Makers. Is that also correct?"

"I'm actually a full member," Cole said.

The lawyer smiled and handed the piece of paper to one of the team of people behind his desk. Cole didn't follow the paper all the way. He didn't want to face the other people sitting there—

"At least, I *was* a full member," Cole added. He wasn't exactly sure what his status with the Order was anymore. He noticed his lawyer frowning at this and wondered if he'd made a mistake.

"So, let's be clear about this." The lawyer turned and faced the two rows of jurors. "You, Cole Mendonça, were a full member of these *Miracle Makers*." He stressed the words and wiggled two pairs of fingers in the air. "You were, on the morning of the—let's just call it an explosion for now—you were perched on what you yourself admitted was the perfect vantage point for your handiwork—"

"Objection," Cole's lawyer said. "He's leading the witness."

"Sustained," the judge intoned.

Cole's lawyer stood up. "Your honor, my client is not the one on—"

"Your objection was sustained, Counselor." The judge picked up his mallet, but used it to point at her rather than bang it. "Please sit."

The crowd in the pews stirred. Their attention returned to Cole.

"On the morning of the . . . *explosion*, you were in a spot with an uncanny view of the new research institute, *and* you were with another member of the Miracle Makers." The lawyer walked over to Cole's witness stand and placed his hands on the wooden ledge before him. "Where did you go immediately after the event?"

"I went to church," Cole said. He wanted to look at his lawyer with every answer, but figured it might seem as if he wasn't sure or was being coached. He knew perfectly well what had happened that day and why. He kept reminding himself of that. All he needed to do was tell the truth.

"Did you go to pray?"

There was laughter from the pews.

"Did you go to *confess*?"

Cole shook his head. "We went to see Marco. We thought we could help, or something."

"Perhaps you thought you could help build the next bomb?"

"*What?*" Cole looked around the room, all eyes wide and locked onto his. "No, I had no idea about any of that at the time. I thought maybe some of the injured people might need help. Joanna and I went to Marco because he's our group leader—"

"Is that what you call each cell? You call them groups?"

"Cell?" Cole shook his head. "No, it wasn't like that. A group was . . . it was just a *group*. A bunch of kids. I mean, Marco was in charge of us, but he was only like sixteen years old."

The lawyer waved his hand as if to shoo away Cole's words. "The court has already established that age will not be a defense for anyone in this case."

"I'm not defending *anything*," Cole said, hearing his voice increase in pitch and volume. "I'm . . . We went to Marco because we weren't sure where else to go. That's all."

"So you're saying that at this time, after watching the explosion from such a choice spot, you had no idea Marco and the Miracle Makers were the ones who set off the explosion."

"Objection."

"Sustained. Rephrase that, Counselor."

The lawyer cleared his throat. "Are you saying— and please remember that you're under oath—that you went to Marco with the *belief* that he was uninvolved with the events of that morning."

Cole nodded. "I had no clue," he said.

"Are you also going to tell me, again while under oath, that this explosion was *not* your idea?"

Cole felt his jaw unhinge. He looked to his lawyer, whose hands were splayed out over the papers before her as if she needed to pin into place all the facts she thought she knew. Cole wanted to keep turning, to scan the room. He imagined Marco sitting off to the side, a mad grin on the boy's face, but Cole knew he wasn't there.

"Answer the question," the judge said. "And I'm getting tired of reminding you of that."

Cole bit his lip. He reached up to wipe sweat from beside his ear but stopped himself and just let it run down his jawbone.

"Was the explosion and the corresponding blast in New Zealand in fact all your idea?" the lawyer asked.

"I don't think so," Cole said. Of all the questions he had feared to hear in court, he never expected this one to come up—the one that had been haunting him for weeks and weeks.

"You don't *think* so."

"I had nothing to do with the bombs," Cole said.

"So you were more of the cell's planner, then?"

"Objection," his lawyer shouted, her voice shaky.

"Overruled. Answer the question."

"It wasn't like that."

"Tell us what it was like."

Cole wrung his hands together. "It was just a conversation," he said. "It was an astronomy book. I didn't mean for anyone to get hurt."

The lawyer spread his arms wide. "And yet here we are, Cole. Now, you've already admitted to killing a boy in cold blood, a member of your little cult, and now we know that this *miracle* of yours was nothing more than a terrorist act that you yourself dreamed up."

"No," Cole said. He looked to his lawyer, waiting for an objection, but her face was blank, her mouth hanging open. "That's not what happened."

"Then tell us." The lawyer turned and waved at the congregation. "Tell these good people about your involvement in this cell. Tell them the truth, and tell them that my client had nothing to do with your actions, that these cells were operating without his knowledge, that all this was done by unruly and sociopathic boys hiding behind his cloak for safety."

"But that's not right," Cole said. "He *did* do this, I swear."

Cole finally relented to the pull of his curious gaze and turned to meet the glare of Father Picoult, sitting at the table with the party of suits. Cole pointed. "I'm telling you, *he* was the one who started it all."

•• Six Months Earlier ••

"So, are you feeling at home yet?"

Cole looked up from the book winged out across his lap. He was sitting in the church hallway, his legs crossed, his back against the ornately tiled walls of the refectory. Before him loomed the shadow of Father Picoult, the heavy folds of his plain black smock still stirring from his silent stroll down the hallway.

"It's Cole, right?"

Cole nodded. "Yes, Father. And yes, I feel very much at home here. Even more than I did at the orphanage." He smiled up at the priest. "Not that I don't appreciate everything the sisters did for me, of course."

Father Picoult smiled down at him. "That's good to hear. I'll pass along your gratitude, and I'm glad you're making yourself comfortable." The Father nodded toward Cole's lap. "What are you studying?"

Cole looked down at the book in his lap. "Astronomy, Father. With Sister Maria."

"Is that a subject that interests you?"

Cole's head bobbed. "Very much so."

"That's God's great mechanism, you know." One of Father Picoult's hands materialized out of the folds of pitch black and hovered over the book, palm down. "Everything we do is determined by what you study there."

Cole didn't know what to say to that. Nothing he could utter would match the profoundness of what the Father was saying. He nodded mutely. Several older boys strolled past, whispering among themselves. One of them peeled away from the others and took a spot beside the father, and the way the boy stood there, completely at ease in the man's presence, standing almost as if an equal, filled Cole with an almighty envy.

"Father, if you have a moment—"

"Ah, Marco, I'm glad you're here. Have you two met?"

Cole gazed up at the older boy, probably at least fifteen.

The boy looked down at Cole and shrugged. "This the new kid?"

Father Picoult clicked his tongue. His hand disappeared back into the heavy folds of his cloak. "This is young Cole, and he will be a brother to you soon. Sister Dara says he is one of the brightest young lads to pass through the orphanage. Isn't that right, Cole?"

Cole lifted his shoulders. His cheeks and neck were burning under their gazes and from the air of the father's compliments.

Marco sniffed and stirred beneath his cloak, clearly not impressed.

"In fact," the father said, "I think I'd like to assign him to your care. I believe you two will have much to offer each other."

"You want him to become a Miracle Maker?" Marco turned to face his elder, his cloaks doing the same with a swishing delay. "How old is he, like eight?"

"I'm eleven," Cole whispered, his words absorbed by their thick cloaks.

Father Picoult laughed. His voice was soft and powerful at once, and full of warm mirth. "My eyes blinked, and you went from his age to a group leader," he said. "The same fate awaits our young Initiate, here." Father Picoult rested a hand on Marco's shoulder. "Tell you what, why don't you spend the rest of the day with him. Show him around. Ask him about his studies. I assure you, there is much to teach and learn between the two of you. I think you'll be surprised."

"But I was going to ask you about—"

"In time," Father Picoult said. He patted Marco on the shoulder and withdrew his hand, and his great cloak swallowed it once more. With a last smile and nod to Cole, the head of the church turned and resumed his quiet stroll down the gilded halls, the heavy folds and deep shadows hurrying along after him.

"All right," Marco said. He let out an impatient sigh. "Come with me, I guess."

Cole hurried along after Marco, jealous of the older boy's flowing cloak and long, confident strides. The blue shorts and clean white shirt he'd so recently felt pride over now seemed insufficient. He wanted more.

"I take it you've already been shown around." Marco held open one of the double doors at the end of the hall. It led out to the walled garden on the side of the church, with the crowded and crumbling cemetery beyond.

Cole hurried through the door, clutching the large astronomy book to his chest. "Sister Anna gave me a brief tour the other day," he answered.

"Well then, instead of showing you around, let me just tell you how things operate around here, especially since it sounds like I'm gonna be stuck with you." Marco let the door slide shut and rested a hand on Cole's shoulder. With the other hand, he pulled the book out of Cole's arms.

"First off, you can drop the studious act. That got you out of the orphanage, but it won't go far here."

Cole fought the urge to twist away from the hand on his shoulder. He watched Marco tuck the astronomy book under his arm, losing Cole's place in the process.

"I take it you were a slum rat before the sisters adopted you?"

Cole didn't say anything. He continued to stare at the book.

"Hey kid, how old when the nuns took you in?"

"Nine." Cole looked up at Marco. The boy's countenance had changed. Gone was the pious and reverent choirboy, and Cole realized this kid was no different from any of those he'd known on the streets, just better fed and better clothed.

"So how long did you live on your own?" Marco slapped Cole's back and pointed out into the gardens. He walked down the steps in that direction, forcing Cole to follow.

"I was never on my own," Cole said, catching up. "I had friends."

"So you were part of a crew, huh? Petty theft, pickpocket, or did you guys run any complicated scams?"

"I don't know what that means," Cole lied. "We begged and scrounged for scraps."

"I'll bet." Marco stopped in front of a bush drooping with roses. He peeled a single petal off one of the red ones and held it up to his nose. "Listen, kid—"

"It's Cole."

Marco turned and smiled. He flicked the petal away, leaving it to flutter in the air. "Okay, Cole, I think you need to understand something. You're not that special here, okay?" Marco nodded toward the far side of the garden where a small group of kids, all different ages, was sitting in the grass with one of the sisters. "Do you think any of us here came from good homes? Or from *any* kind of home? 'Cause we didn't."

Marco spun around and strolled toward the cemetery. Cole glanced back at the kids in the far grass and then hurried after Marco.

"There's not a kid in here who didn't come from the streets and move through the orphanage. Since we all *lived* on the streets, we all know each other's secrets. Do you get what I'm saying?"

"I wasn't a criminal," Cole said.

Marco stopped in front of the wrought iron gate leading into the cemetery. He pulled Cole's book from under his arm, flipped it open, and riffed through the pages.

"I hope you really mean that," Marco said. "It's a lie, of course, but I hope you really believe it." The older kid looked up at the packed rows of aged and stained headstones.

"There're two kinds of slum rats that tunnel their way into the church," Marco said. "There are the

160

ones who don't feel anything, who can do whatever they want without remorse. Those are the scary ones. Then there's the slum rat like I imagine you see yourself, the one who can rationalize a crime as necessary." Marco snapped the book shut. "Maybe even rationalize a crime as *just*."

He handed the book back to Cole. "Is that how you see yourself, slum rat?"

Cole took the book and began automatically thumbing for his place. "I usually just did what I was told," he said quietly. He was pretty sure that was the right answer, in more ways than one.

Marco turned and beamed down at him, and then he laughed. "The nuns must've eaten that shit up," he said. He slapped Cole on the shoulder and pointed at the astronomy book, which Cole had reopened. "The one part of your act that I actually believe is *that* bit. You really like reading that stuff?"

Cole nodded.

"So you're really some kinda bookworm?"

He shrugged. "Reading lets me escape the barrio, I guess."

"In your mind, maybe." Marco tapped his temple, his hand in the shape of a gun. "But don't get any delusions, slum rat. There's no getting out of the barrio for you and me. Just ask my friends here." Marco swept his hand over the gate toward the listing and tilting pale faces of marble beyond. He laughed some more and then noticed Cole had turned his attention back to his place in the book.

"Hey, I'm teaching you a valuable lesson here, kid. Reading up on those stars and dreaming about being someplace else ain't gonna get you far. In fact . . ." Marco snatched the book away and flipped roughly toward the back. "I've read this book, and the only thing worth studying in it is black holes." He found what he was looking for and shoved the book into Cole's outstretched hands. "*That's* your barrio, slum rat." He tapped the image on the page. "That's your point of no escape, right there. You read up on black holes for me and come tell me what you learned. Consider it your first assignment as part of my crew."

And with that, Marco spun away from the black gate and swished through the gardens, leaving Cole alone with all the quiet tombs.

But Cole didn't mind.

He sat down on the cobblestones and started to read. Black holes sounded more interesting than stars, anyway.

8

THE CHURCH

The next morning, at the first breaking of bread, Cole was sitting with his fellow initiates when Marco arrived with a tray of food. One look, and the bench of boys opposite Cole parted like the Red Sea. Marco's tray landed with a clatter. He sat down, picked up his roll, and dunked it in Cole's soup.

"You learn anything about the barrio yesterday?" Marco chewed while soup trickled down his chin. The other young boys, all in identical white-and-blue uniforms, sat motionless in some form of awe mixed with fear.

"I read all about black holes," Cole said. He pulled his soup closer and stirred it protectively with his spoon.

"And what did you learn about escaping them?" Marco's voice was muffled, his mouth full of a second large bite of roll.

"That it's possible," Cole said nonchalantly. He sipped soup from his spoon but kept his eyes on the older boy.

"Oh yeah?"

"Yeah. It's called quantum tunneling. It can happen when a single atom is near the event horizon and has something real random happen to it—"

Marco reached over and dipped his half-eaten roll back in Cole's bowl. When he pulled it back to his plate, he left a trail of soup between their two trays, a constellation of sticky dollops. Cole watched it happen and fell silent.

"What *else* did you learn?" Marco smiled and took another bite.

Cole grabbed his own roll and kept it in both hands while he thought about what to say.

"Is there any chance of a black hole coming to the barrio and whisking you away?" Marco stuffed the remainder of his roll in his mouth and chewed around a smile. The other boys still hadn't moved.

Some stared into empty spoons, and some clutched their trays in both hands.

"Maybe," Cole said, still trying to act calm. "There wasn't much in that book on black holes to be honest, but I found a ton on the web." He took a bite of his roll and smiled at Marco. "Did you know a black hole might've passed through the Earth hundreds of years ago? One could zip through us right now, maybe suck us and our breakfast right up, and then zoom off straight through the roof."

Cole lifted his roll over his head, and the other boys around him looked up after it.

"We'd be dead, of course, but it would happen so fast, we'd never know it. And we'd all be the same," he added. "Us, our trays, our spoons, all pressed together into a tiny space the size of an atom. We'd travel like that forever, zipping through space and sucking down more and more and more, leaving craters and burning rings of fire behind."

Cole smiled and took a large bite out of his roll.

Marco laughed. "What kooky site did you read that load of crap on?"

Cole shrugged. "I don't remember."

"You're making that up," one of the other kids whispered, his tone one of more wistful hope than accusation.

"It was called the Tunguska Event." Cole turned his attention to the other boys his age. "It was the largest explosion of its kind. It took place in Old Russia, back at the turn of the twentieth. For a long time, scientists thought it was a meteor impact, even though there was no crater. The blast rocked people and houses for miles and miles, and all the trees were pushed over, just snapped off and leaning away from the center of this massive fireball."

"And it could happen *here*?" one of the boys asked. "At any time?"

Cole nodded. He looked to Marco, only to find the boy smiling in a different way; he seemed genuinely pleased.

"How do they know it was a black hole?" another boy asked.

Cole turned to address the kid, suddenly feeling quite older than the other boys his age.

"They finally found the spot where it entered the Earth," he said. "At first, they had looked directly opposite the blast, down in the Indian Ocean, but what were the chances that the black hole passed directly through the center of the Earth? It was silly to look there." He stirred his soup. "But then, in the middle of the twenty-third century, some guys were digging for bones in Africa when they found charred rock that only looked two hundred years old. They thought it was meteor rock, so they called these astronomers in, who took one look and realized a black hole had passed through."

"How would you stop it?" the boy beside Cole asked. "There has to be some way to protect ourselves."

Cole took a sip of his soup, ignoring the fact that it had grown cold and that there were soggy crumbs from Marco's roll in it. "You can't stop them," he said. "They can come anytime and from anywhere. There are probably billions or trillions of the things roaming the universe since the time of Creation. They're like cosmic cattle, grazing on everything."

A new fear settled over the boys, quite stronger than the one Marco's presence had brought. Cole looked to Marco to see the older boy beaming. He winked at Cole and stood up.

"You aced your assignment," Marco said. He wiped his chin with his napkin and then threw it into his untouched bowl of soup. "Be sure to take up my tray as well, slum rat."

And with that, Marco spun and hurried out of the dining hall as suddenly and swiftly as he'd arrived. Cole watched him go, the folds of the boy's cloak swaying wide with his turn and then settling down all around him, the blackness swallowing him whole.

●● Six Months Later ●●

"Do you really expect this court to *believe* that?"

The lawyer in the black suit waved his arm out over the pews.

"Are you going to tell these families that their loved ones died because of an innocuous conversation that took place over some *soup*? Is that also what you're going to tell those families in New Zealand? That this wasn't the work of God, or some coincidence too extreme to trust, but the scheming of some homeless kids taking advantage of the hospitality and kindness of the church?"

"I'm telling you what happened." Cole looked up at the judge. "That's what I swore to do."

The judge squinted at Cole, as if looking for something difficult to discern.

"I move to have this case against my client dropped," the lawyer said. He walked back toward his wide table, staffed plenty with suits. "If this is the extent of the evidence, the hearsay of one boy when the other isn't here to provide his side of the story—"

"Denied," the judge said. He held out a hand to calm down Cole's lawyer, who had risen from her seat and seemed fit to explode. "And I'll caution you, Counselor, not to employ theatrics for my jury's benefit. Now, if you have no further questions—"

The lawyer spun away from his desk. "Oh, if we're going to persist in this, I certainly have other questions." He stalked toward Cole, his finger jabbing the air. "I'd like to probe into the charges that were dropped, the charges that prompted you to turn on the man who so kindly took you in. I think if there's any real conspiracy here, *that's* where we'll find it."

"My client doesn't have to answer those questions," Cole's lawyer protested. She flipped through the papers spread across her desk. "It's clear in the agreement he signed—"

"A boy is *dead*," the other lawyer said, whirling on her. "Another boy is dead, and now his name is being besmirched without him here to clear it."

"There is ample evidence—" the judge began, but the stirrings in the congregation-like crowd made it hard to hear. He reached for his gavel and banged the wooden puck on his dais so hard it leaped up in the air.

"Order," he demanded. "Settle down, or I'll clear every last one of you from my court."

Cole watched the scene from the stand, his hands clasping the ledge before him as if the room itself might start spinning.

"The jury deserves an answer if they are to take this witness seriously," the lawyer said. He approached the judge's bench, his hands raised and his shoulders up by his neck.

The judge pointed the gavel at him. "I'll allow you to proceed, but do so carefully."

"Your honor—" Cole's lawyer began.

"He may establish the witness's reliability as long as he does not ask the boy to indict himself."

The lawyer in the black suit grinned.

"Proceed," the judge said.

The male lawyer cleared his throat. He walked up to the side of Cole's witness box and rested his elbows on its ledge. He leaned toward Cole's microphone and looked out over the audience and the jury box.

"Please tell us," the lawyer said, his voice slow and amplified by the microphone. "Tell us why we should trust you, when you admitted to the cops that you *killed* this other boy, this Marco."

"Objection, Your Honor!"

The gavel rang out like a gunshot.

"Why did you kill him?" the lawyer shouted into the mic.

Another gunshot, the round gavel block leaping up like a spent cartridge.

"*Order!*"

Hundreds of simultaneous gasps seemed to suck the air from the room.

"*Order!*"

Another crack of wood. Grumblings turned to shouts.

"*Order in this court!*"

The only people sitting still were Father Picoult, his arms crossed over his chest, and poor Cole, his memory tumbling with awful answers to the question. To that question, and questions he was thankful nobody knew to ask—

9

THE BARRIO · TWO WEEKS
AFTER THE BLAST

"Do you wanna do burritos?"

Joanna tugged Cole toward one of the open stalls lining the busy marketplace. A group of men stood by the ordering window eating wraps the size of soda cans.

"I don't eat there," Cole said, shaking his head.

Joanna looked from the large menu above the ordering window to Cole. "Why?"

"The owner's name is Mendonça," Cole said.

Joanna pointed to the man behind the counter with the stained white smock and cook's hat. "That's your *father*?" she asked.

"I have no idea," Cole said. "I never knew my dad. My policy is to not do business with anyone named Mendonça, just to be sure."

Joanna seemed deflated, then confused. "But that's gotta be like, the second most common surname in the barrio."

Cole shrugged. "There are lots of places I don't go."

"So you really don't know who he is? What about your mom? Or any siblings?"

"Jeez," Cole said.

"I'm sorry." Joanna stepped under the cover of an awning pasted with Chinese symbols. She stuck her head in the ordering window and then turned, smiling. "Definitely not a Mendonça," she said. "Is Chinese okay?"

"Sure." Cole raised his hands. "As long as you're paying."

"I told you I was." She winked at him and smiled. Cole let her order for them both while he watched the busy street, everyone going about their business as if the miracle two weeks ago hadn't happened. Or maybe the bustle and energy of the barrio had *increased* from the weeks before. It wasn't as if

nothing had happened to the barrio, but something
. . . wonderful.

"Let's sit over there."

Cole took a carton of noodles with a pair of chopsticks sticking out of the top from Joanna. She sat on
one side of a rickety table, and Cole quickly sat down
on the other to balance her out. Joanna extracted her
chopsticks but didn't dig into her noodles. She held
them in the crook of her hand, her delicate fingers
cradling them, the tips opening and closing like a
butterfly's wings. Cole shoved a mouthful of noodles
in his mouth and watched her. The smile on Joanna's
face filled him with a warmth he thought he understood, but a dread he couldn't quite place.

"Thanks for lunch," Cole said between bites, wondering if maybe he wasn't being gracious enough
and that was the reason for her mood.

Joanna nodded. She still hadn't touched her food.
"You're welcome," she said.

"You said you wanted to talk about something?"
He took another bite.

Joanna looked up at the underside of the tat-
tered canopy with the Chinese script. Cole saw a film
of tears coat her eyes, and he wondered why that
seemed to perfectly match the dread he was feeling.

"I'm pregnant," Joanna said.

Cole gasped, sucking a noodle down the wrong way. A coughing fit ensued. He pounded his chest and looked around for water. Joanna ran and grabbed a paper cup and filled it from a hanging orange cooler. As Cole hacked and wheezed—his throat scratched and itching something awful—he considered the ridiculousness of Joanna tending to *him* at that moment. He seized the water gratefully and drank most of it in a rapid series of desperate gulps.

"Slowly," Joanna said. Her smile hadn't changed, but the tears were gone from her eyes, even as a different set of them rolled down Cole's cheeks from the burn in his throat.

"Who?" Cole wheezed, his voice a dry rasp. He knew it wasn't his. They'd only kissed the once, and just barely. He was pretty sure it took something other than a kiss. Right?

Joanna sat down beside him, threatening to teeter them and the table right over. She rubbed his back with one hand and took the empty cup away with the other. Cole felt the years between them yawn wide as she tended to him. Or maybe it was that he still largely felt like a child, and Joanna was saying she was *with* one.

"It's nobody's," Joanna said with a smile. "It's . . ." She shook her head and let out a little laugh. "Well, I don't even want to suggest it," she said, "but it must be a miracle. I've never . . . done *that* . . . with anyone."

Cole glanced down at the empty cup in his hand. Joanna grabbed the cup, twirled from the table, filled it back to the brim from the cooler, and returned. Cole took a sip, letting the cool, crisp water coat his throat. The man behind the counter yelled something about one cup per meal, and Joanna apologized.

"How do you know?" Cole asked. Now that the shock of her revelation was wearing off, his rational mind was assuring the rest of him that she was simply wrong, or perhaps she was lying about having never done . . . *that*. Whatever *that* was.

"Sensors in the toilets look for these things," she said. "They notify the nuns. It takes a couple weeks for the hormones to change."

"A couple of weeks," Cole intoned.

Joanna nodded. She reached for her noodles and then stopped herself and folded her hands together instead.

"Who else knows?" Cole asked.

"Father Picoult. A few of the sisters, I suppose. Soon, I expect everyone will. Cole, they're gonna make an announcement next week. I'm . . ."

The tears returned, welling up at the bottoms of Joanna's lids and spilling over. Cole put his cup down and wrapped his hands around hers, an act of intimacy they had shared often in the past weeks.

"What's wrong?" he asked. He suddenly felt as if this person he was infatuated with, whom he'd known for scarcely more than a month and had barely spent time with until two weeks ago, was so much older and different than him. Cole wanted to wrap her in his arms and run away from her all at once. His stomach and heart were at odds.

"I'm scared," Joanna finally said. She brushed the tears off her perfect cheeks and wiped her hands on her shorts. "I mean, I'm excited and all, but I'm terrified of what this means."

"I don't understand," Cole said. "What *does* this mean?"

Joanna laughed, but it wasn't a laugh of humor— it was more like a release of nerves.

"Do you think this is how Mary felt when *she* found out?" Joanna wiped at her cheeks. "Father Picoult said she was probably around fourteen or fifteen, and poor, just like me. I've never thought of that before, you know? I think of her later, all powerful and strong and wise and *His* mother."

Cole felt a lead weight sink through his being and settle in the pit of his abdomen.

"Wait," he said. "You don't really think—?"

"I begged and begged, and Father Picoult finally said I could take you to lunch and tell you on my terms, away from the church." Joanna glanced around at the bustling market. "But I don't think we'll be able to do this much more. He said everything has to be perfect with this birth. He said there's no mortal father, but that since you were there with me that day . . ." Joanna's cheeks flushed, and Cole felt his own temperature rise. "Anyway, I think he knows how we feel about each other—"

"How *do* we feel?" Cole asked. His throat tightened.

"You'll be my Joseph," Joanna said, entangling her hands with Cole's. "Can you imagine what lies ahead? I always thought I was destined for nothing in life, but then . . . I always felt *special* somehow. I feel like this was supposed to happen."

"I don't understand how you're pregnant," Cole said. "I mean, if you've never . . ."

"It was a miracle," Joanna said. "Whatever passed through the Earth, whatever hit Zealand and flew through the center of the planet, it came out here in the barrio, and it left a baby behind. *Our* baby. A new King to save us from a universe gone wrong and full of evil."

Cole glanced down at Joanna's stomach, even though it bore no sign of anything, much less a miracle. His gaze lingered there a second before wandering out over the alley, over the crowded markets, the smoke and odor of the meal stalls. Everything looked the same, which didn't match all the new and bizarre feelings and thoughts coursing through his body and brain.

"I'm not even thirteen," Cole said. He didn't know when his real birthday was, but the one he had chosen for himself was another eight months away. This couldn't be happening to him. The black hole had been enough bizarreness for an entire lifetime.

"Father Picoult says men were much more mature at a younger age, back in the olden days. He says that's how they'll need to be again when our son arrives."

"You think it's a boy?"

For an eye-blink, Cole felt that this child, this unborn being they were speaking of, was really his. His heart swelled with the lie.

"Of course it's a boy," Joanna said, her voice cracking. "Cole, you do know who this is, don't you?"

Cole shook his head.

"This will be the Creator Incarnate," she said. "The Maker's Child. The Blessed Return."

Cole recognized the words, but the tongue suddenly seemed foreign. He didn't know people really *believed* that stuff. Then again, what had he seen two weeks ago? A black hole had passed through the Earth, right through its dead center, taking out a hospital in New Zealand that performed abortions and did work with stem cells, and it had exited the Earth right in his barrio, right in front of him. It had destroyed a new research facility set up to study genetically modified foods. That wasn't a coincidence, was it? Could it be? He ran through the odds in his head, coming back again and again to having witnessed an honest-to-Gods miracle. And now this?

"Are you okay?" Joanna rubbed his forearm, her other hand holding his. "It was hard for me to believe at first, but Father Picoult and the sisters will be our guides."

"Our guides for *what?*"

Joanna smiled. The two years she had on Cole suddenly seemed like a dozen.

"Our child will be born of a virgin," she said. "This will be the start of a spiritual awakening. People will *believe* again, and the church will grow strong and guide them. Don't you see? This is why the Gods chose us. You and I are young and unspoiled. We have not yet been tainted by the world of skeptics and disbelievers—"

Cole shook his head. He thought about all the wrongs he had already committed in such a short life. There was no way the Gods would pick him, if anything like Gods really existed.

He glanced up at Joanna, fearful she might sense his doubts. Not just of this crazy pregnancy, but much more fundamental ones.

"You should eat," Cole said. He aimed one of his chopsticks toward Joanna's untouched carton of noodles.

Joanna smiled. "You're right," she said. "I need to eat for *both* of us."

oooo

Cole noticed the change in the church as soon as they returned. The sisters buzzed like bees over the grounds, pruning and weeding and chipping paint. Father Picoult met Joanna and Cole at the gate. He draped his arm protectively over Joanna's shoulders and smiled fondly at Cole.

"Congratulations," the father said.

Cole nodded.

"Now Joanna, why don't you come inside with me? There are some ancient scriptures I would like to go over with you. Very applicable to what lies ahead for us."

Joanna smiled and reached for Cole's hand, as if to drag him along with them.

"Actually," Father Picoult said, "I think Marco has need of Cole." He lifted his eyes and looked beyond the gate. "Isn't that right, Marco?"

Cole turned and looked outside the church grounds, back toward the street. Marco and his young gang of Miracle Makers were strolling up toward the front gate. Cole had wondered during his conversation with Joanna: If her story was true, why would Father Picoult allow the two of them beyond the reach of the church, alone? And now Cole saw that he hadn't. They had been two lambs, guarded by a half dozen shepherds.

Marco came up to the gate and rested his hands on the wrought iron. "Congratulations," he said to Joanna, a wry smirk on his face.

Cole tried to will himself to be two inches taller. He thought he could sense a tinge of jealousy in Marco's demeanor.

Marco looked to Father Picoult. "Does he know?" He jerked his head at Cole.

Cole was about to say indeed he did, when Father Picoult said, "I haven't told him yet."

Cole turned. He watched Father Picoult pull a dark bundle from the shadows of his cloak. With the snap of his wrist, the bundle unfolded into a smaller version of the cloaks Marco and his peers wore.

"For *me?*" Cole asked. He held out his hands and felt another layer of resistance and doubts crumble. They were letting him into an ever-tightening circle of family.

"We've never had a Senior Miracle Maker so young," Marco said. And it wasn't malice that Cole noted in his tone. It was something more akin to awe—or pride.

Father Picoult opened the hem of the cloak, and Cole raised his arms and wormed his way into the heavy fabric. As his head emerged, the first thing he saw was Joanna's brilliant smile and shimmering eyes. Cole wanted to wrap her in his arms right then but refrained from doing so in front of the others.

"All right," Marco said. He slapped Cole on the back. "Let's get started."

"Started?" Cole watched as Father Picoult guided Joanna away, up toward the entrance of the church. She looked over her shoulder and waved one last time, the smile of so much pride and joy still on her lips. "Started with what?"

"Training," Marco said. "You've got a lot more to learn in the next nine months than she does."

10

THE STREETS

Cole hurried after the group of Miracle Makers, his legs feeling trapped and confined in the heavy cloak. He watched their long strides and tried to match them, wondering how they ever got used to the garb, especially in the barrio's afternoon heat.

"What kinds of things do I need to learn?" Cole asked. "Like changing diapers and stuff?"

The other boys laughed at that. They had to stop and wheeze for air, they laughed so hard. At least it gave Cole a chance to catch up.

"I think that's gonna be taken care of," Marco said. He pinched Cole's neck with one hand and wiped tears from his eyes with the other, a wide smile plastered across his face. "Today you're gonna witness another miracle, and you're gonna see how things are done around here, okay?"

Cole nodded—even though he didn't understand.

"Do you understand why you were picked for this?" Marco asked, the laughter and smiles fading around them.

Cole looked down at his cloak. "You mean *this*?" He brushed his hands across the rich, dark fabric.

"No." Marco squeezed his neck harder. "For Joanna."

Cole blushed. "Because I love her," he whispered.

The boys howled even louder at that. One of them slapped Cole on the back of his head.

"No, you twit. Everyone loves Joanna, if you really consider what you're feeling love."

"I love her the most!" one of the other boys said.

"You just lussst her," someone whispered in Cole's ear.

Cole dug his finger in after the tickle of the insult.

"It's okay," Marco said, waving down the others. "It's perfectly natural. But no, the reason you're perfect for this job is because you're smart. And you're one of us."

"A slum rat," someone said.

Marco guided him into an alley and off the busier street. He steered Cole away from several bums huddled together around a makeshift campfire.

"I think you've got a decent sense of right and wrong," Marco said, "but I also think you have a practical mind. You understand that sometimes doing right means getting your hands dirty."

Cole thought about how many meals he'd stolen over the years. He looked back toward the homeless men, thinking about how he always foresaw his old age just like that.

"The world doesn't get better by hoping and praying," Marco said. "But it sure would be nice if more people *thought* that it did."

Cole frowned. "But then wouldn't those people spend more time hoping and less time doing?"

Marco popped Cole playfully on the back of the head. "See? That's the smarts I'm talking about. You see it all at once, don't you?" He pointed to one of the boys ahead in the alley, who was trying to catch a pigeon. "With these idiots, I have to explain everything a dozen times. But you're right. If people thought prayer worked, they'd do less to improve their lot. Which would leave the job to *us*."

"Which they would pay us for, naturally," another boy said.

Marco smiled at the boy who had finished his thought for him. "We call them *offerings*, not payments," he said.

The other boy laughed.

"What we're aiming for is one church," Marco continued, "and not that dodgy one in Rome, or that one in Salt Lake. Portugal will one day be the nexus of all belief, back under one unified roof. Hell, you've seen the difference in just the last weeks, haven't you?"

Cole thought about the crowds in the church even for the last two Wednesday and Thursday services. He had figured it was just because so many people knew someone who had died in the blast.

"Just wait until you see everything Picoult has in store for the church," Marco said. "You're gonna be one lucky slum rat if you play your cards right."

"We're getting close," one of the boys said.

"All right," Marco whispered to Cole. "Quiet now. Think of this as training and as a test of sorts. It's like a slum rat raid, but to do *good*."

With that, the demeanor of the group changed. The boisterous and loud walk transformed into textbook sneakcraft. The kids moved to the shadows and danced forward on the balls of their feet, the heavy cloaks shrouding them in shadow and absorbing any stray noise.

Cole did the same and noticed how well suited the fabric was for silent movement. The heavy material held him fast, constraining any extraneous motion, allowing him to move with an economy of sound. The others pulled their hoods up, and Cole did the same. He slid around a puddle, avoiding a pile of tin cans, and held up as the group coalesced by a closed door.

The boys flattened themselves to either side, and Cole did likewise. Marco knocked on the door while another boy swished a bottle of something into a dark rag. After a moment, a chain could be heard sliding back, a voice inside calling to someone else that she was answering the knock.

As soon as the door cracked, Marco shoved his way inside. The other boys followed, their actions lithe and serious. There were sounds of a scuffle. Cole looked up and down the alley, his heart racing with adrenaline. He felt like running but knew there was no place to go. Someone yanked him inside and closed the door behind him.

Marco lowered a woman to the ground, the dark rag pressed over her mouth. The boards above them creaked as someone walked casually across the second floor.

"Who was it?" a male voice rang out. Marco looked to the others and raised a single finger to his lips. The boy with the canister began soaking the rag again.

"Cecília? Did you hear me? Who was at the door?"

The shuffling steps overhead moved away and then creaked on a stairwell. The clomping descended, wrapping back around toward them. Cole looked at the other boys, terrified and confused. Shouldn't they be running? At least toward or away from this man coming down the stairs? His heart pounded as the footsteps reached the landing and their owner came into view.

The man stumbled down into the small living room and kitchen, his hand brushing the wall. "Cecília?" he asked. His eyes wandered around the room, but they were obviously blind. He felt his way toward the back door, moving closer to the crouched and quiet group of boys.

"You'd better not be giving the last of your copper to them homeless men," the blind man said. He shouted the words as if the woman were out in the alley, behind the closed door. Patting his way through the stools by the kitchen counter, the old man headed their way as if to go out after her. Marco made a gesture with his hands, and the kid with the soaked rag sprang into motion.

It was over before Cole could even think to breathe. Two boys held the old man, smothering him with the rag as he fell unconscious. Another two started carrying the woman up the stairs, one grasping her armpits and the other her knees.

"What are we *doing*?" Cole hissed.

Marco just smiled.

"Grab the legs," one of the boys told Cole, pointing at the man.

Cole did as he was told. They made their way up the stairs with the old man, navigating the twisting stairwell slowly to avoid bumping him into the walls. Upstairs, they found a bedroom with two tiny cots. The woman was already being arranged on one of them.

"They sleep separate," one of the boys pointed out, which elicited a round of giggling. Cole helped arrange the man on the cot, wondering what the hell they were trying to accomplish. He saw one of the boys pull out a black case. He unzipped it loudly and produced a gleaming needle. The syringe was passed to Marco.

Cole moved to intervene. "What is that?" he asked.

"It's so she won't remember," he said. He passed the needle to another boy, who plunged it behind the woman's ear. Cole cringed from the sight of the act.

"And now for the miracle," Marco said. He grabbed Cole's arm and turned him toward the old man. More syringes were produced, one identical to the last and another that was much larger and gleaming with a stainless steel casing.

The boy with the smaller syringe held it out toward Cole. "You wanna do this one?"

Cole shook his head, and several of the others laughed. The needle dove behind the man's ear, and the plunger was depressed.

"Hold his head steady," Marco said.

Two boys knelt by the cot and braced the man's skull. Marco accepted the larger syringe and moved behind the head of the cot so he could lean over and steady himself. One of the boys holding the man's forehead used two fingers to pry open his eyelid.

"What is that?" Cole asked. "What are we *doing* here?"

"We're gonna make the blind see again," someone whispered.

Marco paused before inserting the needle. He looked up at Cole. "It's stem cells," he said, waving the syringe. "Doctors perform this procedure all the time, only these people can't afford it."

"I thought we were *against* stem cells," Cole said.

Marco laughed. "We're against *doctors*, slum rat. People can't afford to pay them *and* tithe at the same time."

With that, he looked back to the blind man's open eye and lowered the large needle. Cole fought the urge to look away as the metal rod slid into the corner of the open eye. The plunger went halfway down, and then the other eyelid was pulled open. The procedure was repeated, the old couple tucked in, and before Cole knew it, they were back in the alley, locking the door behind them.

"What did we just do?" Cole asked.

"Our good deed for the day," someone called out.

The boys had returned to their youthful state, jostling and joking as they skipped toward the end of the alley.

"These people will be approached later in the week," Marco said. "A group of sisters will go door to door, telling everyone in this neighborhood about the church. The sisters won't know what happened here, but they will hear about it soon enough, right from the source. And you can bet this couple will be in church next Sunday. And you can bet Picoult will have them on stage, asking them about this miracle."

"That was a *miracle?*" Cole asked.

"There's nothing like your first one," Marco said. He clasped Cole's shoulder and squeezed. "Congrats again on the promotion."

They hadn't even reached the end of the alley when everything else clicked into place for Cole. The obvious punched him in the gut, taking away his breath and making him feel sick to his stomach. He staggered out into the busy street, leaned on a rusted light pole, and clutched his abdomen.

"You okay?" someone asked.

"I think he's gonna be sick."

Cole looked around for Marco, who moved to his side.

"She's really pregnant," Cole said.

Marco knelt down beside Cole. "That she is."

"Did you do it?" Cole asked.

Marco smiled. "Yeah, but not like you think. She's still a vir—"

Cole's hands clamped around the rest of the sentence, squeezing Marco's throat. The other boys stopped giggling and tensed up. Marco pried Cole's hands away from his neck and slapped Cole across the face.

Cole hardly felt the blow. His body was bristling with rage. All he could think of was Joanna on a cot, pinned down by a pack of boys, needles or worse invading her flesh. He launched himself at Marco, tackling the boy. He landed a few blows before someone pried him off, the other kids a tangle of cloaks around him, all of them grasping and clutching at Cole.

194

Cole felt himself pinned in place. Marco was on his hands and knees, his nose bleeding. The other boys had fistfuls of his new cloak.

"Hold him," Marco said.

Cole sagged down, wiggling his arms out of the wide sleeves. He felt a primal fury coil up in his gut as the lie of the black hole and its explosion dawned on him as well. He thought of the grieving widows and the confused orphans all around the church the past weeks. He thought about how Joanna had cried and cried over their losses. He fell to the pavement, leaving the boys holding his empty cloak, and emerged a free and mad animal.

Cole lunged forward and kicked at Marco's face. He landed a serious blow, but kicked again. And again. He kept kicking, even as the other boys realized they no longer had him and reached to seize him once more. He kept kicking, even as they rained their own blows against him. He was kicking still when the cops came and took their turn at holding him down. Even as they peeled the other boys off him, he kicked. As they shoved him to the pavement and cuffed him, he kicked. He even kicked later as they dressed his myriad new wounds. Cole kept kicking and kicking and kicking at anything he could.

II

THE COURTROOM

The courtroom remained silent long after Cole finished relaying what had happened. Even the lawyer in the dark suit seemed unsure of what to say. He paced over to his desk, slid a few pieces of paper around, and then returned to Cole.

"Is that where the bruises came from?"

Cole brushed his fingers across his cheek, which was sore only when he touched it. The swelling had gone down the past weeks. He nodded.

"So you resisted arrest?"

Cole shrugged. He did remember becoming even more violent when he saw that one of the cops' badges read "Mendonça." He remembered trying to punch *that* officer in the face, but couldn't recall if he'd landed the blow.

"And now you want this court and a jury of your peers to take the word of—what did you call yourself?"

"A slum rat," Cole said.

"Yes, a slum rat. And a murderer. And probably the planner behind the bomb that killed thousands—"

"Objection."

"Sustained."

The lawyer in the black suit smiled.

"I'm not asking anyone to take my word," Cole said. He looked to the jury box, ignoring the lawyer, who was raising his hands, palms out, as if suddenly Cole shouldn't speak. "I'm just telling you what I know. For context. It was part of my deal."

"For *context*?" the lawyer asked. "Context for what?"

Cole's lawyer stood from behind her desk. "When you're done badgering my witness, I'll call my next one and we can get on with this," she said.

Cole looked out to her and saw a smile on her face. He was pretty sure he'd screwed some things up, but he'd related everything the way he remembered it, and that was all they'd asked of him. He watched the other lawyer mumble something and sit, and then an officer led him out of his stand.

Cole shuffled through the small wooden gate and down the aisle between the silent and rapt pews. When he got to the door, another officer opened it, the flash of a badge catching Cole's eye, a familiar face smiling at him above it. Cole looked to the man and saw a patch of dull purple around his happy eye. Cole was glad that the punch had landed.

The door was pulled open, obscuring the officer. As Cole was led out, another familiar face was led in. It was the blind man from the alley house, his eyes much brighter and younger looking than the rest of his weathered face. The man smiled at Cole and nodded. Cole's lawyer called the gentleman to the witness stand, her voice sonorous and confident, and Cole realized how little he'd been needed for how much he'd bargained away.

•• Two Years Later ••

The crowded bus jerked to a halt in front of a tall gate with coils of razor on top. An American in a military uniform stepped out of a guard booth and spoke to the driver through his open window. Soon after, the gates let out a metallic clang and began parting, sliding to either side on squealing wheels.

The brakes hissed as they let go, and the bus lurched forward into Cole's latest in a long string of adoptive homes. Immediately, however, he saw that the Galactic Naval Academy would be nothing like his previous shelters. Low, shiny buildings consisting almost entirely of glass greeted them beyond the gate. White walls, silvery windows, and flawless pavement divided with painted lines that still appeared wet and new—it was the opposite of his home on the dingy barrio streets. And there were no gardens or greenery like the orphanage, no wandering sisters and brothers like the church. It bore no resemblance at all to Lisboa's Military School for Young Boys, his latest home, which had been carved out of a castle complex, crumbling and old.

This new home of his in a state called Arizona was all orderly and new and sat amid an excess of emptiness that would've made any structure in the barrio blush with embarrassment. Cole was in an alien land, as far from any life as he'd ever dreamed of living, and he was giddy with nerves and excitement.

"Look at all them kids."

The boy in the seat beside him leaned over Cole and pointed to a string of buses lined up by the curb. Their own bus took a circuitous route through the parking lot and ended up at the back of the line. The brakes squealed, and the doors popped open.

A man with a shaved head stomped into the bus and began barking orders, the first familiar thing in Cole's new home.

It didn't seem to matter that the boys came from dozens of military academies scattered all over the planet, everyone in the bus knew how to snap to an adult's demands. They knew how to march, and they knew how to stand in perfect lines. They also knew how to communicate with the barest of looks and the timeliest of whispers.

"My name's Cole," he said to the boy from his seat. The two of them had squeezed out of the bus together and now stood shoulder to shoulder in the back of a phalanx of nervous kids.

"Riggs," the other boy hissed, his mouth parting on one side.

They nodded to each other and smiled, the two of them bound by chance proximity in this new world they'd entered. The boys ahead of them began marching off in a column four wide; Cole and Riggs fell in as directed, and the precise line of cadets wound its way through the yawning doors of the GN Academy, down the shiny tiled halls, and into a crowded gymnasium.

Once inside, the large groups were pared down to smaller ones. Officers were everywhere in their crisp uniforms, shouting advice and orders. Cole spotted what appeared to be a few upper-class cadets helping out, boys just a few years older than he was, in uniforms of their own, already decorated with badges and medals.

"That's the support classes over there."

Cole turned to see where Riggs was pointing. Across the wide hall, he saw other groups of kids receiving their stacks of fatigues and falling into cliques that would soon learn engineering and other auxiliary roles. There was a much wider mix of cadets in those groups, a smattering of girls and even a few members of other races. Cole tried to take it all in, but his line was jostling forward, and he had to pay attention to where he was going.

"Step forward!"

The two boys ahead of them shuffled to a line of tables arranged across the gymnasium floor. They gave their names, stuttering and nervous, and cadets riffled through cards in little boxes. Something was checked off the cards, and stacks of clothing were handed out. Cole noticed with no shortage of excitement that a flight helmet was placed on top of each pile of folded garments.

"Next!"

He and Riggs hurried forward and gave their names. Cole held out his arms and flashed back to similar scenes from his past. He remembered much skinnier arms trembling for a clean shirt and a new pair of blue shorts. He recalled the pleated pants from Lisboa's Military School, much nicer than the lifetime of prison clothes the cops had threatened him with. He watched as a folded flight suit, a black uniform, a pair of glistening boots, and a flight helmet were loaded up in his now older and thicker arms. His dizziness and excitement were interrupted as the upperclassman behind the table shouted for him to move on.

Cole followed Riggs out of the gymnasium and down a hallway. The boys ahead of them were already chattering about their new gear and winning shouts from the older cadets directing traffic.

The long line of boys with their clothes and helmets filed into a smaller room full of simulator pods. A hushed awe fell over them as they shuffled into place along the room's interior. Cole noted how much newer these simulators looked compared to Lisboa's. He wondered if he would have to relearn everything he had learned at his last academy. Maybe his above-average scores wouldn't be reproducible here, and they'd send him home as a failure. The first sensation of raw panic stirred in his guts as he imagined being kicked out of flight school. Riggs had to elbow him into place, he'd become so distracted.

The hopeful cadets stood shoulder to shoulder in a long line stretching down the room of simulator pods, waiting. Upperclassmen in flight suits and aged officers strode up and down the line, taking stock of the newest class. Cole studied one of the older cadets, trying to imagine the boy having once been in his place. He tried to picture, years hence, being where *that* boy stood, seeing the fresh and frightened recruits lined up and trembling. He noticed one man who seemed to command the respect of the rest of these older cadets, a fat soldier in a straining flight suit. The officer lumbered up and down the line frowning, his jowls hanging down like a dog's. Cole stiffened when the man walked by and then relaxed and resumed breathing once his back was turned.

"These must be the navigators," Riggs whispered.

Cole followed his gaze to see another file of recruits shuffling in, their bundles clutched to their bellies, different-colored helmets wobbling precariously on top. They filed to the end of the simulator room and turned to face the string of hopeful pilots as the officers and cadets strolled casually up and down between the two lines.

Cole did a quick count of the boys to his side and saw that he was fifteenth from the end. It dawned on him that he was about to be paired up, and not with Riggs, who had somehow become his friend over the course of a few whispers. He counted the other row as they wiggled into place. He searched faces partly obscured by the ridiculous loads they were each carrying. When he got to fifteen, he smiled at the boy across from him, who smiled back. His navigator looked vaguely European, with bushy brows and dark eyes. Cole started to nod in his direction when the cadet beside him caught his attention.

Cole had to look twice to make sure he was seeing correctly. Riggs elbowed him repeatedly, which confirmed it. There was a *girl* in the line of navigators. Her hair was cropped short, but her cheeks and mouth, and especially her bright eyes, betrayed her. Cole was positive he'd heard flight school wasn't open to girls.

"Cole—" Riggs whispered, his tone dire.

"Shhh," Cole hissed. He watched the fat officer deliberately stroll up in front of the girl and turn his back toward her, as if to shun or purposefully ignore her. The older cadets seemed to be doing the same as they kept toward the other end of the room. As the last of the navigators filed into place, another officer entered the simulator room, an older man, supremely thin, with a plate of medals on his chest big enough to stop a torpedo.

"Pssst," Riggs hissed.

Cole elbowed him back.

The older officer walked straight up to the heavyset one and whispered something. The larger man nodded, obviously the lower ranked of the two, and walked toward the end of the room, calling for all the cadets to listen up. As he began his orientation spiel in a booming voice, Cole watched the more local action across from him. He saw the thin man turn around, pausing ever so slightly to look at the girl navigator. Cole caught just the barest of smiles on her lips before she looked quickly away from the senior officer, and then the thin man strode off, a smile on his face as well.

"Cole."

"What *is* it?" Cole hissed.

"Damnit man, do me a favor," Riggs whispered.

Cole adjusted his pile of gear and turned to the side to see what Riggs wanted.

"What?"

Riggs bared his teeth, then hissed through them: "Switch places with me."

PART XIX

HOPE

"Longing is the fuel for dissatisfaction."

~The Bern Seer~

12

LOK · THE PRESENT

Molly leaned forward in her seat as *Gloria's* tail section rose into view. As the rest of the StarCarrier's hull crept over the horizon, she saw that the downed navy ship remained upright but was slightly tilted, her black thruster cones pointing obliquely up at the sky.

"It's a shame we can't just jump straight out to it," she mused aloud. Her hand automatically drifted to the hyperdrive controls, feeling the switches that could move them anywhere in an instant, ignoring all things in between.

Cat, standing just behind the control console, laughed. "I think your friends in black would have a question or two about how we *did* that." She pointed to the cargo cam, where the navy climbing team could be seen shrugging on harnesses and coiling ropes.

Molly pulled her hand away from the controls and rubbed the pads of her fingers together. "I know. It's just hard to see how I'm supposed to have this power and not use it any time I want."

"I ssay we jusst do it," Walter said from the nav seat. He had his helmet on but with the visor open. He leaned forward and fiddled with one of the dials on the dashboard radio. "Let'ss sshut the cockpit door and do it." He jerked his head toward the cargo bay. "We'll tell them we took a sshortcut," he hissed.

Molly laughed—and then realized Walter wasn't joking.

"This is what gets you in trouble," she told him. "You need to work on being more patient—"

"Are we there yet?" Scottie asked. Molly turned to see him squeezing into the cockpit beside Cat, who rolled her eyes at the coincidental interruption. She and Molly shared a smirk.

"She's just coming into view," Molly said. She turned back around and gestured toward *Gloria's* tail cones. "Are our guests clear on the plan once we get there?"

"I think so," Scottie said. "All they know is they're climbing down to the armory for flight suits and combat gear, the stuff they'll need for the raid on Darrin."

"Do they seem nervous at all?"

"About what? The ship falling over or something? I guess they figure if it ain't toppled by now—"

"No, about going back in there," Molly said. Images of the previous day's horror flashed through her mind: the mounds of dead bodies, the stairwell draped in gore, people crushed from toppling Firehawks.

"I think they know what needs to be done, and they're up for doing it," Scottie said.

"Sounds about right," said Cat.

Molly glanced over at Walter as he fiddled with the radio. "I'd really rather you didn't play with that," she said.

"I'm *hearing* sstuff," Walter hissed.

"That's what radios do," she told him. "Now please leave it—"

"But I'm hearing *weird* sstuff. Ssomeone sstrange iss on here." Walter's hand remained frozen on one of the knobs, sensing he should stop but unable to pull away. "Anyway, I almosst decrypted it—"

"Decrypted—?" Molly leaned over and saw Walter's computer in his lap, his arm partially obscuring its screen. She pushed his elbow up and saw wavy lines and moving bar graphs rippling across the display.

Mom!

She slapped his hand away from the dial and then felt along the back of his helmet and turned the internal speakers off.

"Hey—!"

Molly reached up and grabbed her own helmet from its shelf, sending her Wadi scrambling. She brought it down over her head, snapped the visor shut, and reached for the radio switch, dreading what she was about to discover from her mother—

"ʓɾˈɔ teɕˈɹ ξζδρ ς⁊ ʒhʌ⑩"

Molly froze, her hand poised above the radio dials. She looked over at Walter, who had torn his helmet off and had turned away from her. She could see him pouting in the reflection of his porthole. Molly lifted her visor and removed her helmet. She flicked the radio to the external speakers, allowing the strange language to fill the cockpit:

"ℵ⁊⁊τʋ٦ أوْگَلُ ᴕswمفخ ‿puلإ ـتَذَ چ⁊ﬡ٦ش⑩أ"

Walter glanced at the dash, obviously interested in the sounds.

From behind them, Cat cursed.

"What *is* this?" Molly asked Walter. "What did you do to the radio?"

"That's the *Bern* talking," Cat said, her voice a whisper. "It must be from the fleet."

"You've gotta be kidding." Molly grabbed Walter's arm. "Walter, how did you—?"

He yanked his arm away, still pretending to be hurt. Molly realized the *how* wasn't important. She spun in her seat to face Cat. "Do you understand any of this?"

Cat shook her head. "Not a lick. I've heard it plenty in my day, though. Enough to know what it is."

"Is there any way we can translate it?"

Cat frowned. "Everybody I know who speaks that language is . . . well, *gone*," she said.

Scottie smiled. "I can give you a good guess. I bet they're saying 'Bern mother ship, this is Bern baby ship, over. Commence galactic domination on my mark—'"

Cat smacked him on the arm playfully, but the blow knocked him against the bulkhead. Scottie went to wincing and laughing at the same time.

"I wass decrypting the *Englissh*," Walter grumbled. "Not thiss."

"Wait," Molly said. She held up a hand to silence Cat and Scottie's jovial bickering. "What did you say?"

"The Englissh iss riding a carrier wave." He pointed to his computer. "I wass decrypting it. For fun. Before you hit me."

"Oh, gimme a break. I barely slapped your hand away. Now what's this English? Can you play it?"

"It'ss sstill garbled," Walter hissed. He wasn't giving up the pouting without a fight.

Molly took over the flying from Parsona and decreased thrust. She wanted to hear more of the broadcast before they got inside the StarCarrier and the hull interfered with the signal. "Do what you were doing, but play it through the speakers," she said.

Walter made a show of gazing out the porthole.

Molly took a deep breath. "Please, Walter, as your captain and friend, I'm asking you to do this for me."

Walter fidgeted in his seat and brought his feet up underneath him. He brushed some nonexistent dust off his shoulder and then reached for the dash. He turned the volume down on the radio and did something to his computer, which began emitting phrases that were garbled but clearly English.

"They're not happy," Walter said. "That'ss all I can tell." He placed the computer on the control panel, where its speakers could be better heard while he continued to adjust the virtual dials on its screen.

"—nothing we — do for —. Group — and — two — lost. Mo— or went down — Co—. Repeat, form — continue — planned."

"Can't you clean it up some more?" Molly glanced back and forth between his computer and the view beyond the carboglass. *Parsona's* belly was literally sliding through the feathery heads of Lok's tall grasses as she continued to pull back on the throttle and move into a hover.

"I already *did* clean it up," Walter complained. "It doessn't get any clearer."

"— planet Lok. — can — confirm?"

Molly settled *Parsona* into a hover just a few kilometers from the StarCarrier. She keyed the cockpit door shut, and the four of them leaned over Walter's computer. The small group fell silent, concentrating on every popping utterance and trying to surmise the missing gaps:

"Confirm. — am — speaking to?"

"Edi—on. I — member of Dre— —cil."

"— the —"

"Confirm. — are — Exponent."

"Did you hear that?" Molly whispered.

"Too much basss," Walter hissed. He reached to adjust the dials.

Molly waved him off. "Don't. Didn't you hear—? Why can't we get the rest?"

"Approxima— —ordinates —."

"It'ss a carrier wave," Walter said. "It jumpss frequencsiess oncse a ssecond. I'm jumping after it, but the sscanner tracse I wrote hass too much lag."

He pulled the computer into his lap and fiddled with it. Molly looked up through the canopy at the steel cliff of the StarCarrier looming ahead. Something about the garbled phrases kept tugging on her subconscious, begging her to understand. She heard Cat and Scottie whispering back and forth between themselves—and then someone banged on the cockpit door.

"Tell them we need a second," Molly said, keying the door open.

While Cat and Scottie chatted with the climbers in the cargo bay, Molly turned to see how Walter was doing and then noticed her nav screen had gone blank. A single line across the top read:

LET ME HELP_

Molly leaned forward in her seat and reached for the keyboard.

HOW?_ she typed.

LET ME TALK TO HIM_

Molly hesitated. She turned and saw one of the navy men by the door frowning at the unexpected delay. Scottie gestured and made excuses, and finally the man turned away.

"The boys in black wanna know what's taking so long," Cat said.

Molly keyed the door shut. "They're gonna have to wait." She flicked the speakers on. "Go ahead," she said to her mom. "Talk to him."

Cat and Scottie gave her a funny look, and then her mother's voice came through the speakers:

"Walter," Parsona said. "Do you remember me?"

Walter looked at the dash, and then at Molly. "You're Molly'ss friend, right?"

Molly wondered what he meant, and then she remembered her mom's ruse the night Byrne nearly killed her. They had spoken before, but Parsona had pretended to be radioing in from another ship.

"That's right," Parsona said. "Do you remember helping me with the missiles?"

"Yeah," Walter said. "About that, I didn't mean to be ssso—"

"No, that's fine. You did great. Now I want to help *you*."

"With what?" Walter asked. He looked to Molly and shrugged.

"I want you to give me that program you're using. I can do the frequency switching a lot faster than your computer."

"Okay," Walter said. "I *guessss* that'ss okay." He turned to Molly. "Sshould we go and meet her?"

"She's in the computer, Walter." Molly pointed to his nav screen, which had gone black except for a blinking cursor. "She's a part of the ship."

Walter stared at the screen. He reached forward and poked one of the keys on the dash. The letter W appeared, and the blinking cursor shifted to the right.

He glanced over at Molly and then bent forward and typed out the rest:

WALTER_

He hit enter.

HELLO WALTER_

He smiled at the screen and then turned to Molly, beaming. "I thought you were talking to yoursself all thosse timess!"

"Can you type in the program, or do you want to interface with my computer?" Parsona asked.

"I'll type it," Walter said, rather hurriedly. He bent to the task, referring to his small screen several times. Molly looked back and widened her eyes for Cat and Scottie. They both shrugged and remained silent. The Wadi flicked her tongue out into the air.

After less than a minute of typing, Walter sat back, and the nav screens changed. Molly felt her stomach drop a little, realizing she'd just let the Palan write a program into the ship's computer. When the conversation with her mom went blank, her heart stopped for a brief moment, but then the screen flashed and showed a display similar to the one on his portable unit with audio bar graphs dancing up and down.

The same radio chatter as before came through *Parsona's* speakers; louder, though, and without the annoying pauses:

"*—need to fall back. Listen to your translators. Group Two will have the lead from here on out, assuming they make it through. We'll give them time before zipping up the rift. Until then, nobody transmits on standard frequencies. Keep chatter to a minimum on this channel. Follow your instructions and be good Berns until we can sort this out.*"

"*Group Five, affirmative.*"

"*Three, out.*"

The chatter ceased, leaving the cockpit silent. Molly shook her head and grumbled under her breath.

"Why so glum?" Cat asked. "This could come in handy. We'll know what them bastards are thinking before they pull it."

"I know," Molly said. "It's just . . . one of those voices reminded me of someone. I don't know what I was thinking."

She waited for the chatter to return, but the radio remained silent, the bar graphs flat and mocking. Molly let out her breath, drew in a new one, and reached for the ship's controls, pulling *Parsona* out of its low hover and up along the tilted cliff of steel toward *Gloria's* hangar. Behind her, Scottie keyed the cockpit door open and went back to join the climbers.

Walter leaned toward the radio, presumably to shut it off.

"Can you leave it scanning?" Molly asked him. "Just in case the Bern say something important?"

He nodded and pulled his hand away. "Why would they be sspeaking Englissh?" he asked as he returned to his computer.

"They have to be good at blending in," Cat answered.

"They look a lot like us," Molly added. "Do you remember the guy from Dakura who nearly—that you rescued me from?"

Walter nodded.

"He was one of them, but you would never have known it."

Molly saw Walter flinch. He looked at her with a strange expression—fear mixed with something else. She thought she understood how he felt, having been floored by the revelation herself.

"The ssame guy that sstrangled you," he hissed.

"That's right. We don't have to worry about him anymore, but now you know why they speak English. You have to keep all this a secret, okay? People would panic otherwise. Nobody would know who they could trust."

Walter sniffed and nodded.

Molly guided *Parsona* into the Carrier's hangar, high up the ship's leaning belly. As she flew along the downward-sloping floor, she sensed Walter was dying to ask her another question, or possibly tell her something. She nearly pressed him to come out with it, but the more important task of close-quarters piloting required her attention.

She flew at a steep angle down the calm sea of riveted steel, ignoring the craggy reef of ruined and twisted Firehawks piled up at the bottom. Just above the open stairway door, she spun *Parsona* around and lined up the open door with her own ship's cargo bay. As the landing struts settled to the decking, she locked the thrusters and accelerator just right to keep the ship from sliding back or flying forward. *Parsona* was basically in an inclined hover, held fast to the side of a steep cliff with her skids pressing against the bay's decking.

Walter excused himself. He left his computer behind, crawled over the control console, and padded back through the cargo bay. Molly turned and watched him scurry past the climbers and their piles of gear, wondering what had gotten into him. She turned back around and adjusted the throttles one final time, double-checking that *Parsona* wasn't sliding through the StarCarrier's hangar.

Satisfied they were stable, Molly keyed open the cargo door, allowing the muffled anger of *Parsona's* thrusters to invade the hull. She watched the cargo cam as the door opened fully, its rim swinging out and touching down to the StarCarrier's deck.

The navy climbers wasted no time, lowering bags of gear and coiled ropes out the opening and toward the stairway door below. The visual effect was surreal: Objects dangled out of *Parsona* sideways, even as her grav panels kept everyone upright inside the cargo bay. In the vacuum of space, Molly was able to cope with there being no true down, but seeing Lok's gravity have an effect beyond her ship made her head spin.

Scottie and Ryn seemed unaffected by the vertigo. The large human and Callite stood by the open bay door and shrugged harnesses on. The duo watched the navy climbers intently, duplicating their knots and rope-handling, absorbing everything from the first climb that they'd need for the next one.

Molly felt fortunate to not be going on either expedition; she opened a packet of cheese for the Wadi and settled back in her seat for the long wait. She checked the rate of fuel burn from the thrusters and watched the video screen as the climbers scrambled backward out of the hatch, one by one. The navy guys seemed comfortable as gravity took a ninety-degree turn; they bounced along on bent knees, letting the rope slide through their harnesses and gloved hands as they descended like spiders on thick strands of silk. Scottie and Ryn went last, mimicking them as well as they could, feeding the line in fits and starts as they scampered uneasily toward the stairwell. Molly felt a sudden surge of panic as the enormity of the expedition fully set in. She watched Scottie disappear into the doorway last. The collection of ropes twitched across the decking in time with some unseen movement.

The Wadi finished with the packet of cheese and went to work on the wrapper, nipping Molly's finger as it did so. Molly yelped. She was sucking on her finger when Cat joined her in the cockpit.

"How's everything up here?" Cat asked.

"Restful," Molly said, pulling her finger out of her mouth. She nodded to the cargo cam. "I'm surprised you're not going with them. Seems like your sort of thing."

Cat stepped gracefully over the control console and slid into the nav seat. She placed a mug of steaming something in one of the cup holders.

"I think the boys will have more fun without me," she said.

Molly laughed. "You mean without them feeling weak and pathetic in comparison?" She remembered

Cat's display in the opera house and wondered if the Callite couldn't do the climb without a harness.

"Maybe I just wanted some peace and quiet, like you." Cat laughed as she said it, as if there was some inside joke Molly wasn't privy to.

Molly smiled politely and looked over her shoulder to see where Walter was, but there was no sign of him. For the thousandth time, she wished there was a camera in his stateroom. For the thousandth time, she shuddered at the thought and retracted it.

The handheld radio squawked: *"Belay, this is descenders. We're through the stairwell and playing out line to the armory, over."*

Molly checked the cargo cam, only to see a half dozen taut lines and nothing else.

Cat squeezed the portable radio. "Roger," she said.

"Belay and over," Molly repeated, shaking her head. "What is it with men and their love of jargon?"

"I think one of those guys fancies himself a professional climber. You know what a belay is, right?"

Molly nodded. "I did some climbing in the Academy, which is also where I learned how much boys love jargon and acronyms." She pulled the plastic wrapper away from the Wadi and threw it into the small trash bin behind the controls. Reaching into the vacu-seal compartment by her seat, she pulled out her leftover sandwich from the flight out. She only got it halfway to the Wadi before the animal snatched at it greedily, sniffing for the rest. Molly felt as if her poor Wadi had gotten even smaller in just the last day.

"This is Group Four. We're clear of the rift."

Cat reached for the portable radio, but Molly grabbed her arm. She nodded toward the dash. "It's them," she said, indicating the ship's radio and Walter's computer.

"Group Three, copy. Welcome to the party."

"Five, copy. What's the latest on One and Two?"

"Two is queued up, not sure how far out. One is not going to make it, I hate to report. Over."

Molly leaned forward and turned the volume up. *Parsona's* thrusters and open cargo bay made the back-and-forth chatter difficult to hear.

"Copy that. Hold for instructions."

"They sound very calm about taking over our galaxy," Molly said. "As if it were nothing."

"Quite calm," Parsona agreed. Her mother's voice came out of the radio speakers as the hiss-filled chatter ceased.

Cat took a sip from her mug and returned it to its holder. "It ain't their first dance, you know."

"What do you mean?" Molly asked.

"I mean, there's probably just a handful of galaxies they don't already got their mitts on. I imagine this ain't as exciting or novel for them as it is for us."

Molly moved the Wadi to the control console, its tail tracing circles in the air as it chomped on the last few bites of sandwich.

"What do you know about them?" Molly asked Cat. She turned in her seat and pulled her knees up to her chest.

Cat smiled and arranged herself sideways as well, her lean brown legs folded up in front of her. She adjusted the fabric band around one of her thighs and looked over her knees at Molly. "Whatcha wanna know?"

"Why are they doing this? If they have so much, why not just leave us alone?"

"What if we ain't the good guys?" Cat asked.

"Cat, don't you fill her head with any nonsense," Parsona said. "I don't want to hear—"

Molly reached over and flicked the radio speaker off. "Mom, I love you, and you can listen in, but I want to hear what she has to say."

Cat lifted her mug and smiled through the steam, almost as if to salute Molly for taking a stand. She then turned up the lip and took another deep gulp without first bothering to blow across the piping hot surface.

"Your mom's right," Cat said, smacking her lips. "You shouldn't listen to me."

"But I want to know what you mean. What you think. I want to help you, if I can."

Cat laughed. "*Help* me?" She shook her head. "What makes you think I need helping?"

"I—" Molly reached to the side and muted the cockpit mic, silently apologizing to her mom for excluding her fully from the conversation. "I saw you with the rod in the campfire the other night, how you kept making it glow before wrapping your hand around it. I asked Scottie about it, and he told me—"

"He told you to mind your own business, didn't he?"

Molly nodded.

"He's sweet to protect me like that, but I don't care if you know." Cat shrugged. "Hell, I told people all kindsa stuff for years, but they just look at me like I'm crazy." The Callite glanced up at the ceiling of the cockpit, her eyes narrowing to vertical slits. "Don't care if your mom hears, neither."

Molly reached to turn off the mute but then stopped herself. She *did* care about letting someone else in on the conversation.

"What have you been telling people for years?" Molly asked, withdrawing her hand.

"That the Drenards mean no harm. That *we're* the bad guys. Stuff that tends to get you beat up."

"Is that why you say those things? Just to get beat up?"

Cat shrugged.

"You enjoy the pain, don't you? Why is that?"

Cat shook her head. "Naw, that ain't it. I don't enjoy the pain. I just hate the numbness. And I say them things because they're true, that's all."

"So you don't *feel* anything?" Molly crossed her arms and settled back against the panel behind her. "That sounds nice, to tell you the truth."

"Bullshit," Cat said softly. She spread her knees and leaned closer to Molly. One hand came up, a brown and scaly fist. It wavered in the air. "Ain't nothing worse than being numb," she whispered. "Nothing. I—" She took a deep breath and dropped her hand. "I was born with numbness, with problems in both legs. Couldn't walk a lick." Cat leaned back and grabbed her mug. She didn't drink; she just kept both hands wrapped around it and peered into the steam.

"Go on," Molly said, and then felt bad for being pushy.

"I was raised by my grandparents," Cat said. "They hadn't raised their own kids, though. It was like parenting *skips* a generation in my family, you know? Anyway, they were clueless. Didn't know nothing was wrong till I was five or six and still crawling around on my hands and knees. Other kids knew something was up long before. They took to calling me Cat, like one of the strays in the village."

"I thought it was short for Catherine," Molly said.

"Naw, I *lengthened* it to Catherine. No point in fighting every kid in town over something so stupid, so I adopted the name. Soon as they figured that out, they started calling me Cripple. Or Cripple Cat."

"Why would they do that?"

"Spoken like an only child." Cat smiled through the steam rising out of her mug. "I thought you said you went through the Academy."

Molly clenched her jaw. She thought about some of the abuses she'd suffered, but none seemed as bad as what Cat had been through. Still, she got Cat's point about the random cruelty of youth.

"Them kids done me a favor, way I see it. They not only showed me how I was supposed to be walking, they showed me how *not* to be behaving. Family couldn't afford no hoverchair or prosthetics, so I made myself some walking sticks and started working out at a young age. Went health crazy. Started eating nothing but fruit and veggies from a half-dozen planets and drank a few gallons of water a day." Cat slapped her thighs and stared at her bare legs. "Thought I could fix 'em by working hard enough at it."

"And you obviously did," Molly said.

Cat shook her head. "Naw. I was—"

"Belay, we've reached the armory. Bagging up supplies and rigging the ascenders, over."

Cat squeezed the radio. "Copy."

"Make sure they leave the lines," Molly said.

"Be sure to leave everything in place," Cat radioed.

"Copy that. Belay, over and out."

Molly and Cat smirked at each other.

"Where was I?" Cat asked. "Didn't you want to hear about the Bern? How'd we get to talking about my childhood?"

"It's fine. It'll take them a lot longer to climb back up. You were telling me how you learned to walk by eating healthy."

Cat shook her head. "Nope. I never did. Well, not like that. I dropped out of school when I was twelve. Moved to another town and started working in a plant putting buggies together. I could sit in one place with the other Callites while the parts came by, doing the stuff they did, only with a Lokian accent they made fun of me for. Anyways, I made enough not to starve. Won't bore you with the next few years, but I eventually moved up to delivery and learned to fly. Did some local stuff around Lok, and then eventually got assigned to the run between here and Vega."

"You were a pilot?"

"Yeah, something you don't need legs for, apparently. Unless, of course, your shift is short a man one day and you decide to run a shipment solo. Then your boss figures you can do that all the time, and he starts cutting corners and pocketing the savings. Then, one day, your nav computer goes haywire and you need to run to the engine room to hit the emergency shutdown button on the hyperdrive before it jumps with bum digits, but you're crawling through the cargo bay, dragging yourself along, breaking fingernails back on rivets and crying like a sap, and you're not halfway to the engine room before the ship makes a bad jump—"

Cat peered into her mug.

"All that happened to *you?*" Molly whispered.

"Brightest shit I ever seen came next, the light flooding the ship through every porthole and crack. Thought I was in heaven. Thought maybe some sin-tallying machine had gone as haywire as my hyperdrive. Next thing I know, I'm being thrown all over the cargo bay as my ship crashes into a pile of ice. Screwed me up real good. I remember being drug through the snow. I remember when they cut my legs off, but that was about it." Cat took one hand off the mug and rested her palm on the band around her thigh. "Wasn't awake when they put them back on."

Molly shook her head. "Someone cut off your *legs*?" She reached for the Wadi, remembering what Cat had done to save the animal's life.

"I was half dead anyway, the way Josh told it. But then, a few days later, I'm good as new. Legs working and everything. Some egghead ex-navy chap is telling me the water on Lok had done it, that those gallons and gallons I drank every day while growing up had unlocked some old Callite genes from back when our ancestors could regrow their tails. Wild-ass guesses, if you ask me. Science stirred with gobbly-gook."

She took a loud sip, both hands back to cupping the mug.

"The next few years were a blur, sometimes literally, with people moving by so fast. I learned to fight. Learned to fight for *them*. Started adopting all kinds a weird beliefs—whatever they told me, I believed. You see a place like that, you're a fool to doubt anything. Them boys loved me, said I was almost good enough to be human. They couldn't get over the way I could all of a sudden walk around without goggles. And my blood was useful to them. A steady supply of the Callite stuff— well, you saw how bad they needed that for yourself. I thought it was ritual shit—"

Cat looked over and frowned at her language. Molly waved her off.

232

"I thought it was ritual stuff. I shoulda seen what was going on, where the purple paste came from, the fusion fuel, all of it. I shoulda seen it earlier."

Cat took another deep gulp, the bottom of the mug coming up high above her chin. She lowered the mug and peered inside, as if watching would somehow make it refill.

"It took a while for the numbness to return. Didn't notice the sensations going away at first, not till I was just about completely numb all over."

"Who were these people that did this to you?"

"Humans trapped in hyperspace. Remnants and new recruits from an old terrorist group. They think the Bern are onto something. They see aliens as a problem—and that includes themselves and other humans. They're pretty convincing, too. Of course, the *other* side also had a way with words."

"The other side?"

"The Underground. I spent some years with them as well, after one of our raids didn't go so well and I got captured." Cat looked up. "It wasn't long after I fell in with the Underground that your parents came to Lok, but of course I didn't know about that till later. We eventually made a huge push, one of those raids that grows into a war, and it nearly wiped out both sides. The fighting spilled out into Lok, pretty much leveling the village where that rift is now. Most people got trapped on the hyperspace side. Me and a few others got stuck back here. I kept up the fight for a while, tried to talk sense to some people, but kept getting numb to it all. I eventually stopped caring. Hell, now I go back and forth between the two sides, seeing how one's right and the other's wrong, then changing my mind."

"How *we're* wrong?" Molly asked. "Wrong to want to live and be free?"

Cat shrugged. "Free and bumbling around aimlessly. Hell, your side might mess up the universe for a whole load of *future* people. You might unwittingly end life for everyone."

"How would we do that?"

"Buncha physics I can't half understand, but it's possible. The universe goes 'round and 'round, you see? If it gets different enough, it might be the end of everything alive. The Bern basically make sure the universe is kosher for living things each time it resets itself."

"It sounds like they make the world hunky-dory for them, but what about us? And why are you helping me if you aren't sure who's good or bad?"

Cat tilted her mug and tapped the bottom, letting the last few drops fall on her tongue. She put it back in its holder for the final time and wiped her chin with her sleeve.

"These days, I just go wherever the pain is," she said. "And you seem to be doing the same, so here I am. Here *we* are, you and me."

"Belay, ascenders here. Coming up with the first load. Should be able to get it all in two, over."

Cat grabbed the radio. "Roger," she said. "Copy. Belay is over and out. Ten-four."

She smiled up at Molly and winked.

But Molly wasn't finding anything humorous at the moment. She frowned and stared off into space, thinking about the things Cat had said. There was something familiar in the argument, the claim that it might be worth it to sacrifice a few million lives to prevent the possibility of some future, even larger calamity.

"Glemot," she whispered to herself. Cat's claim was that the Bern might have a right to torch them all, just to keep her people from performing some unknown evil in some unseen tomorrow.

Her mind felt fevered at the thought that it all came down to that. Another calculation of risk, another bout of destruction on such a grand and unfortunate scale, and all over a bunch of *what-ifs*.

"What's Glemot?" Cat asked, having overheard Molly's disgusted whispers.

"It was the biggest mistake ever made," Molly said, tears welling up in her eyes at the memory of that beautiful and haunting planet. "It was the biggest mistake in the universe up until *this* one."

13

WALTER'S ROOM

Walter leaned his head out the doorway and peered to the side; Molly and Cat were still in the cockpit, talking. He stole across the hallway, let himself into Molly's room, and moved immediately to her bottom drawer. He caught the hair lodged in the drawer's frame as it fell to the carpet, dug under her clothes, grabbed his spoils, and returned the single follicle to its place. He had raided the drawer so many times, he often worried he'd do it in his sleep one night and get caught.

He laughed to himself at the idea. *There'ss no way I'd get caught*, Walter thought. *Not even in my ssleep!*

He padded out of Molly's room and back across the hallway, the red band from Drenard clutched in his silvery fist. As soon as his door slid shut, he pulled the band on, the seam lined up in back. Walter jumped in his bed and slid under the covers. He started thinking as loudly as he could, wishing the voice on the other side wasn't so fond of always keeping him *waiting* —

○ ○ ○ ○

"Sir? There's a message coming in for you."

Byrne turned to his assistant and waited. The young officer pressed a finger against his ear, holding tight the small radio receiver lodged there. Byrne assumed the gesture helped block out external noises. He could only imagine how such a messy interplay between flesh and machine would work, for he was one hundred percent the latter. His assistant nodded and raised one hand to signal it might take a moment.

Byrne settled back in his chair and looked around the suddenly quiet conference room. If he still had arms, it would've been a fine time to cross them, signifying his comfort with the wait. He would show his creators that he was quite confident in the invasion's progress, dispelling the worries that had drawn them together in the high command ship's main conference room.

"It's from the latest ship to pass through the rift," his assistant said.

The scattered whispers around the table died down as everyone listened for the latest news from the home galaxy.

"Go on," Byrne said. It would've been a fine time to wave his hand in small circles, but he had to sit, an expressionless torso, and pour as much meaning as he could into mere words.

His assistant coughed into his fist and then cleared his throat. "The Senate is not happy with the timetables, sir. They've sent a spreadsheet showing a revised invasion schedule, with or without the, uh . . . the data stored in your arms. I can send the file through to your internals if you like."

Byrne felt his programming stutter at the mention of the damned arms. That was all anyone around the conference table wanted to discuss. His arms. When would he get them back? Why weren't there backup copies of all the intel he'd gathered on the Milky Way? How had he not foreseen one day being without them?

Right then, all Byrne wanted his limbs for was to pound the conference table to bits. He wanted to wave away the criticisms, to dispel the nonsense made by hindsight. He wanted a *fist* to shake.

"So the Senate wishes us to hurry," he said, forcing a smile he didn't feel.

A scattering of laughter floated around the table.

Byrne nodded to the invasion fleet's head physicist. "What's the latest on the rift?"

"The size has stabilized, sir, but we're still showing a massive strain on local space-time with each ship that comes through."

"So there's no bringing them through any faster?"

"No, sir. Not and still give each of the six folded dimensions time to properly recoil—"

"We take your word for it," Byrne said, the interruption feeling rude without a polite raise of his hand. He looked around the table at the various heads of invasion divisions. Most of the eyes pointed his way were of the fleshy variety. Not for the first time, Byrne wondered what they felt of his being in charge. Was he seen as an abomination? One of their tools out of control? He didn't think so. He often felt something more humiliating: That they just looked at him the way they did their communicators after they'd been popped out of their ear canals and set on the table before them.

"I understand the Senate's impatience, and I understand each of yours," Byrne said. "However, if the science says we can't bring the fleet through any faster, I don't see that we have a choice. It's not as if this galaxy poses a threat to us, so we form up as steady as we can right here until the jump data is retrieved."

The personnel chief raised his hand. "But when will that be?" He glanced at the others as they turned to face him. "And it's not that the crews are grumbling about the time away from home. They just want to know when they'll see some action."

"I thought you were expecting your . . ." The weapons officer looked away from Byrne's gaze and glanced at the knotted and empty sleeves at his shoulders. "Your *data* back days ago."

"I was," Byrne said. "I am. The agent I have working on this has our coordinates. I'm just waiting for the delivery."

"While we wait, the Drenard invasion against the humans continues and is taking a heavy toll."

Everyone around the table turned to the other automaton in the room, the only figure among them who didn't look anything like a good Bern. Agent Bodi stood in a far corner, preferring as always to keep his blue-tinted skin in the shadows. As uncomfortable as his presence made the others, Byrne felt a sort of connection to his mechanical brethren, his fellow plant among the enemy. But he also felt a twinge of disgust. So many other, more *primal* circuits inside of him had been designed to loathe the appearance of anything un-Bern.

Cinthya, the fleet's cultural advisor, turned to Bodi. "Are you really worried about the loss of Drenard life?" Byrne thought she sounded more professionally curious than shocked.

"Don't be ridiculous," Bodi said, which caused more than a few spines to stiffen. "The start of our invasion was coordinated to ease the progress of *this* one. If we wait until the Drenards have already wiped out the humans, I assure you we'll have a messier time scrubbing their blue filth out of this galaxy than we would have otherwise. They'll be battle-hardened, and they'll be everywhere."

"Bodi is right," Byrne said. Chairs squeaked as everyone turned their attention back to the table. "But we still have plenty of time before we need to worry, and every passing day, more of our ships arrive from hyperspace—"

"Hello, hello, hello. Testing. One. Two."

"I'm sorry, more of our ships arrive from—"

"Hello? Is anyone there?"

"Pardon me," Byrne told the division heads. He turned to his assistant and nodded. "I believe our agent is making contact."

The young officer jumped up from his seat and inspected the band on Byrne's forehead. "Is it coming through okay? Do I need to rearrange anything?"

242

Byrne wanted to wave him away. As he collected his thoughts, forcing them into the circuits of the Drenardian communicator, he suddenly realized why the fleshy Bern touch their ears while talking to distant people. With all the curious gazes pointed his way, Bern had an overwhelming urge to rest his missing hand along the band's edge, signifying to the others that he was speaking to someone not present—

oooo

"I'm here. Iss that you, Walter?"

Walter nodded. He reached out from the covers and flicked off the overhead lights. He could pretend to be asleep and continue to talk if Molly barged in.

"Walter, iss that you?"

"Yeah," Walter thought. *"Lissten, about that meeting—"*

"Yess, Walter, I wass jusst disscusssing that with my ssuperiorss."

Walter dug his fingers into his ears, as if he could plug the annoying hiss.

"I loaded the coordinatess you gave me into our hyper-drive, jusst like you ssuggessted," Walter thought, *"But sshe didn't make the jump."*

"But you promissed," the voice said.

"I know, but there'ss been a change of planss. I don't think we're jumping to hypersspacse anymore."

"What'ss going on, Walter? I can't promisse you all thiss gold if you can't come through for me—"

"I think we're gonna be jumping individual people to ssomewhere tonight," Walter interrupted. "I'm gonna have to undo the changess I made to the hyperdrive, or they're gonna find out. I'm ssorry."

"Individual people? What do you mean?"

Walter pulled his sheets up over his head. "There'ss thesse sshipss here keeping uss from going anywhere, sso I think ssome friendss of mine are gonna ssend people ssomewhere with the hyperdrive. I'm gonna have to change it back to the way it was."

"Walter, iss there any chancse you could ssend yourssself ssomewhere with the hyperdrive?"

Walter thought about that.

"I'm not ssure," he thought.

The voice in his head was silent.

"Hello?" Walter thought.

"One ssecond," the voice said.

"I don't know what to do," Walter thought miserably.

The intolerable silence grew.

"Okay, Walter, I've got ssome numberss I need you to jot down."

Walter fumbled at his belt for his portable computer. He powered it on under the covers, filling the small tent with an eerie luminescence.

"*Okay,*" Walter thought, as soon as the screen lit up. "*What kind of numberss?*"

"*Thesse are ssome new coordinatess,*" the voice in his head hissed. "*I want you to jump to them asss ssoon asss you can.*"

"*I'll try,*" Walter thought.

"*And Walter?*"

"*Yeah?*"

"*Don't forget to bring Molly along with you.*"

"*Okay,*" Walter thought.

Images and dreams of a cube of gold the size of a moon filled his imagination, as vivid and bright as the voice invading his mind.

"*I promissse,*" he hissed out loud, enraptured by the vision of so much shiny goodness, all of it soon to be his.

14

PARSONA

Molly clipped her harness to the eyebolt by the cargo door and stood ready to haul in bags of supplies. Each of the climbers had at least one black duffel, which they pushed ahead of them using ascenders that ratcheted along the ropes. The sound of the thrusters holding *Parsona* in place erased the labored grunts of the climbers as they made their way up to the cargo bay and handed off the gear. Walter even emerged from his room to help out. He took one of the bags from Molly, nearly dropping the heavy sack as she let go.

The climbers scampered into the bay thankful for the grav plates, which altered the downward direction their bodies felt. Molly joined Walter and Cat in bringing them refreshments, nobody commenting on the bloodstains on their boots and knees, the marks from their climb through a stairwell littered with the day-old remains of their crewmates.

"Are you sure we need another run?" Molly asked. She felt like doing anything she could to spare them another taxing ordeal, physically as well as emotionally.

One of the navy men nodded as he sipped from his thermos. Behind him, Scottie leaned back against a bulkhead, taking deep breaths. Molly glanced out at the system of ropes rigged up across the decking beyond. Because of the grav plates and the thrusters holding them in place, it looked as if she could just stroll out and walk along them. She had to remember the way the Firehawks had fallen the other day to appreciate the forces at play beyond her own decking.

The climbers rested for almost an hour before setting off again. Cat volunteered to spell Scottie or Ryn, but neither would hear of it. After they disappeared down the ropes, Walter made himself scarce as usual, and Molly and Cat returned to their boring duties as radio sentries and gossipers.

As before, they picked up sporadic chatter from the ships overhead, but nothing that seemed important.

It wasn't long before Cat and Parsona resumed the argument they'd been in the middle of before the climbers had returned and interrupted them:

"I just don't see how you can sympathize with the Bern," Parsona said, not for the first time.

Molly looked to Cat and watched her shrug. The Callite turned to gaze out her porthole. "I didn't say they can do no wrong. All I'm suggesting is that the Underground might be the rebellious upstarts, and the Bern maybe got a right to try to quash them."

"Now it's *them*, huh? What happened to *us*?"

Cat waved her hand. "What's it matter in the long run? Can you really think in absolutes like this? It's like—"

Molly smiled and fed some of her protein bar to the Wadi as Cat struggled for the right word.

"It's like what?" Parsona asked.

"Aw, hell. I was gonna say it's like you can think like a computer, or something, but it wouldn't have come out right."

Parsona and Molly both laughed.

"I don't mean to be obstinate," Cat said. "I guess I've just thought on these things so long that I'm pretty sure there ain't an answer."

"Wait a second, you two." Molly leaned forward and turned up the ship's radio.

"Affirmative, group designation four. Maintaining coordinates relative to—"

"It's nothing," Cat said.

"Yeah, it's just that voice. I swear it reminds me of someone—"

"—approximate vectors. Edison out."

"Flank me," Molly whispered.

"No," Parsona said. "It can't be."

"You two wanna fill me in?"

"Can we can transmit?" Molly asked.

"Yeah," her mom said. "We're riding the same frequency in order to listen in. I'm patching it together right now. But you don't really think—?"

"I don't know." Molly shook her head and reached for the mic. She thought for a moment, then squeezed the transmit button. "Hello? Does anybody read me?"

The radio popped, and then a voice announced: "Carrier frequency compromised. All groups switch to secondary."

A round of "copies," followed, and then the radio fell silent.

"Well that sucks vacuum," Cat said.

"Give me a second," Parsona told them.

They waited.

"Try again. I think I have it, but there isn't any chatter right now."

Molly bit her lip and thought about what to say. "My transmission is scrambled too, right?" she asked her mom.

"Yes, but if the entire fleet is using this carrier wave, they'll all hear you. Keep that in mind."

Molly keyed the mic. "Mechanical bear, this is the Wadi queen, over."

The same voice from before responded immediately: *"Frequency compromised. Switch to tertiary."*

"Copy."

"Negative," a gruffer voice said. A *familiar* voice. *"Break, break. Fifth group is maintaining secondary carrier frequency."*

Silence. Then a different voice. Higher. Softer. Still familiar.

"Molly? Is that you?"

Molly swallowed and blinked back tears.

"Anlyn?"

The trepid male voice returned: *"This is group command, switch to tertiary frequency immediately."*

"Command, this is Group Five," Anlyn said. *"That's your commander's daughter. Please hold."*

"Anlyn," Molly said into the mic. "Are you in that fleet up there? Can we talk? What are the Drenards doing with the Bern? How did you—What's going on?"

"These aren't Drenards, Molly. We—it's complicated. We're with some people from hyperspace. We control three ships up here—hold on a sec."

Molly stared at the dash, waiting. She could hear her own heartbeat.

"Sorry, Edison had to say something on the other radio. We have command of three of the ships up here. There's a few hundred people scattered between them."

"What? Like refugees?"

"No. Warriors. They have a plan to close the rift but weren't expecting the fleet to just be hanging out here. None of the Bern ships seem to be moving on, and we can't act until they do."

"They've been like that for weeks, just holding formation and shooting down anything that moves." Molly let go of the transmit button and then squeezed it again. "About this Underground . . . are they from Lok? Do you have . . . ? Is—?"

"I'm sorry," Anlyn responded quickly. "We just learned what's been going on ourselves. Another ship is still queued up to come through the rift. Your dad and Cole—" Anlyn paused. "It seems one of the ships went down on the other side."

Molly gasped. Her heart pounded through her flight suit. But still, she was just as thrilled to hear someone relate their recent condition as she was dreading whatever had gone wrong. After keeping her thoughts and fears pushed into deep recesses for so long, she could feel them suddenly popping free, stirring and agitated and impatient.

"Reduce chatter, you two." It was the other voice from the fleet.

"He's right," Parsona told Molly. "A constant stream is easier to stumble onto and hack."

Molly looked at the mic in her hand, trying to sort out what was most important to say, what information she needed to best assist their combined efforts to defeat the Bern.

"How did the Underground infiltrate those ships in the first place?" Parsona asked, throwing one of her own queries onto Molly's heap.

"My hunch is that the Bern are staging up here to protect their supply chain," Cat told her. "You should probably tell them that."

"Gimme a sec," Molly told them. "I can't think."

She knew what she needed to say. She needed to speak to this other voice, to tell whoever was in charge up there that they were all in this together and that they needed to work that way. She tried a few phrasings in her head, then squeezed the transmit button.

"Command, we are with the Underground as well." She looked over to Cat, who nodded, approving. "We are currently working on a plan to take out the large ship up there and possibly the rest of the fleet. It's imperative that we talk."

"Negative," the voice said. "Any movement up here, and we're sitting ducks. Maintain radio silence until the fleet moves out of this system. Nobody acts until then. Over and out."

Molly cursed. Having friends so close and not being able to speak with them was going to drive her insane. She looked to Cat. "Any ideas?"

Cat shook her head.

"Molly, Anlyn here. We're coming to you. I need coordinates for your cargo bay, and then I need you to clear out. Wait. Hold on—"

Molly heard voices conferring on the other side of Anlyn's connection.

"Molly, make sure those coordinates are for a space one meter off the deck. And make them exact."

Molly pulled up her nav screen to get her current position.

"How exact?" she asked.

"Edison exact."

○ ○ ○ ○

Molly heard the air in *Parsona's* cargo bay pop, and then a figure materialized a meter off the deck—it just blinked into existence. The person hit the ground in a ball and rolled out of the way. Molly couldn't believe her eyes. She started to get up from the crew seat, but Anlyn ran her way, telling her to stay put.

A louder pop, and a bundle of fur wrapped in tunics crashed to the ground, sending a vibration through the hull. Edison stood up and lumbered her way as Anlyn threw herself into Molly's arms.

Molly held her friend—tears coating her vision—as yet another man appeared in her cargo bay.

"How many are coming?" she asked Anlyn, pulling out of the embrace and wiping at her eyes.

"Just us," Anlyn said, smiling at her. Edison came over and wrapped them both up and lifted them off the ground. Past his shoulder, Molly saw Cat run to the third person who had arrived, screaming his name and nearly tackling him.

"Edison, you're smothering me!"

He dropped them back to the ground. "Sincerest apologies," he said. "Irrationally, my exuberance overcame my ability to forgo immediate gratification, I—"

"I love you, too," Molly said, leaning into his tunics and wrapping her arms partway around him.

"What are you guys *doing* here?" she asked Anlyn. "I thought you were on Drenard."

"Well, what in the galaxy is Cole doing in hyperspace?"

Walter popped out of his room. He hissed in alarm at the sight of Edison.

"Walter!" Edison said, stomping over to greet him.

Cat approached Molly from the opposite direction, pulling along a short, bald, bearded man. Molly felt dizzy from the amount of activity and the number of things she needed to ask Anlyn about. First, though, there was an outstretched hand waiting to be shaken.

"Ryke," the man said. He accepted Molly's grasp and pumped it warmly. "Lotsa folks call me Doctor Ryke, but I done nothing to deserve it."

"I'm—"

"I know who you are," Ryke said, smiling at her. He continued to hold her hand as he gazed around the cargo bay, appraising it as he might a home he had once lived in, or helped to build.

"You know my father," Molly whispered.

"Yup. Good man. And I wouldn't worry none about him. He's fond of grand entrances."

"So he's okay?" Molly turned to Anlyn. "How's Cole?"

"I haven't seen him," Anlyn said. "I just recently found out where he was."

"He set off to help Mortimor get out of hyperspace," Ryke said. "What we need to be working on is getting that rift closed up as soon as he does.

Before we get to that, though . . ." Ryke looked at Molly expectantly.

"I'm so sorry," Molly said. "Do you guys need food or water? The bathroom? If you need to rest before—"

"Naw," Ryke said, looking back over his shoulder. "You reckon I could sneak off to your engine room, just to see her?"

"See *who*?" Molly asked.

"The hyperdrive," Ryke whispered.

Cat wrapped her arms around Ryke's broad shoulders and leaned over to kiss the top of his bald head. "You haven't changed a lick!" she said.

"Sure," Molly said. "Help yourself." She turned back to Anlyn and then realized how difficult it was going to be to explain the presence of all these people to the navy climbers when they got back.

"Oh, Ryke? I'm gonna need you guys to stash away in the crew quarters in less than an hour. You'll have to stay there while we fly back to this clearing we've set up camp in. I'm with some men in black."

"Navy?" Ryke looked around as if she'd warned him of snakes.

"They're fine. I just don't want to have to explain how you got here."

Ryke scratched his beard and nodded, and then he hurried off toward the back of the ship.

Walter continued to gab with Edison near the door to his room. Molly flinched when she felt the Wadi scurry up her leg to her shoulder. Normally, the thing wouldn't leave the back of her seat if she put her there. The animal twisted around her neck and jabbed its tongue out at Anlyn.

Anlyn's eyes lit up at the sight of the colorful Wadi. She came close to Molly, reaching her hand out to it.

"By the lights of Hori," she whispered.

"Another reason I'm glad you're here," Molly said. "I think there's something wrong with her." She removed the Wadi and held it out to Anlyn. "Gods, it feels like there's so much I didn't get to say before we left Drenard. I . . . ." Molly watched the Wadi curl itself around Anlyn's neck. "Exactly what happened after we left? I hear your people are pushing out into Terran space and attacking our planets."

"She's pregnant," Anlyn said, rubbing the Wadi's head with two fingers.

"She . . . Wait, *what*? The *Wadi*?"

Anlyn nodded.

"But she's getting *smaller*."

"Has she been drinking a lot?"

"Kiloliters."

"Well, she's laid her eggs somewhere, and now she's feeding them. Big ones, from the looks of her tail."

Molly leaned forward and looked at the wisp of a tail as it circled in the air. "How can you tell?"

Anlyn looked around the cargo bay. "I can't believe you haven't seen them."

"I can't believe you're standing in front of me! What've you been up to? We—Oh my Gods, I have to tell you about what happened on Dakura, and we got captured by the navy, and Walter broke us free, and then I nearly got killed here. Oh, and we're currently inside a StarCarrier that crashed, and it's like sitting vertically in the air, and you remember Saunders? That guy from the Academy I told you about? He's here and not trying to kill me anymore."

Anlyn beamed and waved Molly down. "Slow down, you're about as easy to follow as Edison right now."

"I'm sorry." Molly went to the galley and filled two cups with water. She glanced over at Edison to see if he needed a drink and saw him studying one of Byrne's severed arms. Walter had dragged the morbid things out to show them off.

"Here." She held a glass out to Anlyn.

"We just ate about an hour ago, but thanks." She accepted the cup. "So, you said you had a plan for getting rid of the fleet? I hope it's a good one because I had to pull royal rank to risk the hyperdrive trace and have us sent down here."

"It's the best we've got, but it'll take a few days to pull off." Molly nodded to the empty spot in her cargo bay where Anlyn had appeared out of thin air. "I just recently learned that my hyperdrive can do that as well. I'm sending a group of Callites and navy personnel straight to Darrin, just like how you guys showed up. They're gonna nab a fleet and then jump back here and put up a fight. Meanwhile, we're gonna send every missile in this Carrier up to take out that massive ship. We think it's the one that's been downing enemy crafts like it's nothing."

Molly took a deep breath and winced at how crazy the plan sounded spelled out like that.

"How're you planning on stealing the fleet at Darrin?" Anlyn asked. Her face had grown quite serious, as if the rest might be workable.

"That's why we're here." Molly pointed to the black duffel bags from the first climb. "We're raiding the Carrier's stores for armor, weapons, flight suits—"

"Not like what you'll need," Anlyn said, shaking her head. "At Darrin, you're gonna come up against personal barrier shields that'll deflect any kind of bullet or bolt fired at it. Trust me, I know."

"Albert," Molly said, remembering the blow Edison had landed to the weapon dealer's head that the man hadn't even felt. "Maybe we can just sneak aboard the ships and blast our way out?"

Anlyn shook her head. "The controls for the force-doors are on their belts. You'll be sending people to their doom, Molly. One-way."

"Well, hyperspace," Molly said. She raised her eyebrows. "Maybe there's enough missiles in here to take out several of the smaller ships before they start jumping away?"

"No," Anlyn said. "Your plan for the Darrin fleet is a good one. You just need something better than these guns to take it from them."

"Yeah, I need some of what *Albert* stocks."

Anlyn smiled. "Actually, according to Edison, we might have something even better—"

Before she could explain what that was, the portable radio squawked from the cockpit, announcing the return of the navy climbers.

"We'll figure it out later," Molly said. She took the Wadi back from Anlyn, allowing the animal to curl itself around her neck. "Grab Edison and Ryke and hide out in your room. Try to get some rest."

Anlyn squeezed Molly's arm and smiled. "Don't you worry on that last bit," she said. "I feel like I haven't slept in ages."

15

LOK

Several hours later, Molly lowered *Parsona* into the now-familiar clearing just as Lok's speedy sun began to slip over the horizon. Yet another brief day on Molly's alien home had felt like several. The longest part for her had been the flight back from the StarCarrier, tormented by having Anlyn and Edison stowed away in their old quarters and unable to talk to them. Her only solace was in hearing how badly all three of them needed some sleep. Still, there was so much she wanted to tell them and to hear in return.

Their first stop in a long round of flights had been to drop off the climbers and their gear. Molly had then used another supply run to Bekkie as a chance to catch up with her old friends and an excuse for how they had arrived. Now that they were returning to the clearing, Molly realized the unthinkable task she had before herself: she needed to introduce a navy admiral to a member of the loathed Drenardian race. And with a Glemot crammed in the room for good measure!

Parsona touched down into her well-worn depressions in the wooded clearing, one strut squeaking a little. Her cargo door opened to let in the night sounds of forest whispers and chirping insects. Molly followed Cat into the cargo bay, where another round of supplies had been arranged. As soon as the hatch met the crackling leaves of the clearing, Callites and humans stomped up together to help unload. Molly left the physical labor to her friends. She squeezed past Ryke, whom Cat was introducing to several Callites, and set off in search of Saunders.

She didn't have to go far, as the portly admiral was already stomping up the loading ramp to find *her*.

"Everything go okay?" he asked. Molly watched him search her for signs of trauma, yesterday's adventures in Bekkie still seemingly fresh on his mind.

"It went fine. We got enough food and water to last the Darrin squads both ways, and I was able to buy extra flight gear off a few other ships for next to nothing. It appears that cash is king right now."

Saunders looked over the bundles of packaged food and the crates of fluid packets with a frown. "Are you sure this will be enough?"

Molly pulled him out of the way of the supply chains and back toward the crew quarters.

"More than enough, actually. I picked up some friends in town, and one of them, a Doctor Ryke who grew up near my home village, knows a way to shorten the trip back from Darrin."

"Even more than the route you picked out? I thought you had it down to four jumps or something like that."

"Drastically shorter," Molly said. "And it'll be even safer, trust me." She led him down the hallway and stopped just outside of Edison's room. She slapped the door twice as the insanity of what she was about to do fully set in. The daunting task wrapped itself around her chest and made it difficult to breathe. She turned to Saunders.

"Molly, what's wrong?"

She shook her head. "Nothing, I . . . I just need you to stay quiet and calm, okay? Some of the friends I picked up in town . . . they might not be what you're expecting."

A hurt look spread across Saunders's face. "I'm fine with the locals," he said. "Just so you know, I was a naval ambassador before taking the job at the—"

He stopped. His eyes darted back and forth, scanning Molly's face. Whatever he saw there had given him pause.

"What could you possibly show me—?"

There was a knock on the other side of the door.

"Just be calm," Molly said, trying her damnedest to follow her own advice. She keyed the door open, and it slid back. The lights inside were off, the portholes shuttered. Molly ushered Saunders inside and closed the door. They had worried over whether or not he'd even *enter* the room if he saw what awaited him.

When the lights flicked on, Molly noted her worries had been justified. Saunders flinched back, reaching for Molly or possibly the door behind her. Molly steadied him; she felt his frozen muscles tremble beneath his copious bulk. She watched as the ruddy color of his neck drained white, and she worried he might pass out again, just as he had when he'd found out about the Bern threat.

As Molly watched his reaction, hoping he'd be okay, she recalled the first time *she* had seen Anlyn. Her body had responded similarly, freezing and fumbling for Cole. She certainly knew what he was going through, and how far her own fears had come in such a short time.

"She's a friend," Molly told Saunders, hoping to calm him. She moved to his side and placed a hand on his back. "And this is Edison, another very good friend of mine."

"D . . . Dre . . ."

Anlyn rose from her bed and bowed slightly. Molly was relieved to see Edison stay put, his bulk fearsome enough just hunched over on the small bunk.

"My name is Anlyn Hooo, and I greet you on behalf of my empire—"

Saunders collapsed, his legs folding neatly, Indian style, as he sank to the deck. Molly steadied his shoulders to keep his head from going back against the dresser. She stepped around, knelt down in front of him, and saw his eyes focusing on Anlyn, his mouth open.

"Sir? Admiral, I need you to stay with me."

His eyes moved slowly to Molly's.

"Are you okay?"

He shook his head, his jowls jiggling left and right. He made little circles with his chin, transforming the shake into a nod.

"Are you or aren't you?"

"I need water," he said, his voice thin and raspy.

"I can't send either of them—" Molly nodded to her two friends. "Do you want me to leave you and get a glass?"

Saunders considered this. He shook his head.

Molly felt Anlyn's hand on her shoulder; she turned to see her friend sitting down across from Saunders. After she got settled, Anlyn folded her translucent blue hands into her lap and smiled at the admiral.

Molly moved aside and sat likewise, occupying the small plot of floor still available, each of her knees nearly touching one of theirs. Edison remained quietly seated on the bunk behind them, and the silence within the room became more palpable by the steady thump of activity in the cargo bay beyond. Together, the three crewmates rode out the old man's shock, respecting the awkwardness they had induced.

"Admiral Saunders—" Anlyn eventually began.

"You speak English," he said, interrupting her.

Anlyn nodded. "Molly told you why our people are at war?"

"Because of *them*?" Saunders asked. He pointed up at the ceiling and presumably to the Bern fleet beyond. His eyes darted away from Anlyn and settled on Edison. "Is . . . Is that one of . . . *them*?"

Molly stifled a laugh and then felt sorry for Saunders. His face was still ashen, his jaw slack with confusion. She reached out and put a hand on his knee. "Edison is a Glemot. He's harmless," she said, ripping the truth in half, grinding it to shards, and setting the fragments on fire. "The Bern look like *us*, remember?"

Saunders nodded and blinked rapidly, relearning old news.

Anlyn held up her hands, showing her pale-blue palms. "Admiral, war has been declared on your empire by mine. There are agents in both of our camps that do not have the best interests of their own people in mind. Do you understand?"

"I do," he replied, some of the color returning to his cheeks.

"I did everything I could to prevent these most recent hostilities, both as a member of our highest council and personally."

"You don't want to fight us," Saunders said.

"That's correct. I don't. Many of us don't." Anlyn adjusted her tunics and then folded her hands into her lap. "We share a common enemy, your empire and mine. One that has been trying its mightiest to drive our people together so they can then sweep through the debris and lord over the ashes. That enemy is gathering right here above this planet. Do you understand this as well?"

"The Bern."

"Admiral, do you understand what needs to be done? That this enemy must be stopped at all costs?"

Saunders nodded. Molly could see his throat constrict as he swallowed. She should have planned better and had some water in the room ahead of time.

"We have a plan," Saunders said meekly. He turned to Molly. "We have a plan, right?" He seemed desperate for a confirmation of this feeble hope.

Molly patted his knee. "Admiral, we need you to do something important, okay? Anlyn has it worked out."

"I am next in line to the throne of the Drenard Empire," Anlyn said.

Saunders's face remained blank, but Molly felt goose bumps ripple up her arms from hearing her friend say such an outrageous thing, even if it was true.

"I am not in a position of military power," she went on, "and I will never rule my people, but I do have certain *inherent* foreign relations rights. Further, I happen to be on an ambassadorial mission sanctioned by my ruling body, entrusted with the right to establish first contact with races not previously negotiated with and enter into negotiations with any such races encountered."

"I . . . I'm not following," Saunders said. He looked to Molly for help, but she just nodded to Anlyn, trying to keep him focused.

"My hope was to make contact with the Bern," Anlyn said. "It was my reading, my interpretation of an old prophe—an old *document* passed down for many generations. But I believe I was meant to do *this*. Right here. Right now. *We* are the races meant to unite under the shadow of a rift, human and Drenard, not the Drenard and Bern."

"Do *what?*" Saunders shook his head as if trying to clear the confusion. Molly noticed both his hands were clenched fists—knuckles pressed against knuckles in his lap, as if he could grip the air and somehow hold his senses firm.

"My people never made official first contact with the Bern *or* the humans," Anlyn said. "I have the power and the rights to do this, to enter into formal negotiations with either race."

Saunders shook his head again, the folds under his chin swaying.

"She means that she can make it official if you declare—"

"I can certify it if you would choose to—"

Neither of them seemed to know how to come out and say it.

An awkward silence began to form as they looked to one another for help.

"Surrender immediately," Edison growled, his gruff voice dripping with impatience.

"Do *what?*"

Saunders popped to his feet with a litheness that defied his bulk and an injection of energy that cut through his former stillness.

"*Surrender?* Concede the war with the *Drenards?*"

Molly and Anlyn both stood as well, holding their hands out to calm him.

"Hear us out," Molly said. "It's not just about stopping the fighting, which we don't think it'll even do, it's about exposing the people on both sides who *want* this war. It's a formality, nothing more."

"It's a way to smoke them out," Anlyn said.

"I don't . . . Even if I had the authority, which I don't, the most I could do is surrender my fleet, the entire crew of which can fit in this single ship!" Saunders threw his hands up.

"That's why we need you to go to Earth," Molly said. "We need you to explain what's going on—"

"But I don't even *know* what's going on!"

"Sir, all you have to do is recount the loss of your fleet and the unwinnable nature of this conflict. Persuade the Galactic Union to terminate its offensive. We need to see who would want the fight to continue, even if it means utter defeat. *These* are our true enemies."

"But what *then?*" Saunders asked. "What will it matter when the people who actually wiped out Zebra group are still around to mop us up? I need to stay here with my crew." He reached out and grabbed Molly's arm. "We'll attack with the Darrin fleet, just like you said. I'll lead them into battle myself."

Molly patted his hand and shook her head. "The attack will be carried out as planned," she said, "but you won't be leading it. The mission to Earth is more important. It'll solve the problem of finding the Bern among us without causing panic or worse."

Saunders turned to Molly. "So I won't be leading the attack back here? Then who will? *You?*" he asked.

She shook her head again.

"Who, then?"

"Me," Anlyn said. "*I'll* be leading them."

PART XX

ANLYN

"A child howls—and the canyons fall silent."

~The Bern Seer~

16

DRENARD · TWELVE
YEARS AGO

Tears streamed down Anlyn's cheeks. She tried her best to blink them away while yanking the control stick left and right, up and down, but nothing she did helped. No matter which way she dodged and spun the Interceptor, her fiancé Bodi was able to match her. Twisting and turning, swooping and diving, jittering her ship nervously in space, she did everything she could to shake him, all to no avail.

Her stolen flight suit did what it could to minimize the Gs, its small pockets of anti-grav fluid coursing through the suit and removing as much of the force on her body as they could. But no technological marvel existed to remove the pressure within her: that clawing at the hollow of her stomach born by a day of far too much tragedy.

"Anlyn Hooo, that is *enough*."

Bodi's voice came through her helmet clear enough to twist her heart in knots. The disgust she felt at the sound of his words was another sort of nausea the grav suit couldn't touch. Anlyn ignored his commands — she was utterly sick and tired of his commands. She kept yanking on the stick, hoping to create enough space to jump away. She needed to get away from Drenard, away from her home. She desperately needed to get away from the emptiness her father's sudden death had left, both in her heart and upon his throne.

"Don't make me shoot out your thrusters," Bodi warned.

As if *she* were the one inconveniencing *him*.

Anlyn glanced down at the dash, where so many lights and knobs twinkled in her tear-blurred vision. Royal flight training had only touched on the basics — a professional pilot had kept his hands on the stick at all times while he showed her how to jump, taught her the rudiments of SADAR, and allowed her to transmit over the radio. It had been just enough instructional ceremony to satisfy ancient traditions of Drenardian royalty without exposing one of the empire's precious women to an iota of potential harm. But now, without someone pointing out which switch did what, Anlyn felt overwhelmed by the dizzying array of readouts and blinking indicators.

"The royal guard is on their way, Anlyn. Take your hands off the controls. You're embarrassing me."

Anlyn looked up through the canopy where Bodi flew inverted, matching her every movement. She could clearly see the glint of his visor just a dozen paces away. Yanking back on the stick, she tried to throw her craft up into his, her hot side stoked by his constant badgering. Bodi moved out of the way easily; he fell back around her and then looped up on top. She dove the opposite direction, but he matched her move for move.

Giving up for a moment, Anlyn allowed her craft to straighten itself out while she took a few deep breaths not encumbered by the squeezing of her gravsuit. She wondered how she had gotten herself in this position. She was pretty sure it had started with her Wadi Rite, not that long ago. Things had been different between her and Bodi after that. And then her father—it felt like weeks since she'd learned of his passing, days since she had fled to the Naval base and commandeered a ship to run away. It had probably been a few hours—she had no idea.

She looked to her display screen, where she had the hyperdrive help file pulled up. As far as Anlyn could tell, she had the drive cycled properly and good coordinates for an empty patch of space plugged in. Still, the blasted engage button wouldn't work. A flashing indicator kept blinking "proximity alarm."

Anlyn scanned the help file while Bodi continued his jabbering: "Very good, Anlyn. Stay on that course. I'm going to lock my ship to yours. Steady, now."

Anlyn ignored him and read something about a jump override. There were two pages of cautions and warnings before it got to the explanation. She scrolled down, ignoring the paragraphs about "slingshots" and "unintended arrival coordinates." Nothing in the universe turned her brain off like tech-speak and such gibberish.

"Steady, now."

Bodi said it as if he were chiding a youth. She hated that tone, especially when he did it to her in public. He had always spoken to her that way when her father, the king of their empire, was around. She had long dreamed of the day she would stand up to Bodi in front of her dad and her uncles. Now, that would never happen. Her father was dead, and she would be forced to marry an evil man, a cold and fiery man. She scanned the override instructions—and then heard a metallic bang as his ship touched hers.

Anlyn's hand flinched, just as if he had touched her body. Just *like* when he touched her body. She yanked her flightstick the other way, worried he might lock the two Interceptors together. As she created a few paces of space—and before she could reconsider—she followed the instructions in the help file and typed in the override commands, entering them in triplicate and agreeing to all the warning messages.

The jump switch finally turned from black to solid blue.

Anlyn punched it without hesitation.

○ ○ ○ ○

The twin suns of Hori disappeared, replaced by a blanket of alien stars and a maelstrom of violence. Plasma blasts the size of solar flares ripped through the distance, arcing toward a blazing ball of destruction the size of a planet. Anlyn saw, just in time, that similar plumes of racing fire were heading her way. She slammed the thrust forward as the columns of sure death slid by in silence.

Where have I jumped? she wondered. It certainly wasn't the empty space she'd been aiming for.

Besides the large rivers of marching plasma fire, Anlyn saw that the cosmos around her was peppered with a swarm of racing ships and the less powerful streaks from their cannons and missile pods. She banked her own ship around—still getting used to the feel of the controls—and searched for a way out of the commotion.

But the chaos was everywhere; it seemed whatever star system she had jumped into was embroiled in an outright orgy of war. At first, she thought it was a trinary star system, an alien land with one more sun than even her own Drenard, but eventually she recognized the other two glowing, fire-stricken orbs to be planets. Former planets, anyway. Both were being devoured by all-encompassing blazes, almost as if the crust of each had opened up to reveal the molten mantle beneath.

Anlyn headed up the star system's orbital plane, hoping to escape the flat battleground where most of the activity was taking place. She threw the accelerator all the way forward and felt her body sag back into her seat with the ever-increasing velocity.

What have I done? she thought.

Red alarms winked across her dashboard in answer. Anlyn fought to unravel them, her eyes darting from one to the next, none of the alarms ever having come up during her brief training regimen:

MISSILE LOCK_ HOSTILE TARGETS_ PLASMA SIGNATURES_

Her hands shook as they hovered over the hundreds of keys and knobs on the dash, so few of which she knew how to operate. The trembling worked its way up her arms, through her shoulders, back into her heart, and all the way to her legs. Anlyn wrapped her arms around herself, trying to hold her body still, trying to prevent herself from flying apart like the distant planets, quaking from their onslaught. She pulled her knees up to her chin, dug her heels into the seat, and tucked her head down, quivering and crying.

And then the first missile struck.

The ferocious blast vaporized one wing and ripped the fuselage in half. Anlyn was slammed into her flight harness, the pilot's suit coping with a majority of the Gs, but not all of them. Her head whipped to the side, her arms and legs fortuitously protected by her tight fetal position as the wounded Bern Interceptor spun out of control, the whirlwind of disintegrating machinery exploding into the cosmos.

A bolt of plasma ripped through the Interceptor next, punching a clean hole, ringed in red and dripping sparks, right through the ship's body. Anlyn heard her visor snap shut automatically, cutting off the banging of steel and the whine of a dozen alarms. The sound of air moving, of a tiny fan somewhere in her suit circulating her precious oxygen, was all she heard besides her heartbeat.

The end had come for her, she realized. Bodi had been right. She wouldn't last a second out in the galaxy alone.

The next missile cruised her way, its red tip armed and hungry. As it plowed through the cosmos after a warm body to devour, a countdown in Anlyn's Interceptor ticked toward zero. It was a warning, giving her the chance to override an automatic safety system.

But Anlyn wasn't aware of it. She tried to hold herself together as her ship screamed and was wrenched apart. The missile drew near, pushing through the fuzzy sphere of her Interceptor's already-expanding field of debris. The counter on the safety system reached *one*, the alarm high and pleading, begging to be overridden before it did something that could not be undone.

It finally reached *zero*.

The auto-eject systems fired, launching Anlyn—still strapped to her flight seat—out into the cold blackness of space.

But that vacuum didn't remain cold for long. The second missile finally found its prey, consuming itself and all else in a bubbly froth of fire.

17

DRENARD · A LONGER TIME AGO

In Anlyn's dreams, the fan inside her helmet was a roar. It was the roar of the Wadi winds, those never-ending blasts of air that flowed over her planet, etching the canyons from solid rock. Her heartbeat became her footfalls—the clomping of her hunting boots on the dry stone. Anlyn incorporated these sounds and constructed a dream world. A world that existed only in her memory, in her not-too-distant childhood.

There were five of them in her exclusive Rite group when Anlyn went to claim her Wadi. They were cousins, all. None of them were as near to the throne as she, if measured by begottens, but her three male cousins were light-years closer for *other* reasons. Anlyn didn't mind. She had no desire to sit where her father sat; she couldn't stand the thought of giving speeches for a living or having to decide matters of galaxy-wide importance. Her ideal life involved moving to a frontier planet, something along the rim of the Drenard arm of the Milky Way, and finding some peace and quiet to surround herself with.

She had imagined her life there a million times in a million different ways, but every variation revolved around common themes: They started with a large plot of land, something not constrained by perpetual night on the one side and day on the other, but spread out. The land would be rolling in places and flat in others. At least one gurgling creek would pass through, playing and skipping over the rocks in little white leaps. The grass would be kept tall so it could wave to and fro with fickle, unpredictable gusts of wind, nothing like the perpetual hurricane roaring around her home world.

And there would be *days*. There would be a growing light expanding in the morning to swallow the sky. The sun would move through the air, shimmering and becoming white hot as it rose to its peak. Then the nightfall would come to cool the sweat from her neck. She had heard about days from her uncles who governed distant planets. She had heard and imagined for herself the gradual sinking of suns, like balls of molten lava, crashing through the horizon.

Supposedly, the colors weren't as severe on these other planets when their suns rose and set—they weren't nearly as beautiful as what she'd grown up with on Drenard. But she could do without the frozen sunset of her home. Maybe, as the sight varied with each day, she would love the lesser spectacles even more. Their temporary nature might make them dearer, if drearier. She had heard as much from elders visiting from other planets.

And after the setting of the sun on her dream world, the night would come. It would be like the dark side of Drenard, but not deadly. The world would cool, shedding itself of its aura of trapped heat. The stars would begin to flash and twinkle, the sight of them temporary and fleeting. Anlyn and her husband— chosen by *her*, and they would be madly in love with each other—would lie out in the waving grasses and shiver and snuggle up together as their land began a plummet in temperature.

But the cooling wouldn't go on forever. It wouldn't freeze like the always-night on Drenard. Before the land could continue to grow cold, that forever-moving sun would race back around, hurrying through its task of warming the far side of her planet, keeping everything lovely and temperate by constantly orbiting and heating things just a little piece at a time.

Anlyn loved to imagine a sun doing that: *Moving*. She knew it wasn't what really happened, that other worlds just spun in their orbits so fast that they experienced day and night, but the illusion would be hard to ignore. And it made her imaginary sun, this sun on her dream world, feel as if it had a noble chore to perform, like a spotlight of energy working tirelessly to evenly distribute its powers across all the lands.

"Hey, we're here."

Anlyn snapped out of her sleepy dreaming and found the shuttle had stopped. Her cousins were already out of their seats and following the cluster of guards and officials toward the exit. Outside, her uncles and her aunt strode toward the Royal Wadi hut. Anlyn gathered her things—just a small pouch of good-luck items her mom had left in her will—and hurried after her cousins.

The interior of the Wadi hut was very different from the ones Anlyn had visited in museums and on fieldtrips. Instead of bare walls and confined spaces, it looked more like a getaway mansion for a Circle member. Blue and purple finery covered the walls and furniture; there were even hints of real wood trim framing the large windows and doorways. Anlyn would have liked to pretend the differences between the huts were due to the eras in which they were built, but she knew that wasn't the case. While most of her friends from private school were riding subways to *normal* Wadi huts, she and her cousins were being coddled in royal finery. And where the males would be allowed to hunt *real* Wadi, Anlyn and her cousin Coril would be relegated to snagging eggs, making them Drenards in the most limited of ways. In name only, really.

As they gathered inside, out of the feisty wind, their escorts gave them a brief overview of the hut, showing them the ready room and their private quarters. Anlyn and Coril picked out neighboring rooms while the boys fussed about in the ready room clashing with Wadi Lances, to the chagrin of their poor escorts.

"It sucks Thooo eggs to have to wait a whole sleep," Coril told Anlyn as the two made their way back to the lounge.

"Are you feeling anxious to get going?" Anlyn asked.

Coril nodded. "Just to get it over with. This whole charade seems like a waste of time."

Anlyn didn't say anything. Part of her agreed with Coril, knowing that their coddled female version of the Rite did nothing but make a mockery of what the old Wadi hunts were used for. In the days of thin living—many Hori cycles ago—the band of hospitable land on Drenard between cold night and hottest day made population growth a real concern. Back then, the Wadi Rite served a sick culling purpose, a twisted and sanctioned system of eugenics designed to weed out the weak. Now, with offworld settlements and two wars absorbing as many offspring as Drenard couples could make, the Rite had become a hierarchical selection process for some quasi-meritorious caste system. Except, paradoxically, it now meant bureaucrats and office workers were selected for their physical prowess, their tendency toward risk-taking, and their aggression. It was a trifecta of traits that had predictable consequences for the ruling of Empire: the hot-headed now dominated discussions and stifled other sorts of progress.

In Anlyn's much *cooler* opinion, at least.

"You've been awfully quiet on this trip," Coril pointed out. "You're not scared or nervous, are you?"

Anlyn shook her head. "No. I think I'm like you, just wondering what we're doing here."

Coril looked out at the colors wavering above the canyons. The two cousins were currently much closer to the twin stars of Hori than normal, which made the light shimmering through the air look different.

"You're not bummed about the throne one day moving off to another family, are you?"

Anlyn shrugged. "Maybe a little. But not because I'd ever want to be king, or because I wish I were a boy. Maybe I just feel a little guilty, or something. I guess I feel bad for my dad for only having *me* to pin his hopes on."

"I would never want to be king," Coril said. "All they do is get blamed for everything."

"Yeah, but if you were king, nothing would ever go wrong," Anlyn joked.

The two girls laughed. Everyone said Coril could do no wrong—that problems rolled off her like wind on marble.

"Oh, I'd make *plenty* of mistakes if *I* were king," Coril said. "Don't forget, I'd have to be a *boy*."

They laughed even harder at that, the two of them bending over, panting, and wiping at their eyes. Anlyn peeked back at the hallway and saw one of their uncles leaning against the doorjamb, frowning.

"I think we're supposed to be taking this more seriously," Anlyn said.

"Yeah? Well, then they should take *us* more seriously, first."

o o o o

Anlyn spent that night tossing and turning, her head full of nightmares of large empty eggs and hatched

Wadi scratching at rock. She awoke from one of the nightmares with a start, her heart pounding and her mind overwhelmed by the sensation of a nearby presence. She sat up, clutching her sheet—and a large figure at the foot of her bed shifted, as if startled by her movement.

Anlyn flinched.

"Gil? Is that you?"

"Not so loud," he hissed.

Anlyn leaned closer, blinking away the sleepiness and peering at the dark form sitting at the foot of her bed. "Gil, what in Hori's name are you doing in here?"

"I can't do this," he said softly.

Anlyn saw him shake his head, her eyes gradually adjusting to the soft light filtering in from the hallway. Gil had always been one of the few male cousins Anlyn didn't mind being around. He rarely teased her, possibly because he was familiar with being on the receiving end so often. At the age of two Horis, he was just barely double the size of a female youth, which put him on the small side among his more manly classmates, who rarely let him forget it.

"You'll do fine on your Rite," Anlyn told him. "Our uncles wouldn't send you into any trouble you couldn't handle." *And certainly not us girls*, she thought.

Gil scooted closer, forcing Anlyn to tuck her feet up under her.

"But I don't think I can do it at all. I mean, kill a real Wadi."

"It doesn't have to be a big one, Gil. You can always—"

"I know, I know, size doesn't matter for me. My dad's got a cushy job waiting no matter where I end up ranking. It's not that. And it isn't the moral objections, I mean, I fantasize about killing one as big as my dad."

"And *shaped* like him, too?"

Anlyn and Gil had to stifle their giggles. The two of them scooted even closer.

"I'm scared," Gil said flatly.

The cousins sat in silence, digesting the concept.

"I think I've always known I couldn't do this. I don't know how I even *got* here." Gil reached out and fumbled for Anlyn's hands. She squeezed him back.

"Is there anything I can do?" Anlyn asked. "Anything I can say?"

Gil shook his head. "I wish you were bigger so we could swap places. No one would know with our Wadi suits covering us from head to toe."

Anlyn felt a sudden sadness for her cousin as she realized just how terrified he must be to utter such craziness. She rubbed his arm. "And I would do it,

Cousin, but the escorts would know. And anyway, I've heard rumors that they use tracking devices to make sure nothing bad happens to us. But I promise, if there was a way . . ."

Her voice trailed off, and the two of them sat together on the bed, their brains consumed with shame and pity.

"I should go try to get some sleep," Gil said. "Thanks for talking."

"You're welcome," Anlyn said, but she felt like a fool as soon as she uttered the words. She couldn't remember saying anything that might've made him feel better. She only began to conjure up decent reassurances as Gil slid out of the room, his large silhouette hunched over and sad as it turned out of sight.

18

???

Anlyn woke when it became hard to breathe. It was her body's way of jostling her into consciousness, telling her to *do* something. It was a warning that the air in her suit had grown too thin.

As she came to, she had a moment's doubt about where she was. She had been dreaming of her Wadi Rite, and now she found herself floating in space. All around her were bright stars and pyrotechnics—the flash and silent explosions of a major war.

A circulating fan whirred near her ear, moving air around her helmet, but her lungs told her that precious little oxygen remained inside. Her breathing had become wheezing—each laborious inhalation a vaporous disappointment. Her suit was kind enough to filter out her toxic exhalations, but it couldn't create oxygen from nothing. Gradually, a vacuum was forming within her suit to match the one embroiled with fighting beyond.

As she spun around in her ejected pilot seat, Anlyn got a sweeping view of the action taking place around her. She could see bolts of plasma the size of Drenardian skyscrapers coursing through the cosmos. They traveled near the speed of light, but the distances they crossed meant their path could be followed, actually *watched*. Anlyn tracked them with surreal detachment. One of the bolts hit the bright orb of a nearby planet. The cylinder of energy punched through an atmosphere choking with smoke. It struck land, already little more than magma, and a red crack appeared in the crust. Chunks of the planet's continents exploded away with enough force to drive them into orbit. Some of these jetted through space, glowing and trailing coronas of fire. Others fell back to the surface, throwing up destructive echoes of the initial blow.

Amid this chaos, two fleets swarmed, intertwined. The crafts seemed impossibly fast and agile, but they *all* were, and so a continuous stream of them winked out in puffs of spectacular coordination and aim.

Dozens of orbital stations seemed to be the targets of these buzzing attack fleets. Swarms of missiles agitated around each one, brought down by equal swarms of countermeasures. Another column of hellish plasma erupted from a nearby station and began its lightning-quick stampede toward another planet in the distance.

Anlyn sucked in fruitless gasps while she lost herself in the swirling battle. Her head had already begun to throb with dizziness. When she spun around in the direction of her ship, she marveled at the cloud of debris it had become. Flashes of light caught on the tinsel and confetti of the craft's remains. All that was left of any substance was half of one wing, blown off before the second missile struck. There was that, plus Anlyn and her ejected flight seat.

She labored for another breath. Her chest swelled with effort, pushing on the harness restraints pinning her to the seat. Since the flight seat no longer served any purpose, Anlyn unbuckled herself and floated away from it. She tried, once again, to wick some oxygen from what little air swirled inside her helmet. As her gasps quickened into frantic, shallow pants, Anlyn felt her mind slipping away. She had a sudden impulse to pull off her helmet, a hallucinatory feeling that it was the thing constricting her breathing, keeping her from taking in the air that surely must be all around her. She felt as if she were underwater. Drowning. She needed to come up. Needed to kick and swim and break the surface of her awful torment.

Anlyn fumbled for the latches on the sides of her helmet. She fumbled for them, even as some receding and sane part of her screamed not to do it. She groped along her collar with her too-big flight gloves, the unwieldy padding making it difficult to do anything. Her lungs burned as they starved for air.

And then the hallucinations grew worse. Something like a ship, but silver and gleaming and fluid, danced in her vision. It hovered in front of her, windows like giant eyes, like a metallic and curious face watching her die. Anlyn screamed. She beat her hands on her helmet, her palms smacking her visor. She was frustrated she couldn't open it, couldn't pop it off to take in a deep breath. She pawed at her gloves, trying to tear them off, but her fingers had already grown tingly. Her entire body was becoming numb. She shook her arms, and a spasm vibrated through her chest. With a throat deadly empty, she took one last feeble pull on the thinning air. The great metal face sat there, watching.

Watching as the black fell over her eyes once more.

•• DRENARD ••

"Girls to the right."

The voice filled Anlyn's head, relayed through the D-bands worn by each of her Rite mates. Anlyn and Coril exchanged looks but obeyed. The three boys jockeyed for position to their left, lining up to receive their great Wadi lances. Gil flashed a quick, sad glance Anlyn's way and continued his half-hearted charade of excitement as he shuffled closer to the other boys.

"Settle down, you three."

One of Anlyn's uncles—a former member of the Circle—joined the other Rite leaders by the lobby's window. Anlyn assumed it was he who had spoken the last, though it was improper for her to guess. During the Rite, all were supposed to be equal, the questions and answers made diffuse by the power of the bands.

"Come forward to take your maps."

The boys scurried toward the Rite leaders as the Drenard adults reached for a table that had been draped in layer upon layer of blue honeycloth. They each picked up one of the fabric maps laid out on top and turned to present them to the boys.

Anlyn and Coril approached a smaller table to the side where their Aunt Ralei stood. Anlyn accepted her map blindly; she was distracted by the flurry of excitement around the boys' table as they took their own maps. Gil turned and met her gaze, and a shiver of fear leaked into her band. Her poor cousin was doing an awful job of concealing his inner thoughts.

Something pinched Anlyn's hand, drawing her attention away from the lads. She turned to find her Aunt Ralei giving her a severe look. Her aunt's eyes darted down to the map she was pressing into Anlyn's hands.

Anlyn looked. The map had been folded over several times, leaving one section exposed. It showed an intricate tangle of Wadi canyons.

Her aunt's finger moved from Anlyn's hand and slowly traced one of the canyons. Anlyn felt Coril leaning against her arm to see, and her Aunt Ralei twisted the map to better facilitate this, showing both girls some specific route through the labyrinth. Anlyn wasn't sure what she was supposed to be looking at; the bands were silent, no thoughts leaking through them save for a twinge of Gil's fear.

She watched her aunt's finger tap one spot in particular, and then the same finger slid to the edge of the map and up the back of her Aunt Ralei's arm, pulling her cloak back to expose a pale-blue wrist.

It was there that Anlyn saw what her aunt was speaking of. Trailing out of the woman's sleeve were three parallel scars, the knotted flesh heaped high and sinister, looking like white ropes laid into her skin.

Anlyn gasped at the sight of them; she felt her deep thoughts leak out as she looked up to her aunt's face. But gone was the scowl her aunt had been giving her earlier. It had been replaced with a grim smile. Her aunt now bore a look of happy, hopeful, and raw determinism.

•• ??? ••

When Anlyn passed out the second time, gasping for air, she had felt certain it was her last moment of life. Her final thoughts had been like a sliver of shimmering oxygen, piercing the black suffocation coiling itself around her. She had thought how nice it would be for the end to come, to find an escape from the slow torment. And if there was something beyond—a peaceful afterlife for those with sound souls—she thought, right at the last, that she was about to discover it.

She came to once again to find her journey had been delayed.

Her helmet was off. She could feel something pressed over her mouth and nose and the pinch of tight straps wrapped around the back of her head. Above her, the silvery curve of a ship's hull arched up, its surface spotted with portholes of varying sizes. Through these, Anlyn could see the bright bolts and explosions of a battle still raging beyond.

Someone leaned over Anlyn. She blinked and tried to sit up, but a gentle hand kept her in place. Large, wet eyes blinked slowly, her own reflection clearly visible in the black dome of them. When the head pulled away, Anlyn recognized the race immediately, even though she'd only ever seen them in books. It was a Bel-Tra, the mysterious surveyors of the universe.

Anlyn tried to say something, but she managed only a groan. Her head felt as if it had been split in two. Now that she was out of her flight seat's harness and back in gravity, she could feel how traumatized her body had been by the explosion that destroyed her ship. She felt bruised all over and completely empty of air.

The Bel-Tra brushed Anlyn's forehead with the back of its hand and then reached to its side. Anlyn turned her head to follow and saw that she was lying on the spaceship's decking. Clear tubes led away from a mask over her face and trailed to a small canister by the Bel-Tra's side. The figure freed a device—one of many hanging from its belt—and slipped it over its wrist. It looked like a flat rectangle of some sort, like an LCD display. When the Tra turned it around for Anlyn to see, words were already marching across the screen:

I DID NOT DO THIS.

"I know," Anlyn whispered. She saw, down in the lower part of her vision, that her spoken words did no more than frost the inner coat of her mask. She reached up and pulled it to the side, then let her hand drop to her chest.

"I know," she said again. She closed her eyes and tried to summon back her voice. "Thank you."

She couldn't tell if the Bel-Tra could hear her, didn't know if it even understood Drenard. She opened her eyes to see more words flitting across the screen:

I MEANT TO SAY: I DID NOT RESCUE YOU.

Anlyn read the words several times, but they made little sense. They disappeared before she was ready for them to.

WE ARE ONLY SUPPOSED TO WATCH.

These new words came fast. They seemed to pulse with extra light, giving them an urgency of some sort. Anlyn realized the device was something like her people's bands, but different. She lifted her arm and reached for the Tra. "I won't tell anyone," Anlyn said, finally understanding.

The Bel-Tra clasped Anlyn's hand. The slim creature's large eyes blinked, pale lids snapping down over Anlyn's reflection. When they reopened, Anlyn saw thick tears welling up at the base of them. They ran out over the lower lids and dashed down the Tra's long and narrow face, past a small mouth, pursed with thin lips. The alien squeezed her hand and then pulled the device up in front of her, blocking her view of it crying. New words slowly worked their way across the screen, the light behind them dim, each one coming hesitantly, as if wary of being seen:

I AM SORRY.

Before Anlyn could ask what the Tra meant, or even begin to puzzle it out herself, the alien took hold of her mask and put it back in place. Anlyn tried to shrug it away, no longer needing it, but it was pressed down too tight for her to resist.

She caught a whiff of the gas that had replaced the flow of oxygen, and the apology began to make sense. As the darkness gathered, squeezing down around Anlyn's vision, the last thing she saw was the face of the Tra, tears dripping off its chin, and the bloom of her own complaints frosting the mask in the tightening edges of her consciousness.

19

DRENARD

The winds howling out of the Wadi canyons were deafening. Anlyn and Coril had begun their march by angling away from the Rite shelter, and once they were out of the building's lee, the flap of their Wadi suits in the stiff breeze had begun to erode their hearing. They soon pulled back their thin and shimmery hoods, tucking them into their collars to keep the fabric quiet. Walking side by side, they let the gusts push at their backs, driving them toward the deepening canyons while they discussed the looming Rite.

"I'm pretty sure Aunt Ralei meant for us *not* to go there," Anlyn complained, still trying to convince her cousin that revealing the scars had been a warning of sorts.

"You can go wherever you like," Coril shouted. "*I'm* going to catch the Wadi that scratched her."

Anlyn turned and looked back over her shoulder. Even squinting into the wind, she could feel it desiccating her eyes. Off in the distance and laboring to catch up to them, Gil's bulky form stood out on the horizon. The poor kid had followed along after the other two boys for a thousand paces before finally breaking off in the girls' direction. Anlyn felt a hollow tugging in her chest. All she *should've* been thinking about was the completion of her *own* Rite and getting back to her studies, and now she found herself dealing with a frightened relative on the one side and a zealous and overeager one on the other. It was like the hot and cold sides of Drenard hemming her in.

"If you're gonna insist on hunting Wadi, you might want to wait for Gil. He's at least got a proper lance."

Coril looked back at their larger cousin, still quite a distance behind them. She didn't slow her pace. "He'll catch us before we get to the dayline." She looked down at the egg graspers and sunshields the two of them had been given. "You make a good point, though."

Sure enough, Gil caught up to them a dozen or so paces from the dayline. He arrived huffing, his eyes wide.

"Thanks for waiting up!" he said, his sarcasm nearly lost between his pants for air.

"Aren't you supposed to be doing your Rite alone?" Coril asked with a mocking tone.

Gil looked back and forth between his female cousins. "Well, why do *you* two get to hunt together?"

Anlyn shrugged. "That's the rules, Gil."

"Well, I don't *like* the rules. Besides, what're they gonna do to me if I come back with an egg? Tell me I'm not a Drenard? So what?"

Coril shook her head and turned away from the two of them, seemingly disgusted by her cousin's attitude. She walked toward a near section of the dayline that stretched across the wide and deepening canyon. Anlyn patted Gil on the back and hurried to catch up.

As she joined Coril, Anlyn saw her cousin had her map out and folded in thirds to keep the ends from flapping. Ahead of them, the canyon split off in two, a sharp wedge of a cliff rising up in the center and bisecting the dayline. Coril stopped and surveyed the tall feature. She looked back down at her map and then rotated it to match the direction she was looking.

"I think we're at the edge of the egg canyon," Anlyn told Coril. She pointed off to one side where a shadowpath hugged the base of a cliff, the first smattering of Wadi holes visible along its smooth face.

"You can go down there if you like," Coril said. She looked up and pointed around the other side of the narrow wedge. "But that's where Aunt Ralei was telling us to go."

"I still think she was warning us to *not* go there," Anlyn shouted above a ferocious gust of wind.

Gil lumbered up beside them, still short of breath from the long and hurried hike. "Who warned you of what?" he asked.

"You should go with Anlyn," Coril said. She folded her map and tucked it into her supply belt, right behind her thermos. Reaching up to her shoulder, she unstrapped her sunshield and brought it around in front of her. Her egg graspers were attached to the back of it. She pulled the device out of its clips and held it out toward Gil.

"Take this."

Gil looked at the graspers, which were just a long set of telescoping rods with a trigger on one end and a padded set of clamps on the other. He reached out and accepted the graspers and then glanced at his Wadi lance. Coril held her hands out for it.

"I'll need it back," Gil said, so quietly they could barely hear him over the wind and the howling of the canyons.

"I'll even clean the blood off it for you," Coril said snidely. She took the large weapon from him and pulled it toward her. Anlyn couldn't help but notice how it dipped down and nearly touched the canyon floor, the heft of the thing taking Coril by surprise.

"What about the sunshield?" Gil asked.

Coril looked to the path leading off toward the egg canyon. "Do you really think you'll need it?"

Gil peeked down the canyon as well. He shrugged. "Maybe."

Coril sighed. "All right then." She handed over the shield.

The three of them stood still for a moment, and Anlyn's mind raced as she tried to sort out what was about to take place. This was *not* how she had imagined her Rite going. Gil turned away from Coril's glare, pulling on Anlyn as he went.

"Hold on a second," Anlyn told him.

"C'mon," said Gil, urging her toward the egg canyon.

Anlyn pulled her sunshield off her back and rested its edge on the ground. The top came up to her waist, and the thing was only two hands wide with its panels retracted. She kept one hand on it and reached around to unclip her thermos.

"Take this," she told Coril, holding out her full vessel of water.

Coril glanced down at it, and then back up to Anlyn. "Are you really not coming with me?" She didn't move to accept the thermos.

Anlyn felt her shoulders sag as her cousin's disappointment swirled around her on an eddy of wind.

"Who do you think you're gonna impress?" Anlyn asked. "Do you really think this will change anything? Do you think a single door will crack for you if you do this? Because it won't. What few paths you do have will just slam shut."

Coril frowned. Gil tried once more to tug Anlyn away.

"I don't give a flying Wadi about *any* of that," Coril finally said. She stepped closer to Anlyn and pushed away the thermos. "I don't care how they measure me by this. I really don't. I simply mean to measure *myself*."

She clasped Anlyn's arm. Her face flashed a glimpse of seriousness before her famous smile came back to wash it away. "Good luck on your Rite, Cousin," she said.

With that, Coril lifted the heavy lance in both hands and trotted away, aiming for the shadowpath on the other side of the tall wedge.

Anlyn watched her go, fearing it would be the last time she ever saw her dear cousin alive.

"C'mon," Gil said. He pulled Anlyn toward the egg canyon. "Don't worry about her," he shouted into the wind. "Nothing bad ever happens to Princess Coril!"

Anlyn reluctantly turned away. She followed after Gil as her large cousin strode toward the dayline and the wide path of shade snaking along the base of the canyon wall. She unclipped her egg graspers from her sunshield and tried to remember where she was—what she was supposed to be doing. Looking back, she saw Coril had already rounded the wedge of rock, disappearing up the canyon her aunt had shown them. She felt a powerful urge to run after her, to either bring her back or to join her, but not knowing which was the right action somehow paralyzed Anlyn into doing neither.

So instead, she simply followed Gil down the dark path ahead, past that line in the rock where eternal day abutted an endless night.

20

???

The pitch black of Anlyn's unconsciousness was shattered by a brilliant flash of light. She awoke to find herself lying flat on her back, the same tumultuous war from earlier roiling above as darting ships and blooming explosions popped in the distance. Nearby, the gleaming and curvy ship that had rescued her from the vacuum of space began to rise, pulling away from some sort of a landing pad that Anlyn had been left to one side of. The Bel-Tra's ship lifted in complete and eerie silence, and noticeably without the flare of chemicals belching from any sort of thruster. It just floated higher and higher, departing as mysteriously as it had appeared.

The stomping of heavy boots thundered all around Anlyn, chasing away the quietude. Figures appeared in her peripheral. A group of men—humans!—garbed in dark suits formed up around her. One of them shouldered a large weapon of some sort; he raised it toward the departing ship, and Anlyn heard something click.

There was a swoosh and a spit of fire before a lozenge of metal popped out of the weapon. The projectile paused, seeming to struggle against gravity, and then took off in a flash, spiraling up after the Bel-Tra's ship. Beyond the craft, Anlyn could just barely make out the shimmering curve of a dome of some sort, whatever material was holding in the atmosphere around the landing pad. Even in her dazed and confused state, she felt a pang of fear for the Tra as the craft seemed to be pinned between a hard barrier on the one side and a dangerous projectile on the other.

And then, with what was either a miraculous display or a desperate and suicidal leap, the Tra's ship disappeared. It winked out with all the suddenness of a hyperspace jump, despite the threat of matter and gravity all around.

One of the men above Anlyn shouted something—something in a tongue that was alien and yet familiar. The rocket continued to chase after the missing ship, finally slamming into the dome and erupting in a ball of orange hellfire.

"Gotammeet," one of the men said, as phonetically as Anlyn could place it. As the fire drained away and the smoke cleared, she could see the dome itself hadn't been scratched. The men in the strange cloaks—with clinging bottoms fitted to each leg and tops that met in vertical seams left open—turned from the dissipating fire and looked down at her.

Their reactions were sharp and immediate. All four men jumped back, eyes wide. What were obviously weapons became trained on her, and the men began shouting back and forth. Anlyn couldn't tell if it was *she* they were shouting at, or each other.

She tried her best to sit up, but her stomach felt like one giant bruise. She raised her hand. "Sheesti Looo," she said in Drenard, knowing it would be ineffectual.

One of the figures pushed the others back. He fiddled with something on his belt, and suddenly the fabric of his suit began to shimmer like a tunic made of honeycloth. He came forward with his arm out, his palm reaching for Anlyn's outstretched and much smaller hand.

"Sheesti Looo," she said again, this time with more relief than fear as the weapons were returned to the folds of the strange and open cloaks. She sat up further and pressed her hand into the human's—

Something electric jolted through her body with the contact. A burning fire shivered up her arm, into her chest, and down through her thighs. It filled her with a trembling power, a surge of agony higher and harder than any pain she'd ever known. Her body became paralyzed, and her muscles seized up.

It wasn't until the jolt rattled her brain, knocking Anlyn unconscious once again, that she found some sort of escape from the pain.

●● DRENARD ●●

"I can't feel anything."

"That's because there's nothing there."

"Let me try one more."

Anlyn blew out her breath, but the gesture was lost among the stiff wind and the shrill howl of the Wadi canyon. She watched as Gil removed his egg graspers from the small hole and inserted them into one farther down.

"Gil, I'm telling you, no Wadi in its right mind would lay its eggs in there."

Gil reached in as far as his thick, boyish arms would allow and fiddled with the trigger. It was obvious he'd never practiced with a set of graspers.

"How do *you* know where they'd lay them?" he asked.

Anlyn leaned away from the canyon wall and looked back to the dayline. It was still visible in the distance. "Because it's too close to the nighttime," she said. "This would all be in the shade during the slightest of cycles."

Gil ran his tongue across his lower lip, concentrating. After a pause, he pulled the graspers out and shook his head. "Okay," he said. "*You're* in charge."

Anlyn pulled out her map. "Our best bet is to go to the end of this canyon. It terminates in a pocket several thousand paces from here, and that's where the females would most likely go to lay their eggs. There's plenty of shade on this side."

Gil moved to her side and peered at her map. Anlyn pointed to the spot where their canyon dead-ended.

"See? The rock on the other side gets a full blast of heat from both Horis, which means plenty of condensation inside for the eggs. There's probably a lot of convection currents and watering holes in there."

Gil scratched his neck and wiped his hands off on his shimmering Wadi suit.

"All right," he said. "Lead the way."

o o o o

They walked in silence. Anlyn left her graspers clipped to her sunshield and strolled along by the edge of the shade, marveling at how hot the air blowing through the canyons felt. The high-pitched wails on all sides seemed to resonate with the deeper groans echoing from farther ahead—the sounds of larger Wadi holes.

The noise gave her chills, even as she reminded herself that male Wadi would be rare in an egg-laying canyon; supposedly, the smells and pheromones were enough to keep them at bay. Anlyn tried to picture all those scents traveling up and down the dayside on the heavy winds. She wondered what the world must look like to a Wadi. It must be so different from how she saw it, mostly through sights and sounds. She wondered if the Wadi ever pondered in kind just how the world appeared to these silly Drenards stumbling through their canyons in their silvery suits.

As she walked along and pondered these things, Gil lagged a dozen paces behind, despite his longer legs. Her cousin seemed wary of their journey into the deepening canyon, preferring to hang back and stick close to the canyon side of the shadowpath. Anlyn glanced back periodically to make sure he was still with her. They'd walked a few thousand paces already, and Anlyn had consumed roughly half her water. Then again, if she read the last bend in the canyon correctly, the map showed them almost to the dead-end. Once they rounded the next curve, they should be able to see it.

The next curve, unfortunately, proved to be one they couldn't just walk around. On the other side of the bend, the canyon wall arched back the other way, putting its face in the full sunlight of the two Horis. There was a shade bridge crossing to the other side, so Anlyn waited for Gil, testing her sunshield while he caught up.

"You didn't say we'd have to cross a bridge!" Gil said.

Anlyn turned to see him resting by the wall, one hand clinging to a hole in the rock. He still had his graspers out, his fingers working the trigger over and over without seeming to realize he was doing it.

"I think we're almost there," Anlyn told him. She looked to the bridge. "Besides, it's a wide one. Just stay low and keep your shield ready." She turned back to see him probing a Wadi hole with his graspers.

"Gil, seriously, we need to keep moving."

"Fine," he said.

Anlyn shook her head. She wished—and not for the first time—that she'd gone with Coril. She held her shield out and pushed the deploy switch a quarter of the way down its glideline. The top and sides of the shield immediately grew, the overlapped panels sliding away from one another. She adjusted the switch until the shield was wide enough to cover her in a crouch but not too big to catch excess wind. Once she was satisfied, she stooped down and crept out onto the bridge.

They were called bridges, but of course she walked across bare rock hardly different than the last thousand paces of stone. The actual bridge was a metal column embedded in the canyon walls much farther ahead. That column spanned the canyon horizontally, positioned in just the right way to throw a shadow back to the exact spot a path was needed. On the other side of the canyon from Anlyn, the bright sunlit wall ended, and another shadowpath began right at the bend in the rock. Anlyn knew that in most cases, the shade bridges were situated at turns in the canyons just like this one. The shift in angle brought an end to the shadow on one side of the valley just as it began creating a new one on the other. The bridge simply allowed them to move across the boiling hot wasteland in between.

Once out on the beginnings of the bridge, Anlyn waited for the wind to pick up a little more. It was dangerous to cross during the lulls, for the lulls never lasted for long. All they would do was make her complacent, causing Anlyn to relax her muscles before the gusts came. She waited until the howls sounded about average and then shuffled out, keeping the sun-shield sideways to the wind ahead of her.

Anlyn had practiced with the shields on windy rooftops where the force was steady, but had never operated one in such unpredictable gusts. She had very little warning before a stiff blast of wind hit her. There was a slight increase in pitch from the shrill calls upwind—just enough to make her adjust the angle of the sunshield—and then the mighty breeze wrapped itself around her. Anlyn fell to one knee and placed a hand out on the rock; she angled the shield to provide suction, just like an atmospheric fly-er's wing, and used the flow to pin herself in place. Behind her, she heard Gil curse. She glanced over her shoulder to see that he had already started out on the bridge with her.

One at a time! Anlyn yelled in her head. But of course, without their D-bands, he couldn't hear her.

The distraction of him crowding the bridge caused her to lose focus for a second, and she felt the stiff-ening breeze claw at the edge of her shield. Anlyn got it back under control as the wind passed, the breeze dropping down into a dangerous lull. Before she could steady herself, preparing for the next gust, Gil thundered by. He ran, fully upright on his long and powerful legs, knocking Anlyn out toward the sunside.

She fell, off-balance. She nearly threw her hand out onto the sunrock to stop her fall, but some innate sense of self-preservation caused her to swing her sunshield out and dig its edge into the floor of the steaming rock. Her hands and arms went into the full fury of the Horis, but the suit easily reflected their sunshine. It was the rock in the always-heat that could hurt her.

Pushing off with the shield, Anlyn threw herself back into the shade of the bridge. She heard a cry from the canyons, heralding the arrival of more wind. Her legs, already shaking from the near-fall, kicked off, responding in fear just as Gil had. She retracted her shield and ran. She ran like a fool Wadi being chased by a pack of males.

21

DARRIN

The first weeks of Anlyn's captivity in the Darrin system were the worst in some ways but the best in others. Best, of course, being a relative term. The bad parts came from the confusion. Anlyn was kept in a cell by herself, the other cages around her packed with as many as a dozen aliens, mostly humans. She was treated as a curiosity by a few and as a scourge by most. Even the younger humans spat at her between the bars, using words Anlyn could figure for cussing just by the energy and invective put behind them.

Lots of adult males came and paid visits; they were always careful to shimmer their suits before they stepped in the cell with her. Anlyn learned quickly not to put up a fight. If she thought there was a chance of hurting her captors—or possibly ending her own life with the effort—she would have. But any sort of kinetic blow just shocked her with more of the electricity, jolting her like a blast from a Drenardian guardlance. And so she allowed the humans to inspect her, prodding her in the most humiliating fashion in front of the sneering, spitting spectators.

When her captors weren't around, Anlyn spent her time huddled, her knees to her neck and her back to the lone solid wall. They had taken her flight suit and left her with the short undertunic she'd put on so long ago, back when her father was still alive and only one person ever touched her against her will. She sat like that, enduring the odd cycle of artificial light and dark, as she watched the humans and the others come and go from their cells, their energy to yell at her and spit at her seeming to fade with time.

It wasn't until much later—many, many sleep cycles later—that Anlyn would see anything good about those first weeks. It took her that long to understand the confusion as a blessing, to appreciate how wonderful it could be to not know what was going on around her.

After at least two dozen sleeps, the men in the dark tunics with the thread-thin stripes began pulling her from her cell, just as they did the others. They first led off a group made up mostly of humans. They paused before bringing Anlyn out and marching her off in the same direction. The sight of her along a new stretch of prisoners elicited fresh howls and new volleys of saliva. The humans banged their palms against the bars, a sound that wouldn't have been too loud if there had only been a few of them doing it. So much anger directed at her made Anlyn cower deep inside her own skin. But then, some other part of her wished she could speak their language. She wanted to yell at them, to let them know that they were only alive because of *her* people. She felt an urge to spread the seeds of doubt among them, to detail the treacherous nature of the Bern and explain that they were likely infested with them.

Had she known English at the time, she probably would've yelled all of that and more. And of course, she would've been ignored as their enemy and as a raving lunatic.

Outside the hallway of cells, her captors led her through several gates and down a long corridor. They finally passed through a door at the end and into a wide room humming with electricity. Anlyn could feel heat from the machines hanging in the air—the stuffiness that came from cabinets of computing power inadequately ventilated. Along the far wall, the other prisoners were already being situated, made to lie flat on their stomachs on padded beds. A dozen men in the dark, tight-fitting tunics cinched straps across their backs and clipped wires here and there. White helmets studded with more tangles of multi-colored wire were strapped down on the prisoners' heads. Some of the humans tried to twist away; they shook their heads in an effort to resist the procedure. Others seemed to prefer *not* to get the small jolts from the shock-devices that came from putting up a fight.

As Anlyn was pulled toward one of the padded tables, she felt a compulsion to disobey, to kick out at her escorts, to put up enough of a struggle that they'd be forced to kill her—but her body was too fatigued to do her bidding. Or perhaps it disagreed with her mind's wish to have their combined life snuffed out. Before she could summon her courage, she felt herself being lifted up and shoved flat on the padded table. She turned her head to the side as they strapped her painfully in place.

A man in a white tunic—a proper one with a flowing bottom—rushed over. He seemed to be arguing with the ones in the dark, open-front tunics. There was a lot of shouting and then the pinch of straps across her back and the bite of more straps into her legs. The man in the white tunic was shoved away. More yelling followed. Painful pricks bit Anlyn's skin as wires were clipped, unclipped, and reclipped. Several people seemed to want to be in charge at the same time and disagreed on where things went.

The helmet came on last. They held her head in place, being rough with her as they strapped it beneath her chin. Anlyn shouted her own string of curse words, unleashing a fury built up over so many imprisoned sleeps that the time seemed to stretch back into forever.

She cursed at them and was still cursing at them when her first nightmare began.

o o o o

It was a chasing dream. As it would turn out, they would always be chasing dreams. It took Anlyn so very many of them before she figured out what was going on, how they were using her. At first, she thought it was just for torture. She thought every bad piece of propaganda she'd ever heard about humans was correct, that they were tormenting her for the mere sport of it. It wasn't until much later that she learned the truth and realized the propaganda had been tame in comparison.

The machine tapped straight into her fears. It placed her in immediate danger, turning her loose in a dream world and leaving her to survive on pure adrenaline. Her brain was made to feel the worst sort of panic, its entire computational powers melding with her most primal fears. And so Anlyn found herself in a Wadi canyon, chased by a horde of scratching, clawing, hissing males. The nightmare was so powerful, so *real*, that Anlyn could feel with complete surety that she would die if they caught her.

And so she ran.

She ran faster in the dream world than she could in real life. Her brain was alive with terror and made powerful by a surge of hormones. As the Wadi came after her—a handful, a dozen, hundreds—Anlyn twisted and turned, dashing along the shaded paths branching out in a knotted web before her.

She looked left and right as she sprinted along, trying to make sure she saw them all. Wadi were everywhere: darting and leaping, pawing the air where she had been just moments before.

Anlyn became consumed with the awareness of them. Her autonomic fear response—her overwhelming urge to live—told her where to cut and dive and dodge to avoid them. The scenario set up by the nightmare felt impossible to survive, but it became ever *less* so the longer she ran. Eventually, the hundreds of Wadi dwindled to dozens, then down to a handful of the biggest and sleekest ones. Several times, these ultra Wadi grazed her, nicking her leg as she spun out of the way a blink too slow, gashing her arm as she swung it out for balance or to fend off another attacker. Each time, the pain was real—she could feel Wadi toxins spreading through her nerves with painful electricity. Anlyn dug deep, summoning every drop of will she had to outrace the rabid animals. She pounded her feet, choosing one turn in the shady paths after another, running toward a hole she somehow knew was just ahead, a hole only she would be able to go through.

When it came into sight—this magical place where she would be safe—there was only one Wadi left behind her. Anlyn felt a powerful urge to forget the beast and run straight for the hole, but a smarter part of her knew it would mean her death. If she were to forget the danger for even a moment, if she were to make the mistake of dreaming too fondly for an end to the nightmare, her foolish hopes would surely just worsen the torture. She knew without knowing *how* she knew that a twisting path would be shorter in the end.

With renewed vigor, she darted to and fro, cutting a mad and winding course across the flat rock. The last Wadi skidded behind her, slipping now and then, cutting across the sunrock when it had to, its scales gleaming in the fury of her nightmare Horis.

Anlyn lunged left and right several more times, her thighs so heavy and sore that they threatened to collapse with each powerful juke. She forced her feet to grip the stone, forced her arms to pump along with her legs, took one more spin, faked to the side, and then dove, headfirst, through the hole of her imagined and longed-for safety . . .

o o o o

When the helmet came off, there were even more men around her than before, more in the dark suits and especially more in the white tunics. They were yelling even louder, but no longer at one another. They seemed to be cheering. The wires came off her skin with sharp stings. The straps were pulled away, and Anlyn was forced up. She could see that the room was empty of other prisoners; all the padded beds were vacant, which left her with the impression that she'd been in the nightmare for much longer than it had felt. Then again, in other ways, it felt as if she'd been in that horrible place for several sleeps.

The humans were obviously happy with their experiment. A large group of them continued to speak loudly with one another as her escorts led her back to her cell. Along the way, there was more spitting and yelling. This was followed by more hours of sitting alone, hugging her shins, and then another sleep during the confusing cycle of light to dark. The only change was in the quality of her water and the amount of food she was given later that night. Neither, however, was enough to overcome the residual shaking the nightmare had left in her bones.

The next day, they did it to her again. It was another Wadi nightmare, similar to the last one. The fear and pain did not lessen, but Anlyn at least knew what was expected of her. She made it to the hole once again, cut up and bleeding by the time she got there. The dream wounds felt so real that her flesh was tender as they dragged her back to her cell. She half expected to find actual scars or dried blood on her somewhere. She slept with real aches and with the perpetual fear of the nightmares finding their way into her cell.

And so it went: Wadi dreams for a dozen sleeps. Anlyn became exhausted by the ordeal, which at least meant she was able to pass out for the entirety of her imprisoned nights. During a subsequent march down the cell-lined corridor, one of her escorts lashed out at a spitter, which was different. Anlyn hardly cared. She liked it better when they left her alone in her cell.

During the next nightmare, she learned something new: the Wadi could be turned on one another. Not purpose-minded, but on accident. She could taunt them along on colliding vectors, sending the imagined animals into one another, which made them vanish even quicker than outrunning them. At the beginning of the dream—when there were lots of them giving chase—this tactic worked well to thin the herd. It was after a few days of experimenting with this that she reached the hole for the first time without getting touched, with nary a nick. The humans were oddly silent after that dream. A group of them huddled together, their heads bent close, as she was led out. It was also one of the few times that other prisoners were still strapped to their beds when she awoke. She saw them twitching with shocks of pain as the guards marched her out of the room. She tried to feel some twinge of joy at seeing the spitters get their own, but she couldn't quite manage it.

And even though Anlyn hadn't gotten nicked in that last dream, she was already losing her sense of feel. She could hurt while not being touched and feel numb as she was struck. It left her in a confused, permanently anxious state. Her environmental cues did not match her feelings.

After that first untouched nightmare, the humans gave her a sleep cycle off. The following day, they took her to a different room, one with more of the white tunic men and fewer of the black-suited ones.

That was her first day of learning English, one word at a time. They used pictures and repetition. They showed her words made of letters, the shapes of which she recognized as human, just as she knew the florid script of the Bern. Her meals were served as she followed along, the two feedings framing the extremely long sessions. Even though her mind was numb from her conditions, Anlyn fought to absorb the lessons, knowing that communication was the way out. If she could explain who she was, perhaps appeal to their leaders, she might be able to return home.

And so she learned. And the next day they forced her to suffer a nightmare. And the next day she learned some more.

And so it went for many sleeps.

And what they were teaching her was war.

22

DRENARD

Anlyn was glad she and Gil had only one shade bridge to cross, for his moment of panic had nearly gotten them both hurt—or far worse. She was already furious, her hot side dominating, as she dove into the shadowpath ahead of the next strong gust of wind. Before she could vent her anger, however, Gil fell to his knees before her, panting.

"I'm so sorry," he said, over and over.

"It's okay," Anlyn said, though she didn't mean it.

"I just got scared." Gil wiped at his face, a sheen of sweat mixing with his tears.

"We have to be more careful," was all Anlyn could say.

He helped her up, and they walked together the last few hundred paces, a tense silence settling between them. Their quiet left just the canyon moans and the whipping winds and the flapping of loose bits of their Wadi suits to pace their march.

Anlyn let Gil walk ahead of her, perhaps to keep an eye on him, perhaps because her excitement for the Rite had abated. She took another swig from her thermos, careful to not drip any, and looked through the Wadi holes to her side.

The animals' tunnels had grown in size over the last few thousand paces, moving from something a single fist could get caught in to holes almost large enough for a young child to squeeze through. The wall was also quite thin, being a part of the narrow wedge that had divided the canyon in two. Some of the tunnels went straight through to the other side and were lit up almost all the way across. Anlyn knew that these were getting to be a better size for grasping eggs, but the canyon's pocketed dead-end was visible just ahead, which should offer them a bounty and save them time in hunting.

"This is gonna be embarrassing," Gil yelled over his shoulder. He held the egg graspers to his side, the pinchers clicking together nervously.

"You're just now realizing that?" Anlyn asked.

Gil shook his head slowly. He stopped and waited for Anlyn to catch up. "Well, maybe I am," he said. "All the other boys are gonna have stories to tell."

"We'll make up something heroic for you," Anlyn told her cousin. "C'mon, let's go get our eggs."

"*Anlyn?*"

The voice came through a Wadi hole, high and tight, nearly lost among the cries of the wind passing across the face of the cliff. At first, Anlyn thought she'd imagined it.

"Anlyn!"

There it was again. Anlyn stopped and leaned close to one of the holes beside her.

"Hello?" she called into it. "Coril? Is that you?"

"Hey!" Her cousin's voice came through with an echo and a crispness borrowed from the cool stone. "I'm on the other side of the wall!"

Anlyn ran back to the hole her cousin's voice seemed to emanate from the loudest. "How are you?" she yelled. "Have you got your Wadi yet?"

"Go back another hole," Coril shouted. "I saw you guys go past a second ago."

Anlyn looked ahead to see that Gil had already begun rummaging in one of the holes with his graspers. She moved back down the cliff face, peeking through caves high and low and looking for one straight enough to see all the way through.

"Go back," Coril yelled.

Anlyn moved the other way and bent down. There, across from her and through a half dozen paces of stone, was Coril.

"Hey, Cousin!"

"Hey," Anlyn said. "So where's your Wadi Thooo?"

"I had one," Coril said, "but he got away. There's a ton of watering holes in a pocket canyon over here. You really should've come with me. We'd both have one by now."

"Probably right," Anlyn said. "Well, I'm already half done with my water, so I'd better find an egg."

"Okay. Keep an eye out, though. The one I wounded went into this system somewhere. I heard him fighting with some females, so he's probably pissed."

Anlyn looked away from her cousin's dim face to see if Gil had heard; she'd rather not have to deal with him if there was a male Wadi loose. She turned back to whisper through the tube to her cousin, only to see something dark descend across the hole. Anlyn leaned close, thinking Coril had pressed her face to the other side, when her cousin screamed. She let out a blood-boiling wail of fear and pain.

It was the sound of someone being *attacked*.

•• Darrin ••

When Anlyn accidentally jumped into the Darrin system, she did more than simply jump into the middle of a civil war, she jumped into a universe of nightmares and pain. And the more she tried to avoid both, the more curiosity she aroused in her captors—and so the more things began to change for her. After another dozen sleeps, and another half-dozen untouched nightmares, the English they were teaching her began to hone in on its target. It veered away from the rudimentary basics of communication and made aim for a vocabulary of armaments and defenses. They taught her about missiles, about thrust velocities, about tracking systems. They taught her how projectiles flew and every way to defend against them.

The lessons frustrated Anlyn. It wasn't just that she loathed technobabble, it was more that she wasn't learning the kinds of words she needed in order to plead for her release. And no matter how hard she struggled to alter the course of the lessons, she found her instructors just as reluctant to budge. So she satisfied herself with what she could glean from the sentences they spoke between each other. Along with snippets she overheard in her cell, the instructors' banter helped flesh out a language heavy on the hate. And in the meantime, she continued to allow the humans to drag her into the room with the padded tables and strap her down. She even learned how to stay calm while the buckles were being cinched, how to make herself "swell out" so they didn't feel so tight afterward. She learned to relish the few moments of peace she had lying there, face down, cheek to cushion, before each descent into the tiring chases.

She had no idea how long that routine went on before they showed her what she was really doing. It could've been for what she had come to learn was a "month." It could've been several of them.

Nothing seemed different about the apparatus. She still had to suffer the wires being clipped to her skin, each spot on her body sore and tender from the habit. The helmet came on last, Anlyn lifting her head so they wouldn't do it too rough. But this time, instead of an immediate plummet into nightmareland, one of the humans in the white tunics knelt down in front of her.

"Red is for rockets," he said in English. He held up a white card with a red rocket on it. Anlyn felt a wash of confusion at the break in the routine. It was reflected in the human's face as what she now knew to be annoyance. She nodded as much as the helmet straps would allow her, letting him know she understood.

"Good," the human said.

It was a word they used a lot, which made Anlyn doubt she truly understood what it meant.

"Blue is for bolts." Another card came up, this one showing a blast of plasma fire leaping out of a cannon. The barrel of the cannon and the plasma were both blue, even though she'd never heard of the weapons firing in that color. She nodded anyway.

"Green is for good." The last card came up. It was a drawing of a young human, colored green, getting up from the padded table, his helmet coming off. He was surrounded by men in white tunics all beaming with joy.

Anlyn nodded. She realized why the bolt was blue and the rocket red. It was the same sort of tool they had used to teach her basic words, with the beginnings of each pair starting in the same manner. She expected some final instructions, but the man nodded to someone else and stood up.

And another nightmare began.

o o o o

Once again, Anlyn was launched out of a Wadi hole, a handful of angry beasts on her tail. Over the past few nightmares, the scene had changed a little, perhaps as she learned new things to be frightened

341

of. Now and then, the canyon walls were lined with bars; spitting humans clutched them and waved their arms through the gaps to grab at her and hold her down for the Wadi. There was some of that in this dream, and even a human or two chasing among the Wadi, but most of it was more of the same. It wasn't until she had dodged around the first few creatures, sending them smashing into one another, that she noticed what had changed.

A bright circle loomed in one corner of her vision. It was outlined white and full of colored blobs. Anlyn puzzled over this and then felt something slash across the back of her leg. She stumbled, dodged out of the way, and went back to her zigzag patterns, cursing herself for her break in concentration.

She shook her pursuer and sent two others into each other. With a bit of space created behind, she took a moment to glance back at the circle hovering in the corner of her vision. There were even more blobs inside, just as more Wadi had appeared behind her. It didn't take long for the pattern of shapes—the way they were moving, emerging, colliding, disappearing—to make sense. The blobs were the things running after her. She could see them all in one place, just like the ship's tactical display from her rudimentary flight training.

The red ones seemed to go with the slower, dancing Wadi. They were the ones that could leap up a wall, circle around, and then come for her in another direction. Slow, of course, was relative only to the blue Wadi, which came fast and in straight lines, or with just a little curve. These were the bolts. The others were the rockets.

The connection kicked in another level of awareness for Anlyn. She suddenly knew what she was. She finally understood what they were doing with her. She looked down at herself, at her running form, and saw that she was red.

She was a rocket.

One of the Wadi swiped at her, punishing her for another lapse of concentration. Anlyn felt the gashes across her back; she felt herself wobble, losing momentum. She pressed on, drawing two of the red Wadi into the path of an oncoming blue one, the three of them vanishing from her nightmare and also from the display.

After that, she used the vectors from the circle to help her with the beasts chasing behind. She knew what the game was now. She wondered if people from some enemy prison were virtually strapped into the *other* rockets, the ones chasing after her. She wondered what that enemy was using to stoke their fears and make them strain as hard as she. She wondered if that was why she could always outrun them, finding that safe spot at the end. Maybe it was her extra fear that made her special. Maybe it was a lifetime of Wadis and Bodis and forever running.

And that made her wonder just what the safe spot was that waited for her at the end of each canyon run. What was the hole she dove into at the end of her nightmares? Just where was she guiding these rockets day after day, sleep after sleep? And why did she sense that they were safe places, but only for her?

23

DRENARD

"Coril!"

Anlyn peered into the Wadi hole, which was now unobstructed and lit with a dull glow. She could see out the other side and through to the brightly lit canyon's far wall, but there was no sign of her cousin. She yelled Coril's name through the hole again, and by the time her echo dissipated, her cousin's screams had come to a sickening halt. Anlyn could hear the thrumming of her own heartbeat over the canyon's cries.

"What happened?" Gil asked. He arrived by Anlyn's side and peered into one of the holes.

"A Wadi . . . " Anlyn gasped. The rest of the thought remained unformed in her head. She looked upwind, back toward the distant nightside, and thought about how long it would take her to get around, even at a full sprint. She turned and scanned for the largest of the holes, but none were quite the size she needed to crawl through. She looked up and considered the ludicrous.

"What do we do?" Gil asked.

Anlyn secured her graspers to her sunshield and slung them both across her back. She reached for the highest hole she could grab, stuck her foot in another, and lifted herself up. The next hole was a lunge, but she got a firm grip and found a spot for her other foot. Higher up, the holes were smaller, but more tightly packed. The wall was completely shaded all the way to the lip; she hadn't thought any further than that.

"What are you *doing*?" Gil yelled up after her.

Anlyn looked down at him through her feet. She was already quite a few paces up, enough to not want to fall. She was about to answer when Coril's screams resumed. It sounded more like someone waking up in a nightmare than a person engaged in a fight for her life. After a few moments, the screams changed into more of the latter. There were shrieks of surprise and pain. Anlyn froze. She watched numbly as Gil dropped his gear and ran off toward the nightside, running with the same mad panic he had displayed earlier on the shade bridge. Anlyn cursed him and reached for the next handhold, clawing her way toward the top.

A dozen paces higher, she ran out of safe spots to put her hands; her arms were already sore and shaking from the climb. She wasn't sure she could hold on with one hand to do what she needed next, so she reached inside a small hole up to her elbow and made a fist. Leaning back on her arm, she felt her expanded hand wedge itself tight, allowing her to hang from her bones and give her muscles a break. She let go with her other hand and found herself comfortably secure, if quite a ways up.

There was no way to grab the hot stone over the top of the canyon wall—*that* rock sat in the light of both Horis day after day. It would melt her skin, right through the suit. She did know, however, that the suit could take the brunt of a full-on shine for a minute or more. She just needed a way to get across a few paces of rock without touching it. She reached behind her head and pulled the graspers off her shield and stuck the long device inside a hole near her waist, leaving just enough sticking out to form a step. Anlyn pushed down on the arms of the protruding graspers, testing them. Satisfied the device would hold her, she lifted one foot and placed it on the graspers. Still leaning back on her expanded fist, Anlyn lifted her other foot and balanced fully on the small handle. With her free hand, she pulled her hood over the top of her head, all the way down to her eyes. She wiggled her chin in the lower half and then pulled the sunshield off.

She had no idea how this was going to go. She could imagine roasting alive, could picture falling to the solid rock below. She could see herself tumbling off the other side. As Coril's screams stopped for the second time, she wondered if the effort, the risk, even mattered. But she was going on autopilot—acting without thinking. She had forgotten the Rite and all else. All that mattered was her cousin.

Holding the shield with her free hand, she slid the lever to "full open" with her chin. The shield extended to its maximum length and width, nearly pushing Anlyn off her perch in the process. She had to swing it out wide to give the panels room, which let it catch the wind like a sail, twisting her around painfully on her trapped fist. Anlyn nearly let go of the shield to keep from falling, but it banged into the side of the canyon, its sharp edge digging into the rock. She steadied herself, grunting with effort, and finally managed to push herself back into place.

Before she exhausted any more energy, or her persistence wilted, Anlyn lifted the shield to the top of the canyon wall and let it slam down flat. The heat on her exposed hand was sudden and surprising. Hesitating would make it worse, so she stood up on the lodged graspers and extended her upper body into the two suns. With a shove, she forced her trapped fist deep, relaxed it, and pulled her hand out. Both hands went up to the top of the shield, which was already warming but was much, much cooler than the forever-exposed rock. Anlyn pressed down and launched herself from the graspers, jumping up onto the shield, leaving her Wadi tool behind to poke out of its hole.

The dual suns began heating her suit immediately. Anlyn looked to the end of her fully extended sunshield and saw that it wasn't quite long enough; the thin wall's other edge was still a few paces away. Holding the shoulder straps below her feet, she scooted forward, throwing her weight up while she shot the shield along the surface of the rock. Each lunge won her a few fractions of a pace. Her thighs soon burned with the effort; they had already grown sore from the climb up.

Another fraction of a pace with another lunge. A few more fractions. Bit by bit, Anlyn jittered across the top of the Wadi canyon's narrow wall, totally exposed and hardly aware of the inhospitable vista around her. All she cared about was the edge of her shield and the end of the sun-soaked wall. She threw herself forward, bringing them a fraction closer. Again and again she went, sweat pouring from her hood. Her face was on fire. Her legs had grown numb, moving only by a repetitive act of iron will. Anlyn yelled at herself to keep it up. She grunted with pain and exertion. And finally, the edge of the shield shot out enough to hang in the air on the other side.

Anlyn felt like crying out in relief, even though she had done little more than strand herself halfway to her goal. She moved to the edge of the shield and looked down. She could see Coril far below, lying on her belly, unmoving. There was blood everywhere, tracks of it leading across the ground in curvy patterns. The heat on Anlyn's suit forced her to stop gawking. She spun around and lowered herself over the cliff, careful to grip only the edge of her shield. Even that, however, had now been in the suns long enough to singe her fingers through her Wadi suit.

Dangling her legs, Anlyn found a hole for her foot and rested for a moment on a locked knee. She reached down for the nearest hole and held the bottom edge of it, which was shaded a little by the top. The wall she clung to was sunlit for the first half of the climb down, but the inner parts of the Wadi holes were shaded. She only had to brush her knee against the lit rock once to know not to do it again—the Wadi suit hissed in complaint and melted, sticking to her flesh. Anlyn considered dropping the rest of the way but knew she'd break or twist something in the fall.

Still, she went down faster than she should have. It was a mad, desperate scramble, running toward the pull of gravity but fighting the urge to give in altogether. Once she hit the shaded part of the wall, she was able to go even faster. She flattened herself out, resting her poor legs by applying friction across the whole of her. When her feet were head-high off the ground, she dropped the rest of the way, her numb thighs giving out and leaving her in a heap beside her cousin.

"Coril—"

Anlyn crawled next to her. She reached out and tugged on Coril's shoulder, oblivious to the pain in her blistered hands.

"Cousin, wake up." She crouched by Coril's still form. She lifted one of her shoulders, trying to roll her over, but her body had all the heft of a thing that would never again move of its own accord. Purplish blood was everywhere, and the imprints of Wadi marks trailed away and into a nearby hole.

Anlyn wanted to cry in frustration. She wanted to shout the canyons quiet. She wanted to pound her fists into something. Rage and fury leaked out of her, trailing off as rich and powerful pheromones on the

wind. She couldn't see the columns of smoke she created, of course. She was oblivious to the bright trails
of emotional screaming her pores leaked out around
her.

Anlyn couldn't see these things. But the creature
lurking nearby, licking blood off its paws, certainly
could.

24

DARRIN

The Darrin Civil war lasted just over a year. Anlyn spent most of that time remotely guiding missiles for Darrin I, sending them to various targets on Darrin II, especially its heavily defended orbital stations. Even though the command structures on both sides of the conflict were too fractured for any one person to have a full grasp on what went on where, how the war had even started, or why it had come to an end, there were many on both sides who knew of Anlyn, even if by rumor. Word of a captured Drenard, who had been left like a gift by a mysterious Bel-Tra, became the stuff of unbelievable legend. Despite the swelling gossip, and the growing doubts that soon followed to swallow them, there were many who would swear to their last day that the war would've ended sooner without her—but that it would've been a Darrin II rout.

Anlyn wouldn't learn of this until later, long after her months and months of bad dreams and worse wakings. The pattern that formed around her made little sense on the surface. All she knew was that she had to avoid the ungodly pain the wires clipped to her flesh could bring, and so she needed to guide her missiles well. The motivation to do so—the fear that kept her senses sharp—meant her nightmares couldn't end or let up. Her captors found themselves in a tricky game of keeping her both informed and full of fear. It meant Anlyn's reward for her continued success was a gradual deterioration in her conditions. Her captors could be heard urging on the spitters on either side of her cell, even as they looked to her for salvation. The only way they could reward her was with more hate, lest her abilities become dulled by a diminishment of fear.

Often, as Anlyn lay on her padded table, she considered giving in to the wires and their electricity. She wondered if there would be enough pain to kill her, even though she doubted it. She would have gladly martyred herself if she'd thought it possible.

She would have steered her guided missile right back around on the very installation they held her in—if only she knew which Wadi hole represented it. But her fear and the pain kept her forever running.

Over time, the nightmares changed. The Wadis completed their morph into scrambling, spitting humans. The canyon labyrinths became mazes of cell-lined corridors. All that remained constant was the primal fear of bad things descending upon her neck and the allure of finding that safe place. It was always about that safe place, even long after she understood what sort of explosive death it meant for someone else.

Along the way, Anlyn forgot who she was. She forgot where she came from. A pampered childhood spent skipping through rooftop gardens with her cousins became a dream, something that couldn't *possibly* have ever actually happened. Not to her. Wadis became something mystical that haunted her occasionally in nightmares, not something that she had once hunted. Bodi nearly transformed into the memory of someone she would seek solace beside. *Nearly.*

Anlyn lived in a shell. She curled into a ball when she was left alone. When called upon, she did what was expected of her with all the pent-up ferocity she could muster. She was an animal, docile and meek if untouched, embroiled and calculating when threatened. Those who could use such a thing mastered the art of threatening her and aiming her rage.

It all came to an end with little warning. Looking back, Anlyn could possibly see that her pursuers had become fewer in number, but it was all as much a blur as the blue bolts. One day, all she knew was that there were no more nightmares to make. The war was over. Now there were just papers to sign.

Anlyn was brought along to the ceremonies as some sort of display. They led her out in front of the dignitaries, and she rattled her chains dutifully. The electricity her handlers could send through her shackles kept her in line.

One of her original captors—one of the humans in black who had watched the Bel-Tra ship disappear—seemed to be a major player in the treaty proceedings. His suit shimmered and caught the reflection of the bright stars, the alien constellations barely visible beyond the overhead dome, occluded by the new debris field Anlyn had helped create. The large gathering of humans all stood on what was left of one of the orbital stations and seemed pleased with themselves for what their efforts had won: two belts of barren rock, chunked and splintered and all but uninhabitable.

Some of them, of course, had won something more. Part of what Albert—the man in the shimmering suit—had won was Anlyn. After papers were signed with many pens and much smiling, he took her in the inferior ship he had bartered for to the inferior asteroid he had bartered for and bragged about having bartered so wisely.

He would be right in the long run. It didn't take long to translate Anlyn's finely honed skills and reflexes to ship flight. Soon, Albert's home and spacecraft began their steady incline of upgrades as Anlyn wrangled in more customers than any dozen pilots combined. Before long, she was the most feared thing in the most fearsome corner of the Milky Way, a thing rumored among its inhabitants but hardly believed. She was whispers in the darkness that sent chill bumps up the arms of other pilots. She was the sort of bluff that caused nervous laughter among hardened men, eyes glancing around to see if anyone believed, or if anyone else could smell their fear.

The years went by, and Anlyn gradually morphed into a thing that lived in *other* people's nightmares.

All of it made possible because she could never escape her own.

•• DRENARD ••

Anlyn was leaning over Coril's motionless body, her heart bursting with sorrow, when the Wadi lunged at her from above. She turned as soon as she heard its claws cracking stone. It flew at her in a flash of shimmering scales, catching and scattering the very shade. It landed all-claws before she could turn to defend herself, slicing into her back through her thin Wadi suit.

The toxins leaped through her veins, jolting tired and numb limbs alive with the bite of their poison. Anlyn lurched to the side, her body spasming and jerking reflexively.

The Wadi lost its grip and skittered across the rock. Anlyn spun around and tried to locate the beast before it could strike again. She moved to the other side of Coril and tugged at the lance pinned beneath her cousin's body. It wouldn't budge. She was trying to roll Coril away when the Wadi once again became an airborne blur.

Anlyn tried to move, but the creature slammed into her chest, knocking her backward. Snapping jaws came for her neck, teeth scissoring open and shut in anticipation of her flesh.

Anlyn's arm was pinned. She yanked it free, but her hand caught on something—*her thermos*. She yanked the small cylinder free and shoved it in the animal's face, and the Wadi bit down, crunching through the metal skin and leaking what remained of her water.

The Wadi shook its head, the thermos caught on its teeth. Water sprayed out into the sunlit part of the canyon, evaporating as soon as it hit. Anlyn scrambled away, eyeing the creature and the pinned lance. The Wadi took a step forward; it rested one paw on Coril's back and tried to use another to pull the thermos off its fangs. Anlyn didn't think it would take the animal long to figure it out. She moved to grab the tip of the lance, but the Wadi howled in its throat and swished its tail at her. Anlyn glanced around but didn't have her grippers, her shield, or anything.

She looked up. The edge of her shield was still sticking out over the lip of the wall, high above.

Anlyn turned and grabbed the holes in the cliff. She climbed up, willing her weary limbs to operate, ignoring the burning gashes on her back as she stretched out for the next hold. She lunged from one to the other, scaling the shady portion of the wall as fast as she could. She glanced down only when she heard her empty thermos clatter across the rock. The Wadi howled, its jaws free, and then shot up the wall after her.

Anlyn climbed even faster. Dangerously fast. She reached the edge of the shade halfway up the pocked rock and continued on, careful now to keep her body and knees off the steaming wall. She felt something brush against her foot—she pulled her leg into the sun and then looked back. The Wadi hung from a hold down in the shady part, its head bob-bing from side to side as it rocked on its eager arms. Anlyn remained still, watching it. They both studied each other. Anlyn's legs trembled with fatigue. Her suit began to heat up in the light of the Horis.

The Wadi broke away first. It darted into one of the holes.

Anlyn froze. She heard the clicking of claws deep within the hole near her head. She looked up at the shield, its razor-sharp edge poking out above. She thought about how hot it must have already gotten from sitting there so long. The clicking near her head grew louder, the Wadi worming its way through the warrens. Anlyn let go of her hold and grabbed a lower one. She raced down the wall as if it were no more than a ladder, reckless and brushing against the blistering rock, the suit melting and sticking to her flesh in ever more places.

She ignored it. When she hit the shady portion, she began a half-fall, half-plummet down the face, clutching at holds just to slow her descent. Her boots hit the rock floor with a jarring thud, forcing her knees up into her chest. She dove toward Coril as a frustrated wail erupted from above. Throwing her weight into her cousin's body, Anlyn rolled Coril to the side; she grabbed the large Wadi lance, unsure of how to even wield it. Lifting the sharp end—unable to pick it all the way up, her muscles were so weary—Anlyn kept the hook on the rock and rose shakily, looking to the sky—

The Wadi Thooo was a blur of falling claws and open jaw. Anlyn braced herself; she pulled the lance between her and the Thooo. She felt a jolt of electricity as the Wadi screamed, its open throat yelling right by her ear.

But the scream was one full of rage and fear—a wail of the dying.

Anlyn fell to the rock, exhausted and unable to hold the lance.

Something heavy collapsed on top of her, moving and groaning. She pushed herself away and scrambled deeper into the shade. When she looked back, eyes wide, fear still gripping her throat, she saw what she had done: She saw the Wadi lance had pierced the wild animal's stomach and had erupted out its back. One last wicked groan, and then its twitching arms fell still. The Wadi was dead.

Anlyn Hooo had killed it.

○ ○ ○ ○

When Gil finally reached her, Anlyn was passed out, her head resting on Coril's back. She had fallen asleep in the shade, her body too weary to move, the last of her adrenaline scurrying away.

Gil woke her and held his thermos to her lips. He was panting heavily from his long run around the wedge-shaped wall, his breathing dry and labored. Anlyn took deep gulps from his thermos and then pushed his hands away so she could breathe. She watched him survey the messy scene.

When his eyes fell back to hers, the two of them sat in silence, looking at each other, no words large enough to fill the mood. Gil gave her more water, which Anlyn accepted eagerly. She held his hand while she drank, and then he helped her sit up.

"What now?" Gil whispered. He worked the cap back on the thermos, his hands shaking and a paler shade of blue.

Anlyn looked back at Coril, the youth and vitality of her small frame incongruent with its stillness. All she knew was that she needed to get her cousin home, but there was no way she could do it alone. She looked to the Wadi, which was just as motionless as her cousin, the lance still shoved through its body. From tip to tail, it was almost two paces long. Big, but not so big she couldn't carry it.

"What do we do?" Gil croaked.

Anlyn turned to him. "We do each other a favor," she said sadly.

25

DARRIN

Anlyn's homeworld of Drenard had forever been shaped by its cycles, by the slow orbit of its two great stars swirling around each other like two beads on a circle. Known as the Horis, these twin suns dominated her planet's environment, its weather, even its culture. They burned one half of the planet and left the other to freeze. They would slowly wobble across lands out on the border of the planet's habitable halo, parts that burned at times and cooled during others. There, the rocks cracked open and the blowing sand found wounds in which to sift. It was these unpredictable parts that Drenards looked upon with skepticism and worry, more perhaps than the frigid night and burning day.

Those changes occurred over a Hori cycle, the time it took for all things to come back around to where they had started. It was a cycle of burning followed by a cycle of cooling. Some temperate average may have been held over time but rarely in any one moment. And so Anlyn's burning years, her great and wasted adolescence, ended how they began: With two ships matching move for move, one trying in vain to latch on to the other.

Only *this* time, Anlyn was flying expertly amid the rubble of Darrin, not above her home world of Drenard. And unlike her mad run from Bodi—her desperate escape from her father's death and her forced marriage—*this* time Anlyn was the hunter rather than the hunted.

She closed in on the old GC-290 ahead of her, leaving Albert's many competitors behind. It had become a familiar sight: Her ship chasing down the customer of Albert's choice while the rest of the pack scavenged for leftovers. Anlyn went into each pursuit with a detached calm. Her body had shriveled on a Wadi's diet of water and nothing else, leaving her fractured and tormented mind to wither. She had her fear, her sensitivity to pain, and her fine war skills etched back to razor sharpness—but only shadows and ashes of her true former self. The long burning had charred her down to her blackest essence.

She was halfway to the GC-290, only a few other pilots keeping up, when she realized she actually needed to concentrate. The pilot of the 290 had nearly shaken her by setting up a false pattern. He had teased to port before juking starboard, the sort of habitual twitch even expert pilots had a difficult time avoiding because they were normally unaware of their own tells. After a few false habits like this, the pilot did the opposite, which sent two of Anlyn's companions into each other and nearly made her lose ground.

The skilled fighter in her awoke, coming out of its autopilot daze. It had been many years, going back to the civil war, since she had faced a worthy adversary. Anlyn pressed in farther, ignoring the complaints and grunts from Albert in the nav seat as excess Gs wracked his body.

The 290 pilot changed tactics again. He was employing a vast array of strategies in rapid sequence. There was skill in the maneuvers, but a hint of desperation as well. He wasn't trying anything long enough to see if it would work, preferring instead to toss all his tools out into space, hoping one would fit and secure his escape.

Anlyn knew the strategy was foolish; regardless, she couldn't help but admire the shape and precision of each tool. This pilot wasn't playing around if he was trying to make sure he attracted the Darrin salesman with the best gear. Anlyn pushed hers and Albert's top-of-the-line grav suits to their limits as she pulled in tight to the 290. She darted around it, mere paces away, doing what Bodi had once tried so many sleeps ago. She readied the airlock to grab on.

When they finally collided and *Lady Liberty's* hull latched on to a ship identified as *Parsona,* Anlyn felt the tension of piloting drain from her limbs. Her job was over, and Albert's was about to begin. It had been an unusual skirmish, a challenge to awaken something within her, some worm of her former self wiggling deep beneath the ashy layers. She didn't feel quite alive, but she sensed the stirrings of something that *could* be once more. At the very least, she felt some of the stiff tension exiting her body, perhaps leaving room for an old vitality to return.

What Anlyn didn't know—what she *couldn't* know at the time—was that her feelings of release were far more than mere tension leaving her body. The moment she locked with this other ship signaled the momentous end of one great cycle for Anlyn Hooo.

And the silent, inauspicious beginnings of another.

•• Drenard ••

Anlyn and Gil stopped half a thousand paces from the Wadi shelter. Anlyn lowered the Wadi she had been carrying, and Gil did the same with Coril. There was no way she could've carried her cousin so far; she wasn't even sure she could make what few paces were left.

Gil bent over, exhausted, and rested his hands on his knees. He coughed several times into his fist, wheezing for breath. "Are you sure about this?" he asked, his voice nearly lost on the wind.

Anlyn nodded. She was sure.

She stepped in front of Coril's still form and crouched low. Gil lifted Coril and rested her on Anlyn's shoulders. The extra weight on her open wounds—the deep claw gashes in her back—made each of them sing out, sending a chorus of cold pain down through her arms. Anlyn ignored it. She held her cousin's wrists in one hand and wrapped her other arm behind her bent knees. Shifting the weight more up her neck, where so much seemed to already weigh on her heart, Anlyn tensed up wiry muscles already weak from so much ordeal—and gradually, haltingly, stood.

"You've got her?"

Anlyn didn't waste her energy nodding. She took her first lumbering step forward. As she fell into a numb, silent routine of step after step, Gil hurried up beside her, the dead Wadi slung easily over his shoulder.

They were a hundred paces away—close enough that Anlyn could count down the end of her heartbreaking, trying ordeal—when her aunt and several other Rite counselors burst through the door of the shelter. They ran out, the worry visible on their faces even from so far away. When they got closer, that worry morphed into fright and disbelief. Coril's closest uncle clasped his hands over his face, ran up to Anlyn, and seemed about to remove her burden.

Something in Anlyn's demeanor, however, held him back. Instead of moving to help, the counselors formed a rough circle, a bubble respecting the Rite. Anlyn trudged the last dozen paces as moans and wails from her elders joined those from the distant canyons. A door was held open, which she stumbled through. She collapsed to her knees on the worn carpet and twisted to the side to lower her cousin flat. The adults went to Coril immediately, even though there was nothing they could do for her. Gil fell to the carpet beside Anlyn and sprawled out, his chest heaving from the long hike with so heavy a burden.

When Anlyn looked up, her aunt Ralei was standing before her. Tears streaked down the woman's face, flowing around an expression of shock, or shame, or something of both. When their eyes met, Anlyn knew the ruse of Gil's Rite would not last. The new hardness she felt inside her was reflected in the way her aunt stood before her, her adult carriage tense with respect. As the counselors removed the Wadi from Gil's shoulder, they too looked from it to Anlyn, and then to the drying, heat-scabbed wounds across her back, exposed beneath her shredded suit.

The room stood silent, stuffed with sorrow and thick with somber respect. It pressed in on Anlyn, as stifling as the canyon heat. It filled her lungs, stung her eyes, burned her wounds with the stitch of healing.

The severity and importance of the moment— the loss of her cousin's life mixed with the awesome power of her own survival—concocted a rapturous joy smothering under a blanket of regret. Anlyn was too happy to cry, too sad to smile, too guilty to exult. She felt near to bursting with all the conflicting emotions.

And in that moment, it suddenly occurred to Anlyn that whatever happened next, whatever followed for her, it wouldn't be *anything* like all that had come before.

She was sure of it.

PART XXI
THE PROPHECY

*"Things don't come true.
They are true, or they aren't."*

~The Bern Seer~

26

LOK · THE PRESENT

Mere hours after Molly dealt with Saunders's reaction to Anlyn, she found herself faced with an even more daunting proposition: now she had to introduce her friend to an entire crowd, a crowd that had been raised and taught to loathe her kind.

She cupped her hands around her face and leaned against the cargo bay's porthole. Beyond, in the dim glow of *Parsona's* landing lights, she could see the surviving navy crewmen and the remaining Callites seated in rows, listening to Admiral Saunders speak.

"I'm nervous," Anlyn said beside her.

Molly turned to see her friend's face pressed up against the adjacent porthole, looking out.

"It's not too late to back out," Molly said. "You don't have to lead this mission if you don't want. I could go, and you could take *Parsona* to the Carrier for the missiles. You'd be hidden there—"

Anlyn shook her head but continued to gaze out through the carboglass. "I'm not nervous about that," she said. "Going back to Darrin, flying in combat again . . . I think I can handle those things—"

"Are you nervous about facing *them*?" Molly pressed a finger to the glass.

Anlyn turned away from the view outside. "Let's put it this way: if you didn't have all the guns stored away in *here*, I don't think I'd feel safe going out *there*."

"They'll be fine. The admiral is breaking the news to them gradually, so there won't be the same degree of shock." Molly looked back out the porthole. "I hope," she added quietly to herself.

Saunders looked as if he was just warming up, his arm-waving reminding Molly of her academy days and all his energetic debriefings after simulator missions. Like all his former cadets in the audience, she could tell when he was nearing his final point by how high his hands got in the air. They fluttered like featherless, wounded birds flapping for altitude. The poor things hadn't made it past his shoulders yet, so she went to see how Ryke's engineering lesson was going.

Molly joined Edison in the aft hallway and peered into the engine room.

Two of the new arrivals from the Underground—warped down from another of the captured Bern ships just hours earlier—were also in the hall. One was a Callite, an old recruit from Lok and a friend of Dr. Ryke's. The other was a race Molly had never seen before, a smaller version of the Bel-Tra, thin and hairless. The two of them quietly chatted together, paying little attention to the lesson going on inside the engine room. Molly hoped their distracted affect meant they already knew what they were doing.

She patted Edison's arm, and he moved aside enough for her to peek in. Ryke stood in front of *Parsona's* hyperdrive. He had the control panel off, with wires hanging everywhere. A large electrical schematic was taped to the side of the open drive, and Ryke waved a soldering iron in the air as he spoke. Molly listened in for a minute; she watched several of the gathered nod their heads as they absorbed the step-by-step routine. Counting Edison, they had a total of seven engineers who would soon know how to make alterations to hyperdrives, giving them the potential to jump from any one place to another while ignoring gravity and all obstructions between.

The only other piece they needed to make it work was Ryke's secret nav program. It was at that point in his earlier conversation with Molly that she had balked. Her preference had been to wave off the entire mission and take their chances with the long way back rather than risk trusting anyone with such powerful knowledge. But Ryke had just grown more excited, explaining the alterations he could make to the code to create an absolute failsafe.

Each drive they altered, he explained, would be good for a *single* jump. Four of the tap wires soldered by the engineers would have nothing to do with making the modification work. They would fire when the hyperdrive engaged, but they would be connected to the control board that housed Ryke's program. The ship would make its solitary jump from Darrin back to Lok, but the *business* end of the hyperdrive would jump somewhere else entirely.

Molly stood by the engine room door and watched Ryke conduct the lesson. She smiled as he paused now and then to scratch his beard or brush his hands across the schematic. The Lokian dialect seemed an odd match with the subject matter. Combined with his squat build, the jarring mix of pure genius and provincial upbringing made him instantly lovable.

"I think they're almost ready for us," Anlyn whispered.

Molly turned to see her friend at her side, her pale blue face scrunched up in what she recognized as Drenard worry. She nodded and then reached past Edison and waved at Ryke.

"Five more minutes," Ryke said, holding up his grease-streaked hand, his stubby fingers spread out.

Molly patted Edison on the back and followed Anlyn into the cargo bay. In the cockpit, she could see Cat leaning back against the console, her lips moving as she conversed with Parsona. Molly snapped her fingers and waved, and then pointed toward the cargo ramp. Cat nodded and held up one finger. Someone slapped on the outside of the hull.

"You ready?" Molly asked Anlyn.

"No, but let's do it anyway."

Molly keyed the loading ramp open. The lip swung away toward the dirt, gradually revealing the faces of those standing in the back rows and then those seated on the ground. A palpable wave of shock washed over the bodies of those gathered, human and Callite alike. Molly could sense two conflicting emotions in *Gloria's* survivors, both of them borne of military training. There was the primal and uncontrollable fear reaction of seeing an enemy in the flesh, and then there was the stoic formality unique to a gathering of those in uniform.

Anlyn stepped cautiously onto the ramp, her boots joining the whistles of the night bugs as the only sounds. The regal tunics she had been wearing for weeks had been replaced with her old *Parsona* flight suit, which she and Molly had agreed would soften the visual blow and help the gathered see her as a pilot and one of them.

Anlyn held up both of her slender arms, the lights from the cargo bay filtering around them and into the dark forest beyond, casting large and hazy shadows.

"Greetings," she said. "My name is Anlyn Hooo."

Molly watched her friend scan the crowd, amazed at the poise and bearing of what she had once seen as a fragile girl in slave chains.

"I wish I could greet you in peace," Anlyn said, "but I bring you tidings of war instead. War against a common foe that has, for too long, brought our races together in conflict. Your commander has just told you the nature of the threat above us, these glimmers in the night sky that shot down your friends and loved ones. Know then, that I was raised to fear the sight of *you*, just as you were trained to loathe the visage you see standing before you tonight—"

"We're supposed to *trust* you?"

Anlyn stopped speaking, her arms frozen mid-gesture. The gathered grumbled, turning to look among themselves, but no one took credit for saying it. Saunders stepped toward the cargo ramp, his face lit up crimson in the light spilling out of *Parsona*.

Molly waved him off and stepped forward, taking a spot beside Anlyn.

"Do you trust *me*?" she asked the crowd.

There were nods and a chorus of assents, none among either of the groups easily forgetting the nature of their rescue.

"Yeah, but you're one of us!" someone shouted.

"Am I?" Molly asked. She took another step forward. "Am I one of you? As most of you know, I was recently locked up on your very ship for murder and for treason. Am I one of you? I was kicked out of the academy for being different. I never graduated as you did."

"You're asking us to follow a *Drenard* into battle," the anonymous voice protested.

"Would you follow *me*?" Molly asked. "A girl, not yet eighteen, with no military credentials to her name. Would you follow *me* into battle?"

The chorus of assents was louder, the back few rows of seated rising to their feet.

"Well, *I* am a Drenard!" Molly shouted, pressing her fist to her chest. "I have been to their home planet. I have participated in ancient rites, and I am just as much a Drenard as she." She pointed to Anlyn, and the crowd hushed. Even the night bugs ceased their twittering.

"The only difference between Anlyn and me is that I'm not half the pilot she is. I don't have a fraction of the familiarity with where you're going. She—" Molly took a step back up the ramp and put a hand on her friend's shoulder. She lowered her voice. "She was held captive, a slave, by a human from the Darrin system. She has more reason to hate our race than we have of hating hers—but she is able to see past this. And now I beg of you to show the same restraint." Molly scanned the crowd, pausing to catch her breath. "Anlyn is my friend," she said simply. "If you trust me, you can trust her."

The crowd remained still. Saunders stood frozen between them and the ramp, only his head moving as he turned to look back and forth from the duo to the assembled crowd.

Anlyn squeezed Molly's shoulder and then took a step down the ramp. "The present is defined by history," she said softly. "Hate burns from fires set so long ago that their source has become charred and forgotten—it has become a mystery. There is so much more to fear here than simply each other."

She pointed to the sky. "*There* is our doom, whether it is on the battlefield of tomorrow or our gradual defeat a generation hence. Look at how few of you remain from your previous encounter. Just an inconsequential fraction. Well, our distrust of each other is just as meaningless. We have a chance, however slim, to succeed—to take down even a handful of those great ships above. And even if we fail, even if we join the already fallen, our actions, taken together, will be the locus of a *new* fire, one that might spread through the generations. One of trust and hope rather than hate and fear. *Today* could eventually become the *new* past that shapes a better tomorrow."

Her soft voice faded out over the crowd and among the trees. The night bugs resumed whistling, softly at first, testing this strange intrusion into their habits. Molly watched the crowd as they turned to one another, whispers growing into murmurs as the twilight chirping swelled to its own chorus. Molly feared the solid stone of military formality had been cracked by their doubts, fear and rage seeping through the fractures. She feared the Callites would see more empty promises, more potential letdowns.

But the whisperings and murmurs didn't grow any further. They didn't rise with a mad hiss interspersed with shouts for violence. The hushed sputtering remained calm and grew calmer. The crowd seemed to be accepting—*believing*—or at least wanting to.

Saunders strolled up the ramp, his eyes sparkling with wetness as he glanced toward Molly and Anlyn. He took his place between the two girls, his poise and carriage several light years from the shocked pile of jelly he'd been earlier that afternoon. He looked out over the Callites and what remained of his fleet, his throat bobbing as he fished for his voice.

"For the *Gloria*," he finally said, his words cracking with emotion.

"For the *Gloria*," someone whispered.

"The *Gloria*," Molly said.

The chant grew, finding its rhythm, gathering its voice even among the Callites, who had their own, smaller shuttle crashes to consider. These aliens rose alongside the meager group of survivors of a once-great ship, stirred by the cheer, all of them defying the silence of the night. They stood and shouted in the openness of that wooded clearing, daring the menacing fleet above with the audacity of their plans and with the power of their full-throated promises of war.

27

LOK

After the stirring rally, the attack plans on the Darrin asteroid belts were reviewed for the final time. Squads were formed, gear equipped, rations portioned out. Molly busied herself among the fevered activity, helping where she could, her own mission to the StarCarrier lingering at a lower level of thought. She had no time to fear her involvement in the next day's plans — she was too busy worrying over the impossible task she was about to send these poor, bedraggled survivors out to perform.

Perhaps, she wondered to herself, this was too much for any of them to absorb and process all at once. Most of the raiders had only a few hours' training with the bizarre swords sent down from the Underground ships. The vast majority of the navy pilots had never flown a real mission outside a simulator. And with their paltry numbers, they only had crew and supplies for forty ships with an average of three crew members per ship—a minimum verging on unsafe.

Molly went over the plan in her head one more time, taking each stage individually to remind herself how doable might be the whole: Using the data from *Parsona's* recent visit to Darrin, each squad would jump inside one of the asteroid bases, just on the other side of their force fields. Teams of three would then storm each weapons shop, commandeering any ships they might find. Once secured, the crews would jump out to the predetermined rendezvous point where they would lock up in pairs, moving Ryke's engineers from one craft to another as they modified the hyperdrives. If any of the ships need more fusion fuel, or any of the crews needed medical attention, that would be taken care of at the same time. Meanwhile, the pilots could familiarize themselves with the ships' controls and test the weapons systems.

They had set aside a full eight hours for the Darrin phase of the plan, with two hours reserved for the rendezvous and modifications, which meant—thanks to Ryke's modifications to the drives—they would be back at Lok by local sunup. That should give Molly and her crew plenty of time to set up in the StarCarrier and begin bombarding the Bern command ship with teleported missiles.

Going through it slowly, it seemed almost too simple. However, as she watched navy brass squeeze their bellies into combat armor and Scottie show Callite civilians how to load firearms, the plan seemed destined to fail. Molly helped one of the crewmen secure a Velcro strap around the back of his armor, getting it as tight as possible; she then walked around *Parsona* to see how Ryke and Walter were coming with their "rift."

"You guys about ready?" she asked, walking out to where they'd set up a few floodlights.

Walter nodded without looking up from his computer. He typed furiously, wires trailing from his handheld to a control console that had been jumped down from one of the Underground ships. The device had been one of the five originally meant for closing the rift on Lok. The Underground command was still waiting until the bulk of the Bern fleet moved off before risking a flight to the planet's surface. They had sent the console reluctantly, seeing the distraction gained from the Darrin mission as a greater boon than the loss of one more backup platform.

The number crunching for the jumps to Darrin would fall to Parsona, who had the SADAR data from their recent trip to that system in her memory banks. With the mass of the 120 or so crew members and their gear, they had more than enough fuel for the one-way jump, with plenty left over for the missiles. All the fusion fuel Molly had longed for and bartered for, and had nearly used to jump to hyperspace, would go instead to this mission. The consequences of her decision, the reality of having fully made it, dawned on Molly for the first time as she watched Walter and Ryke work. *This* was the thing she had wrought, whatever happened next. *This* was her plan, with real lives at stake. *This* was what she had chosen to do, rather than rescue Cole and her father.

She suddenly felt pregnant with doubt.

Stepping past the console, she checked on the appearance of their fake "rift." It was nothing more than a gap between two trees that had been smeared with the droppings of mooncrawls, giving the halo a pale glow. Molly found the getup ridiculous, but she figured it seemed ominous enough. Besides, once people started disappearing as they walked through the "rift," there would be no doubt that it was working. And work it would, thanks to the jump platform sunk into the ground between the trees and the four insulated wires snaking from it to *Parsona's* hyperdrive.

Molly saw Walter had covered the platform with leaves, even though he must know they would only be sitting there until the first jump. After that, she guessed everyone would be too nervous to see that they were passing over a flat, black pad on the ground.

Satisfied with her inspection, Molly turned back to the console. Ryke looked up from its display screen, his face lit with an eerie, green glow.

"It'll be almost two in the morning Darrin local time when they arrive," he told Molly.

"Perfect," she said. Molly squeezed Walter's shoulder. "Are you set?"

He nodded without looking up from his computer. Molly had given him a supervisory role of making sure the rate of escaped fuel was matching their projections—nothing he could cause trouble with but something that made him a part of the greater plan. Over the past day or two, perhaps ever since the StarCarrier incident, he had seemed overly eager to lend a helping hand. It was something Molly wanted to foster as much as she could.

Seeing that she wasn't needed around the rift, Molly walked back toward her ship, steering for the small planning group that included Saunders, Anlyn, and several of his senior staff.

"How long?" Saunders asked as she approached.

"We can go at any time. We just need to get everyone lined up in the correct order so we know who we're sending where."

"Quite lucky to have one of these rifts so close," Lieutenant Robinson said. Saunders's chief of staff flashed Molly a friendly smile.

"No luck involved," Molly told him. "That's how my friends even knew this clearing was here. Besides, the rifts are everywhere, you just have to know how to look for them and how to open them up."

The lies came out like honey, sweet and smooth. Molly felt an odd sense of déjà vu, remembering another time in a wooded clearing when she'd been shocked at the ease with which lies could be told. The flash of recollection settled like particulates in water, arranging themselves in a thickening film. She suddenly remembered Cole lying to Orville on Glemot, how she'd barely known him back then — not as a civilian, anyway. She recalled how shocked and disgusted she'd felt, afraid even, of Cole's ability to lie so well and so easily.

And now it's a new power for me, she realized. Molly watched the staff members nod to one another; they seemed to think her explanation was the only rational one. Robinson continued to smile, obviously buying it as well.

"Well, I think we're due a little luck," Saunders said grimly.

The rest agreed with him while Anlyn pulled Molly to the side.

"Everything okay?" Molly asked.

Anlyn nodded. "Fine. People are actually going out of their way to be nice to me. I think they're over-compensating a little." A grave expression washed over Anlyn's face, one that filled Molly with dread.

"What is it, Anlyn?"

"Edison and I switched assignments with group thirteen," Anlyn said.

"But I thought you two were going to retrieve *Lady Liberty*."

"I know. But then Edison and I got to thinking that it just made more sense this way. We're both familiar with the layout of his base, and I know what kind of ship he would have replaced her with—"

Molly shook her head. "This is about revenge, isn't it?"

Anlyn didn't say anything. Her eyes didn't waver from Molly's.

"You're even more familiar with *Lady Liberty*," Molly pointed out. "I mean, you've flown her into combat a thousand times. And besides, there won't be any fighting involved in picking her up. She's right where we left her, and we can't afford to lose either of you—"

"I'll still command *Lady* for the flight here," Anlyn told her. "We'll transfer over when Edison goes to modify the hyperdrive."

Molly ran her fingers through her hair. She looked up through the clearing at the stars overhead.

"And you're right," Anlyn whispered. "It *is* about revenge."

Molly stared at her, agape. "You admit it?"

Anlyn nodded.

Molly turned away from her friend, disappointed by the decision. She watched the dozens of small squads as they formed up in a jagged line stretching from the console and back around her ship. In the glow of Parsona's work lights, she could see flat hands zooming through imaginary space, dogfighting one another in mock battle as old lessons were dusted off and honed to something approximating sharpness.

Anlyn moved by her side; her tiny hand settled in the small of Molly's back.

Molly started to voice her objection, but Anlyn interrupted.

"Look at them," she said quietly.

Molly swallowed her thoughts. She watched as hands soared in mock battle and eyes were cast upward toward the fleet that had taken away the friends and family of those gathered.

"This whole mission is about revenge," Molly said. "Isn't it?"

Anlyn's small hand moved from Molly's back and went around to her side, squeezing her. Their bodies rested on each other as the two friends pulled themselves close.

"It is," Anlyn said softly. "So let me have mine."

28

THREE JUMPS

Anlyn and Edison stood side by side, the only squad comprising just two members. The argument had been that Edison counted twice, if not three times. And not just for his ferocious power, but for his navigation and engineering skills. With Anlyn's abilities at the flight controls, the duo almost seemed like overkill.

Standing close to her fiancé, Anlyn could feel the warmth radiating off him. Edison kept scratching the back of one paw through his flight gloves, a habit she hadn't seen before. It made her wonder if he might be more nervous than he was letting on.

Anlyn certainly was. She had briefed the groups earlier, after their weapons training, to let them know about the slight chance that they might jump into empty hangar bays, and not to be alarmed. Darrin, she knew quite well, didn't operate on a steady schedule. It was more like an orbit of competing fire-houses that were on watch at all hours of the day, the difference being that they were poised and ready to go out and *start* fires.

Anlyn had instructed them to proceed as planned if their asteroid was empty, to just move in and set up ambushes. In many ways, it might make for a smoother mission.

The line moved forward as another squad filed into the fake rift. The members of each group went in two seconds apart, just like when she, Edison, and Ryke had jumped down from the Bern ship to *Parsona*. As they shuffled forward, the nervous chatter in each group fell silent. Ryke, Walter, and Molly stood by the glowing control console to one side, overseeing the coordinates being fed into the platform.

There was another surge forward, and Anlyn could clearly see the groups ahead disappearing into a dark cleft between two glowing trees, a convinc-ing illusion. Yet another surge, and then there was only one group left ahead of them. Ryke waved his arm, directing each member forward while Walter peered into his little computer, a sneer lit up from its dim glow. The coordinates were changed, and the group ahead moved into the rift one at a time.

Six seconds later, she and Edison were up. Ryke waved. Anlyn caught a darting glance from Walter and saw a worried smile on Molly's face. Each image was a flash from her surroundings, giving her a strobe-like consciousness of all that whirled around her. She gripped her pistol tightly with one hand and pulled her visor down with the other, just in case the garage was open when they arrived. Edison lumbered ahead and into the rift. A perfect shadow took him.

Anlyn counted:

One.

She whispered a call to the Horis for luck.

Two.

And she followed.

○ ○ ○ ○

Admiral Saunders and his two highest-ranking officers comprised the last group of three to step through the rift. Saunders remained skeptical about the mysterious object, even as the long queue ahead of him was swallowed up. He half expected to step between the trees and find his crewmen on the other side, stumbling around in the darkness.

But then it became his turn, and the one they called Doctor Ryke waved him forward. Saunders strode through the glowing gap . . .

Half a galaxy away, Saunders fell to Earth. He had just enough time in the air to feel a twinge of guilt for the nature of his arrival. He materialized a meter off the ground and landed with a squishy and awkward thud on top of Senator Kennedy's grave. Along with his burning conscience for such a rude, albeit necessary, landing came a dozen internal stings from the rain his body absorbed out of the Washington sky. Becoming one with the droplets caused flaming sensations like heartburn, only in every part of his body: his arms, legs, and one in his head that felt like an ice-cream headache.

Saunders grimaced in pain as the air beside him popped, followed by a wet splash. He peered through the rain at Commander Sharee as she fell to her knees on top of Robert Kennedy's grave, her face contorting in agony as she suffered the same internal burns. Lieutenant Robinson came in next, right on John Kennedy's plot. Saunders's second-in-command landed gracefully, a puddle splashing up around his navy blacks, his face as stoic as ever.

Molly's rift had worked. Defying everything he knew about interspace travel, the three navy veterans had been magically whisked clear across the galaxy, back to the epicenter of their Naval Empire and the Galactic Union. Saunders's tactical brain couldn't help but think what a military boon such knowledge would bring. He had to force himself to remember the importance of his *current* mission, his brain whirling with potential uses for these rifts.

The three crewmembers checked in with one another, grim smiles on all their faces. They then trudged through the soggy grass toward one of the many twisting concrete paths, their boots and pants mud splattered and their hair soaked. In a heavy silence, they marched up a wet walkway through Arlington National Cemetery, white tongues sticking up through the green hills all around them as if catching the rain.

Just as they had expected, the cemetery had been a perfect place for them to arrive. It was the nearest known coordinates to the GU's capital where taboo could be relied upon to keep the air obstruction-free. Of course, Saunders was expecting plenty of *other* sorts of obstructions as their mission advanced. He and his two commanding officers might've been too old and unfit for the sort of combat the others would see, but they were well familiar with the bureaucratic dogfighting ahead of them.

As the trio stomped up the windy path, they headed for the kind of fight with which they were

more familiar. Fights where desktops were their bat-
tlefields, words their weapons, intrigue and decep-
tion their tactics, and lives were lost by the *billions*,
rather than the thousands.

○ ○ ○ ○

Molly watched the final group step into the rift
and fade into nothingness. The ensuing silence, the
heavy emptiness pressing down on the wooded clearing, nearly smothered her. The past day had been
a whirlwind of anxious thoughts, of competing chatter, of stomping boots and gun chambers clacking
back and forth. There had been a constant chorus of
Velcro being adjusted and readjusted . . . and now
all that remained was a comparative silence, making
the residual buzzing in her head all the louder. The
severity of what their small group had begun, the mission on which she had just launched so many brave
souls . . .

Molly shuddered and looked up through the canopy at the lights twinkling overhead. To try to crush *that*
fleet with a group camped out in the woods seemed
as likely as destroying a constellation of stars. The
humming in her head continued. In the silence of the
vast woods, she could begin to hear her doubts.

"I reckon that went well," Ryke said. He flicked a series of switches on the console, and its displays faded to black.

"What's the damage?" Molly asked, referring to their fuel supply.

"Only used up twenty percent of the tank. More than my calculations, but not by much. Each squad took more heavy gear than I would've liked."

Cat came up to help lug the large control console back into *Parsona*. They had only a few hours to put everything away before flying to the StarCarrier and doing it all over again with the missiles.

"But we still have plenty of fuel for the fireworks?"

"You bet."

Molly nodded and moved to collect the jump platform from between the trees, but Walter grabbed her arm before she could get there. She turned and saw his reflective skin glowing in the light of his portable computer. He looked up from its screen to face her.

"What is it?" Molly asked. Her Wadi flicked its tongue out at him and then scampered down her back and into one of the cargo pockets on her hip.

"The person in the computer needs you." He pointed to his handheld device. Molly reached for it, but he pulled it away.

"Inside," he said.

Shrugging, Molly went to collect the wires so she could spool them up on her way to the cargo bay.

"I'll get that," Walter said. "Ssee what your friend wantss."

"Thanks," Molly said. She rubbed Walter's head with one hand, his newly buzzed stubble scratching her palm. She had no idea what had gotten into him, but he had become incredibly helpful of late.

Molly hurried toward the ship, past Ryke and Cat. She kept one hand on the Wadi's pocket to minimize its jouncing. When she got to the cargo ramp, she saw Scottie and Ryn arranging the climbing gear across the deck in preparation of their descent through the Carrier.

"You guys about ready?" Molly asked on her way to the cockpit.

"Getting there," Ryn said.

Molly gave them a thumbs-up over her shoulder. Entering the cockpit, she made sure the speakers and mic were both switched on.

"Everything went well?" Parsona asked.

"From what we can tell, yeah. What'd you wanna see me about?"

"About?"

"You said you needed to speak to me."

"I did?"

"Yeah, Walter said you wanted me in here."

"That's odd. I'm looking at my recollections right now, and I don't see that exchange anywhere."

"That *is* odd," Molly said. She glanced over her shoulder as Cat and Ryke brought the control console inside.

"Maybe he's just playing games with you," Parsona said. "I saw him fooling around with those gruesome arms earlier. I really wish you'd get rid of—"

Molly missed the rest. She stomped through the cargo bay, her skin electric with the paranoia that Walter was up to no good. She swore, if he let her down one more time, she wouldn't care how many jams he squeezed them out of—she would kill him with her bare hands.

Stepping into the night air, she tried to calm herself by taking a deep breath. She didn't want to jump to conclusions. She felt the Wadi twirl in her pocket, trying to get comfortable, or maybe tumbling after its tail.

"Hey, Molly," Walter yelled, calling her from the other side of the ship.

She ducked under the starboard wing and followed the black wires as they rounded the thrusters and headed off toward the imaginary rift. One of the work lights was still on; she could see Walter standing in its pool of photons, his skin reflecting much of it back her way. He stood there, as still as he could be, holding a bundle against his chest.

It looked like a lumpy towel. Some leaves and small twigs stuck to it as if it had been dropped. Molly was storming in his direction, preparing to grill him for answers, when he spoke out, hissing:

"I wanna sshow you ssomething."

Two more long strides, and Molly saw it: the way the leaves were piled up ahead of her—one corner of the jump platform sticking out—the wires doubling back along the ground.

She saw it, but it was too late. Her feet hit the platform, and Walter's face flashed as he pressed something.

His computer screen winked to life.

And then Molly winked out of the woods.

29

DARRIN

The sensation of complete displacement rocked Anlyn's senses.

Jumping through hyperspace in a ship was nothing. The cockpit remained the same, even the view from the canopy was normally no more than a jiggling of lights as stars jolted like startled insects. Earlier that day, she had jumped from one cargo bay to another, but even that couldn't compare—the environs of one locale and the next were too similar.

With the jump to Darrin, however, her senses were totally rocked. The dark, cool forest exploded into light and heat. A fully lit hangar popped into being around her. She could feel air kept warm against the vacuum of space through her flight suit. It was like waking too fast from a deep dream. Anlyn's eyes struggled to adjust.

Crouched in front of her, she saw a blurry Edison. His visor was up, his eyes blinking rapidly. She nodded to let him know she was okay.

Edison moved to the side, and Anlyn saw a looming wall of thruster cones beyond him. It was Albert's new ship, a replacement for the one she'd stolen what seemed like forever ago. It had five thrusters, which she immediately pegged as one of the Darrin II designs. Not quite *Lady Liberty*, but then business probably wasn't going so well since Anlyn's emancipation.

She sized the ship up as she and Edison stole around it and toward the entrance to Albert's shop. They moved quietly and swiftly, or as much of the former as Edison could muster while Anlyn pushed her limits on the latter.

The door to the shop was unlocked, which meant Edison didn't need to use his sword to cut their way inside. The door slid back noiselessly, and Edison took the lead. And not just because of his bulk and the power of the strange weapon he carried, but because he had actually spent more time freely exploring the asteroid's corridors than Anlyn ever had. In a few days of being Albert's guest, he had been given access to the arms dealer's house in a manner never extended to his slave of so many years.

They passed through the lobby and opened the door to the living quarters, which squeaked as it recessed into the jam. Edison glanced back, and Anlyn thought she could see his flight suit rippling with nervous fur underneath. He shrugged, and they moved forward through the dimly lit hallway past the kitchen, leaving the kids' rooms behind.

They headed directly for the master bedroom.

○ ○ ○ ○

Albert woke with a start. Some noise—probably Luke rummaging in the kitchen—had disturbed his dreams. He listened to the sound of his wife breathing: deep, peaceful snuffles. He rolled over gently, pulled the covers up to his shoulder, and wiggled his face close to her hair to breathe in the calming scent of her shampoo.

Then the bedroom door opened, letting in a spill of light from the hallway. Must've been Jenni who woke him, having trouble sleeping again. With a deep sigh, Albert rolled to the other side, pulling back the comforter to let her in, resigned to an evening of no sleep, to another long night of bruised shins from her infernal, nocturnal, kicking—

The light in the hallway went out. Not out, exactly—it became *blocked* by something. Beneath Albert's confused and sleepy surface thoughts, something triggered an alarm. Some part of him knew, from night after night of repetition, that the amount of light shielded didn't match his little Jenni.

He reached for the lamp beside his bed, but the overhead light came on first.

And the thing from the hallway rumbled closer.

○ ○ ○ ○

The plan was to be generous, to give Albert the quick death he had done nothing to deserve. One shot from Anlyn's gun to the chest, another to the head, nothing said to his wife. No kids would be involved if it could be helped. They would grab the force field controls, get the ship, and make it to the rendezvous point. Quick and uncomplicated.

Edison did his part, bursting through the door, hitting the lights, making sure the room was secure, and getting to one side so she would have a clear shot.

But the barrier between her pistol's plasma and Albert's heart wasn't a physical one. That wasn't what stopped her. The real barrier, one she hadn't foreseen, was some internal system linking her brain and the tendons in her finger. It wouldn't allow the

406

latter to constrict. Anlyn took several steps forward, as if proximity would help her overcome the paralysis, but it just made things worse. She thought it would be easy, that the years of abuse, pain, and torture would steer her toward release, but the opposite was true. Albert's power over her came trembling back, reminding her how meek and subservient she had been.

Albert's eyes, meanwhile, grew wide as the terror of recognition coursed through him. His wife rolled over, one hand patting him, wanting to know why the light was on.

Albert remained speechless, but Gladys didn't. She squinted at the intruders, gasped, and then yelped and covered her mouth in surprise.

"You—" Albert muttered.

Anlyn's hand quivered. It was the same hand that had pulled so many other triggers, reducing man and machine to dust. It was once a hand infamous for its ability to kill, all at Albert's whim.

But she couldn't. Even as she focused on the years of starvation, of subsisting on a Wadi diet of nothing but water, she couldn't. Anlyn tried to feel the shackle around her withering ankle, tried to see Albert for all he had done to her, but all she saw was an old man in bed with his wife and two burglars standing over them.

Her hand slid down. The gun pointed away from Albert's chest.

Albert's arm moved beneath the blanket, a small mound creeping toward his waist.

The first to utter something was Edison, just a grunt of alarm. His hand moved swiftly as Anlyn screamed for Albert to hold still. Gladys yelled "Wait!" with her white and wrinkled hand extended over her husband, fingers splayed, body begging.

Edison roared.

He swung his arm down, whizzing past Anlyn. There was a loud pop, a surge of electricity in the air that Anlyn could feel through her flight suit. Edison flew back, grunting, the scent of charred fur coming from somewhere.

Gladys got hit by the surge as well. She flew from the bed with a yelp, taking the blanket with her.

That left Albert at the epicenter of the discharge, unmoving at first, his body exposed. He wore a set of pajamas Anlyn knew well, and she recognized the shimmer of his personal force field all along them, the glisten of hardened air and energy just like the barrier that gated his hangar bay.

Albert's hand rested on his belt, on the device that controlled the fields. His other hand moved up and down, patting his stomach, almost as if looking for something he'd misplaced. He tried to sit up—and a strange groan leaked out of his lungs.

He collapsed back into his pillow.

Something in the air caught Anlyn's attention. She saw it as Gladys began whimpering and sobbing. It was the handle of Edison's sword, hovering in midair, the end of it pointing directly at Albert. Following the tip, Anlyn focused on Albert again and saw where he was patting himself. She watched blood ooze from a crack in his form and gather behind the shimmer along his body, pooling up inside the force field that was doing more to hold Albert *together* than it was to protect him.

Edison reached over the bed and pushed Albert's trembling hands away. He deactivated the device on Albert's waist. When the force field released his buck-blade, the handle fell to the ground. Edison and Anlyn both jumped back from it, lest the invisible sword do something effortless and awful. On the other side of the bed, Gladys's soft whimpers grew to wails as the thin line seeping blood around her husband's waist opened like a purse.

Her wails blossomed to shrieks, and then to mad screams. Gladys reached for her husband, ignoring Edison as he removed the device from Albert's waist. She grabbed one of Albert's hands and pulled it to her cheek, but the movement just made things worse.

Albert's body yawned wide, spilling things. The mad screams turned to gagging noises and pants for air, to nausea and hyperventilation, to the sounds of primal fear and disgust.

Anlyn had hardly moved through it all. She watched in detached confusion, the gun in her hand still pointing somewhere between Albert and the floor.

"Vacate with haste," Edison said, reaching down to scoop up his blade and turn it off.

"I—"

"We have to go," he said in Drenard, pulling her toward the door.

Anlyn felt herself dragged back, away from the terrible scene, away from Albert's wide and motionless eyes staring up at the ceiling. Terrifying shrieks and accusations lanced at her as she stumbled back, shuffling and transfixed and trying to come to her senses.

It only got worse in the hallway, where they ran into the kids. Luke and Jenni stumbled out of their rooms with sleepy eyes and frightened mouths to see what was wrong with their mother.

Edison shouldered them aside. Anlyn followed in his wake, the look on both of the kids' faces seared into her memory as sudden recognition seized them, their young brains putting together the horrific sounds from the bedroom with the unexpected presence of their father's former slave, running free.

Anlyn hurried after Edison. A dozen words of regret and apology choked up inside her, all crammed in her throat as they tried to swim past the labored gasps of air heading the other direction.

Out in the hangar bay, Edison found the ship unlocked, just as they'd expected. Not needing to cut their way inside meant they could finally remove their helmets. Anlyn popped hers off as she made her way to the cockpit. She finally managed to swallow down a gulp of air, her first in what felt like forever.

Edison brought up the ramp and got ready to lower the force field while Anlyn settled into the pilot's seat, her body still quivering, her mind continuing to race over what had just happened.

Then she thought on what lay ahead of them, the mission to return to Lok and face the Bern, and she settled on an awful truth:

This had been the easy part.

30

LOK

"Molly? Walter?"

Cat swept the portable spotlight across the edge of the clearing, looking for any sign of them. She'd found the jump platform where one of them had dropped it halfway back to the ship, but she could find no trace of where they'd gone afterward. She played the light across the trees one more time, throwing shadows deep into the woods, and then powered it down to save the battery. She returned to the platform, disconnected the four wires, and carried it back to the ship to share her lack of results with the others.

"Nothing?" Scottie asked.

Cat shook her head.

"Were they . . . ?" Ryn made a rude gesture with his hands, which Cat broke up with a slap from hers.

"Absolutely *not*," she said.

"How'dya know?" Scottie asked.

"Because we've had girl talks," Cat said.

That was too much for the boys. They roared with laughter.

"You . . . " Scottie snorted. "*Girl* talks?"

More guffaws from both of them.

"Youguysareassholes.I'mworriedaboutourfriends, and all you—"

"Hey, Cripple!"

Cat turned to see Ryke standing in the entrance of the cockpit. He waved her over with one hand, his other one tugging on his white beard. He was the only person who could, in some magical manner, call her "Cripple" in a way that sounded nice.

"Where'd you go?" she asked Ryke. "I thought you were gonna help me look for them."

"I was. I mean, I *am*. Or I did." He stepped to the side and ushered Cat into the pilot's seat.

"There has to be some kind of mistake," Parsona said through the radio.

Ryke waved Parsona off as if she could see him. He pointed to the SADAR screen in front of Cat.

"What is this?" Cat asked. "Signature traces?" She dialed out the range and got rid of two of the overlays. The controls were similar to ships she had run, but with way too many options and readouts for her to see past.

"Two jumps," Ryke said, pointing. "Here and here. Both less than forty kilos. Both to roughly the same spot."

"Is that a moon?"

"It's that big ship up there."

"Do *what*? Why would Molly jump there? I don't understand."

"She wouldn't," Parsona said.

Cat turned to Ryke. "Did you know about this? How did you think to look here?"

He gestured to the screen. "Because this is where I always look for people." He said it with a hurt tone. "And plus, there was something about that boy—"

"You don't trust him either?"

"I don't know about that, only . . . he said we had twenty percent of our fuel in captivity." Ryke held up his small reader. "I show nineteen point nine two eight."

"So he rounded up?"

Ryke looked at her as if she'd gone mad, or had struck him with a physical blow. "You think he's the sort to *do* that?" The whiskers above his lip flapped with a disgusted puff of breath.

Cat rolled her eyes. "Oh, gimme a break."

"Molly hinted to me many times that Walter couldn't be fully trusted," Parsona told them.

"When was this?" Cat asked.

"Let me check our prior conversations . . . Forty-seven times over the past four and a half weeks. Most recently, yesterday at eight thirty-two. Another time earlier that morning at—"

"Okay, I get it," Cat said. She looked to Ryke. "So, how do you read this?"

He leaned forward. "Two objects, less than forty kilos each—"

"No, not that. I mean, do you think the Palan is working for the Bern? Did he make a mistake? Is he looking for adventure, what?"

"Oh. Hmm. Hadn't thought about that. I was just excited to have found them."

"That's not *finding* them." Cat jabbed a finger at the SADAR. "That's locating where they *used* to be!"

"What in the world is going on in here?" Scottie asked, squeezing into the back of the cockpit.

"More *girl* talk?" Ryn hollered from the galley, followed by snorts of laughter.

"Shut it," Scottie told him. He turned to Cat, all the levity drained from his face at the sight of her. "What's going on, Cat?"

"Molly's gone."

Ryke tapped the SADAR. "Jumped into orbit," he said.

"Do *what?*"

Ryn squeezed in behind Scottie. "Who's gone where?"

"Why would she *do* that?" Scottie asked.

"She *wouldn't*," Parsona said again. "She's been abducted."

"So what do we do?" Cat asked the others.

"We need to tell the Underground," Ryke said.

"And what? Have them put out a missing persons report?"

"No, but they have all our translators. They can at least keep an ear out. Besides, they need to know she's in that big ship."

"We don't have time for this," Ryn said.

"I'll be damned," said Cat. "Don't you start on—"

"No, he's right," Scottie said. "How many hours before the pilots jump back? At dawn, right? If that monster is still in the sky, and if the navy geeks are right that it's what sent them crashing down, then we need to get to the StarCarrier's missiles—"

"Flank that," Cat said.

"Cat, be reasonable for just a second. We need to—"

"You wanna send bombs in *after* her? You wanna blow up the thing she just jumped into? Flank you, Scottie."

Everyone fell quiet. Old friends looked down at each other's boots.

"I'm sorry," Cat whispered. "It's just—"

"No, I'm sorry, too," Scottie said. "But we started a war tonight, Cat. We've all been here before. Hell, you especially. And look, we're friends and all, but we knew the chances going into this, right? We know what happens to friends in war—"

"Yeah," said Cat, finishing his thought for him. "Friends die."

31

NEAR DARRIN

The hijacked ships jumped into the rendezvous point near Darrin, one after another. Each successful arrival was celebrated, and they held out hope for the others. But after three hours, the gathering fleet realized two of the crews wouldn't be joining them. There weren't any reliable reports to explain what had gone wrong, but one of the squads saw an asteroid base explode as they were leaving the system, which accounted for one group. Anlyn gave the other missing group as much time as she could while the rest of the ships locked up, swapped engineers, made modifications to the drives, tended to small wounds, and distributed the fuel and supplies evenly.

The newly trained mechanics moved from one engine room to another, following Ryke's wiring schematics and uploading the new firmware he'd provided. They were short one Callite engineer, who had been in a group gone missing, which meant extra work for Edison. Anlyn ferried him from one ship to another while his dexterous claws made quick work of the modifications. She looked for any sign of trauma in him, any hint that he had been affected by Albert's death the way she had, but it was either missing or very well hidden.

The third ship they locked up to in their queue of modifications was *Lady Liberty*, which had been retrieved from its hidden orbit deep within Darrin II's asteroid belt. As Anlyn and Edison switched ships with the crew, she noted a hint of guilty relief from the others at having gotten the safer assignment. Little was said between the two groups as they filed past each other in the cramped airlocks.

Anlyn hadn't expected it, but walking through *Lady's* cargo bay and entering the cockpit felt nearly as bad as her first flight in that Bern craft, back at the Great Rift so many seeming sleeps ago. Gone were the slave chain and the eyebolt that had held her for so many years, removed by Edison prior to Molly and Cole's trip to Earth. But everything else was intimately familiar: the controls and readouts, the screens and portholes, all the walls of her old prison that somehow seemed to contain an entire other life she'd known. It was like walking back into some prior existence that had been stolen, that she could never get back, even after the death of the man who had taken it from her.

As she settled into the worn seat, Anlyn was thankful for the task of locking with more ships while Edison performed modifications on the remaining hyperdrives. She needed to do something rote with her body while her mind scrambled for purchase. Looking down at her hands, how they trembled so, Anlyn couldn't imagine going into battle in such a state, much less attempting to lead so many others. The sudden lack of confidence was unsettling. For countless years, she had flown into combat knowing she would win, and she had been able to do so almost on autopilot. She had formed a habit of warfare in order to avoid punishment and pain. She had fought without caring, and so fought without fear— without fear of failure.

As she went over the weapons systems, each powerful device a trophy from her days as the best customer-wrangler in either Darrin, she confronted the awful taste of preparing herself for a *different* kind of fight: a fight she cared deeply about. A fight she would be crushed to lose.

The difference was light years apart.

"Gloria leader, Wing Two."

Anlyn snapped out of her cold thoughts and keyed the radio on her helmet. "Wing Two . . . " Her words came out as whispers; she swallowed and tried to find her voice. "Wing two, go ahead."

"Requesting permission to assume command of one of Wing Three's ships," the pilot said. "The two missing flight crews were both in our wing, leaving us with eight."

Anlyn hesitated. She didn't know any of the pilots and only knew what a few of their ships were armed with. As skilled as she had been in a cockpit, she had always flown into battle solo, never with even so much as a wingman. Her stomach sank; she could feel the back of her neck thrum as her heart raced and pounded.

Molly was meant to do this, she realized. *My thirst for revenge has cursed everything. This has all been a mistake.*

Lady Liberty seemed to do a barrel roll as her mind reeled. She even wondered if she'd upset the prophecy somehow. She was no human, just a Drenard. Did that *mean* anything?

"Gloria leader?"

Anlyn keyed her mic. "Uh, negative, Wing Two. I'm transferring two of my squadron to you. Wings Two through Four will go in with a full complement of ten. All wing leaders copy?"

"Four copy."

"Three copy. And we have just one drive left to modify over here."

"Wing Two, here."

"Two, go ahead."

"Gloria leader, that leaves you with just eight ships."

"Copy that," Anlyn said.

She silently wished she could give up even more.

•• Lok ••

"We could just as easily argue about this on our way to the Carrier," Scottie told the others. "We need to get a move on before the fleet from Darrin gets back and finds that big ship still up there."

Ryn grunted. "Hell, *they* can argue about it all they want. *We'll* be climbing down to the armory."

Ryke stared up at the ceiling and scratched the thick, white tangle of beard below his chin.

"What's on your mind, doc?"

"Nothing. Just . . . theoreticals."

"Well let's hear 'em," said Cat.

"It doesn't apply, sorry. It's just a problem Arthur and I were working on. This would've been one of its uses if we'd ever gotten it to work."

Cat took a step closer. "Do I have to throttle it out of you?"

Ryke shook his head. "You wouldn't understand half of it. Besides, it ain't workable."

A look from Cat, and he held up his hands, preparing to explain.

Scottie and Ryn must've seen the look as well—they stopped their impatient shuffling and crossed their arms, hugging themselves still.

"We were working on a way to bring people back from raids instead of using the skimmers." Ryke turned to Cat, who had been on her fair share of raids in hyperspace. "We had just lost another lad due to a frozen locator, so we started thinking outside the box in a big way. The idea we came up with was to create a small rift, like the kind I made back in my house, the very kind the Bern are using now—"

"What, and you would just step through that rift and grab someone from the other side?"

"Theoretically. Problem is, we never figured out how to make a rift that isn't grounded to hyperspace on one side, but not the other. When one object is scurryin' about—like the surface of Lok for instance—you can compute the blasted equations and link up between here and hyperspace. But between two *moving* objects, like Lok and that ship up there, it just can't be done. It's like in physics, going from a two-body solution to a three-body—" Ryke frowned and narrowed his eyes. He rubbed his whiskers. "See? I'm losing ya, right?"

"Well, what was your idea, then?"

"It's useless, really. The idea was you could open a rift from your location to hyperspace, jump someone to the other point, and have them open a rift to the same spot in *hyperspace*." Ryke meshed his fingers together. "Basically, you would try to sandwich the two rifts together, allowing you to step right through."

"Like the two rifts we used in your house that one time?"

Ryke nodded. "Only the rifts would be far apart over *here* and near together in hyperspace, the *opposite* of what we did back then."

Cat ran her hands up over her face. "But you'd need a console on both sides, right?"

Ryke nodded.

"So this helps us none."

"That's what I tried to tell you!"

Ryke scanned their faces. There was no sound in the cockpit for a long while. He scratched his beard.

"We need to try *something*," Parsona said, her voice cutting through the tense silence.

"I know," said Cat.

"But what?" Ryn asked, shrugging. "Wouldn't Molly just want us to continue on? I mean, this *was* her plan."

"I know what we need to do," Cat said.

Everyone turned to her.

"You guys need to go ahead to the Carrier. Take out as many ships as you can with the missiles. Try to wound the big ship, maybe send some bombs up, but away from where Molly jumped."

"And what're *you* gonna do?" Ryn asked.

"You guys are gonna send me up first. Right now. With the platform."

"Where?" Scottie asked. "To that big-ass ship? You want us to send you up *after* them?"

Cat nodded. "A meter or two from their coordinates, to the side and up." She turned to Ryke. "I'll radio back her condition and coordinates. Maybe it'll be something you can use."

"No," Ryke said. "No way. It won't do any good, and we'll just be tossing your life after hers. Besides, you're the only one of us who can fly this ship, so even if you have a death wish, you aren't as expendable as you like to pretend."

"Actually," Parsona said, "that's not true."

The gathering looked toward the dash, as if meeting the ship's gaze.

"What's not true?" Scottie asked.

"That Cat's not expendable?" Ryn laughed.

"No, that Cat's the only person here who can fly me," Parsona said. "*I* can."

426

32

FINAL BETRAYAL

Molly stomped toward Walter in the black of wooded night, preparing to grill him about why he'd lied about her mom needing her—and then the world vanished in a flash of light. She suddenly found herself floating, her legs pedaling for the forest floor, but finding nothing but air.

Bright air.

Her brain rebelled from the jarring assault, from the sudden and drastic change in environment. Her vision seemed off; the pungent odor of the forest was gone; even the feeling of the cool and damp air on her skin had gone away. Her every sense lurched, groping for what wasn't there, recoiling from the new things that were.

And then that discombobulated instant, that frozen moment of unfeeling confusion, was shattered as Molly's toe caught steel decking. Her knee crashed down, her palms smacking cold steel, her body sprawling clumsily after.

The air went out of her lungs. Molly rolled over, clutching her knee, a small cluster of dried leaves crackling at her back. Her startled Wadi bolted out of its pocket-cave and shook its head, its scent tongue whipping through the air.

Above her own groans, Molly heard a muted pop of air followed by the thud of another body crashing into steel. Lifting her head and squinting in a harsh light her nighttime eyes had not yet adjusted to, she saw another form through a glass partition:

Walter.

Molly sat up, her head still spinning from the jarring relocation. She cupped one hand above her eyes, shielding them from the overhead lights while they adjusted. Three walls of glass and one of steel surrounded her. Walter looked at her through one of the clear walls; he was in an adjoining holding cell of sorts. By his side he held a towel with a thin arm— one of Byrne's arms. With the other, he slapped at his prison walls, his complexion shiny with confusion.

"What have you *done?*" Molly yelled at him through the glass.

He seemed as clueless as she. He glanced around as if he expected to see something or someone. Then his face lit up; he patted frantically at his flight suit, reached into one pocket, and extracted a bit of red fabric.

Molly rocked back on the balls of her feet and fell onto her butt. Her mind reeled. She watched Walter through the glass as he lined the seam up in back, pulling the band into place. His brow furrowed in a mask of concentration, of thoughts forced to the surface. It was a look Molly remembered well from their time on Drenard. But nothing else about her predicament made sense. The Wadi turned circles in her lap, obviously agitated. Molly turned to the hallway beyond one of the glass walls. Sensors and cameras twitched on extended arms, their eyes winking with red lights. She wasn't sure if it was the cameras or Walter's thoughts that brought them, but their hosts didn't take long to arrive.

Four uniformed men strolled into view, weapons lolling in hip holsters. They lined up along the hallway and stood frozen as statues.

Through the transparent cubes stretching off beside her, Molly could see a fifth figure walking their way. He was a stick of a man, and his long strides seemed a bit . . . *off*. It took Molly a moment to realize it wasn't his legs that made the gait seem strange: it was the lack of swinging arms.

He marched past Molly's cell without even looking her way. He nodded toward the glass wall before Walter.

Two of the uniformed men moved forward. One of them waved his hand in the air, which caused the partition to lift into the ceiling. Walter seemed relieved. He brushed imaginary dirt off his flight suit as if removing the embarrassing stain of having been unfairly incarcerated.

His smug expression melted, however, as the guards seized him. They produced a set of restraints—metal bands with a silver cord between them—and clasped them on Walter's frantic wrists. They then pulled him into the hallway.

Molly could hear him hissing in frustration through the thick glass partitions. She watched as one of the guards bent and retrieved Byrne's arm. He rummaged around in the towel and extracted the other and then turned to the former owner of the arms, smiling, and Molly realized where she was. She was with the Bern, up in their fleet. The fact registered without making sense.

Byrne nodded to the man holding his arms. He jerked his chin to the side, and Molly watched intently, wondering if they were going to reattach the things right there, if he was going to torture her with them once again, if her destiny was to be choked to death by those hands and somehow she had teased fate or delayed it.

But the guard didn't even pause by Byrne. He ran urgently past Molly's cell and on down the hall, as if those arms would save someone's life if they arrived and were transplanted in time.

One guard was left holding Walter by his restraints. Two others came for Molly. The glass wall slid up, and they entered her cell brandishing another set of the metallic cuffs. Byrne stood behind and between them, helping form a wall. Molly backed up against the steel panel behind her, feeling her body tingle with the urge to fight, to claw and lash out, to scream and kick, to die in that box rather than be taken anywhere. A million ways to move surged through her at once, all the lessons she'd learned at the Academy, the new things Cat had taught her, all those things canceling one another out.

She stood—frozen and bewildered—as they reached for her. The only thing she was aware of was the Wadi, which had returned to its cave in her hip pocket. She could feel it in there, vibrating and unable to act—just like her.

The only other thing spinning through her mind was this latest act of duplicity from someone she had thought was her friend. *That* was the true paralyzing force, the thing that made it impossible to move, to resist the guards as they reached for her. It was the powerful shock brought on by this betrayal, this *final* betrayal perpetrated by the infernal Palan known simply as . . .

Walter Hommul.

PART XXII

WALTER

"Not all that shines is golden."

~The Bern Seer~

33

PALAN · THE RAID

Heavy clouds pressed in over the solitary continent of Palan, draping a deeper level of darkness onto the black city below. Shadows upon shadows clung to Walter like a film of oil. They slid across his metallic skin in dark pools as he stole through a dimly lit alley. Just ahead of him, two senior pirates led the way, their twisting route curving through the blackest part of the Palan night. Behind, two junior pirates-in-training could be heard padding along after. Walter hurried to create some distance. He already considered himself more like those *ahead* of him than his fellow inductees behind.

Overhead, another roll of thunder tumbled through the city, reverberating off storefronts shuttered for the rains.

A chill ran up Walter's skin in response to the noise, his silvery lining pleading with him to get indoors. He ground his teeth and ignored the temptation to hide. There was more at stake for him that night than a mere promotion to full pirate.

The two figures ahead paused at an intersection and signaled for the others to stop. One of the moderators peeked around the corner while Donal and Pewder half-collided, half-clung to Walter's back. The two boys, both Walter's age, were frequent allies in his illicit raids. They had just enough potential to be useful to him—but not so much potential that they could try out for a clan higher up than the lowly Hommul.

Walter felt an unusual degree of annoyance at their presence. Almost as soon as the final test had begun, they had morphed in his unsettled mind into something other than onetime allies and future clan-mates. They had become rivals to be dispensed with, mere pawns in a game meant for much bigger things.

"Okay, let's go."

The lead pirate dashed across the empty street, leaping over the wide Palan gutters with practiced ease. The rest of the column followed; they ran between unoccupied cars leashed to floodposts and across old cobblestones worn smooth by the floods. The five shadowy forms slithered like a single snake into the alley behind the navy headquarters and gathered amid bags of rotting trash. The two instructors calmly indicated the locked comm box bolted to the rear of the building.

A grumble of thunder rattled nearby windows. The group had little more than half an hour for all three of them to pick the lock and hack their way through the human navy's defenses. If they passed this final test, they would win full status. If not, it would be another year of junior pirate menial duties and zero pay.

Walter leaned close with his pick set and noted the scratch marks around the locking mechanism where previous teams had conducted their tests. That year's graduation challenge was to piggyback the navy's long-distance array and send a prank message to Earth HQ. It was elementary stuff. The *hard* part was to perform with the rains looming and the moderators watching.

Walter chose the proper pick from his set, but before he began his work on the lock, he patted the ID card in his chest pocket to make sure it was still there. Nobody but him knew it yet, but that year's challenge was going to be quite a bit different from what the Clan leaders had planned. There was more to promote that night than Walter's status. The entire *Hommul* clan was about to be lifted by the floods.

And not even Walter knew how far . . .

•• TWO DAYS EARLIER ••

UNAUTHORIZED COMPONENT DETECTED_
PROGRAM WILL TERMINATE_
END OF TRIAL PHASE_

Walter hissed at the computer. He slapped its side with his silvery hand. Bending over the terminal, he tried another hack.

The machine beeped. The words INVALID ACCESS_ flashed across the screen, and then the entire unit began shutting itself down.

Now Walter was pissed. He shoved the keyboard aside, pulled out his multi-tool, and ducked behind the whirring unit. There was an access panel there. The first three screws came out easily enough—whoever had last worked on the thing had barely taken the time to hand-tighten them. The last one, though, was stripped bare; the business end of the screw was bored out and smooth, completely ruined by the previous attempt to fix the unit.

"Explains why they tossed it," Walter murmured to himself. He folded his multi-tool away and pried back the opposite corner of the panel with his deft fingers. He kept yanking on it, bending the panel in half until the head of the last screw snapped off and skidded across the floor.

"Flood me," Walter said.

He tossed the stupid panel aside, pulled his multi-tool back out, and shone its light into the Automated Breathing Machine's cavity. A motor inside began dying down, whirring to a pathetic stop. Soon after, the loud air pumps ceased operating. Walter could hear a cooling fan continue to run along in a wheezy rattle, the only other sound besides a steady beeping from the display screen warning him that the machine was powering down for good.

Walter traced the ribbon cable from the display back to a control board. The first thing he looked for was the line out to the speaker cable. He found it and gave the wires a quick snip, shutting the flank out of that stupid beeping.

With it stopped, Walter found he could breathe again, his flush of anger subsiding. Part of him wanted to reach in and mangle the blasted machine, but he couldn't do that. He needed to get it working again, and fast. He thought about it logically: The ABM was just an artificial lung, right? Beyond the security systems that forced users to pay the lease and upgrade the software, it was just a device for purifying and moving air. He felt along several wiring harnesses and tried to deduce their function. Entire mechanical systems had been replaced in the machine's belly over time. It looked as if three generations of Palans had been cobbling the device along from a poor selection of scraps. He could see parts that belonged to taxicabs, parts that might as well be in a space-ship, parts that looked as if they were hand-made right there on Palan. As for the pumps, there were two of them, but the original was little more than a rusted ball. The new one seemed to be working fine, but some sort of trial period had ended, and now it was being rejected like a poorly transplanted organ.

Walter studied the problem. He pulled the knife out of his multi-tool and scraped some of the rust off the original pump. It looked as if water coolant from above had dripped all over it for a period of time, destroying the mechanism. Even the electronics board was toast, all the solder connections black, bubbled, and touching. Walter forced his head into the cavity and studied the board more closely. Above him, the last cooling fan sighed to a quiet stop as the machine fully booted down. Walter felt a bead of sweat run through his stubbled head and trickle behind his ear. He stuck the point of his knife behind one of the sock-eted chips in the original pump board and gently pried it out.

The chip popped free, and he could see the socket had remained dry, even though the connecting pins were completely shot. He turned to the other, newer pump and found the corresponding chip. He pried it out and replaced it with the original, hoping to fool the component detector.

Nothing.

Walter smacked the pump with his fist and cursed. He had another vision of tearing the guts out of the machine, but the sensation soon drained away. He went back to the old pump and scraped around the base of another chip. He wasn't sure what he was doing, but at least it was *something*. At least she wouldn't be able to say he hadn't tried. He pried out the second chip, a little less delicately this time, and the small black rectangle of integrated circuit fell to the bottom of the unit.

"Flanking flanker!" Walter spat. He reached through the tangle of wire and hoses for the small chip and heard his mother groan in agony.

Walter pulled his head out of the machine and peered around its side. His mom, a half dozen tubes and wires snaking all around her bed, had begun to stir from the lack of air. She clawed feebly at the mask over her mouth, her eyes wide with fear. Walter felt the blood boiling below the surface of his skin. He felt a powerful urge to run to her, to hold her hand while she finally slipped away, but he couldn't. He wouldn't let the flanking machine outsmart him.

He dove back into the bowels of the antiquated unit, a medical outcast from some Terran world, no doubt donated to the residents of Palan to assuage away human guilt for otherwise ignoring them. Walter parted the cluttered web of wire and shone his light into the deep pit of the machine. It looked as if the floods themselves had once settled there. Bits of broken plastic and metal formed a jumbled layer in the bowels of the unit. The metal shavings from numerous drillings and cuts were sprinkled over everything, the shiny flakes turning to rust. A black slime seemed to hold it all in place, the drippings of grease and hydraulic fluids having turned into some tar-like substance. Walter played his light back and forth across it all, looking for an innocuous bit of black IC chip. He grumbled to himself while his mother gurgled behind him, asphyxiating. The machine seemed to spin around his head, his world tumbling out of control.

And then he saw it: a speck of black on a ball of orange rust. Walter reached down, his hand shaking with anxiety. He clasped the chip with trembling fingers, even though he had little hope that the piece would actually fix the flanking unit. It didn't matter. He just needed to be doing something, anything, fixing whatever he could.

He blew on the back of the chip to remove the flecks of rust before turning to the new pump. With his knife, he pried the corresponding chip out of the working control board and let the thing fall into the bottom of the unit. He pressed the rescued chip into the empty socket and waited.

Nothing.

Walter hissed to himself. He turned to his mother's bed, ready to deal with what he'd been putting off emotionally and mechanically for so many years, when he noticed he wasn't the only thing hissing. There was a whir of air coming from the breathing unit. A fan had begun spinning, and then a motor chugged to life. A worn belt squeaked over a poorly balanced flywheel. Walter turned to the screen, his heart thumping, and saw green phosphorous text burst across the display:

RESUME? YES/NO_

Walter hurriedly jabbed the "Y" and hit enter. The tubes leading away from the machine lurched and kicked as fortified air surged through them once more. He spun around to his mom, following the wires and tubes, and saw her arms falling to her bed and away from the fogged mask over her mouth. Walter let out a cry of relief, of sorrow and frustration and anger. He sat on the edge of the bed and held his mother's thin, feeble hand.

"It's okay," he told her. "Everything's fine."

As Walter consoled his mother, he looked from the blue veiny web beneath her silvery skin to the machine that had nearly let her down. He watched it chug and whir dutifully, and pictured himself ripping the flanking thing to pieces.

○ ○ ○ ○

Once his mother was settled and Walter had regained some semblance of trust in the machines keeping her alive, he stole out through the back door to get some air. The night was already muggy with the looming rains—it had the foul odor of mildew Walter had come to associate with poor pickings. What little tourism Palan got from nearby planets came in a rush right after the rains. Locals on Palan called the foreign invasion "second floods," and the great mounds of alley trash and filth deposited like seeds by these off-worlders would soon grow until they threatened to clog the streets in their eventual tumble toward the ocean.

For most junior pirates-in-training, the humid stench was a sign to lay low and watch for the rains. For Walter, it was a chance to have the city to himself, just him and the locals with their empty pockets and heads full of rumors. It wasn't that Walter had a dislike for money—nothing could be further from the truth—it was just that he had a powerful lust for anything valuable. And information could be a wondrous commodity.

Walter exited out of his mother's alley by the Regal Hotel. He glanced toward the lobby to see if the homeless and low-liers had begun moving in, but there was just the normal number of stragglers milling about in the flickering fluorescent lights. For him, the Regal lobby was the ultimate barometer for the weather. You could listen to several dozen predictors and prognosticators to try to time the next rain, or you could look to the Regal for a grand average of all those resources. It was a curious thing, a mob. They tended to heighten aggression, which made them look stupid, but they could also be more accurate than a lone expert, their individual ignorance somehow canceling one another out.

Walter watched one of the lobby's occupants stumble out into the street and nearly fall headfirst into the wide gutter. He shook his head at the thought of so many idiots providing him with reliable information.

He looked the other way down the street and considered heading toward his uncle's hideout, the Hommul clan's inglorious basement headquarters. If everyone was asleep, he could do some snooping or get started on the programming assignment he should've completed a month ago. That was what he would do: get cracking on his finals hack.

First, though, he decided he should go by the market to see if any of the booths had been left untended. He figured it wouldn't hurt to put off the programming another few hours. He turned toward the spaceport, padding softly past the sleeping cabbies in front of the Regal lest any of them wake and demand what fares he owed.

Walter's jaunt to the market played out like a pirate training session of sorts, complete with arbitrary and false-serious rules: the sporadic cones of light shining from overhead bulbs were to be avoided at all costs; loose pavement and noisy rubble needed to be spotted ahead of time, lest he be heard by any others roaming the night. Walter practiced these things as if his mother were watching him, the looming specter of her disapproval forcing him to hone the trademark abilities of a Palan pirate. No book reading for him, no sir. Not when anyone was around, anyway. It was hacking until you slept in a haze of code. It was picking the dozen locks on the front door while she watched from her bed, and doing it until he could make it slick as a key. It was going on raids, and smash-and-grabs, and in-and-outs, and bang-you're-deads with his uncles. It was whatever it took to keep her alive and happy. Walter had become just one more machine chugging and hissing and propping up her sickness, delaying the inevitable.

He wouldn't have minded the career he'd been born into, of course, but if only he'd been born into it someplace else! Anywhere but Palan, that world of filth built on a bedrock of lies and peopled by a race who had evolved the ability to smell a fib. What did that say about the last few million years of their biological development? Nothing good, that's what.

For a long time, Walter had complained about the irony of his people's heightened olfactory sense and the malodorous nature of their planet. Then, one day, it had dawned on him with the suddenness of the floods: the stench they made with their garbage was no accident. It was a blanket, like the shroud of darkness he stole through toward the market. It was fostered by the collective unconsciousness of so many habitual liars, all terrified of anyone sniffing what they were thinking. The putrid stench that drove everyone else away? It was the smell of Palan guilt hiding under a fog of rot.

And Walter hated it. He hated the idea of living out his life on the planet's only natural continent. To him, the butte of bedrock rising out of Palan's oceans was no cleaner than the massive rafts of detritus that drifted to and fro on the water's rough surface. If it were up to him, he would use his wits in other ways. He would've stayed in school, kept acing his tests, and won a minority scholarship to a Terran world, a world where he could reek of guilt and nobody would ever smell it. A world so ripe with easy pickings, he could steal without even knowing he was doing it.

His mother would kill him for even considering such a scheme. The worst beating he'd ever gotten from her was after she'd found his stash of books in the ceiling tiles. Of course, lying about them had contributed to the blows, but she was plenty angry to start with.

"Out to enrich just yourself, are you?" his mother had asked him. "Don't care about the clan your father made, is that it? Ready to run off and live like a human boy, pink and stupid?"

"I was gonna sell them," Walter had said—a lie far too ripe for a day so soon after the floods.

Years later, Walter had to grind his teeth as he recalled what had followed. The memory made the moist Palan air adhere to his skin, beading up and dripping through his clothes. Walter wiped his forehead and smeared his palms on the seat of his pants.

"Floods take me," he murmured to himself. "Floods take me the flank out of here."

Walter skipped over the last gutter and entered the markets. He quickly scanned the quiet booths and sparse crowds. There weren't any shuttles standing upright beyond the collection of tents, no passengers coming or going, so the nighttime trading appeared to be as slow as it got. On the surface, at least.

He knew from accompanying his uncle to other, more clandestine deals, that this was a busy time for lucrative transactions. Walter cared little for such senior pirate scheming. Who was in charge which month meant little to him and impacted his life almost none. His own clan was too small for it to matter which table the crumbs tumbled from, if they even tumbled at all.

Weaving his way through the center of the market, Walter scanned the shabbier tents for easy pickings. Each one had a guard posted out front, usually a family member from the tent's clan, but like Walter, all boys couldn't be expected to care for the family business. He was looking for someone shirking his duty when he felt a bad presence nearby—a faint whiff of ill intent drifting up from behind.

Walter scooted over to get behind a bald Palan walking slowly in the same direction as he. Surreptitiously, he glanced up at the back of the man's silvery head and scanned the fishbowled reflection of the crowd behind him.

There! A figure slid over in Walter's wake and ducked behind another late-night shopper. Walter matched pace with the bald man while he scanned the crowd ahead of him. He needed someone fat. Why weren't there more fat people on Palan?

Ah, a man in a trench coat, the next best thing. Walter took a last glance at the silvery dome ahead of him and then slid around the bald gentleman. He used him for cover as he angled for the guy in the trench coat heading the opposite direction. As soon as he passed the second man, he whipped around and fell into his shadow, heading back the way he'd come. He hugged the Palan's elbow, swinging wide as whoever was tailing him strolled past behind his or her own escort.

As soon as his stalker went by, Walter jumped out and jabbed the kid in the ribs, his knuckles pointed sharp. The unsuspecting youth jumped and hollered with the fear of discovery. Walter smacked him on the back of the head for good measure. "What the flank are you *doing*, Dugan?"

"Godsdamnit, Walter, that hurt!"

Walter jabbed him with another knuckle between the ribs. "I asked you a question."

"Floods, man, I was just practicing for next week. I was gonna come ask you if you wanted to play some Rats with me and the other trainees."

"You were coming to ask me to play a game of Rats," Walter repeated.

"Yeah, I swear." Dugan jerked his head toward the deeper markets. "Dalton's uncle has the gambling parlor shut down until after the floods. He's letting us use the pits."

"And I'm invited?" Walter sniffed the air while Dugan thought about his answer.

"Of course," Dugan said.

Walter smiled. He forced himself to think about cool baths and empty alleys and all the refreshing, happy things he kept at the ready. He exuded positivity and peace for Dugan's nose. It was the Palan way of thinking: Sustain a world of lies on the mind's surface and dwell on them while conversing. Use the back of your brain to *hear* the words of your speaker and form a reply, but do not actually *think* on them. Thinking on them causes the body to know it's lying. If, however, you think on *other* things and just spit out your replies without truly contemplating them, you come out smelling fresh as a flood. Walter was better than most at pulling the trick off. One more talent for his dearest mother to be proud of.

"Lead the way," Walter told Dugan with a smile. As he said it, he pictured being taken to piles of gold and heaps of fresh food—not to his fellow trainees.

o o o o

It wasn't Walter's first time in the casino, but it certainly felt like it. Without the haze of smoke and the perpetual dinging and clacking from the luck boxes, the place had an altogether different vibe. The absence of a crowd made the stained and threadbare carpets, littered with tables and silent machines, feel like a warehouse just storing things. Walter followed Dugan through the deliberate maze of gambling stations, back toward a distant ruckus.

As they rounded the poker tables with their individual, airtight, and odorless Palan-proof playing pods, Walter saw what looked to be his entire training group, three dozen junior pirates or so, gathered around the Rats pits. Those not playing were yelling advice to their comrades, pointing and shouting. Walter followed Dugan as the boy strolled up to the pits and weaved his way through to the railing.

"Look who decided to join us," someone close by said.

Walter ignored whoever it was and leaned out beside Dugan to see who was winning.

They were playing one-on-one, just two boys matching wits and skill. Each of them had a long Rats pole in his hands with its small, flat paddle on the end. The pit between them was full of a few feet of water that had turned brown and foul with the signs of several rounds played. There were two rats paddling on the surface of the water, their noses twitching for air. One had been painted silver, the other black. The goal was to drown one's own rat before the opponent killed his.

Walter watched with some interest as the two boys jousted from opposite ends of the oval pool. Neither kid seemed keen on playing straight offense by just holding his rat under. They took turns reaching out and knocking the other boy's paddle away from his rat while corralling their own animal closer. Wielding sticks a dozen feet long was taxing after a while, so both boys had the same strategy of trying to get the rats to *their* side of the pool where they could wear out their opponent by forcing them to use a longer reach.

Someone bumped into Walter from behind.

"Excuse me, your heinous!"

Several of the boys nearby laughed.

"I mean, your *highness*."

Walter turned and gave Dalton the finger. He'd know his distant cousin's dry voice and even drier wit with his nose cut off.

"So, the pirate queen extended your curfew, eh?"

Dugan turned from the action in the pits. "Flank off, Dalton." He yelled it over a sudden round of jeers from the boys paying attention to the match.

"I'm talking to my *cousin*," Dalton said with a wry smile.

"You're being a dick," Dugan said.

"Nonsense. Why would I be rude to my future king?"

Walter ignored him and returned his attention to the pits. Both rats were gone, the boys' paddles jostling beneath the water's surface. He couldn't tell who had what, but the crowd was furious with excitement.

"Forget him," Walter told Dugan. He pointed up to the scoreboard where the vitals for the silver rat could be seen. Its heartbeat was racing. The betting line began to tilt in that boy's favor, and a flurry of wagers took place all around, little of it with any potential payoff now that the end was near. The boy with the black paddle released his rat and began pushing and prodding the silver paddle, hoping to free the drowning Earth mammal and win it a precious breath. The silver player had excellent control, however. He leaned into his end of the paddle, flexing it as he poured on his weight.

The black rat bobbed to the surface and began panting furiously for air, kicking at the turbulent water with its tiny paws. The silver rat breathed its last. A steady buzz and flat pulse relayed its victorious demise.

Cheers and groans mixed as the game went final. Walter watched money fly back and forth between the boys, the sight of so much of it making him feel a rush of giddiness. Despite the half-truths of Dalton's jabs, the reality was that Walter stood to inherit the poorest clan in the history of Palan pirates. What little his father had been able to forge had just as quickly been scrapped by the ineptitude of his uncles. And his mother, despite her drive and brilliance, had been sidelined by a type of pneumonia likened to a slow, inexorable drowning. The running joke, for those who were able to laugh about it, was that her clan was going to go down with her.

Dalton, meanwhile—the descendant of a Hommul clan outcast from so many generations ago—had now been born into the once maligned and now dreaded Smiths clan, which had ruled Palan for dozens of floods. The ironic reversal was not lost on Walter at all. Perhaps that was why he longed to be exiled from his own people: He was envious of what that long-ago action had done for Dalton's great-grandfather and by extension his greatest rival.

While Walter mused clan history, he scanned the crowd of forty to fifty boys arranged around the uneven rail of the Rats pit. He wondered which of them his uncle and mother would be able to land for the looming finals. The Smiths, by currently holding power, would get the top picks. The Savages would get next, and so on. None of the higher clans would take Walter, no matter how highly he had scored in prior examinations. Too many clans had been sabotaged from within as distant kinsmen wrested power for their own blood clan. At least it meant Walter didn't have to do anything to try to impress the clan leaders or his peers. There *was* that.

"You're nexsssst," Dalton hissed into Walter's ear, in English.

Walter reached back, shoved the boy away, and then dug into his ear to remove the invasive whisper.

"I challenge Walter Hommul!" Dalton yelled over the pits.

Walter watched the group of boys look up from settling their bets.

Murmurs grew to cheers.

Dugan elbowed Walter and hissed some foul-smelling good luck.

"I just *got* here," Walter complained.

Boys normally waited hours for their chance to play.

"And it's my uncle's place," Dalton said, "so I can challenge whoever I like."

With a dozen prods and pushes, the gathering of boys ushered Walter toward one end of the pool. He hissed at the crowd but found himself slotted into the little jut of railing leaning out over the black side of the pit. A ratpole was placed in his hands, and someone thumped him on the back of his head.

Above the pit, the scoreboard was reset to zero and the names "Hommul" and "Smiths" blinked across the LEDs. Dalton took his place in the silver slot and grabbed his paddle from another boy. He waved the long pole out at Walter, taunting him.

Walter held his own pole out and tapped the surface of the mucky water a few times, getting a feel for the heft of it. He'd played enough Rats in his day to wield a paddle with some skill. He could hold a twenty-foot pole with a ten-pound paddle at arm's length for half a minute, no problem. He also knew Dalton played every day and could do the same with one hand and for twice as long.

A countdown began on the scoreboard, and the crowd chanted along with the falling numbers. Walter tightened his grip on his paddle and glanced up at the underside of the scoreboard to follow the countdown. Dalton whacked Walter's paddle smartly, and Walter nearly dropped his pole into the water. He tightened his grip even further. When the crowd got to zero, a hole opened in the scoreboard and two rats fell out, each covered in paint. The animals clung to each other in a feisty, hissing, midair ball as they tumbled down and splashed into the pit.

The crowd erupted, and Walter and Dalton sparred from opposite sides, using their long paddles to draw the two frightened creatures closer to their own ends.

It was apparent from the start that Dalton was too strong for Walter. Walter could feel the boy's tugs and shoves through the shaft of his paddle. Already, the two splashing rodents were being drawn toward the other side, and the farther away they got, the less leverage Walter would have. He leaned against the rail, the unforgiving metal digging into his ribs, and locked his ankles around the posts to either side.

Dalton separated his silver rat out and pinned it underwater. Walter's black rat clawed at the surface, its whiskers twitching with deep gasps of air. Walter pushed the animal under, careful not to slap it on the head and get a foul called.

A groan erupted from the crowd as it appeared the two boys would play a game that tested the lung capacity of their rats rather than the wits of the players. Dalton had his rat underwater first, but more depended on what sort of breath each animal had gone down with and their individual lung capacity and tendency to panic while drowning. It did little to satisfy the spectators, but Walter felt perfectly comfortable with the game plan. If he lost, he could blame his defeat on the rat and no credit would go to Dalton.

"How much on yourself?" a boy yelled in his ear.

Walter looked at the betting board. The odds were almost even; Dalton had just a hair of an edge.

Even though Walter had only a few bucks on him, he couldn't *not* bet on himself.

"Two," he shouted over his shoulder.

As soon as Walter made the wager, Dalton changed the game, almost as if he'd been suckering him into betting. He let go of his own rat and slashed underwater with his paddle, whacking the side of Walter's pole. Walter felt his paddle slip off his rat. Both animals briefly bobbed to the surface, and the crowd erupted.

Walter fumbled for his rat, but Dalton had already pulled it farther away. The larger kid deftly shifted back and forth between both scrambling swimmers, waving them toward his side. Walter managed to push his rat under, but Dalton slapped him off it. Walter made a grab for Dalton's rat, but again was knocked aside. Back and forth they went, both animals heading toward the silver side of the pit.

There wasn't much Walter could do, he quickly realized. The bigger boy could always overpower him, doing pretty much whatever he wanted, especially as his leverage improved. He smacked Dalton's pole in frustration. Dalton pushed back and then quickly pinned his silver rat below the surface of the water. Walter did the same with his, but now he was using much more pole than Dalton. It would be child's play for Dalton to knock him off his rat and repin his own before it could break the surface and suck in another breath. It was the classic endgame for a dominant Rats position, and one that would cost Walter double his bet.

Dalton didn't disappoint. He slid his paddle to the side and whacked Walter's rat free. He then fumbled underwater for his own struggling animal as it bobbed toward the surface. He must've caught it, for he leaned back into his pole with no sign of the silver rat.

Walter's rat, meanwhile, bobbed to the surface before he could corral it. He got his paddle on its head and pushed it back down. His brain whirled with some way to overcome the boy's strength and leverage. As he pushed his rat to the bottom of the pool, he steered it nearer Dalton's paddle rather than try to pull it back closer to himself. As soon as it reached the bottom, he felt Dalton strike his pole again, pushing him off the animal.

Walter acted quickly on a sudden idea, a way to use Dalton's strength to his advantage. He felt his rat bobbing for the surface and pushed it back down, but not to pin it. He touched it to the bottom and then slid over and pinned *Dalton's* rat as it tried to swim up. He held the other boy's rat in place and waited while Dalton performed his own maneuvers beneath the murky water. No rat bobbed to the surface. Walter took his eyes off the poles and watched Dalton, who was sneering with concentration. He was holding *something* down right beside Walter's paddle and seemed intent on crushing it. Walter waited. Just as Dalton was about to look up at the scoreboard to check his rat's vitals, Walter yelled out: "Twenty on black!" Far more money than he had on him.

The crowd hissed. Dalton narrowed his eyes, and Walter could see his face grow dull with nerves and confusion. Walter's rat had half the breath of Dalton's, making it an odd wager. The other boy acted swiftly, taking another good swipe at Walter's pole, and Walter felt his paddle fly off the silver rat.

Dalton's rat.

He stirred the water furiously as if groping for the struggling animal, and the crowd began to chant Dalton's name. Walter caught a glimpse of the rat below the water's murky surface. He moved his paddle clumsily all around it, whipping the dirty water into a froth of wave and bubble, his seeming desperation a ploy to keep the color of the animal hidden while also allowing it to regain its breath. He fought the urge to yell out an even higher bet, knowing that would appear foolish and suspicious. Instead, he hissed and cursed at himself as he pretended to struggle with the long pole. The chants of "Dalton" and "Smiths" grew furious, the last filling the room with a powerful English-like hiss, which made the hair on Walter's head stand on end.

Walter had a brief moment of panic when individuals among the crowd began pointing up to the scoreboard and tugging on their neighbors. Walter didn't look himself, fearing Dalton would grow suspicious. He concentrated on his efforts to conceal the boy's rat while Dalton unknowingly worked to drown Walter's.

The end of the game was a confusing, riotous affair. When the flatline buzzer sounded, most of the kids erupted to celebrate their friend's victory, and money went flying from hand to hand. An observant minority, however, began working to undo the celebrations. The winner's light pointed toward *Walter*, and the scoreboard reflected a truth incongruent to their own eyes.

There was a moment of stunned silence before the next wave of yelling—of *angry* yelling—began. The kids shuffled bets around and looked sternly in Walter's direction.

Meanwhile, in the pit itself, a black rat bobbed up, its arms curled and lifeless. Nearby, a silver rat pawed at the rippled and muddy surface, looking for a way out.

Walter dropped his pole into the pits and did the same.

34

THE PITS

"You'd better run," a boy beside Walter suggested.

It sounded more like a threat than a warning. Walter scanned the crowd and realized it was a good idea. He also realized he wouldn't be seeing the $240 he'd just won on the twelve-to-one odds against. Nobody was amused with how he'd played the game.

As his pole splashed into the pit, Walter pushed his way out of a crowd still correcting their bets. Kids hissed and shouted at him as he forced his way through, but they weren't about to give chase until their money was squared. Walter ran up the steps toward the luck machines, turned, and scanned the crowd for Dalton. He saw the boy still in the silver out-crop, gripping the rail with both hands and sneering down into the water. For Walter, it was worth at least half the bet he was leaving behind. He spun around and wove through the maze of machines designed to rob men of their money and confidence, and out to the market beyond.

Walter blended in with the light stream of late-night shoppers and worked to slow his breathing. In the hush of the Palan night, the roar of the mob he'd just escaped rang as echoes in his ears. He had left his apartment looking for a bit of excitement and found more than enough to sate him for a day or two. Leaving the markets behind, he skipped over a gutter bridge and shadow-hopped his way back home.

Walter was in such a good mood as he passed the Regal and turned into the alley by its side that he nearly made a serious junior pirate gaffe. He entered the alley with a loud walk, along the edge of a cone of streetlight. There were only a few apart-ments behind the Regal, so the daily habit of finding it empty had him growing sloppy over time. If he hadn't seen the figure at the alley's end moments before the man turned around, Walter would've missed out on the heist of a thousand lifetimes.

By the time the man turned to survey the noise, Walter had flushed his skin to dull the sheen of his exposed flesh and moved quickly and silently into the alley's darkness. He stood motionless, his back against the rough brick of the Regal, while the man at the far end peered past him and out into the quiet street.

Walter waited.

Nothing on him moved, save his eyes. He picked out several darkened routes to his apartment door, just in case. He also sized up the figure crouching a hundred feet beyond his stoop. By his bulk, Walter pegged him as human, which was out of the ordinary for this time of the rains. He watched the man wipe his brow—and even though the humidity was creeping up, Walter sensed the gesture was as much from nerves as condensation. He took in deep sniffs of the alley's air, but the figure was too far away for him to pick up anything.

After a long moment of staring his way, the man turned back to something at his feet. Walter took immediate advantage. He danced through the shadows along the blackest route, halving the distance between him and the stranger. Crouching behind his apartment's crumbling landing, he peered through the flood-rusted rails and watched the man sift through the detritus in the alley's dead-end.

Finally, the man stood and scanned the alley. He shuffled noisily in Walter's direction and could be heard mumbling to himself as he passed. Walter tried to catch a glimpse of the man's face, but the figure happened to be glancing over his other shoulder as he hurried by. When he reached the end of the alley, the human looked one direction, started to head off the other way, stopped, and then hurried toward the Regal's entrance.

The pathetic display did nothing to undo Walter's disdain for humans. That such a dull, noisy, numb-nosed race prospered while *his* people languished could only be attributed to the unlucky geography of his planet. He knew from his own studies that Earth had many continents and very little ocean. Rains there came sporadically and rarely flooded. Give his people such a place and see who's naming other people's stars, then. Oh, he would *love* to hear a human throat attempt to gurgle his native tongue. And to think of never needing to hiss English again!

Walter stood from his hiding spot and glowered after the departed figure. His joyous mood from the game of Rats had eroded, marred by the presence of the human. He turned and crept down the alley to see if the man had left any traces of his curious actions, sniffing the air as he went.

The first thing he noticed was a reek of paranoia. The man had left behind a braided odor of lies of such density, only one living in abject terror of discovery—discovery of something *bad*—could have created it. That certainly got Walter's attention. He followed the scent to its locus: a heap of alley trash seemingly no different from the rest.

Walter stooped to inspect the bag. He wiggled its white plastic mouth open and peered inside. It looked to be normal trash: rotting fruit rinds, balls of paper, a tin can. Walter picked the bag up to look under it, but it was caught on something. He moved some of the neighboring trash out of the way and saw that the bag had been tied down to an iron rod poking out of the pavement. Someone didn't want the bag moved, even in the floods.

Walter peeked back inside at the garbage. He considered running to his apartment for gloves so he could sift through the foulness and then noticed something odd about the mouth of the bag. There were two layers. A bag within a bag!

Walter's heart raced with the series of discoveries. He knew, as surely as stumbling across a wallet in the market, that he was about to uncover treasures. He glanced over his shoulder at the mouth of the alley and began digging between the two plastic liners.

At the very bottom, behind the cool dampness of the mucky filth sitting inside the inner bag, he felt a cloth bundle. Walter pulled it out to see what he had lucked upon.

Clothes. A stupid navy uniform, but the pockets felt heavy. Walter reached in one and came out with a radio. He felt the urge to twist the power on, but radios were poison, too easily traceable. And besides, they were worthless unless you had friends with the same models. He chucked the thing over the wall at the end of the alley, taking delight in the sound of its splintering demise on the other side.

In another pocket, Walter found a neat surprise: A gun. Navy issue. He figured it would fetch at least what he should've won at Rats. He slipped the thing into his waistband and rummaged through the rest of the pockets.

Nothing. There was a row of medals above the breast of the jacket, so he took those, just in case any of his friends would be dumb enough to trade for them. He then flicked the useless jacket over another heap of garbage.

Walter patted the pants down next and felt a single item. At first he thought it was a credit chip, and his mood again waxed. When he saw it was a navy ID badge, his stomach sank and swelled at once. He'd seen them before, mostly from wallets lifted off soldiers on training furlough. They were like lottery stubs, always with the allure of high-ranking passcodes and first-class tickets off Palan, but usually coming up as worthless as the plastic they were printed on. Part of Walter knew that he would access the chip and find useless codes he could just hack in his sleep if he wanted. But another part, the hopeful gambler inside, imagined the man was an admiral with codes that could summon havoc-wreaking forces with a single dispatch, or admit him to a distant university on some foreign aid GI bill.

Walter clutched the plastic chip, which may or may not contain his dreams, and tossed the black pants as far from him as he could. He thought about rushing to his mother and telling her about the curious man in the alley, but he needed to get to a computer first. There was no point exciting her weakened heart only to let it down when nothing came of the find.

Walter slipped the chip into his favorite pocket, the small one with the silent zipper that he greased daily. He trotted down the alley and considered which computer to use: the one at the library kiosk, or the one at Hommul HQ? And should he try to pawn off the gun immediately, or spread some seeds among his friends to drum up the price? Or should he just keep it?

Walter was so distracted by the decisions as he slipped past his apartment door that he didn't notice it opening. Nor did he note the three large Palans sliding out into the night after him.

oooo

"Walter? That you, boy?"

Walter's heart skipped a beat. He slid to a stop in the alley. He was looking for the deepest shadow to dive into when a powerful, meaty hand slapped down on his collarbone, fixing him in place.

"Aren't you out a little early to be on a proper raid?"

Walter turned and met the squinty gaze of his uncle, and then he saw the old man was escorted by two of his large goons.

"And aren't you a little early to come pay your respects?" Walter asked. He nodded toward his apartment door. "She's not dead yet, you know."

His uncle laughed and slapped his back. "Not yet, you are quite right. Doing a fine job of tending to her, I see."

Walter shrugged. "Some *other* clan leaders pitched in equipment," he said.

His uncle wagged a finger at him, and the two brutes to either side shifted their bulk as if eager to put some of it to use. "Careful," he said. "You know I'd do more if the clan wasn't hurting like it is."

The clan wouldn't be hurting if you did more, Walter thought.

"What's this?" his uncle asked. One of his fat hands darted toward Walter's belly and came away with the pistol.

Walter flinched, but it was too late.

"Hey—"

"Very nice," his uncle said, turning the gun around in his hand to inspect it. One of the brutes stepped closer to get a good look. Walter's uncle beamed. "Excellent find. I'll add it to the clan coffers."

"But that's—"

"You'll get your share, of course." He sniffed the air. "Was there something *else* you wanted to tell me about?"

Walter shook his head and thought of mintberry shakes and shiny new laptops.

His uncle smiled. "Don't overdo the pleasantries, Nephew. I'm liable to think you're plotting my demise." He handed the gun to one of his goons, his eyes never leaving Walter's. "Now tell me, junior pirate, since you obviously think I'm performing below the watermark—If *you* were running Hommul clan, what would you do differently?"

One of the goons chuckled. The other looked over the gun before stuffing it into the shadows of his jacket.

"I'd invest in ships," Walter blurted out. His thoughts on the matter were no secret. He watched the gun—his *treasure*—disappear.

"You'd sink us with a fleet of ships, would you?" His uncle laughed. "No clan has ever prospered by wasting their spoils on ships."

"No clan has ever led without them," Walter said. He looked back to his uncle.

His uncle laughed even harder, his throaty bellow filling the alley and flooding out beyond.

"You think this is about *leading*?" He pointed out the alley. "Do you think the Smiths own their ships? They don't. Terran banks own their ships, and they own the Smiths with their interest payments. What do the Smiths get in return? The headache of managing this flooding place and the thrill of first recruits, that's what. You think this is about who's in charge? Boy, you have no idea. This is about who can pay the rent, who can raid enough to get by. Scrap and salvage, boy, that's what'll see us through the rains, not your blasted *pirate* ships."

Walter clenched his jaw lest his mouth get him in trouble. His uncle stepped to the side and waved at his apartment's flood-high stoop.

"Now get along. Go see to my sister in case it's the last chance you get."

Walter was glad to. He squeezed past his uncle and between the two towers of goon.

"And no more talk of ships," his uncle called out after him. "Nobody ever made a dime on the blasted things. They're just holes in space that suck your money away."

More laughter filled the alley. It chased Walter up the steps and mocked him for being stupid while he fumbled uncharacteristically with the locks. He hurried with them as fast as he could and took longer as a result. After working the last lock loose, he slipped inside with his mom and the machines, slamming the door shut to block out the awful and humiliating stench in the alley.

35

THE RAID · TWO DAYS LATER

Walter concentrated on the locked comm box attached to the back of the navy building. With another deft tickle from his lockpick, he felt the final tumbler click into place, his torque wrench slid to the side, and then the human-built Master lock popped open smoothly.

"Who's the masster *now*?" Walter hissed. He smiled over at the moderators and pushed the lid closed with a soft click. One of the mods ticked an item off on his clipboard while Pewder switched places with Walter and took his turn at the suppos-edly impregnable lock. Each kid had two minutes to get the hatch open. Walter had taken less than thirty seconds. He glanced up at the dark and roiling sky and hissed with impatience as Pewder struggled with the mechanism.

After what felt like an hour, the lid to the comm box popped open, and Pewder pumped his fist and turned to beam at Walter. Walter pushed Donal forward, wishing they could just skip to the good part.

It took Donal almost the full two minutes. It felt like longer, but Walter watched as one of the moderators counted down the final seconds with his hands. It was all Walter could do to not reach forward and finish the job himself.

Finally, with seconds to spare, the lock clicked open. Donal started to push it closed again, but one of the moderators caught the boy's wrist and waved Walter forward.

Walter sneered. *Finally*. He pulled out his small pouch of electrical gear and freed his alligator clips. First, he placed a button LED inside the comm box and tapped it on. The small lamp put out just enough light to reveal the interior of the box, but not enough to spill past and alert anyone to their presence.

He then attached the alligator clips from his card reader to a set of wires—red to red and black to black. Walter liked to think of the reader as a second type of lockpick, one that slid dexterous programs into the tumblers of electronic firewalls, jiggling them loose. For this final test, each trainee would use his reader to load a hack he'd been working on for weeks. Or, in Walter's case, for the last two days.

In one of Walter's pockets, he had a card with his actual assignment on it, just in case anyone checked. With one swipe, it would bypass four layers of firewall and two security checks before routing a message through the large navy containment tower a few blocks away. That tower was full of entangled particles whizzing around inside fibermagnetic wires. Those wires were connected to a Bell phone, which could send the message instantly to Earth, millions of light years away, where the sister entangled particles would accept the transmission. The transmitted code would then seek out and hack a certain mainframe, taking down the Galactic Union homepage and displaying that year's pwned message for his moderators to validate.

Walter had written the program just that morning, and he knew it would work. But he wouldn't be using the backup card that held his pristine hack. No, he would be using the one he had written *earlier*, the one saved on the navy ID badge pulled from the alley two nights prior, the one that promised to solve Hommul clan's ship deficiency by making sure *no clan* had ships.

Walter sneered in the pale light emanating from the comm box. He reached into his favorite pocket and pulled out the card. He held it up to the reader fastened with its alligator clips and prepared to swipe it—

•• TWO DAYS BEFORE ••

Walter hurried down the alley steps to the basement entrance of Hommul HQ. His family's pirate offices were drastically below flood level, yet another embarrassing result of his uncle's maniacal drive to cut costs. He pulled out his pick set and knelt down before one of the dozens of locks on the door. If a non-member picked the wrong one—or even threw the tumblers too far in the *correct* lock—alarms would sound and deadbolts would engage. In order to enter the headquarters, clan members simply had to pick the correct lock and do so gently. There were few things more humiliating than setting off alarms on one's own door.

Walter clicked the mechanism aside with practiced ease. As with most skilled pirates, fumbling for a key on a crowded ring would've taken him longer. It was much slicker in any case to simply carry a single key for every lock, which was how he thought of his pick set.

Pulling open the door, Walter was greeted with a billowing rush of warm air, a sign that the air conditioner was on the fritz again. He stepped inside and yanked the door shut behind him. The thrum of water pumps vibrated through the walls as he hurried through twisting corridors. It was good to hear the pumps running with the rains looming in a day or two. Hommul HQ had been flooded out twice in the nine years they'd been in the new space. Walter frowned at the thought as he snuck past the junior pirate bunkroom. The lights inside were off, the darkness bearing an unoccupied stillness. Walter knew where most of the junior pirates-in-training were—he'd just left them around the Rats pit. The senior pirates were probably out staking heists and prepping for the upcoming finals. Whatever the reason, Walter felt giddy to have the place to himself.

His mood sank, however, when he entered the computer room. The place was a wreck.

"What the floods?" he hissed.

He waded through an ankle-deep layer of candy wrappers and empty tin cans of Pump Cola. The two computers had been left on; their fans whirred with an annoying clatter, and both machines were adorned with a half dozen twinkling, blue lights. The chairs in front of each were sprinkled with cookie crumbs and the telltale orange smears of Chedder Puffs. The room also reeked of sweaty Palan, of worry and agitation. Walter even nosed a bit of raw dread, the sort of smell he associated with the soon-to-be-dead. He'd seen some nasty last-minute hack sessions in his time, but the scene before him beat all. As he lowered himself to the edge of the less-ruined chair, he noted someone's code had been left up on the monitor. One glance, and he pegged its owner for the one reeking of death-dread. The code was more of a mess than the room.

Walter fought the urge to clean the code up a bit, knowing it was an irrational compulsion and very un-Palan-like. He closed his eyes, bent forward, and blew out as hard as he could across the keyboard. Bits of pizza crust and flood-knows-what-else peppered his face. He wiped his cheeks with both hands and shivered. Part of him considered sabotaging the water pumps prior to the coming flood, just to give the joint a good rinse.

Reaching inside his best pocket, Walter extracted the ID badge, his only remaining bit of loot from a night full of complete busts. First, his winnings at Rats had been denied him. Then, his blasted uncle had nabbed his gun, probably worth an easy two hundred. "You better be worth it," he told the plastic chip. He shook the card so it would know he meant business.

With a deft one-handed flourish, Walter called up a few macros he'd stored in the computer, and his private card-reading program booted up. He inserted the ID into the scanner. With a hesitant swipe, he ran the magnetic strip through—silently hoping for something good. A ticket off-world was almost too much to dream of, but some info he could sell would be nice. Anything to make up for the night's losses.

The card's code flashed across the screen, filling the smeared monitor with lines of green-phosphorous text. Walter's beady eyes flicked from side to side, trying to tease out the pertinent from the mundane.

Gradually, a glimpse of what he'd stumbled onto began to coalesce out of the lines of code, and Walter realized just what he had.

And he realized he had not been dreaming big *enough*.

•• The Raid ••

The two moderators crouched close to Walter and peered down at their computers as he slid the card through the reader and loaded his program. He watched the moderators press their refresh buttons over and over, expecting his successful hack to appear on the GU website at any moment.

It will, Walter thought. But his complex program had a few other tasks to perform before it did anything as mundane as sending messages off to Earth.

He remained perfectly still and tried to exude calm, even as another roll of thunder boomed in the distance. While Walter waited, he imagined what was going on in the ethereal realm of code and connected computers. With his eyes closed, he pictured his elegant hack zipping off through cheap copper wire. He traced its route through Palan, knowing where the main trunks were buried from so many datajacks over the years. The program would round High Street, dash down River Avenue, and then course up Cobble. That's where it would enter the navy's Bell phone containment tower—

Walter's heart raced as he suddenly realized his code could not be recalled. His actions could not be undone. He had pulled a trigger of sorts, knowing what the fired bullet would do, but only after he had done so did the repercussions fully seize him. Entire clans would be heading to Earth, taking their ships with them. Or was it the other way around? The play on words evaporated Walter's dread, replacing it with a sudden urge to giggle. He opened his eyes and looked to the moderators, wondering if they could sniff his mix of fear and humor. Hoping to replace the scents, Walter focused on the fact that his secondary program would soon dutifully reach Earth and perform a successful hack of the GU site. He also reminded himself that his program, swirling in the entangled particles of the navy's containment tower, would not be there for much longer. Soon, the floods would come and wash them away, the turbulent waters taking all signs of Walter's duplicity. He thought of these happy, calm facts and tried so very hard to refrain from thinking about what his program would do in the meantime . . .

•• Two Days Before ••

Simmons. The card owner's name was uncomfortable to even *think,* leaving a residual hiss in Walter's mind. But that wasn't what really stood out about the ID badge. What was weird was that the human had *two* official names. He seemed to go by Drummond while he was on Palan—at least to the markets, the Regal Hotel, the passenger shuttle office, and the cabbies. To the navy, however, he went by the name of Simmons, and as far as Walter could tell, he wasn't even supposed to *be* on Palan. He was on what Walter would call a rogue mission, and what the human navy referred to as "clandestine."

It was the first time Walter had gotten to rummage through the file of anyone in Special Assignments—the first time he'd heard of anyone getting the *chance.* But that wasn't the big surprise, either. The big surprise was how unbelievably sloppy Simmons was to be so seemingly well connected. Walter hit a goldmine when he came across a file named "Passwords. txt." He had thought it was some sort of joke until he opened the file up and saw its contents.

The next thing he had to do was immediately raid the snack closet for some Chedder Puffs and a warm Pump Cola. Like his trainees before him, Walter was about to pull an all-nighter.

Simmons, it seemed, answered directly to a navy admiral, one Wade Lucin. Their entire message history was logged in a navy database, opened as slick as grease with the contents of the passwords file. It appeared Simmons was on Palan to secure a "package" of some sort. He even had two accomplices heading his way from Earth. Walter scanned these messages, but none of it seemed too terribly interesting. What caught his eye among the terse lines were the words "username" and "password." For some reason, the admiral had given Simmons temporary access to his own account. It was a one-time login and no longer any good, but it was enough to get Walter guessing the admiral's full-time passcode. He knew from hacking human laptops that all their passwords were slight variations on a single theme—either their limited noses kept them ignorant to the threats swirling all around them, or they just couldn't hold more than a few tidbits in their brains at any one time. Walter suspected it was a blend of both.

It took fewer than a dozen tries to log in to the navy database. All the admiral had done was transpose the two words in his password and increase the four-digit number by one. When the login screen disappeared and the master account page popped up, Walter nearly spilled his can of Pump. He whipped around to make sure nobody was behind him, his entire body tingling with the thrill of found treasure. Pulling the keyboard into his lap, Walter began flipping through account tabs. The overwhelming choice of devious tasks to perform made his head spin.

Walter scanned the Personnel page first. The admiral had almost complete control over what looked to be thousands and thousands of humans. Walter briefly considered transferring every staff member with an S in his or her name to the front line. He laughed to himself at the thought. There was a massive subpage for humans ranked as mere "cadets." With half a thought, Walter could've flunked or expelled whichever brats he chose. He thought about changing some grades, or possibly admitting himself to flight school, but like the frontline transfers, these were all ideas that would arouse suspicion and turn out to be no more than practical jokes. Annoyances, sure, but with no real outcome, no payoff other than a locked-down account and someone in human IT lecturing the admiral on how not to be so stupid with his passcodes.

The best solution, Walter knew, was going to be to just sell the account to someone off-planet. Take someone's money and let *that person* deal with the heat. He went to the admin page and set up a few secondary logins so he could access the account even if the primary password was changed. He then went to the admiral's inbox and deleted the automated messages warning of the account changes. He also opened the IT log file and removed the entries for his actions and reset the time stamp for the last logon. Satisfied, Walter went to log out, but after closing the IT tab and just before he exited the admiral's inbox, something caught his eye: An older message entitled "Delete After Reading."

But it *hadn't* been deleted.

And with a title like that, there was nothing Walter could do *but* read it.

OOOO

TO: Adm. Wade Lucin

FROM: IT Specialist Second Class Mitchell

Admiral,

The alterations to the simulator were completed today, and I even stamped Hearst's name on the modifications in case anyone looks. I promised I wouldn't ask about these mods, but I want you to know how hard that promise is to keep. I'm dying to know. Anyway, everything was done remotely and I covered my tracks well. I expect to see those reprimands expunged from my files like we talked about.

As for the hyperdrive question, I can only assume you're talking about hypotheticals. For the sake of dis- cussion—assuming for a moment you had a drive that could ignore gravitational permutations—there are ways to remotely input jump coordinates and bypass the navy control boards. It isn't easy, but it's doable. The radio inter- face for sending out coordinate verification can be turned around the other way, but you'd have to come up with a master key for the hack to work. I just don't see why you'd want to. Why not input the jump arrival directly in the nav computer, as per usual? The only thing I can think of is not wanting a log of the jump—or maybe wanting to avoid those annoying alarms. Does that qualify as a question? Hey, I didn't make any promises about not inquiring into this. Feel free to tell me more if you need help with this. I'm insanely curious.

Attached you'll find a classified white paper on jump drive overrides, which might help. I also threw in the hardware schematics you wanted. On second thought, whatever it is you're doing over there at the academy, I'm thinking it's best I don't know. Oh, and I'll be pulling my internal affairs file up in a few weeks. It had better be a lot thinner than the last time I looked at it! ;-)

From one war dog to another: Be Easy.

-Mitch

○ ○ ○ ○

Walter frowned at the message. It sounded like a bunch of military stuff, but the Mitch guy was obviously a coder of some sort. Even if it was boring, he was pretty sure there was something in there for a nice piece of blackmailing—it just wasn't as juicy as he'd hoped, especially for something with a dire warning to be deleted. He clicked on the attachment, wondering if the schematic might be something he could fence.

The first file was a technical paper, almost indecipherable even to him. There were also schematics labeled "Hyperdrive," the drawings making even less sense, as they were perfectly laid out and didn't have a dozen replacement parts tacked on willy-nilly as he was used to. He scrolled past them, annoyed and disappointed, until he came to the lines of code that followed.

Programs. Written in G++. The formatting was perfectly clear, with nested levels of indentation, just the way he liked to lay out his own code. Even better, the code was full of detailed comments explaining what the next few lines did for whoever might be maintaining it. In fact, Walter saw that there was more than one person involved in the writing of the code. As neat and standardized as they tried to make it, some of the lines bore distinctive imprints of their author. One coder stood out from the rest with a much higher degree of elegance. Walter could almost see the program coursing through a piece of electronics somewhere; the syntax practically sang to him, giving him goose bumps.

After scrolling up and down, following the snippets of code as it bounced routines from one module to another, Walter got a decent grasp on the overall function. It even helped to make sense of the schematic attached above. What he was looking at was basically a cryptographic system that took one set of numbers and converted them to another—that was pretty much it. A quantum gate was used for randomization, and there were numerous security measures, but he saw how it went together. The input for the program could be any three-number Cartesian coordinate, pretty much an exact location in space, and the output would be a string of numbers and letters that a physical circuit could format back into a location. It was obviously meant to go into the machine laid out in the neat plans above.

Suddenly, the contents of the message made sense. Walter was looking at the human navy's solution to making their hyperdrives unhackable. The master key was hidden right there somewhere!

Walter had to sit back in his chair and consider the implications. He ran his hands over his head, tickling the stubble there.

"Flood me," he whispered.

Somewhere down the hallways of the HQ, a distant door slammed, and loud voices echoed their way into the computer room. Walter pulled out one of his flash drives and plugged it into the computer. He copied the attachments over and wrapped them in his very best encryption. He logged out of the navy database and erased his steps from the computer's history one final time. He deleted the entire Simmons account from all navy servers as well, just to cover his tracks further. His last step was to run a sniffer program from his flash drive to make sure nobody had installed tracking software on the computers in an attempt to cheat for their finals. A quick scan came up clean.

Walter yanked out his drive and tucked it in his front pocket. He kept his hand on it while the voices faded away, eventually pinched off by the slam of another door.

Walter's brain tumbled. He thought about what could be done with the knowledge in his pocket. Selling it seemed like the obvious thing, but for how much? And was simply selling it really the most elegant solution? Would it give him the most long-term benefits? Or would it mean that someone *else* would have the knowledge that for the moment *he alone* possessed? And how long would it be before the navy found out their program had been compromised and they changed their design? Would the buyers then come looking for a refund in the worst, most Palanesque way?

The questions swelled, growing like moist yeast and pushing on Walter's skull. There had to be something better. Something that didn't require sharing the knowledge. Some way to keep it *his*.

The obvious predicament was that he had no ships to try the code on, so he didn't see how this windfall did him any personal good. Of all the Palan clans, his Hommul family was the only one holding out on the relatively new technology. When the GN had arrived, all the other clans had been quick to jump on the new transportation boost. Piracy had left the wide Palan oceans where veritable islands of floating debris were the only scraps worth fighting over and had moved out to space, where far greater treasures seemed to beckon. Could Walter use this code to persuade his uncle to buy their first ship? How would that even help? How could he ensure that his clan matched the level of the others? He couldn't see any way his new bounty would even lift his prospects an inch from his planet's surface.

Ah, Walter thought, *but that's not the only way to level a playing field.* Just as in that night's game of Rats, there were two ways of winning any contest. One was to lift yourself up to the level of your competition. The other was to bring them down below you, crushing them in the process.

Walter thought about how he had cleverly won at Rats earlier. There was another option available to him, a way to secure Hommul's place among the clans. And it was a plan so delicious, Walter couldn't help but lick his teeth.

36

THE RAID

Walter waited while the moderators stared at their handheld computers. One of them frowned, obviously disappointed in the amount of time Walter's hack was taking to display itself on the GU website. His eyes flicked up to Walter's and then darted over to the comm box before finally settling back on his computer. Walter held his breath, imagining all that was taking place in the background. A peal of sharp thunder cracked in the distance. The other two trainees shifted nervously, everyone growing uncomfortable with the delay.

Finally, the glow from one of the computer screens dipped and then brightened as the page refreshed with Walter's hack. The second computer did the same. The two moderators frowned but nodded over the results. One of them quickly turned the screen so Walter could see, and then waved him aside and pointed to Pewder, letting the boy know it was his turn.

Pewder tossed Walter a snide look as he brushed past. Walter just focused on thoughts of pure honey. He imagined himself unboxing a new powersurfer, still wrapped in plastic. He thought of anything good he could conjure, keeping all worries of what would follow to himself, even though he knew not much would happen until after the floods.

Another rumble of thunder grumbled much closer to the city. For once in his life, Walter urged the Palan rains along, impatient for them. He fidgeted in place while the other two boys uploaded their hacks, attempting to replace Walter's web update with one of their own.

Pewder's worked without a hitch, updating even faster than Walter's had. Donal's program may have worked, given enough time, but that was part of the test. The poor boy flushed as the moderator's fingers ticked down, counting off the last seconds of the half hour. When his fist clenched, the other mod give Donal a slight nod, as if to convey hope for next year. Donal couldn't even turn to face Pewder and Walter, both of whom were bundles of nervous excitement—even if for different reasons.

The first splatter of rain punctuated the end of the exam, snapping the small cluster of pirates out of their reflections. The lead moderator pointed down the alley, his fingers twisting in the shape of "single-file, fast over quiet."

Donal trotted off first, more wet on his cheeks than could be accounted for by the occasional drops of rain. Pewder went next, beaming with pride, his entire carriage more erect, taller, more confident than it had been when they'd entered the alley.

Walter let the two adults go next, even as they hesitated and tried to wave him along. He stood alone in the corner of the alley, looking back toward the swirling charcoal rainclouds obscuring Palan's starry night, and felt a drop of rain smack the top of his head and weave its way through his short hair. Before he turned to follow the others, he caught one faint glimpse of a blinking red light, high atop the navy's containment tower. As the light was swallowed by the storms, Walter had a sudden surge of doubt. Had he sliced far enough through the flood diverter's cables? Was there any chance the rushing wall of floodwater would fail to knock them down? Would they hit with enough force to carry the containment tower away completely?

What might become of the tower worried him more than his program, which at the very worst would do nothing, and then nobody would ever know it had been there. But if it worked! Walter felt dizzy with the potential consequences, the assured fallout among what remained of the clans. He imagined those ones and zeros he had arranged swirling through the air around him, coursing up through the mighty clouds, racing off to find eager receivers and hyperdrives to infect. He thought about the hapless pilots, inputting jump coordinates to the annual clan meeting and being whisked off to Earth instead!

Too delicious, Walter thought. He licked the rain from his lips and finally turned to hurry after the others, chased along by the patter of heavy drops of rain and the thoughts of the shift in power that was about to occur. The shift *he* will have created.

○ ○ ○ ○

The streets were thick with rain by the time they arrived back at Hommul HQ from the finals raid. The wide gutters gurgled with temporary rivers, their turbulent surfaces dotted with loose trash and debris. The examination group hurried down the stairwell and stood in several inches of water, steady falls cascading down the steps and already overwhelming the gated drain below their feet. Walter fidgeted in place while one of the moderators fumbled with the lock. It was all he could do to not shove the man aside and open it himself.

Finally, the door popped open, and the small group of Palans squeezed into the mildew-laden air. The excited chatter of another exam group rumbled down the hall ahead of them. More thunder growled outside until the stairwell door slammed shut, cutting it off.

"Just in time," Pewder said, smiling and shaking the wet off his hands. His excitement was lost on Donal, who hurried off toward the showers and bunkroom. Pewder shrugged at Walter. "Always next year," he said.

Walter smiled and nodded, but he felt more in common with Donal at that moment. Passing the stupid finals had never been in question for him. The *real* nerves were just beginning to creep up as he considered what he had done, the very real consequences that were now out of his hands. While other junior pirates would spend that night worrying about their scoring reviews and placement, Walter would agonize over what the future had in store not just for his clan, but all of Palan. He hurried down the hallway toward the bunkroom to change into dry clothes, the comfort of being locked inside for a flood at least affording him the time to rest and contemplate.

"You boys cut it a little close, didn't you?"

Walter turned and saw his uncle standing in the doorway of his office. The old man's eyes were the dullest silver, the look of someone who'd stayed up all day.

"Donal and Pewder maxed out their times," Walter lied. He shrugged and turned to hurry off.

"I heard *your* hack took its sweet time as well."

Walter turned back. His uncle was smiling, one hand resting on the side of his ample belly, the other clinging to the doorframe. Walter sniffed the air, but the mildew was too strong. He wondered if the odor was as much due to laziness as he always assumed, or yet another noxious cloud to occlude guilty thoughts.

"Why don't you step inside for a second," his uncle said. He moved into the hallway and waved Walter toward his door.

Walter hesitated. He looked down at himself. "Why don't I go change first?"

"I've got a towel inside."

His uncle took a step toward him, one meaty hand reaching for his shoulder.

Walter hissed; he ducked past his grasp and into the office. He *hated* the way his uncle liked to pinch his shoulder, hurting him while pretending to be nice.

Inside, he found the office partly lit and fully wrecked. There were piles of papers everywhere: stacked high on the desk, mounded up in the corner, spilling over and suffocating a computer monitor. The only clear surface was his father's old couch, which looked recently slept on. A dented pillow was wedged by one armrest, a bedsheet knotted up at the other. Walter scanned the room for the promised towel and spotted it hanging from a hook, nestled between two rain slicks. His uncle entered behind him and shut the door. He adjusted the dimmer up a tad while Walter retrieved the towel, sniffed it at arm's length, and used it to dry his head and neck.

"I've been thinking about our conversation at your mom's place the other day."

His uncle weaved his way around the desk and lowered his bulk into an old wooden swivel chair.

"In fact, I've been thinking about it a lot."

Walter ran the towel down his arms and then turned and hung it back up between the slicks. He was having a hard time remembering what in the hell conversation his uncle was talking about. All he could recall was the loss of his blasted gun.

"I may have found our clan a ship."

Walter turned. *That conversation*, he thought.

His uncle powered on the monitor, casting himself in a broad cone of greenish light. He reached for the mouse and slid it back and forth. Walter wondered if he was supposed to step around the desk and see something on the monitor.

"I thought you were against taking out loans like that." Walter glanced at the sofa, considered sitting down, but decided against it. He stood and scanned the carpet for clues among the papery detritus.

"I finally found a ship we can afford." His uncle sat forward, the chair squealing as he did so. He reached for a sheet of paper and held it out to Walter. "I called in a few debts so we'd be able to pay cash. She's not much, no arms and no real defense, but she'll get us to the off-planet clan meetings for the first time in forever."

That last bit sent a shiver up Walter's spine. He stepped forward and took the piece of paper, but his body had turned cold, his ears full of cotton.

"When?" he barely hissed.

"When what?"

Walter looked at the piece of paper. "When were you thinking of doing this?"

"Already have." His uncle stood, grabbed a loose heap of paper, and began tapping the sheaf on the desk to straighten it. "The sale went through earlier today. We own our first ship."

Walter looked at the piece of paper. It was a proof of sale for a GN ship, a class 290. He searched the document for any information on the hyperdrive, but the only details listed were gross tonnage, thruster ratings in Newtons, how much freshwater she held.

Nothing on the engine models. He couldn't believe the awful timing—that his uncle had given in to his idea at the very moment he'd found a different way to level the playing field—

"Something wrong?" His uncle sniffed loudly and set the stack of papers back where they had been. The neat pile slid off the mound and returned to its natural, jumbled state. "I expected a whiff of excitement," his uncle said. "Not this . . ." He waved at the air between them. "This *dread*."

Walter collected his thoughts. He held the bill of sale back out to his uncle. "It's just, I don't want to get the blame if anything goes . . . *badly*." Walter glanced at the couch. He reconsidered his uncle's offer and sat down heavily.

His uncle walked around the desk and leaned back on its edge, precariously shifting the mounds of paper behind him. "It won't go badly," he said. "Your mom and I discussed this last night. We won't build a fleet that can sink us, and we won't be taking out any loans. Just one ship. No weapons. We might try some salvage work when fuel rates are low, but it'll mainly be for status, you know? No more sitting here and twiddling our thumbs and waiting to hear what status the clans relegated to us in their meetings. *This* time, we'll be joining the flotilla in our own craft."

"*This* time?" Walter's voice was the barest of gurgles.

"Yeah, why wait another year? We wouldn't have rushed the sale for any other reason. Of course, we're gonna have to hire a pilot, but that won't be a problem. Tomorrow morning, while the floods are cascading over Felony Falls, we'll be soaring up in our very own starship. The ship *you'll* soon become a full senior pirate inside of."

His uncle beamed with pride. For a moment, Walter assumed it was the thrill of the sale, and then he remembered the exam he'd completed not an hour ago, the looming promotion, how much all of that meant to his mother and uncle. And then he realized the purchase of the craft was not merely due to his age-old pleadings, but to his graduation! For all he knew, they had been planning this for years and years, all while he bitched and moaned about Hommul not having a ship of its own.

His uncle stepped closer, sniffing the air.

"You feeling all right, Nephew?"

Walter nodded. "I'm fine. Just . . . a little space-sick thinking about it, that's all."

Walter's uncle loomed over him. He slapped Walter on the back. "Don't you worry. After a few flights, your belly will be hard as steel. And if not, you'll soon be running this joint, so you can send whoever you want up into space *for you.*"

Walter dipped his head. He tried to think of normal dreads, like his fear of the floods, hoping to maintain the ruse of being afraid to fly. He buried deep his thoughts on the following day—the idea that his grand plan had been for naught, that soon he would be whisked off to Earth with the rest of the Palan fleet.

The irony of it all was nearly too much to bear. He'd always wanted to escape to the mystical planet of freedom and riches, but it had always been with a mind of getting *away* from the other clans. Now he had discovered a way to send them off, surely to be captured in Earth orbit and rounded up while he and his Hommul clan took de facto control over a shipless Palan.

But now Walter was going to get *all* of his wishes. He was going to get a ship; he was going to visit Earth; he was going to become a full pirate, and all on the same day. And all those tasty treats were doomed to mix together like the putrid slop of a restaurant's flooding alley.

37

ABOVE PALAN

"Look at all that water. You could flood the *hyperspace* out of something with all that water."

Walter leaned close to the porthole and peered dutifully out at his receding home. It was a sight he had longed for many times, but now he wanted to be elsewhere. Anywhere.

"You can see more clouds already forming over there." Pewder jabbed a finger against the glass, pointing to another flood forming on the horizon as the last rains dissipated out at sea. Walter looked from these new clouds to his mud-colored continent, which sat like a dollop of dirt on a bright-blue sphere.

The clouds were probably less than a week away—a rare double-flooding—but already they appeared big enough to swallow all the lands. The new perspective had Walter marveling that all of dry Palan hadn't long ago been washed away completely.

He turned away from the sad sight, the fragility of his home too great to contemplate, and surveyed the cargo bay one more time. "I sure hope you didn't pay too much for this," he told his uncle. He thought about the fact that it would soon be impounded in Earth's orbit, anyway.

"We got a fine deal. In fact, I think the Smiths were eager to ditch it."

Walter sniffed the musky air trapped in the old ship. "Ownership dispute?"

His uncle shrugged. "There was a human in here this morning claiming the ship was his. The man reeked of lies, though."

The ship jittered in a pocket of turbulence—or perhaps a bout of poor piloting. Walter's uncle swayed, his arms out, while he and Pewder clung to the handles by the portholes. They all threw scowls and hisses toward the cockpit.

"This human," Walter said. "He didn't have any ownership papers with him, did he?"

His uncle shook his head. "Forget him. It was just another crazy human thinking everything not tied down is his." He waved his hand. "Now why don't you boys go do some proper snooping. See what's in the bunk rooms."

Walter lit up at this. He had been looking for an excuse to see if his hack of the ship's drive could be undone. He turned away from the porthole with its dreary view of Palan and headed toward the back of the ship. He hissed at Pewder as the boy raced past, nearly knocking him down.

Pewder turned into the first room he came to and let out a loot-cry of "Spacesuits!"

Walter stuck his head in the small room, which looked like a place to change clothes. Full-body suits hung on one wall, and there was a sky hatch or something in the ceiling. He turned away while Pewder began patting down one of the suits.

Across the hallway, Walter found what he was really interested in: the ship's hyperdrive. The unit was bigger than he would've thought, having seen only schematics of the main board. It looked like a boxy taxicab, and it sat close to the back wall of the small room. There was just enough walkway around the sides to circle the unit, allowing access to all the panels and hatches screwed tight over the unit's innards. Walter approached the machine, his skin tingling at the sight of it. It was so . . . *purposeful*. So whole and complete.

Nothing seemed out of place or tacked on over years and years of intermittent operation. Pipes led where they were bent to lead, as if molded for their foreseen purpose. Wires were trimmed to the proper length, routed neatly in parallel lines, and even—floods take him—*labeled*.

Walter reached out and ran his hands along one of the riveted panels. It felt cool to the touch. He had somehow expected it to be warm, or thrumming with contained energy. Instead, he saw it as a perfectly engineered marvel—a thing with frightful and awesome potential. A means of escape, to take him anywhere he chose.

Walter strolled around the side, looking for model and serial numbers. He found both on a silver plate screwed to the back of the unit. It had the place and year of manufacture, the requisite numbers, and all kinds of cautions and warnings.

"You don't have to tell me," Walter said to the plate.

Pewder stuck his head around the rear corner of the drive. "Tell you what?" he asked.

Walter waved him off. "Go check the bunk rooms, you bolthead."

Pewder sniffed and then padded away without a word.

Walter pulled out his multi-tool and his card reader. He hoped to hyperspace he knew what he was doing. Or *undoing*, as it were.

oooo

Over a hundred pirate ships from all the clans were gathered at the first rendezvous point when they arrived, with more of them streaking their way over from the Orbital Station and up from Palan. Each pirate clan tended to cobble together as many functioning craft as they could for the annual promotion ceremonies. The size of their fleet said much about the potential ranking of the clan and the power they would wield that year, resulting in some absolute clunkers puttering through space.

Kinda like ours, Walter thought as he looked around the cockpit of their own jalopy.

"Looks like the Smiths've been boozing it up on the station."

Walter's uncle pointed from the navigator's seat toward a sizable fleet heading their way.

"How long before we jump out?" Walter asked the pilot impatiently; he wasn't sure if he'd overridden the Earth coordinates properly, but he was anxious to hurry up and find out.

"They're already queuing up for the jump," the pilot said. He pointed to a display on the dash where each ship stood out as a bright blip. It made it easy to see how the dozens of craft had formed a straight line with more forming up at the rear.

"See? That's the Palan system's L1 they're heading toward." The pilot tapped a finger at a blank spot near the end of the line. The lead blip moved under the pad of his silvery digit. When the pilot pulled his hand away, the ship was gone.

Walter lifted his eyes and searched through the windshield, but whatever had just happened was already over and done with, obscured and pulled off with the timing and mystery of a magic trick.

"Ell *what*?" Pewder asked. The smaller boy tried to squeeze in past Walter, but Walter stood firm, keeping the kid out.

"A Lagrange point," the pilot said.

"I wanna see!"

Walter ignored Pewder and leaned closer to his uncle. He wasn't sure what the Lagrange business was all about, and he didn't care. He tapped his uncle on the shoulder. "Hey, Uncle, do you think we could do our promotions right here while we wait our turn?"

His uncle laughed and shook his head. "We might have to jump out one at a time, but promotions are always done together. If we were down on Palan, I'd still be making you wait until the set time. And don't worry about your friends beating you to full pirate—the others'll wait for us."

Walter watched another blip wink off the screen on the dash. He thought about the young and hopeful Palans on each ship, them and their uncles and fathers having similar conversations. The thought created some new sensation in his stomach, something similar to the dread of the floods. It only seemed to register, though, when he was thinking on how many Palans were out there in all those ships, how they would soon find themselves rounded up by Earth's orbital defense. Walter nearly laughed out loud when he thought about how it would look. The humans are gonna think Palan is invading them!

"Why do we jump out to the *moon* for the promotions?" Pewder asked, interrupting Walter's thoughts. The younger boy's pestering hands were all over Walter's ribs, trying to find room on one side or the other in order to see. Walter shifted as needed to keep him away from the prime spot he had claimed just behind the ship's controls.

"It's the same reason we used to sail out over the seas to do it, back when I was your age," Walter's uncle said. "Part of the ceremony, sure, is welcoming a new group of youth into the clans, but what you boys don't see is how much jockeying takes place among us elders."

The heavy Palan shifted around in his seat and looked back at the two boys. "When I was promoted, I remember thinking the entire ocean revolved around me, that *this* was my day—Pewder, are you back there?"

"Walter's *blocking* me."

"Son, let the boy see."

Walter gave him a two-inch vertical shaft of visibility.

"You see, the trip out over the water proved much more about the clan's health than the new members they were about to induct. Hell, it was ten times harder sailing the stormy seas after a flood than it is cobbling a ship together and hiring a pilot."

He turned to the pilot. "No offense," he said.

The pilot shrugged.

"What did it prove about us that we had to do our own ceremony on Palan all these years?"

His uncle turned in his seat and gazed out at the stars beyond the canopy.

"It wasn't fun for me, I'll tell you. But hell, I've been against the move to space from the beginning." He held up his hands and looked at his great, meaty palms. "As soon as we stopped sailing, the clans started getting soft." He sighed. "Then again,

I suppose one of my ancestors would've been angry that *my* old ship had hydraulic steering and synthetic sails, like I was some kind of wimp compared to him. Time moves like the floods, boys. You either lift your feet and drift along on the surface, or you drown trying to stay in one place."

"So there's really no way we can do the promotions before we jump out?" Walter was dying to at least be a full pirate in Earth prison, if that was his fate. He'd be sure to rub that in Dalton's face— through the bars if he had to.

"You've waited an entire year for this, Walter," his uncle said. "What in hyperspace is another hour gonna do?"

Walter cringed at the thought.

If only I knew, he thought.

OOOO

As befitting the status of their clan, the lone Hommul ship was the last to arrive at Palan's primary Lagrange point. A very light smattering of commercial traffic stood nearby, patiently awaiting an end to Palan's annual swarm around the safe jump point so they could resume their normal business.

Walter had completely forgotten about the non-pirate ships that might be passing through their system. He had never considered the possibility that other craft might get caught up in his web and be sent off to Earth with the clans. He shrugged. Unintended consequences were just a part of life.

He was thinking this and looking out at the distant collection of waiting ships when their newly purchased GN-290 winked through hyperspace. The commercial ships disappeared, and the stars beyond jittered to new positions. Off to one side of the canopy, the farthest moon of Palan popped into being silently and sat motionless, its bluish surface dotted with craters and streaked with ejecta.

"What in the . . . ?"

The pilot's confusion was drowned out by Pewder's thrill of partially seeing the jump take place. He screamed in Walter's ear, and Walter's uncle added to the commotion, clapping his hands together as if his risky purchase had somehow fully redeemed itself with a safe and successful jump.

Walter's heart pounded with relief. The override of the *override* had returned things to normal. He had unscrewed himself. The tension in his body slid out like jelly through his arms, which tingled at the sight of all that empty blackness ahead.

The pilot was not having the same reaction to their being alone. He cursed and fiddled with his

514

instruments. Moments later, Walter's uncle finally noticed that something was missing.

"Where *is* everyone?" he asked. He looked down at the display that had been full of green blips. The pilot adjusted some knobs.

"Where *are* they?" he asked the pilot.

"I have no idea," the pilot said. He pulled up another screen and turned to Walter's uncle, his posture and voice suddenly defensive. "These are the coordinates you gave me. This is where we're supposed to be."

"What kind of trick *is* this?" Walter's uncle shook his fist at the vacuum beyond the carboglass, like a sailor cursing the sea.

Walter, meanwhile, was overjoyed. He took in a breath, realizing he had been holding it for what felt an eternity. To him, the empty space outside the ship stood as perfect verification of his accomplishment. It was the ultimate programming rush: He had hacked an entire fleet! He had written a program—sent out via Bell phone—and it had infected every ship in a star system. Anything with a GN hyperdrive board had received his commands, and they had all obeyed him.

He imagined those hundreds of ships in Earth's orbit right then, clan leaders scratching their heads while they were surrounded by the human navy. And that was when a new fact hit him: the only ship to not show up would be the obvious culprit. Oh, how delicious that they would know it had been Hommul who—!

"What did you *do*?"

Walter's uncle was out of his seat with a speed that belied his bulk. He came across the controls between the seats and seized Walter by the neck, pushing him against the bulkhead. Pewder screamed and stumbled out of the cockpit, his arms windmilling for balance. Walter got out half a hiss of alarm before his windpipe was squeezed too tight to breathe.

"What in hyperspace have you done?" his uncle demanded. He leaned close and sniffed Walter's cheek, taking in the reek of his excitement and guilt.

The scrutiny just made Walter ooze more of both.

"I didn't—" Walter tried to croak.

"Tell me!" his uncle roared. He throttled Walter, lifting the boy's feet off the decking.

"I can't breathe," he squeaked.

The pilot twisted in his seat and reached for the two of them. "Hey, there's no way the boy could've—"

"Stay out of this!" the senior pirate thundered. He shook a finger back toward the pilot, allowing Walter to gasp for a breath.

"It was an *accident*," Walter whispered.

His uncle's eyes flared. Disbelieving hands loosened their grip. "Tell me," he said softly.

Walter looked beseechingly to the pilot, but the other man sat rapt in his seat, his eyes searching Walter for an impossible explanation. Walter, still pinned to the bulkhead, looked the other way to see Pewder standing in the doorway of the cockpit, rubbing one elbow he must've bruised in his fall to the decking. His uncle seemed to sniff the collapse of Walter's resistance. The hands clenched around his neck relaxed further until they were simply draped on his shoulders. Walter looked to the leader of his clan, his mother's brother, his sometime stand-in of a father, a man he used to know simply as Karl, and he saw in his terrified and shock-glazed eyes the forgotten fragility of the old man. There was a stunned horror there that Walter couldn't match up with his own fear of his uncle. He couldn't conceive of the possibility that *he*, little Walter, had engendered that fear.

"I just wanted to rid us of their ships," Walter breathed.

He searched the three faces turned his way.

"I didn't think we'd be up here." He widened his eyes for his uncle. "I didn't know we were getting a ship!"

His uncle's large hands left Walter's shoulders and moved to the sides of his head, as if he had suddenly been seized by a headache.

517

"I thought you didn't *want* ships," Walter told him, the excuses beginning to gather like the floods. "This way *none* of us would have them. We'd be equal." A new reason popped into his head, and Walter added it to his premeditated list: "You said Terran banks owned them. All I did was send them back."

"To Earth?" the pilot asked.

Walter nodded.

"From *here*? With one jump?"

More nodding. The pilot slumped down in his seat.

Walter's uncle turned and sniffed the air. The stench of fear from the pilot hit Walter a moment later.

"What is it?" the senior pirate asked.

"We'll never hear from them again," he said. The pilot looked back over his shoulder at Walter, an odd mix of fear and shock on his face as well. "You can't jump like that," he said. "People who try are never heard from ever again." The Palan pilot waved toward one of the screens on the dash. "There's *procedures* you have to follow. There's way too much stuff between here and Earth."

"So how long before they come back?" his uncle asked.

"Aren't you listening?" The pilot waved his arms. "They're not *ever* coming back. They're dead."

"What the floods?" Pewder mumbled to himself.

"I thought you'd *like* this," Walter begged of his uncle. The pilot's words weren't registering with him at all. He couldn't think of the possibility that thousands might be dead when he was still facing the possibility of being in trouble.

"I thought I'd be promoted to full pirate and Hommul wouldn't be at the very bottom of the clans. But now look!" He waved toward the empty space beyond the windshield. "We'll be at the top!" Walter exulted.

Walter's uncle looked out toward Palan's most distant moon. He seemed to chew on the consequences of Walter's actions, on this new power vacuum as real and great as the void of space. He looked to the pilot with a frown, then to Walter, then Pewder. His face grew suddenly serious.

"By the might I have vested in me," he chanted, "by my wiles and my guiles, by the authority of a clan all mine, I now bestow the privilege of full pirate to you, Pewder Hommul."

Walter watched Pewder positively glow from the hasty but proper proceedings. It wasn't with all the pomp and circumstance the boys had imagined, but the occasion was no less momentous. Their lives, everything they did and said around Palan, it was all about to change. They were moving from boys to men, and it didn't matter to Walter how exactly that had to take place—

"You." His uncle turned to face him. "You can wait another year. You're grounded."

"What . . . ?"

His uncle stepped back and reached into the folds of his jacket.

"How can you ground me?"

A pistol came out. Walter immediately recognized it as the one he'd found on the Simmons guy.

"Wait," Walter said, raising his hands. "Uncle, please, think on what you're about to—"

His uncle's arm came up, the gun pointing out. He swiveled to the side, and with a concussive roar made mighty by the confines of the cockpit, he shot a bullet, point blank, into the side of the pilot's face.

Blood and bone scattered, adhering to the dash and windshield in a wide cone of gore. The smell of burned powder stung Walter's nose, the ringing in his ears cutting off the first of what his uncle said next.

" . . . so that nobody ever knows what you did." His uncle turned to Pewder. The gun did as well. "Is that understood?"

Pewder's head nodded so hard, Walter imagined it could pop right off.

"Okay. Now." The senior pirate of the Great Hommul Clan, highest and mightiest of them all, turned to survey the mess Walter had made. "The first job for you, junior pirate, is to clean this man's blood off my spaceship." He looked back and forth between the two boys, waving the smoking gun at the ship's controls as he did so. "After that, I might need you to tell me how much you remember of what this man was doing with all these gizmos and knobs to get us out here."

38

NEAR PALAN'S
FARTHEST MOON

By the time Walter had the dash clean—filling two large garbage bags with nasty wads of paper towel in the process—the three Palans had argued enough over the ship's controls to realize they had no idea how to get themselves home. Pewder and Walter took turns pointing out that their uncle could just as easily have shot the man *after* they'd landed back on Palan. Their Uncle Karl didn't want to hear any of it. And during the argument, Walter was dismayed to see how quickly Pewder had begun talking down to *him*.

"You missed a bit of skull there, Junior Pirate."

Walter grabbed the offending piece, imagining it a gold coin to keep the kill scents out of the air. The next year would certainly be the longest of his short life, he realized.

With the dash clean, the crew of three began to deduce the functioning of simpler systems. The changing room turned out to be an airlock. Once they dragged the pilot's body inside, Walter took great pleasure in figuring out the hallway controls and opened the outer hatch. The vacuum sucked hungrily at the body, the arms and legs whacking limply at the jamb as it was yanked out into space along with a misty fog of crystalized air.

One of the only other devices to succumb to their combined wit—the hyperdrive being something not even Walter could summon the courage to fiddle with—was the radio. It soon transmitted a load of lies and the honest promise of future reward to any pilot willing to come fetch a poor, stranded crew in distress.

The flight back was a deathly silent affair, the smells of rotted flowers and dirty dishes wafting through the confined space. Walter spent the time dizzy with the wrongness of his punishment. He had given his uncle power beyond the wildest hopes of his schemings, and the reward had been practically a demotion from the true rank he'd honestly earned. That, plus a year of being grounded. Not to mention a year of hearing it from Pewder, and of now never being able to outrank him in seniority, even when he eventually took over the clan!

Thoughts like that were too much to take. Walter practically vibrated from holding it all in.

Their new pilot set the ship down in the space-port, and Walter was the first out the ramp. He ran across the tarmac and through the market, bump-ing off busy shoppers as he went. He ran out into the streets, the pavement still shimmering from the passing floods, the gutters gurgling the last inches of water down their drains. He skipped over the crumbling bridges and through the crowded side-walks, churning his legs for home. He had one last chance to make things right, to get the rewards he deserved for bringing all of Palan's pirate clans to their knees while lifting Hommul above the rest. His mother, surely, would understand what he'd done and duly lavish him.

He ran past the Regal Hotel, disgorging its lobby of low-lifers, and then around the corner and into his alley. Walter wheezed as he clomped up the steps to his door. His picks shook in his hands as he tried to unlock the deadbolt.

"Momma, I'm home!"

He yelled the greeting through the stubborn slab of wood. Tears of frustration were already welling in his eyes as he secured the first tumbler.

"I'm back from promotions, Momma!"

Walter still wasn't sure how he was going to break the news that he hadn't been promoted. The next tumbler succumbed to his frustrated machinations. Walter bit his lip and concentrated on the third and fourth, his damned hands shaking like a junior pirate's.

Finally, the lock clicked open. Walter threw his picks in his pocket without bothering to arrange them back in their case. He shoved the door open and rushed straight for her bed, not noticing how quiet the machines were as he weaved around them.

"Momma," he gasped, wiping his nose and plopping down on the foot of the bed. "You've gotta do something about Uncle. You've gotta talk to him. The Hommul Clan is—"

Walter reached for his mother's hand but stopped himself just before grabbing it.

"Momma?"

The plastic bubble of a mask stood over her nose and mouth, its surface dry and clear, not fogged with her breath as it normally was. Walter could see the dull shimmer of her slightly parted lips through the clear shell.

"Mom?"

He shook her knee. His mother's body felt like part of the furniture: still and lifeless, absorbing his movement and dissipating it to nothing. His mind, already stunned by the day's disappointments, could not wrap itself around the obvious.

"Momma, wake up. I need to talk to you."

Walter slid up the bed and wrapped both hands around one of hers, holding the wires and tubes along with her fingers. So much of the apparatus had become a part of her, anyway.

"No," he said. He shook his head and patted the back of her hand. "Momma, wake up."

He turned to the machines around her. One or two were still running, monitoring the awful. Walter could've read their screens and graphs at any other time, but right then, the silence was deafening. His head thrummed with the lack of whirring; it roared with the absence of kicking tubes and fan-compressed air. There was a whole lot of nothing going on in the room. The machines that kept his mother alive had all gone dead.

Dead.

It was the first time his brain nudged up against the concept. He pushed away from the bed and stomped toward the breathing machine. The screen showed an auto-shutdown procedure, responding to an input from the pulse monitor. It wasn't Walter's prior nemesis that had let him down—it had been another machine.

Walter turned to the pumps that kept his mother's lungs dry. That machine was also calling out at him with its silence. Its screen showed an error message, an indecipherable code of digits and letters that might mean something to whoever possessed the manual. Walter spun around to the back of the unit, his multi-tool materializing in his hand. He fumbled for the screws, his mind spinning.

"Hold on, Momma," he said. "Hold on."

Tears coursed down his face, obscuring his vision. He dug and gouged at the screws, working them loose in fits and starts.

"We're gonna get those lungs dry," he told his mom. "Don't you worry. You just hang in there."

He ripped the panel free once the last screw was loose. Walter threw it out of his way, sending it clanging and skidding across the cracked tile floor. The stench of electrical fire, of charred silicon chips, wafted out of the machine. Walter shone his light into the bowels of the pump unit, scanning the mishmash of cobbled gear, antique spares, hasty wiring, and deep scratches haloed with rust. He sniffed hard, tracking the odor to the offending part, and his cone of light caught a tiny gray wisp of coiled smoke rising from an electrical board.

Walter stuck his head in and turned to the side so he could get a good look at the board.

It obviously didn't belong.

The board was affixed in place with ugly gobs of yellowed and aged glue. In fact, the board wasn't even being used for its original function. It was a piece-board, something Palans did when they wanted to use individual components on a PCB board without taking the time to remove the pieces. A tangled web of colored wires were soldered to the board here and there, hijacking the use of a resistor or a capacitor, three wires soldered to what looked like a timing chip. Walter felt a wave of relief as he realized he could just replace the components with spares ripped out of one of the other monitoring machines.

"You hang in there," he told his long-dead mother. He reached in and pushed the wires to one side so he could see which unit would need which transistor or rheostat. He bathed the board in the full glare of his light, memorizing the location of each component—

And that's when he saw for the first time just what he was looking at.

The board.

He was seeing it straight-on, all the chips arranged just so.

And he'd seen it before. He'd seen it in a schematic, laid out so pretty and clean. It was just the sort of navy hardware that made for a perfect piece-board. Just the sort of top-secret, unhackable device one could only use for a spare part, a resistor or two.

Walter gazed at the barest whiff of smoke rising up from the fried unit. He watched it spiral its way out of his cone of light, up into the darkness of the machine's innards.

The hyperdrive board sitting before him was dead. It was as dead as the hyperdrive boards in all the other ships in the Palan system. It was as dead as his mother.

And Walter had killed it.

39

FELONY FALLS PENITENTIARY

One of the wheels of his food cart spun with a mind of its own. It would rise from the uneven floor of the prison hallway and do a spastic dance. It would make contact once more, jittering the cart sideways. Then it would squeal out, jump back in the air, and do it all over again.

Walter watched the unbalanced wheel go through this routine. He kept his head bowed, the weight of his shoulders supported mostly by the other three wheels as he pushed the cart along. He followed the crazy wheel's rise and plummet, its howling complaint, its inability to do what the other wheels did, and he wondered—as if the wheel had a mind of its own—why it bothered.

On top of the cart, tin cans sloshed water dangerously up their sides. Other cans of brown food pellets rattled as the unappetizing nuggets did their little dance, jiggling themselves deep into their brethren while other pellets jostled up to take their place. Walter scrutinized this interplay for a while, imagining each pellet like a pirate clan enjoying its brief stay up top before it was swallowed by the rest. He thought about how long that ordeal had persisted— probably as far back as the time when his people had grown legs and crawled out of the muck.

Walter shook his head and sighed aloud. None of the metaphors were apt any longer. He had seen to that. Palan was in chaos. The loss of pretty much every ship in the system was nothing compared to the clan heads who had gone missing along with them. The pilot of their own ship had been right: None of them were heard from. They didn't show up at Earth. They were just *gone*.

And now junior pirates were trying to be senior pirates. Outcasts were muscling back into old clans. And the coming of a second flood so soon after the last had been seen as an omen of sorts, a harbinger of more turbulent years ahead. Already, the meteorologists and armchair prognosticators were saying many more floods were on their way. What had been a slow year was now forecasted to be one of the most severe in centuries. They said it was a thousand-year cycle, but Walter knew better. All it had been was a hack with the best of intentions. A program that had come with unintended consequences.

But unintended consequences were just a fact of life, Walter thought.

He let out another sigh and watched the kernels of food jostle, all of them going in circles.

The wheel of his cart set down and screamed, then rose back up, spinning idly and silently, if only for a moment.

Walter pushed his cart.

He had new prisoners to feed.

He figured he always would.

PART XXIII

THE BERN AFFAIR

*"Nothing ends up where it began,
for it cannot survive its journey unchanged."*

~The Bern Seer~

40

NEAR DARRIN · THE PRESENT

On the fringes of the Darrin system, an unlikely fleet formed and found its footing. Manned by navy personnel long in the tooth and short on combat experience, and Callite refugees with little time even as shuttle passengers, they came together and tested their systems in a rising cloud of confidence. They had already done something previously thought impossible: they had pulled off a raid on the most feared system in the galaxy and had walked away with a fortune in hardware.

And now, what the new fleet lacked in numbers—counting less than fifty craft total—they almost made up for in raw power. The arms and defenses in each of the ships had evolved in a system famous for warfare. A system that had reduced entire planets to rubble.

Inside one of these ships, Edison put the finishing touches on the last of the hyperdrives, giving it one-time powers similar to *Parsona*'s. He surveyed the changes a final time, screwed the side panel tight using an index claw shaped like a Phillips head, and then left the engine room, waving good luck to the ship's crew as he stepped through the airlock and returned to *Lady Liberty*.

○ ○ ○ ○

Once Edison was aboard, Anlyn waited for the hatch indicators to show a good seal and then decoupled from their last ship. As she peeled away, she felt an immense pride in him for modding two more of the drives than any of the other engineers. His extra efforts had helped keep the Darrin fleet on schedule.

Overall, Anlyn was more than satisfied with how well the plan was unfolding. Even counting the loss of two full raid crews, the mission to steal and assemble such an advanced fleet had gone surprisingly well.

She spun *Lady Liberty* around to face the staging area, where pilots were putting their new ships through their paces. Several groups were engaging in weapons-lock dogfights with other ships in their wing, getting used to how the craft handled and how many Gs the crews could take in their ill-fitting flight suits.

Anlyn watched as a few laser bolts were shot off into the distance. She had given them permission to test fire the cannons but had told them not to waste rockets. Meanwhile, navigators contented themselves with dialing through menu after submenu, memorizing the location of defensive routines and practicing with locking onto neighboring ships on SADAR. This also helped the other crews get used to the sounds of their new warning alarms so they wouldn't startle as easily in real combat.

Anlyn kept *Lady Liberty* above the action and watched. She saw a few good things within the maneuvers, but much wrong. The three real Firehawk pilots Molly had rescued from the Carrier stood out immediately as being head-and-shoulders above the rest. Each had been given command of one of the other three wings, and two of the pilots rode with their regular navigators. Saunders had argued the crews be split up, spreading their experience between two of the other ships, but Molly had insisted they remain together. She had assured them that the strength of an old partnership was more than double the advantage of each person on his own, and the way she had said it prevented any serious debate from taking place.

Now, Anlyn could tell from the mock engagements that Molly had been right. Those two intact and well-trained crews were dominating in their sparring matches, and they were already helping the others improve their own abilities. Anlyn watched for a moment and then thumbed her radio. "Wing Three Beta, you're inverting your dive like you're in atmosphere. Just spin in place and fire."

"Copy," the pilot radioed back, his voice strained from the Gs.

Anlyn watched the maneuvers continue, offering advice where it was needed. Now and then, she glanced at the clock on her dash, which was counting down the moment to the *real* raid. Soon they would be jumping straight back to Lok and beginning their clash with the Bern fleet.

She could hardly believe what was set to happen next. As Edison settled in the nav seat and began going through the systems checks, she thought about what she was about to do. Anlyn Hooo, young princess, former slave, rogue pilot. She was about to lead a ragtag group of the aged and infirm against the very fleet that had nearly brought all their demises and had literally downed loved ones among both the Callites and humans. She was about to go up against the true enemy of her empire, the shadowy figures of her childhood nightmares, the subjects of so much prophecy, hand-wringing, and empty pronouncements, and *she* was in charge.

The ridiculousness of it all made it seem as if it couldn't take place, as if something must stand in the way to prevent that moment from arriving. Even as the clock on the dash ticked down to the final hour, Anlyn felt almost sure it would happen to someone else, or in a different lifetime.

Then she thought about that massive Bern ship up in orbit around Lok, the one Molly told her had taken out an entire human fleet. She knew that if *Parsona* and her crew didn't have that gravity machine taken care of before they arrived, then none of her worries, none of her pointers to the other pilots, none of it would matter in the least.

Anlyn wondered if perhaps that ship was the thing keeping all her dreams from feeling real.

oooo

Cat prepared herself for the jump into orbit while Scottie and Ryn arranged the hyperdrive platform in *Parsona's* cargo bay. She sorted through the four remaining buckblades, looking for the one with the most solid craftsmanship. Ryke, meanwhile, continued to try to talk her out of going.

"It's suicide," he told her for the countless time.

Cat smiled to herself. The grizzly old scientist had resorted to repeating an experiment while hoping for a different result. It was a sign of how much he must care for her that his brain had stopped functioning properly. She powered on the buckblade, plucked one of her blond hairs out of her ponytail, and swiped the invisible weapon sideways through the dangling strand. The bottom half of the follicle fell away, and the barest tinge of something burned drifted up to her Callite nose. She powered off the blade and hung it from her belt.

"Look." She turned to Ryke and placed both hands on his low, broad shoulders. "It isn't suicide, so stop thinking of it like that. Hell, if everything goes to shit like I suspect, that fleet up there might be the safest place in the universe. And you know me, I'll switch sides in a heartbeat if I have to."

Ryke frowned, his lower lip disappearing into his beard.

"I'm only kidding," Cat said.

She squeezed his shoulder and looked around the cargo bay for anything she may have forgotten. She had a little food and water, a pair of good boots, a radio, and a buckblade. She couldn't think of anything else.

"We're all set up," Scottie told her.

Cat walked over to Scottie and Ryn. She reached out her hand to shake Scottie's, but he just used the grip to pull her into an embrace. She reciprocated, foreign emotions swelling in her throat, making it impossible to swallow.

"You be careful, Cat."

"I will," she mumbled into his shoulder.

Ryn hugged her next, his powerful Callite hands slapping fondly at her back.

"Don't hesitate to send up those missiles," she told the boys. "Don't you think on me and Molly—you worry about that fleet coming back from Darrin."

"We won't let you down," Scottie said.

Cat pulled out of the hug and waved the boys back. She stepped onto the jump platform and sat down in the ready position, her arms wrapped around her chest, her legs pulled up in front of her. She looked up to Ryke to let him know she was ready and caught him wiping at his eyes. The tears that had snuck by glistened in his beard.

"Let's do it," she told him.

He shook his head sadly, but stepped to the relocated control console. Ryke glanced up one final time, his finger poised over the button, and seemed to want to say something. For Cat, it was the first and last time she'd known the chatty frontiersman to be at a loss for words.

OOOO

The jump happened in a jarring, disorienting flash. The cargo bay and her friends winked out of existence, and Cat popped out of hyperspace one meter above and two meters to the side of Molly's hyperspace trace. The idea had been to follow her, but not precisely. With the modified hyperdrive they were using, two dangers were to be avoided: one risk was arriving in the middle of something solid; the other was the risk of arriving in the middle of *Molly*. To minimize both, Cat arrived higher than Molly's head and in as tight a ball as she could manage.

It wasn't tight enough, however, and the direction they'd chosen to offset proved unfortunate. Both of Cat's feet and the entire length of one shin immediately occupied the same space as a solid metal wall. Molecules jiggled as their electrons made room for these incoming strangers, and the two elements fused into a new one—a living alloy of steel, a dying wound of flesh, or something of both.

Cat cried out in shock. It was the shock of pure, raw pain. It was the rape of neurons.

Her body fell back, limp, bending at the waist.

She pivoted around the stuck bits of herself, her back slamming against the steel, her skull cracking against it just a moment later. Cat hung there, upside down, gasping for air. The pull of her weight against the invaded flesh heightened the experience. Through the haze of it all, she could see transparent walls surrounding her, like a cell, but with no sign of Molly or Walter. She could've jumped right on top of the trace coordinates and been perfectly safe.

But then, she would've missed out on experiencing all that *glorious* pain.

More of it lanced out of her foot as neurons too shocked at first to respond finally kicked into gear. Cat ground her teeth as she hung upside down. Her lips quivered somewhere between a grim sneer and an ecstatic smile. She flexed her stomach muscles and hoisted herself up, levering off her trapped shinbone back into a semblance of the ball in which she'd arrived. Glancing down by her waist, she saw her radio had fused with the wall as well. Thankfully, the buckblade swung free from her belt. She pulled the weapon loose and powered it on, careful to keep it pointed away from herself. Working slowly, concentrating on not puncturing the steel wall in case the vacuum of space existed beyond, she moved the blade down across the surface of the steel with the invisible thread parallel to it. She slid the molecule-wide cutter through the top of her knee, hacking her shinbone in two. She watched the flesh part under the weight of her body, the blue insides revealing themselves as her flesh magically unzipped. She continued to cut, upset at having to do it, at having the painless blade move through her gloriously injured nerves, parting their connections to her brain. She would have preferred to hang there, enjoying the agonizing sensation a little longer, but Molly needed her.

So Cat cut herself free, slicing down to her ankle where both feet were taken off just before the heels. With over an inch of meat still to go, her weight did the rest and ripped what remained, tearing the flesh in two. She fell and slammed into the steel decking below, sending out a spray of blue Callite blood tinged with purple.

Cat lay perfectly still, groping in her mind for the throbbing ache, the sensation of hurt. She pawed at it with mental fingers even as she felt the roar begin to fade and slip through her numbed grasp. Lying in a puddle of her own blood, chunks of her former body hanging above and dripping her vitality down the wall, Cat the Callite groaned with dismay at the end of the experience, the end of the welcome and foreign pain, and the beginning of the cursed *healing*.

41

LOK

Parsona flew herself low and fast, the buffeting wind of her approach flattening the grasses ahead and the flame of her thrusters leaving them smoldering behind. Over the horizon, the glow of dawn signaled an end to their short preparation time and the looming return of the fleet from Darrin.

Doctor Ryke rode alone in the cockpit, watching the instruments arrayed across the dash as the mighty ship piloted itself. In the cargo bay, Scottie and Ryn coiled hyperdrive wires, their climbing harnesses already on, carabineers and ascenders jangling as they worked.

"Are you sure you can duplicate what that Palan boy did with the missiles?" Ryke asked Parsona.

"I have total recall, Sam. I'm looking at Walter's individual keystrokes right now. It's a pretty clever hack."

"That means you can arm them remotely, right?"

"I can. I'm just not sure yet if I'll be *able* to, if that makes any sense."

Ryke mulled that over. He wondered if he would be capable of doing what they were asking of Parsona. Would he be able to send those missiles through hyperspace? Could he kill his only child in order to save a galaxy? What about a universe—did that finally tip the scales? It was so easy to expect it from another when looking at the equation from without, but then . . . he didn't know what it meant to have a child, or to be in a position to make that level of sacrifice.

"It *is* a large ship," he reminded Parsona. "It's the size of a moon. We won't send any of the missiles near Molly's coordinates."

"You know that would just be symbolic, Sam. We aim to kill her and Cat both, or all the ships returning from Darrin will go down as sure and fast as Zebra, and all the fleets of all the Milky Way's worlds will soon follow."

"You can't be sure. Let's not think like that—"

"I wish you hadn't let Cat talk you into jumping her up there," Parsona said.

"You coulda stopped her just as well. It's *your* drive and all."

Parsona seemed to hesitate.

"No," she finally said quietly. "You're right. And I'm sorry. Besides, there's no stopping her once she gets like that. I . . . Life is full of hard choices, I guess. Even when you can crunch all the probable outcomes in a blink."

"Yeah," Ryke said, nodding and completely understanding. He looked up through the carboglass as the dark silhouette of the upright StarCarrier came into view. Another few minutes and they'd be there.

"I have to be honest with you, Sam. If it weren't for Anlyn, I'd refuse to do this. It wouldn't even be a question to ponder. The Bern could take the whole flanking galaxy for all I care, just for the chance they'd keep Molly alive afterward."

"Anlyn? The Drenard? I didn't know you guys were that close."

"It's not so much that. Well, that's not true, we are close. She made a huge sacrifice to make this all possible. But the reason I have to save her is because it's what Molly would do if she were here. It's what she would want *me* to do. I don't think she'd forgive me if I chose any other way. Yeah, she might survive if I don't agree to arm the missiles, but she'd be miserable the rest of her life. She'd hate me and loathe her own existence if saving her meant Anlyn came back to an ambush. I couldn't force her to live with that kind of guilt, you know?"

Ryke nodded sadly, understanding the last bit, if nothing else.

"I guess that's it then," Parsona said. "It's one thing to calculate it all, another to voice the decision and feel as if you've really made it." She paused. "The hyperdrive is completely cycled, by the way, and we have nineteen point—"

Parsona's voice clipped off mid-word, like a mechanical trap snapping down over her thoughts.

"Parsona?" Ryke asked.

Without warning, the ship banked hard to port, the thrusters roaring up into the red curve of the gauge. Ryke grunted as he was thrown to the side. A frightening clatter rang out from the cargo bay as piles of gear slammed into one wall, followed by hollered complaints and a bout of startled cursing.

"What in the—?" Ryke began, but the radio cut him off. It came on blaring, with the background hiss of the Drenard Underground's carrier frequency:

"—mayday, mayday, Group Two is going down. Repeat: we have Mortimor, but we are under attack and going down. Group Two is through the rift and going down—"

○ ○ ○ ○

The Bern guards dragged a furious Walter and a stunned Molly down a long corridor of transparent walls. Molly was dimly aware that a heated conversation was taking place ahead of her, but her mind felt too unraveled to participate. She lost herself in the sight of the endless glass cells, thousands and thousands of them converging in the unseen distance. The cleanliness and orderliness of the passageway filled her with a hollow dread. No, she realized, it wasn't the neatness—it was the *emptiness*. It was the horrible sense of what must loom ahead, of what that ship had been designed for.

Molly wondered, if their plan on Lok failed, how long it would take for the corridor and hundreds more like it to be filled to the rim with screaming and crying refugees and prisoners of war. Looking at the empty rooms was like looking at a loaded gun, at chambers of awful potential. It made it somehow easier for Molly to see what things would look like once they failed, once the barrel was smoking and spent, once a thousand worlds had succumbed to that invading fleet, and once all those rooms were full of the people she had let down.

Her imagination tortured her with such thoughts until the guards pulled them inside a lift. Molly was actually thankful to find herself within its confines. The sliding doors pinched shut on all those waiting and empty rooms.

And that was when Molly realized how tired she was. She tried to remember when last she'd slept. She had spent the previous night planning what now must be falling apart. The night before, she had been dealing with the Callites. The night before that, she had been strapped down and unwillingly giving blood. And now, she could feel her sense of where she was and what she was supposed to be doing slipping away from her. Through her numbed senses, her environment took on a dreamlike quality. One of the only things she was aware of was the Wadi trembling against her thigh.

She also heard Walter, his hissing dulled by the fog in her mind. She heard him vaguely arguing about mountains of gold and promises broken. The flanking Palan hadn't shut up since their arrival. Then she remembered where she was and why. As she watched Walter beg and plead—his promises and lies mashed together in a pathetic blabber—some inner, resigned, shameful part of her hoped they were both being marched to their deaths.

At least that would make it impossible for her to ever make the mistake of trusting him again.

○○○○

The Wadi's scent tongue flicked out of the soft cave, tasting the air. Trails of emotion—bright columns

552

of drifting feelings like chords of raw communication—flashed in the creature's head.

Something was wrong.

The good person's scent was as black as she'd known it, and the bad one's was as guilt-ridden and empathetic as it had ever been. The two constants in her environment, the bright smells that were always there like the twin lights of her home, seemed to be *converging*. Would they shift, taking each other's place just like the rays that soaked her canyons often did? It wasn't time yet for that change, she thought. This must be something different. Something new.

And there were other smells. Some were similar to the good one, the same type of animal or very close. Their emotions were easy to read: Ingrained duty, blind faith, the stubbornness and self-righteousness of male Wadi. If her constant companions had her confused, these others did not. They were the enemy. They were big and strong and doing harm they could justify. They were doing it without flinching. Just as the male Wadi had done to her so many cycles ago.

○ ○ ○ ○

Cat didn't wait for her toes to fully form—she didn't know if she had the time. Standing on her crippled feet, slipping in her own blue blood, she reactivated her buckblade and hobbled toward the glass wall between her and the corridor outside.

Her reflection greeted her in the glare of the clear material. She saw dried blood coating her legs from the knees down, the white of half-formed bone still visible through her stitching flesh. The rest of her was pale with so much blood loss. Her brown, webbed skin looked almost tan and human-like from the drain. Cat felt a surge of dizziness from the sight of it all. She flicked her wrist, and a rough circle of the cell wall fell away, taking the reflection of her with it. The clear slab landed on the metal decking outside with the chime and heft of solid diamond.

Cat sniffed the air, searching for the scent of the Palan or the Wadi, two quite distinguishable odors. She turned left, following a weak trail of fear. Behind her, she left her own sign of passing as the decking of the hallway became marked with smears of blue blood, dotted between them with wavy traces of splattered drippings.

Most of it was residue, the actual bleeding nearly stopped and the front edge of her shins regenerating with the practiced ease of a good brawl. Her pace evened out as she moved. The pads of her feet and then the stumps of her toes began to emerge anew as genetic code, junk DNA, holdovers from swerves in her evolutionary lineage, did their thing. A past adaptation from a distant, tree-dwelling ancestor had been unlocked by too much Lokian water, too many of the little life-loving critters inside that couldn't leave well enough alone.

Cat healed as she hurried, healed even as she snuck up on the first guard station. It quickly became a mess. Not so much because of the two corpses splurting crimson in arterial arcs, but because she'd nearly let one of them reach out and activate an alarm. The blood loss had her fighting sloppy, unable to concentrate. Cat took a deep breath and tried to steady her nerves. She searched both guards and came away with swipe badges and a radio, the latter useless with her rusty Bern. What weapons they had on them paled compared to what she wielded, so she left them behind and danced away from the spreading pools of red blood, running down the corridor, resolved that the next guard station would go smoother. Or less *messy*, in a way.

oooo

The lift shuddered with a sense of great speed, taking them on what felt to be a very long ride. Molly endured it in silence, her thoughts racing as well. After a minute or more, the lights beside the lift doors lit up, and they opened to reveal a long ship-docking port.

Molly immediately recognized the layout as the guards dragged her from the lift. She would have known what it was even without the revealing glimpses through the large portholes to either side.

Ahead of her, a long corridor stretched out with airlock hatches staggered in a classic docking bay pattern, allowing each ship's wings to occupy the void created on the opposite side. Through the wide portholes, Molly could see various hulls locked to each hatch. Judging by the distance between hatches, and the length of their elevator ride, she felt certain they were in the biggest Bern ship, but she still didn't understand why Walter had brought them there. She sensed that he thought, on some twisted level, that he and Byrne were on the same side, or that there was some sort of reward for bringing her along.

As the group of men dragged her forward, Molly caught a glimpse of Lok far below, its bright film of blue atmosphere wrapped around the prairie brown. It looked like a Drenard's translucent skin encasing bone. The view was just a flash, the sight gone as quickly as it had come, blocked by the wing of a hanging ship. Losing the sight made Molly struggle against her captors for the first time; she pushed back against the guard, itching for one more peek of her old home before it and everything else was gone forever.

The guard shoved her forward, denying her a second look. But Molly felt, in that brief struggle, the strength of muscle and tendon in him and not the iron clutch she'd once felt with Byrne. Unless they were being gentle on purpose, these other men were different. More *human*. She filed this away as the guards stopped by one of the airlock doors. It was keyed open, and Byrne stepped inside, his armless form at once powerful and confident, yet totally reliant on his helpers.

Molly and Walter were pushed after him, the guards guiding them through the airlock and into the wide bay of a sleek and smaller craft.

Once inside, the inner hatch was closed and sealed. Byrne said something in a foreign language and then bent forward while one of the guards adjusted a red band around his head. They all stood there for a moment while Byrne's face contorted in a grimace of concentration, as if communicating with someone. After a while, he said something more to the guard, and they continued forward toward the cockpit.

"Where are you taking us?" Molly asked.

Byrne did not respond.

One of the guards folded jump seats out of the cockpit wall, and Walter and Molly were strapped in. Safety webbing was fed through their restraints and the seat's flight straps, making it impossible for them to reach the release handles on the buckles. One of the guards helped Byrne into a seat just forward of them and then took up position in the pilot's chair. The other two guards made their way back through the ship, busying themselves noisily with mechanical checks and other signs of departure in the cargo bay.

"Why are we leaving?" Molly asked, not really expecting an answer.

"We're not," Byrne said, startling her with a response. "The fleet is leaving soon. We're staying in orbit, where I belong. There's trouble down by the rift that I'd like to oversee. And of course, there's an invasion to conduct." He turned and smiled at her, and then he nodded to the pilot.

The ship shuddered, and a loud mechanical clank reverberated through the hull. The grav plates kept Molly's stomach from traveling up into her throat, but she knew with a pilot's innate sense that they were away, falling from the great metallic orb above them toward the much larger and earthy one below.

42

LOK

Ryke glanced at the cargo cam to see how his friends were faring in the cockpit. *Parsona* was pulling several Gs as she responded to the mayday call from the Underground ship, but neither he, Scottie, nor Ryn had on proper flight suits to cope with the acceleration.

"Parsona, you can't do this," Ryke said, his voice strained as his back sank into the pilot's seat.

"I'm sorry," Parsona said.

"We help everyone the most by downing that big ship up there. We *need* to get to the Carrier."

"Those equations already had a great deal going against them," Parsona said. "A few more minutes of thrust like this, and I'll let up and fall back to one point five Gs. You'll need to get the console ready, and you might want to lengthen those wires—"

"No," Ryke said. He tried to shake his head, but the acceleration kept it pinned to his seat. "Closing the rift is *not* our job. One of the Underground ships will do that. We're the only ones who can clear the way for that fleet coming back from Darrin—"

"Listen," Parsona said. The volume on the radio rose, allowing Ryke to listen in to the chatter between the various Underground groups up in the Bern fleet, none of them in agreement on what to do next. As soon as Mortimor's ship had passed through the rift and crashed into Lok, the leadership of the Underground had fallen apart, everything suddenly in question.

"They're dithering," Parsona said, "rather than acting. I'm not being unreasonable, I assure you. I'm heading for the rift, not Mortimor."

"I don't believe you," Ryke said with sadness in his voice. "I don't blame you, but I don't believe you."

"I accept that, but the Underground's cover was blown the second Mortimor's ship crashed through. I've got targets on SADAR heading down to mop them up and probably garrison the base of the rift. Now that the Bern know it's threatened from this side, we'll never get another chance at it. It's us or it's nobody. And that paltry fleet above us pales to what will gather if we don't act now."

Ryke chewed on that, crunching the odds. He eventually realized she was right. Everything was falling apart all at once, but if they could close the rift, there was at least a chance that future battles could whittle down the Bern ships that had already come through. He wouldn't be alive to see it, of course, but walling off the galaxy was the top priority, something the Drenards had discovered long ago.

As he thought of them, that old empire he had reached out to so many years ago, Ryke realized how important Admiral Saunders's mission to Earth had become. Even if the efforts at Darrin and on Lok failed—and it appeared that they would—at least his treaty with Anlyn might provide a long-overdue spark. Maybe humans and Drenards would stop fighting each other, wasting all those lives and resources, and join forces. And if Ryke and his friends could plug the hole he'd created on Lok, perhaps those future generations, banded together, could eventually win the war.

o o o o

Ominous black clouds hung low over Washington, DC. They oozed a steady patter of rain, soaking

Arlington Cemetery. As Saunders and his two subordinates trudged up the paved walkway, he couldn't help but be aware of the significance of the national monument around him. He had recently lost enough men and women to account for every tombstone in sight, a truly sobering and depressing thought. But if his mission failed, or if the plan on Lok fell apart, there wouldn't be enough green grass on Earth to hide the dead. Saunders chewed on that, growing ever more determined to succeed, as they slogged their way up the hill.

When they neared the outer gate, two figures in uniform rushed out of a small guardhouse nestled among the black wrought iron. The soldiers raced down through the rain to meet the trio, nervous hands resting on holstered guns. As they drew closer, Saunders could see the confused expressions on their faces as they struggled to account for the presence of three intruders on the *inside* of their carefully protected perimeter.

Saunders glanced around and realized for the first time that he and his companions were alone among the sad monuments. Normally there would be one or two family members, even in the rain, their umbrellas domed above their grief. It must've been a local Sunday, or perhaps the Drenard invasion had federal properties puckered tight. Whatever the reason, Saunders made sure to reach for his credentials slowly.

"Arms up," he told Robinson and Sharee, before the guards had a chance to ask them less politely. Sharee reached for her credentials as well, but Saunders assured her his would suffice.

The two guards arrived in a wary trot, their hats encased in clear plastic and popping with large splatters of rain. One of the guards reached for Saunders's credentials. He waved his scanner over the card, and it beeped cheerily. The soldier's expression quickly went from perplexed to befuddled as he read the results. He frowned at his machine as if it might be malfunctioning.

Saunders imagined not only his rank showing up, but also his currently assigned quadrant, half a galaxy away. Perhaps the machine was even saying he was presumed killed in action. The guard with the scanner twisted the device to show his companion. Both of their bodies tensed with formality.

"Sirs!" the second guard said. He snapped a salute to all three of them.

"At ease, soldiers." Saunders reached forward to accept his credentials back, the rain coursing down from his flattened hair and off his chubby nose. "Now if you would, call for transport and notify the president." He replaced his ID, pulled out another laminated card, and held it out. "This is my clearance badge. It should patch you straight through."

"Which president?" the lead guard asked. He fell in beside the trio as they marched toward the guardhouse and the gate. His partner had already sprinted off in that direction to summon a surface ship.

"The GU president," Saunders said. "Do I look interested in domestic affairs?"

"Of course not, sir. And what should I tell him?"

"Tell him to put down whatever he's doing. He's about to have visitors with very good news."

○ ○ ○ ○

The marine Rynx set down in front of the GU building, the craft's rotors thrumming with the whump whump whump of shuddering air. Saunders gazed out at the great structure. It was a sprawling palace done in the triple-postmodern style from the twenty-third century. Its grand façade, broken up by ornate columns, overlooked the ancient spread of old DC — a perfect vista from which it could watch the monuments of yore dilapidate in time along with their ever-eroding significance.

A contingent of Galactic Guards met Saunders and his two officers by the Rynx's deployed loading ramp. They all wore serious faces and fitted armor that clapped against itself as they hurriedly marched to get in place. Between the two lines of guards hung an anti-grav awning erected against the steady rain. Standing at the base of the ramp was an instantly recognizable figure: Susan Karlton, secretary of the galaxy and a one-time presidential candidate.

Susan smiled when she saw Saunders. "Griffin," she said, greeting him warmly and informally. "I asked them to run your credentials three times. I didn't believe it."

"The hits are gonna keep on coming," Saunders said. He stepped close and clasped Susan's hand. He had seen her as recently as his promotion ceremony a month or so ago, but it felt as if a lifetime had passed since. "Just wait until you see what I'm bringing along." He let go of her hand and patted the chest of his borrowed navy regs, feeling the Drenard peace treaty folded up within.

Susan glanced at his companions.

"Oh, I apologize. I'm not sure if you know my senior officers." He turned to the other two figures huddled under the awning and raised his voice as the rotor overhead continued to thwump loudly. "This is Commander Sharee Rickson and my second in command, Lieutenant Major Robinson."

Susan smiled and nodded at them, then looked Saunders up and down. "You look like shit," she said.

"I feel worse."

"I bet. I'd offer you the chance to shower and rest up, but Marine Two said you wanted to debrief at once?"

Saunders nodded. "It's urgent."

"Very well," Susan said. She waved the trio toward the South wing entrance and continued to talk as they walked, lowering her voice to a reasonable level as the Rynx gradually powered down. "The snippets we've gotten from Lok were hard to believe. I—We saw pictures of *Gloria* nose-down in the dirt. Locals are posting them on the net. I'm . . . I'm very sorry. What exactly happened?"

"I'd rather not discuss that right now," Saunders said, feeling on the verge of getting choked up. "I'm not here to debrief on any one battle. I need to discuss the larger war."

They approached the entrance, and a guard stood ready with a scanner. He tagged Susan's credentials hanging from her chest. Once again, Saunders waved his junior commanders off and used his own ID to validate the three of them. He let the guards fume over the breach of protocol as he and the others stepped inside and out of the humid DC air. Susan picked up the conversation again.

"So, you're not here to debrief on Lok or the loss of Zebra? The president will want to know—hell, *I* want to know what went down out there."

"Bad choice of words," Sharee said.

Susan blushed and continued walking sideways, leading them toward the elevators as she spoke. "I apologize. I haven't slept in two days. I'm pretty much running on coffee and adrenaline right now. But still, the fact that you're standing here is the best news we've had in weeks. We—Well, a lot of your friends had given up on you. *All* of you. How many survived?"

"Not many," Saunders said, shaking his head. He stepped into the waiting elevator. "And we're not here to debrief on that."

"Then what are you here *for*?" Susan asked. She stepped aside and waved the other two crewmembers into the elevator.

Saunders reached inside his coat pocket and drew out a folded document. "We're here for the president's signature," he said. "And we wouldn't mind something warm to sip on while we listen to his broadcast on the cessation of hostilities."

Susan's eyes widened with curiosity. Her gaze drifted down to the documents in Saunders's hand.

"What *is* that?" she asked.

"This one is a formal registration of ambassadorship between the Galactic Union and the Drenardian Empire."

He teased apart one of the sheaves, holding it to the side and watching Susan's stunned expression follow.

"It's a mere formality, of course, but necessary to assure that *this* one is official."

"And *it* is . . . ?" It came out a squeak, all Susan seemed able to muster.

"This one is the immediate and complete surrender of all Allied armed forces and a call for peace, accepted by a member of their War Council, the new ambassador to the Terran forces, and currently the second in line to the throne of the Drenard Empire, one Anlyn Hooo. It's also been ratified by their council member specializing in alien relations, and you wouldn't believe who he was if I told you. Combined, these documents demand an end to a war that's been raging longer than you and I have been alive."

The elevator dinged as they arrived at the president's residential wing, and the doors opened on a sophisticated array of security stations and guard booths. Susan exited and waved the trio forward, her gesture meek and subdued as she seemed to reel from the bizarre claims of her old acquaintance.

Saunders strode out confidently, relishing having had the opportunity to practice his delivery before seeing the president—not to mention the chance to shock an old friend into stunned silence. What he *hadn't* explained was that the cessation of hostilities with one enemy would just be the beginning, a chance to root out the traitors in their midst and align forces for the true threat pouring into the galaxy. Still, the end of a war that had raged for generations was near at hand, a monumental and historical moment. Saunders walked toward the final guard station between him and that slice of history, his mind spinning with the implications, his mood giddy from being so close to fulfilling his portion of the mission.

Beside him, Commander Sharee strolled with a similar bounce in her step, her erect posture and loping gate letting him know that she too was taking no small amount of delight in the significance of their actions.

○ ○ ○ ○

Behind them both, Lieutenant Robinson brought up the procession's rear, preventing the three humans from glimpsing his dark expression. The Bern agent felt along his ribs as he walked, comforting himself with the presence of his internal munitions.

He imagined for a moment that he could feel the warmth of the suicide bomb inside his chest as the two powerful fluids flowed from their lung-shaped sacks to mix together. What once could've passed for two benign organs in any x-ray were slowly coalescing, forming in their coming together a new and deadly mixture potent enough to level an entire city block.

As much as the Bern agent had loathed to watch his fat boss gloat over the end to a meaningless squabble, he had to remind himself that such celebrations were premature and ridiculous. In reality, the *true* mission to Earth had only begun. And it would *not* be a call for the end of violence by their pathetic president. It was very soon to become a bright, gory plume of fire and shrapnel. Another spark in the great conflagration that was destined to consume this damned and pesky spiral galaxy for good.

43

CRASH

Cat followed the Wadi's scent trail to a bank of elevators as the weak odors thinned out to a vaporous nothing. She pressed all the buttons arranged on the shiny column between the lifts, the symbols as meaningless to her as the jabber she'd squeezed out of the guard at the last station. Doubt crept up inside, making her feel stupid for jumping off to orbit all half-cocked as she always did. Of all the things she'd expected to find when she jumped after Molly and Walter, she hadn't been prepared to find *nothing*.

She looked down at her emerging toes while she waited on one of the lifts to arrive. So focused was she on her healing wounds, Cat missed the silent swish of the opening doors. There was just a soft ding, and by the time she looked up, two stunned Bern had already drawn their guns.

One Bern got a shot off before Cat could slice them both in half. The blast went through her chest, right by her shoulder. Cat staggered inside the lift, reeling from the impact of the blow, her nostrils tingling with the smell of burned self.

The doors closed, snapping shut across a new stream of Bern blood. Cat looked for buttons to press, her pursuit having become mad and completely blind. The dizziness from her blood loss worsened with the new wound, filling her with despair but very little pain. She blinked away the cloudy thoughts and realized there were no buttons in the elevator to press, just a badge scanner and four massive knobs beneath it, each of which was ringed with more Bern symbols.

Left or right, Cat thought, peering at the knobs. Either way, she wanted to go to the max. She wanted to be wherever the important shit was. The Callite in her wanted to turn them all the way to the left, knowing that would take her to the top, but these weren't Callites. They shared more genetic code with humans, who loved all things right and clockwise. She turned the knobs that way, all four of them, and then waved each of her plucked ID cards in front of the scanner, not sure which was the highest ranked.

To the max, Cat thought, smiling as the lift rumbled into motion.

o o o o

Cole felt powerless as the wounded Bern craft plummeted toward the surface of Lok. Group Two's suicidal dash for the rift, spurred by a fear for Mortimor's life, had drawn copious amounts of fire from the Bern fleet still in hyperspace. He knew Arthur was in the cockpit doing his best to manage the crippled ship, but as they passed through the rift and screamed down through Lok's atmosphere, the pilot in Cole wanted to be up there in the cockpit doing *something* with the controls, even if that something proved futile.

Around him, the ship's cargo bay had become a physical manifestation of his internal chaos. A wide mix of aliens screamed and shouted as the ship bucked and shivered. Fear had them reverting back to their old, primal tongues. Gear was scattered everywhere and still rumbling about. What remained of a once-noble resistance force was now jumbled, confused, and frightened as it fell out of the rift toward the sucking gravity of the planet below.

Cole stayed wedged between one of the storage lockers and a bulkhead as he held Mortimor, whose body had grown perfectly still. Gone was the fierce and calm bravery he'd seen the man possess during the past days. That vitality had been replaced by the sagging slowness of a man with half his life drained away.

Penny helped Cole hold him in place, the three of them braced together for impact. They were no longer able to do any first aid as the Bern craft rocked from side to side, the screaming of disturbed air audible through the hull. Every now and then, the sight of Penny's severed arm caught Cole's attention—the trailing wires and dripping fluids adding to the surreal nature of his environment.

A loud wail emanated from the cockpit, the shrill call of a collision warning perhaps. The yelling and shouting from the passengers grew in noise and pitch, matching the changing Bern alarm. As it grew in frequency and duration, Cole marveled at the psychological similarities humans and the Bern must share. The clatter of the warning siren eerily mimicked the sound a human engineer would choose to signal impending doom—

o o o o

Doctor Ryke made his way to *Parsona's* cargo bay as soon as the ship leveled off and the Gs relented to a level the grav panels could compensate for. They were still moving at quite a clip, heading back around Lok to the small ruin of a village where the whole mess had begun. The mess *he* had created.

"If only I'd gotten married," he said aloud as he helped Scottie to his feet. His two old friends had remained seated on the deck by the rear bulkhead, pinned by Parsona's acceleration.

"If only you'd done *what?*" Scottie asked.

"Nothing."

"I thought she knew how to fly herself," Ryn said. "You sure it's safe to stand?" The large Callite accepted the help up, but with the wary stance of a man distrusting gravity.

"It should be fine."

"What in the hell just happened?" Scottie asked.

"Mortimor's ship just came through the rift from hyperspace and went down. It looks like our missile plan is off."

"But the crews we sent out to get that fleet—" Scottie said.

"Toast," said Ryke, nodding. He pulled on his beard. "Now help me with that console we were gonna use for the missiles. We've got other things that need doing with it."

"We're gonna leave them to die?" Ryn asked.

"Afraid so, but now it's up to us to slam shut my damned door forever. Let's just hope the end of the many massacres to come will get its start right here."

44

REVELATIONS

"You can go crazy reading into prophecies, you know."

Molly stopped struggling with her restraints and looked up. Byrne had turned in his seat to peer back at her, a wide smile on his face. Beyond him, she could see through the cockpit that the pilot had brought them into formation with a cluster of warships. The surface of Lok hung below, impossibly far away.

"Is this the time of fulfillment?" Byrne asked. He frowned at Molly. "Or did we narrowly miss that just a few weeks ago? Are *you* the one? Is Cole? Does it matter?"

Molly felt herself flush at the mention of Cole's name. She bit her lip and looked down at her lap to see the Wadi's tongue spiraling out of her pocket. She adjusted her elbow to keep the animal covered and felt a wall of resistance building, a shield of silence to keep from giving Byrne whatever satisfaction he was looking for.

"Don't want to talk, huh?" Byrne wiggled around in his seat even farther to gaze at her. In Molly's peripheral, the armless maneuver made him look like an angry snake poising for a strike.

"How about you, my silvery friend? You've gone awfully quiet all of a sudden."

Walter sniffed. "I don't trusst you," he hissed softly.

"And why not?" Byrne asked. "Because I don't reek of lies? There are two reasons for that, my pirate friend. My builders left out such glands when they made me, and I never once lied to you."

The cracks in Molly's new wall spread out in a spiderweb of curiosity.

"Then where'ss my gold?" Walter asked.

"Many jumps from here, I'm afraid. But we'll take you to it once this galaxy is secured. A few months, at the most." Byrne looked past their jump seats to the cargo bay beyond. The other guards could be heard working on the ship, securing items and putting away cargo. They had been at it since the small craft pulled away from the massive, orb-shaped ship above. "As soon as your . . . *rooms* are ready, I'll let you make yourself comfortable while the invasion progresses." Byrne nodded to Molly. "You, however, might want to stay up here and see it for yourself."

Molly turned away and looked back toward the cargo bay. She thought about what she could do if not for the restraints. Perhaps dash back, jam the door behind her, take her chances with the guards in the bay. Maybe she could find an escape pod and risk that they wouldn't blast her out of the sky. She wondered if the pilot or any of the other guards were like Byrne, or if they were flesh and blood like her. She twisted her wrists against her restraints while she ran through the slim options, hating them all.

"There's nothing you'd like to discuss? Strange, because your boyfriend was so chatty in hyperspace." Byrne nodded to the pilot, who leaned forward and adjusted something on the dash. "Perhaps you'd like to listen to some radio?"

The pilot dialed up the volume, filling the cockpit with a crackling static, and then a voice: *"Mayday, mayday, mayday. Group Two is going down. We have Mortimor, but we are going down—"*

Byrne dipped his head, and the pilot flicked the volume off.

"It was a horrible crash," Byrne said.

The fractures in her wall widened.

"I'd be surprised if anyone survived it."

The cracks spread all the way around Molly's shell until they met on the other side.

"Just in case, though, I've dispatched a ship to finish them off and another to wipe out your friends attempting to close my rift."

Molly fought to contain the anger welling up. Shouts and screams were bubbling within, ready to explode through the fissures. She kept her eyes on her lap. She could feel her Wadi vibrating against her thigh, almost as if it were absorbing and containing her rage.

"If only Lucin were here to see how you'd failed him."

The words stunned Molly. Rather than provide that final spark, sending her anger bursting through her wall of silence, they somehow defused it all, draping her with confusion. She felt her urge to scream deflate, even as the shell that had been holding it back crumbled all around her.

"Lucin was a *traitor*," she said, the words lingering as a whisper. She pressed her chin down against her sternum and fought back the urge to cry.

"That he was," Byrne said. He leaned down to the side, his head looming in Molly's blurred vision. "He was a traitor to his own people."

Molly shook her head. "He was one of *you*," she hissed.

"Was," Byrne said. "He *was* one of us. And if he'd been stronger, this would've been *his* prophecy to fulfill. But they sent flesh and blood to do a machine's job."

Molly peered up at Byrne. His mouth was spread out in a rapturous smile. He continued: "The pathetic irony, of course, is that my superiors never wanted to trust machines like me in command positions. The hubris of meat-filled skulls makes them think the things they make can't replace them. But the weakness is in the fleshy heart, not the robotic mind."

The mention of Lucin's heart brought back horrible memories: Images of Cole's bullets tearing through Lucin's back. Rich, dark blood pooling up through the wounds. Earlier memories, like him in the principal's office weeks before, preparing to give her the news of *Parsona's* discovery—

"A machine never falls in love with the enemy," Byrne said. "We never lose sight of our objectives, of what needs to be done. Emotion can't get in the way."

"Lucin was the *enemy*," Molly said. Again, it was almost a whisper to herself. She forgot where she was, forgot about Walter to the other side of her, forgot about the noises from the cargo bay, forgot about the Wadi frozen in the folds of her pocket. All she could think about was Lucin, and Byrne's confusing talk.

"We're pretty sure he turned his back on us some-time during the Dire War, maybe even at Eckers. Something happened to make him never file another report with us. He retreated to the human academy, hiding from his superiors, shirking his duties—"

Molly shook her head. "He was working for *you*."

"Not me. I was sent here to replace him. Lucin failed us all. And if what you said weeks ago is true, you did us a *favor* by killing him."

"No." Molly crushed her teeth together and pinned her chin to her chest. She pulled against her restraints, not because she thought it would snap them, but because her muscles needed something to do, some way to burn.

"He was working for you to the last," she said through clenched teeth. "He was trying to steal my ship. He said he was going to use it to end all wars. He was trying to wipe us out, just as you are now."

She repeated the words in her mind, silently, to herself. She had to remind herself that Lucin was a traitor. She *needed* him to be a traitor. Otherwise, what had she done?

Byrne laughed. "The only war Lucin was work-ing to end was the one between the humans and Drenards," he said.

Molly shook her head.

"Oh, yes. We know exactly what he was trying to do. Our agents in your navy, the ones keeping the flames of war stoked high, had no end of trouble dealing with the waves of tolerant cadets he sent their way, all of them spouting a desire to cease hostilities one day, to find some kind of peace."

"You're wrong," Molly whimpered.

"Am I?" Byrne bent even lower in the corner of her vision. "Or are you just trying to justify what you did?"

He sat back up in his seat. Molly couldn't help it: she turned to follow his movement.

"Is it better for you to remember him as a traitor, rightly slaughtered, than as a hero to your people wrongly killed?" Byrne smiled, his face blurred in the coating of tears Molly could neither blink away nor wipe with her bound hands.

"Maybe that was your true role in all of this," Byrne mused aloud. "How delicious if your great contribution to our victory was murdering our biggest threat and your sole ally!"

The tears flowed freely as Molly's head drooped toward her lap. In the muffled distance, past the thrumming pulse in her ears, she could hear Byrne and the pilot laughing. She could hear Walter hissing in confused annoyance to her side. She licked the salty wetness out of the corners of her mouth and felt more tears course down her cheeks. She could see and feel them splatter on her thighs. Molly tried blinking the blurriness away. She tried to focus on what was real and true, on what was false and a lie.

Why had the discovery of Lucin's betrayal back at the academy stunned her in a way Byrne's words now could not? Why did finding out he was a Bern make her reel, while discovering he may have been a traitor to them seem to resonate?

It was because he had loved her.

She knew that. The hugs and solace, the advice and long talks, the risks he took to help her achieve a life worth living, the sacrifices he had made to win her admission to his school—none of it made sense if he was her enemy, but it all made perfect sense if he was working against them.

It explained why he had no family other than Molly and his wife. She even understood why he would need to keep it a secret, why he couldn't tell her about the ship, about her mom, about the hyperdrive, about *anything*. He wasn't being sinister—Lucin had been *afraid*.

More tears fell, and Molly ground her teeth in frustration. Byrne and the pilot were talking, but she couldn't bother to listen. Walter hissed something to her, but his words were a poison to avoid swallowing.

She cried to herself, chewing on horrible truths, grinding her teeth together, losing her awareness of all that was going on around her, unaware even of her hungry Wadi, who was crying as well, grinding her own lizard teeth and chewing her way through Molly's restraints.

45

THREE SHIPS

Cole came to in a cloud of smoke and a noisy din, the confusion and fog of a mighty crash swirling around him. He heard coughing and groaning. He heard the wailing of the gravely injured, the popping and hissing of electrical fires, and the sickening pealing of the stressed metal as the wings and broken fuselage sagged under their own weight.

Looking down at himself to see if he'd been injured, Cole saw Penny looking back up at him, her eyes wide and unblinking against the smoke. He saw that she had punched her remaining hand through the bulkhead of the Bern ship, anchoring them in place. What was left of her other arm was wrapped around

Mortimor, all three of them having braced together prior to impact.

Cole let go with his own mechanical hand and saw that his fingers had pierced the hull plating as well, leaving behind five black holes in the dull steel. He met Penny's eyes again. They both eventually broke the shocked stare to look down at Mortimor, who lay between them, unmoving.

Cole groped for a pulse with his non-mechanical hand. He wanted to shout to the dying to shut up, to end their racket, to give him a chance to feel.

Penny's hand went to Mortimor's forehead. She brushed his dark hair back and stroked his cheek with one of her thumbs. Cole looked to Penny as he fumbled for a sign of life. Her wild red hair hung around her face, almost seeming like the source of the smoke fogging in all around them. Beyond, the coughing and hacking from the survivors seemed to morph into the crackle of flame. Soot and dirt had lightly covered her face everywhere except for the thin tracks shoveled aside by falling tears.

In his peripheral, surviving aliens moved dimly through the dust, tending to others and pushing heavy equipment off bodies. Someone worked one of the hatches open, letting in a shaft of light that seemed to multiply the smoke. The entire scene wrapped itself around Cole, holding him there, nothing in his awareness truly real other than Penny and Mortimor — an enigmatic and mostly metallic woman revealing to him the first signs of real life, and a man he'd sworn to protect and rescue slowly giving up the last of his.

о о о о

Parsona banked herself wide to approach the rift from the edge. The expanded tear between Lok's atmosphere and hyperspace had the shape of a weather balloon pressed flat: tall and thin, rounded at the top, and tapering to a pinprick at the bottom, right in the foundation of Ryke's old house. The rift was difficult to look at directly, both with eyes and with sensors. The harsh photons escaping from the cone-shaped land had much of their primal fury intact. They faded, however, as they slammed into the different set of physical laws governing the universe to which Lok belonged. Those hyperspace particles quickly wilted as they arrived, melting in the atmosphere along with the sideways-drifting snow.

The strange combination of light and glistening flakes seemed out of place as they billowed over a notoriously dry and dark frontier planet. They seemed, at least at a distance, anything but awful. The entire rift appeared more like some visiting angel from a race of blob-giants, the creature's surface boiling with light and throwing off dying sparks like little fairies.

Suddenly, though, a black lozenge protruded from the angel's rounded head. It looked like a small, deadened tongue by scale, but it was just another Bern ship pulling through the rift high off the ground, continuing the long line of crafts filing out over the planet for weeks.

However, instead of increasing thrust to pull up to orbit, instead of falling into formation with the others, this black shape nosed down, no longer a tongue, but now something deadly spit from the angel's mouth. This new arrival continued its chase of Group Two's ship, arcing toward the downed craft and toward *Parsona* . . .

"Contact on SADAR," Ryke said.

"I see it, but I don't think it's coming for us." Parsona banked a few degrees more to the side, stiffening her angle to swing wider around the rift. The Bern ship stayed on course, heading out over the ruins of the old village and several kilometers beyond.

"They're heading for Mortimor's ship," Ryke whispered.

"You should get back with the others. Make sure everything's ready."

"They're heading for Mortimor's ship," he said again. "They're gonna finish the job."

"Ryke, see to the console. We don't have much time."

Two more contact alarms flashed on SADAR, pressing home the point. Only these two were swooping down from orbit rather than coming through the rift. And their vectors had them heading straight for Ryke's house: the locus of the great tear in space. It seemed the orbiting fleet had finally become aware of the local threat to their rift.

Parsona quickly calculated that she would beat them there, but only by minutes. And the procedure to seal the rift, according to Ryke, would take half an hour, give or take. Fighting the urge to increase thrust, Parsona swooped low over the prairies, constrained by the forces she could inflict on Ryke and the others. For an AI routine trapped in a life of so many eternal seconds, she suddenly felt a level of impatience and desperate anxiety that recalled a more human existence, and not in a good way.

oooo

Lady Liberty popped out of hyperspace in a high orbit over Lok, Anlyn and Edison taking point in the raid from Darrin. The single jump maneuver had worked perfectly, even if the hyperdrive would never operate again. With the press of a button, their ship had moved from one quadrant of the galaxy to another, with no care for what lay in between or how much gravity was encountered upon arrival. Anlyn felt as amazed and grateful as she had during her and Edison's previous experimental jump—the one to the center of that alien star so many sleeps ago, leading them to hyperspace.

Her thankfulness, however, didn't last. They had a problem. It showed up the size of a small moon on SADAR.

Anlyn didn't even need her instruments to know it was there. Glancing up through the carboglass, she could spot the massive vessel with her naked eye, its steel hull reflecting Lok's sun with the brightness of an unnatural albedo. It was shining, not smoking. It was perfectly intact.

The rest of Anlyn's wing began popping into orbit around her, each a few seconds apart.

There's no way to warn the others before they arrive, she thought grimly.

Her SADAR flashed with a targeting alarm, and then a gravity alert.

With little other warning, *Lady Liberty* went dead, just like the navy pilots had said their StarCarrier had. The ship began falling toward Lok in a flat, lazy spin, the pull of some bizarre artificial gravity dragging it out of orbit toward a very real death.

Anlyn's wing of ships followed, spiraling down after her. So too did every other craft jumping in from Darrin, wing after wing materializing in Lok's orbit and then beginning the long plummet down. They were like a flock of canaries appearing in the vacuum of space only to realize they couldn't breathe there— and that there was nothing for their mighty wings to flap against.

○ ○ ○ ○

Parsona's cargo ramp slammed to the grass in the commons, and Scottie and Ryn shuffled sideways through the door, lugging the heavy control console between them. Resting on top was the makeshift cross Ryke had cobbled together. The anxious engineer followed along behind, playing out coils of wire. He dropped the loops to the grass as the three men shuffled toward the foundation of his old home.

As he went, Ryke tried to concentrate on the simple task before him, worrying over the trivial threat of a snag yanking them to a halt. It was better to focus on such things than to fret over the massive ships roaring down to destroy them. Better to note the squeak from one of *Parsona's* struts as the ship's cooling thrusters lowered the rest of her bulk to the commons than dwell on the massive rift he had too little time to close.

"That strut needs greasing," Ryke mumbled to himself.

He wondered if he would die worried about such a minor thing.

Ahead of him, Scottie and Ryn weaved through a gap in the crumbling, rocky perimeter of his old home, carrying the console between them. Ryke followed, dropping his coils of wire where his front porch once stood. His mind warped back to promised dreams he'd had while living in hyperspace, dreams of making it back to Lok and rebuilding his old home from scratch. Dreams of getting his workshop back together and tinkering with hybrid combustion-electric engines, or something equally boring.

His foot caught on a bit of rubble. He nearly tripped and fell but managed to catch himself. As he regained his footing and remembered the task at hand, the wire trailing behind him pulled taut. Ryke dropped the few loops that remained and saw they had just a few more meters of wire than they needed.

Scottie and Ryn left the console in a bare patch, right beside an old work light someone had left lying on its side. Ryke pointed them to the exact spot in a now-nonexistent wall, right over a gap in the foundation where the frame of the cellar door once stood. The boys paid no attention to him, knowing as well as anyone where the old rift lay. They approached the paper-thin opening to hyperspace edge-on to stay out of the harsh glare leaking out to either side. All around them swirled melting flurries of the strange and twinkling snowfall.

Ryke powered on the console and fanned his hands over the top of it, as if the drifting flakes would shoo away like bugs. As the other two arranged the cross at the rift's base, he resisted the urge to look up at the massive hole in the sky above him, at the widening body of that great tear soaring thousands of meters overhead, taking a scale and shape he had known to be theoretically possible but had never imagined coming to life. He concentrated instead on the thin crack right in front of him, on the sliver of light and drifting ice no thicker than foil at that angle and yet the source of so much consternation.

Even though the rift was narrow near the planet's surface, the escaping photons—energized and angry—were difficult to look at. As Ryke concentrated on his console, fiddling with its knobs, he could see a vertical green bar in his vision where his retinas had been seared from just the briefest of glances at the relatively tame leakage. Working as fast as he dared, he began repairing the rift, closing up the old opening for the second time in his life. But now, so many years later and with a ton more experience, it would be different.

"This time," he said to himself, "you'll *stay* closed."

A rumble in the atmosphere disturbed the determined promise. Ryke looked up; he shielded his eyes from the rift and saw the source of the sound. Three enemy ships were screaming through the atmosphere directly toward them. One seemed to be coming from the rift; the other two arced down as if from orbit.

"I guess there won't *be* any this time," Ryke said to himself, sadly.

○ ○ ○ ○

Arthur Dakura staggered from the cockpit and into the smoke-filled cargo bay, shouting Mortimor's name. Cole looked up and saw him, saw the older man's face smeared with blood and grime.

"Over here!" Cole shouted.

Arthur turned, his body stiff and unsure of itself, reinforcing the likeness he shared with his robots. He stumbled stiffly over and sank to his knees by Mortimor's side, groping his neck for a pulse.

Cole shook his head softly, unable to speak.

"Get him flat," Arthur demanded, grabbing Mortimor by the armpits.

Cole and Penny helped, untangling themselves from their crash positions and doing most of the heavy lifting while Arthur cupped the back of Mortimor's head with one hand, lowering it to the deck.

Penny crouched over the scene, her face intent, her eyes wet and wide. Cole settled back against the bulkhead, his ears ringing, both his body and mind weary and sore. He watched with a sort of wounded detachment as Arthur—a quadrillionaire famous for both his obsession with immortality and his lack of real human bonds—dealt horribly with the death of his closest friend.

Arthur locked his arms and began performing stiff thrusts to Mortimor's chest. He stooped now and then to force air into the man's lungs. But the textbook resuscitation methods soon slurred into textbook depression. Perfect form degenerated into pounding fists as denial slipped into rage.

It all took place in slow motion but seemed to happen so fast. Time toyed with them, as if its governing particles could reach through hyperspace with the melting snow and the perishing photons. It seemed to usher along the most wicked of events and then force them to linger at their worst.

A muffled haze filled all of Cole's senses, like cotton balls forced in his ears, his mouth, even a wispy gauze of it over his vision. The coughs in the smoky hull came slow and quiet, the wails muffled to a background hum. Someone's shouts became whispers. He heard it, over and over, someone saying his name, mere whispers—

"Cole!"

He finally heard the shouts when Penny shook him by the collar. She forced his chin up with her one hand, caught his eyes with hers, and then pointed to the side.

"Cole!"

Larkin, the translator from his raid group, stood by the rear of the cockpit hallway. Cole realized the young man had been yelling his name for a long while.

"Larkin," he croaked. He waved an arm to help him locate them in the haze. He felt himself rising from the floor, his back scooting up the bulkhead.

Larkin turned and peered through the smoke. His eyes widened; he ran over and glanced down for a moment at Arthur, who had taken to silently cradling Mortimor's head.

"There are ships incoming," Larken said. He pointed toward the cockpit. "The rest of our squad is gone."

Why tell me? Cole thought. He started to complain and then saw Larkin's countenance: the wild, unblinking look in his eyes. He realized Larkin was in shock and looking for a chain of command to padlock his sanity to.

Cole felt like explaining the futility of it all. He wanted to say that he was no more in charge than anyone, but Larkin pulled him upright before he could complain and tugged him toward the cockpit.

"We've got to get these people out of here," Larkin said. He shoved Cole forward, through an aisle of shattered and sparkling carboglass. At the end of that glittering path he saw Arthur's seat, now vacated but covered in smears of someone's blood. In the other was the pilot from Cole's group, slumped over the dash and obviously dead.

Larkin leaned over the empty seat and pointed up through the hole in the carboglass. Cole squeezed against the dead pilot and numbly obeyed the gesture.

Sure enough: Bern ships. Three of them, roaring down through the atmosphere. Cole nodded, confirming Larkin's assessment of the situation and resigned to have it play out to its end.

"We need to get these people out of here!" Larkin yelled, shaking him.

Cole knew he was right. He knew the translator was trying to coax some sense into him, trying to stir Cole's spirit to action. And from the hollow pit of the cave into which Cole had crawled, he wished his crewmate the very best of luck.

46

LIGHTS OUT

A light by the elevator doors lit up just before the lift slid open. There was even a quiet ding, as if to announce Cat's arrival. Wherever her knob-turning and card-swiping had taken her, she was glad to be there.

She emerged from the long ride whole—almost fully healed—but still pale and covered in her own blood. With the new flesh of her legs and the sticky mess all over, she felt like a fresh babe delivered into the world. A babe made new and not broken as she'd been the first time she was born.

The birth analogy was made perfect by the room that awaited her: scattered with men in clean uniforms and chock-full of machines freckled with purposeful lights, it looked like the sort of place wealthy people gave birth.

The machines were everywhere and expensive-looking, Cat noted. *Very* expensive-looking. And they all seemed to be manned by equally important-looking people.

There was no sign or scent of Molly, however, which filled Cat with a powerful sadness. The ship they were in was far too big for some chance encounter. She had taken a wrong turn and would likely never see the girl again. For all Cat knew, Molly could be at the opposite end of the structure. She frowned at her failure and stepped out of the elevator—a bloody, alien samurai strolling into the scene of some science fiction vid.

None of the uniformed Bern tending to their machines seemed to notice her arrival. Their attentions were fixed on their screens and the constellation of indicators before them, their bored everyday minds not able to register the exciting in their peripheral.

Cat looked out over the assemblage, both of man and machine, and realized that she had gone about her search for Molly in the wrong manner. Completely, horribly, ass-backward wrong. She had approached the mission as someone else might: trying to be sneaky, and to not get caught. There was, of course, no way she could've ever found Molly on that massive ship, but she hadn't ever *needed* to. What she *should* have done was cause some trouble—as much of it as she could—and then wait for them to subdue her, maybe even beat her senseless, and take her to wherever they'd taken Molly.

The old Callite smiled at the plan, one that gave her logical license to flank some shit up. It also held the promise of a severe beating at the end. She wanted to kick herself for not thinking of it sooner.

But then, looking around, she realized it wasn't too late to try, and there was probably no better room on the massive ship in which to start. She had taken the lift to its limits, and that was where she'd wreak some damage. She flicked her buckblade on, wrapped her hand tight around its hilt, and then the grizzled and wounded Callite ran out into the room of blinking lights and swiftly widening eyes. She darted straight into them, cutting man and machine in half with the effortless and unfeeling lack of resistance only a good buckblade could provide. And Cat did it all in a manner and style possible only by someone who could not only feel no pain but had struggled most of her life to overcome that deficiency.

○ ○ ○ ○

The control console hummed beneath Ryke's fingertips like a drum of agitated bees. He adjusted the hyperdrive's gain and watched a needle quiver beneath its window. He released the knob as it settled in at just the right mark, the tip tickling a preset indicator drawn on the clear shield in magic marker. Ryke brought both hands away gently, leaving the machine in perfect balance. It wouldn't matter, what with the ships roaring down toward them, but Ryke didn't know how to do anything any other way. He was a tinkerer and a perfectionist to the last.

And besides, dying anywhere near a poorly calibrated device seemed to him the worst sort of death possible. He watched the needle quiver in synchronicity and felt a sort of peace within himself. Stepping back, he joined Scottie and Ryn, who were squinting up at the sky with their hands shielding their eyes. Ryke reached into a vest pocket and drew out a dark monocle. He screwed it into one eye, kept the other tight, and looked up.

He saw the three Bern ships from before, roaring their way. Two were speeding from orbit, one from the rift. The latter seemed to have a different vector, though.

Ryke twisted the monocle's rim, and green lines projected the foremost craft's destination like an overlaid SADAR image. It seemed the craft from the rift was going to pass overhead, heading out to finish Mortimor's downed ship. The other two, he didn't need to bother tracking. They were both barreling straight for him and *Parsona*, preparing to make a crater where his old home used to lie.

"It's been a good run with you fellers," Scottie said.

Ryke felt one of his friends pat him on the back. The three of them knew what was about to happen, and they remained motionless, waiting for it. They had all been on the other side of their current predicament, and so they knew the running made no difference. The cone of destruction about to be unleashed by the ship's lasers would be wider than the old village, swallowing even *Parsona* in the blast.

Ryke opened his unshielded eye and checked the rift. The narrow crack of light ahead of them had disappeared, the rip in space zipping up from the bottom. It was good to know the device was working, even if it didn't have time to finish the job—

"Watch out!" Scottie said, squeezing his arm.

Ryke flinched and looked up, shutting his naked eye just a tad late. Through the monocle, he could see laser fire lance out from one of the ships coming their way. They were firing from an extreme range, probably picking up the closing of the rift on SADAR and wanting to put a stop to it.

For that reason, maybe, the over-eager shots made some sense. But what *didn't* compute, what Ryke *couldn't* figure, was why the *trailing* ship seemed to be firing first.

o o o o

Cat's balletic dance through the engineering space took a brief intermission when a direct hit from a blaster took her arm off at the shoulder. Her limb spun to the deck, the buckblade still in its grasp. Cat bent over—a brief bow for her audience—and tugged the sword from one set of her fingers with her other hand. She rose, and the performance resumed, an arc of her thinning blood spinning around her as she twirled to dispatch the shooter. The artery closed itself quickly, pinching tight, but she could feel the giddy dizziness from having lost even more of her dwindling supply. She tiptoed through puddles of it, the fresh balls of her bare feet gripping the deck better than her old boots would have. Two more defenseless workers were split open, then another guard, then one of the several Bern whose body sprayed *sparks* when it was cut in half, rather than blood.

Cat kept at the equipment as well, enjoying the fountain of lights that erupted from some of them— pyrotechnics for her show. She felt pinpricks of joyous sensation as burning embers settled on her skin. Warning domes mounted to the ceiling choreographed her movement, all their lenses the same shade of danger-red humans were fond of. Each of them throbbed with an impatient pulse, throwing their cones around and around, sliding over the far walls and rows of hurt Bern and machinery.

Another device as big as a refrigerator was split in half. It was an important-looking one, and Cat's lightheadedness intensified.

Then she realized the machine must've had something to do with the grav panels, as she saw several dead workers drift up from the deck, their body parts propelled like stuttering rockets with a red, arterial plume of exhaust.

Cat's ballet of dismemberment seemed to move underwater as the gravity in the ship lessened and then disappeared altogether. She kicked off a tall server cabinet, propelling herself through the zero-G toward a Bern firing wildly with a plasma gun. She sliced through him and the large machine behind him, and the lights and sirens stopped their blaring and throbbing. She hit another piece of equipment—the one that must've controlled the air moving through the vast ship—and another—one for the overhead lights—and the whirring vents fell quiet and the room descended into near darkness.

Cat's eyes adjusted as she cut through more of the Bern and their machines. She looked around for anyone left to murder, but her raucous audience had become wide-eyed and politely still in the darkened room. She swiped another machine, giddy with the pain coursing through her brain. A blaster wound in her thigh hurt so badly, her leg almost felt numb with agony. It was a sort of numbness she hadn't known in almost forever. She didn't have much time left, she knew. Her head was so light it could hardly corral a clear thought. She had pushed herself far past her body's ability to heal. She had, as always, gone much too far.

Cat slashed through a few more machines, and the remaining indicators and twinkling lights on their panels went dark, signifying the end of her show, her *final* performance. What small amount of blood remaining within her thumped with a rapid, shallow pulse that she could hear in her temples. It beat with the patter of tiny, galloping feet. It was—sadly—the only sound approximating applause that Cat the Cripple would ever know.

But then, Cat had never performed for the simple pleasure of her audience. As her eyelids grew heavy and a final curtain of darkness descended before her, Cat knew that this last hurrah of hers had been, as with all her prior shows, mainly for *herself*.

o o o o

Lady Liberty grew warm as the ship hit the outskirts of Lok's atmosphere. Anlyn and Edison had stopped fiddling with the controls and struggling with the flight-stick long ago. Nothing they did so much as altered their ship's fall through the field of artificial gravity that surrounded them.

Instead, they chose to hold hands.

Around them, other crews were likewise finding ways to cope with their inevitable demise. The entire Darrin fleet had arrived in Lok's orbit intact, and all were meeting the same fate Zebra fleet had: They were plunging toward a fiery reentry and crushing impact below.

It wasn't long before a pale glow filled the cockpit with the first sign of atmospheric reentry. A nasty, tumbling, disintegrating death loomed. Anlyn reminded Edison, once more, of how much she loved him. Her ears popped, the sign of a hull breach somewhere. Another pop, followed by a beep—

And Anlyn realized those weren't pops at all! They were power relays kicking back to life. And the glow she thought had come from the heat of reentry was actually emanating from the dash! When the grav panels came back online, Anlyn felt her body sag in her seat, even as her spirits soared in the opposite direction.

Edison roared with excitement. His hands danced across the dash, giddy and alive. The radio crackled with whooping wing leaders cheering and barking instructions. Anlyn took the controls, and *Lady Liberty* pulled up, her thrusters warming as she rose, a battalion of tear-streaked faces and wide smiles forming up around her.

She aimed for the Bern fleet, and the first thing she saw was that the largest ship had gone perfectly black. All the lit portholes, the observation windows, the red flashing lights atop their spindly towers, all of them were dead and dark. There were no signs of explosions from the missiles, but she assumed they were embroiling within the belly of that beast.

Whatever the reason, she and her wingmen from Darrin were a fleet once more—a grinning fleet full of the sharpest of teeth. The other craft took up their positions around Anlyn, forming up on their wing leaders, and they accelerated toward a formation of Bern ships now in chaos.

The fleet from Darrin moved to wage war.

47

LOK

Cole peered out the maw of the Bern craft's broken windshield, past the jagged carboglass teeth lined up top and bottom, and watched the diving ships head their way. One of the enemy craft had fired on another one, sending it into a smoky spiral. Those two seemed to have been heading toward the ruined village just ahead. The third ship—the one that had been heading straight for them moments ago—began to bank around, racing back to help its wounded comrade.

"That's one of ours," Cole said to himself.

"*That* one?" Larkin asked, pointing toward the closest ship, which was swooping away.

"No, the one firing. It must be one of the Underground groups that came through before us. Has to be." Cole looked down at the dash, which was sprinkled with small broken triangles of nearly indestructible carboglass. Indicator lights winked with power, but only some of them. The screen in front of the dead pilot was still on, the SADAR showing in blinking dots what Cole and Larken could see just as clearly with their naked eyes.

"Help me move him," Cole said, tugging on the pilot. Together, they were able to slide the man's body, once a member of their raid squad, out of the seat and into the hallway. Cole ran back and plopped down in the vacated seat. He closed his eyes, bent forward, and blew a puff of air over the controls to get rid of the sharp dust.

"What does this say?"

Larken leaned over Cole and followed his fingers. "It's a systems menu. That says life support, and that one's for the grav panels, but it looks like they're not selectable."

"What is?" Cole asked.

"Choose that one," Larken said. "It's defenses."

Cole scrolled down to it and pressed the control dial in with a click. Everything seemed to work just as he'd expect, even if he couldn't read any of the gibberish on the screen.

"Anything?" he asked Larken.

"The chaff looks like it works."

Cole laughed. "If we could fly, that might help." He jogged the control dial to the left, and the previous menu came up. Again, he marveled at the familiar design aesthetics.

"What about weapons?" he asked.

"Scroll down," Larken said.

Cole did.

"There!"

One of the menus was lit up. Cole had already begun moving to select it when Larken pointed excitedly.

"What is it?" Cole asked as he drilled down into the menu.

"Oh shit," Larken said. He slapped Cole on the back.

"What the hell am I selecting?" Cole asked.

"You're not gonna believe this," Larken said.

○ ○ ○ ○

"Get those flankers!" Scottie yelled. He and Ryn pumped their fists in the air as the lead ship spiraled out of control, a plume of dark smoke trailing from its rear. Their allies in the Bern craft, one of the squads Ryke had formed up with in hyperspace, had nailed it with a series of laser blasts. As the wounded ship went down, it spat out desperate bursts from its own canons, but the shots flew wide over the old village. Where the bolts of plasma struck the earth, they sent up geysers of dust and soil in fantastic kinetic explosions.

"Aw, shit!" Ryn said. He grabbed Ryke by the shoulder and pointed behind them. The third ship, the one from the rift, had doubled back and taken a perfect bead on their comrades in the ship above. Plasma cannons erupted, furious bolts of pure energy lashed through the sky, and one of the shots clipped the wing of the allied Bern craft.

The hostile ship closed, adjusting its angle of attack. Another round of plasma flared across the gap, catching the ship square, and their friends blossomed into a lumpy ball of orange with a black, smoky fringe.

Gone, just like that.

The attacking ship banked hard, pulling away from the fireball it had wrought, and angled down toward the base of the rift. It had dispatched the only ally Ryke and his friends had nearby, and now it was turning around to do the job of its wounded comrade, which finally reached the ground a kilometer away in a mad, screaming explosion.

The two blasts from the destroyed craft reached them at almost the same time, the roars of destruction deafening and coming from all directions at once. The three friends flinched in unison, ducking from the onslaught of compressed air that followed the explosions. Recovering quickly, they stepped back from the console, watching the remaining ship line up on them, bringing its cannons to bear—

And then another ball of flames appeared, another explosion, right where the enemy ship had been. The orange cloud blinked into existence like an eyelid peeling back on an impossibly large and brightly colored orb. The fire blossomed out, its edge fusing with the billowing smoke from the other ball of airborne destruction, three large ships meeting their sudden end in bizarre and rapid succession.

Ryke scanned the sky, dumbfounded, looking for a clue as to why they were still alive and the Bern ship destroyed. He finally saw, and followed, a thin plume of gray smoke, an ephemeral and dirty rope of exhaust, as it threaded its way through the bright, blue, Lokian sky back to Mortimor's downed ship. It was the spiraling vapor trail of a lone missile that hung in the sky, slowly dissipating but still tracing the flight of its maker to the sad, crashed craft on the horizon.

Group Two's ship sat there, listing to one side, a wing drooping, its body broken, and yet—still very much deadly.

48

BYRNE'S SHIP

As soon as Molly noticed the Wadi chewing through the webbing holding her in place, the creature stopped and looked up at her, its scent tongue flicking out like a whip. Molly blinked away her tears and noticed the sheen of wetness on the Wadi's eyes. The animal blinked at her. Its tongue spiraled out and then disappeared back in its mouth.

Molly looked to her restraints, which were partially eaten through. She tested them, wrenching her hands apart, but they wouldn't budge. She glanced to her side to see Byrne and the pilot conferring. To her other side, she saw Walter watching her and the Wadi with interest. Molly turned her attention back to her lap. She focused on the chewed portion of the harness, imagining herself eating through it. She ground her teeth as she had been doing moments earlier.

Her Wadi resumed its efforts.

Her Wadi could read her emotions!

So much dawned on Molly all at once: The tongue-flicks and the head-bobs, the hiding in her pocket when Molly was frightened, the pawing at the air when she was enraged. All the nuances and small behaviors Molly had superstitiously been reading into for weeks were confirmed! Her desire to avoid anthropomorphizing the animal had blinded her, and now she knew how the sheriff had used her Wadi to attack his deputy!

The webbing holding her into the seat parted, leaving her hands shackled, but her arms free. She thought about having the Wadi test the metal bands around her wrists with its teeth, but worried they would be too much for her jaws. Molly kept her hands in place so she wouldn't alert Byrne and turned and saw Walter eyeing her freedom. He glanced down at his own buckled harness.

Molly looked to the Wadi, who stuck out her tongue and waved it in the air.

Yeah, Molly agreed, *but half an ally is better than none.*

She forced the words to the surface, just as if she were wearing a Drenardian headband, and then realized the Wadi probably didn't use language that way. Why would it know English? She closed her eyes instead and tried to form pictures in her mind that the animal might understand.

It was harder than she thought, so reliant was she on using words to convey instructions and meaning. And then there were the distractions spinning around her and within her that made it hard to think: her father's crashed ship, the returning Darrin fleet and how she'd failed them, Byrne and the news of Lucin, Walter's latest betrayal. The more she tried *not* to think of them, the faster these distractions bubbled to the surface.

Molly pictured a god-like arm sweeping them all away, leaving just the blackness behind her eyelids. She pictured herself there, along with the Wadi. She imagined the two of them high up in the air and glowing white. She then placed the Bern crewmen below them, shrouded in black. She added Walter last, up with her and the Wadi, as painful as the picture was to create.

Molly opened her eyes and looked down at her lap.

Her Wadi stuck out her tongue. The creature's head cocked to the side, almost as if in confusion, or deep thought.

Rather than ignore the temptation to read into the animal's body language as she would have before,

Molly took it all in and interpreted the Wadi's look as she would from a human. Something about her mental image must not be right—it must not make sense to the Wadi. She closed her eyes and reexamined the image she had formed as if she were an alien—and she saw everything wrong with it all at once.

There was no telling if white was good and black was bad to the Wadi. Of course! The animal lived in dark caves, avoiding the twin suns of Drenard. And it lived *down* in the canyons, not up in the harsh air. Molly wiped the image out of her mind, realizing at once that her prejudices were opposite the Wadi's. She tried to start over, concentrating on the very basics, the primitive building blocks of communication. She could feel a sheen of sweat tickling her scalp, could hear Byrne and the pilot talking in the background. She swept her imaginary god-arm across all the wrong images looming behind her closed lids. She tried, for the very first time, *talking* to her pet Wadi piece by mental piece:

She started with an image of her own neck, big enough to fill her imagination. Just her neck and shoulders. She pictured the Wadi on it, tail curled tight, rough cheek brushing just behind her ear. Molly tried to *feel* it. She took a deep breath and tried to exude the calm, good feelings that came from security and safety.

She panned back. She brought Walter into the image. Molly imagined her arms around his back, her head leaning on his shoulder. A tremor of disgust threatened to invade, but she stifled it. She pictured the Wadi moving to Walter's shoulder, feeling safe and content there.

Zooming out even more, she brought in the Bern. She gave them snapping jaws and filled them with aggression. Rather than feel *fear* of them, though, the kind of fear that made her want to retreat into a cave, Molly swelled herself with bravery. She made a show of striking at them, of the Wadi pawing the air at them, but not launching an attack just yet. First, she showed Walter's hands breaking free, the Wadi chewing through his harness. Her final thought was of the Wadi striking out at the pilot while she and Walter went for the armless Byrne. She filled the attack with such confidence, even Molly began to feel it. She opened her eyes to see the Wadi already moving, already biting through the webbing holding Walter to his seat.

It was happening.

Molly had thought it, and now it was happening.

She was about to fight the Bern, in that cockpit, with her bare hands.

Walter's arms came free. He undid the strap across his legs while Molly fumbled to do the same with hers. The Wadi burst off Walter's lap and launched for the back of the pilot, just as she had imagined. Molly jumped up to wrap her bound wrists around Byrne's neck. She yelled for Walter to help, but saw, in the corner of her vision, that he was running the *other* way, out to the cargo bay.

Molly cursed him. She threw her hands over the top of Byrne's head and brought her shackled wrists down to his throat. She leaned back, trying to crush whatever he was made of.

A shriek erupted from the pilot. Molly kept her eyes tight, her jaws clenched. She didn't need to see what the Wadi was doing to know. She'd seen the animal tunnel its way through flesh before.

Whatever Byrne's neck was made of, though, it wasn't flesh. Even with Molly leaning all her weight back and her feet braced on the base of Byrne's seat, she couldn't feel the surface of him budge. It was like trying to strangle a lamppost.

Byrne roared something and began to sit forward, bringing Molly with him. She hadn't worried about him doing harm to her, not without his arms, but she quickly realized she'd been mistaken. Byrne bent at the waist, pulling her into the back of his seat, and then kept bending forward even more, his mechanical spine showing no limit to the forces it could impart.

Molly was crushed and smothered against the back of his seat. She could feel the strain on her shoulders, the bite of the shackles on her wrists, and wondered which joint would give way first and if it would happen before she suffocated. She felt the urge to gasp in pain, but her cheek and neck were twisted against the back of the padded headrest, her jaw forced to the side. With a sickening pop, Molly felt one of her shoulders leave its joint, the tendons and ligaments crying out in pain. Tears formed in her eyes and were trapped there. Molly couldn't breathe. She pictured her death, her failure, her stupidity.

The other shoulder felt as if it could go at any moment, and Molly realized the danger of picturing such things, the sort of pain and confusion she was leaking to her Wadi. With only half a breath in her lungs, she pictured instead her Wadi attacking Byrne. She pictured raw hate and destruction, all aimed at the armless man. She concentrated her fear into fury, her pain into punishment.

Her shoulder was blasted with another wave of torture, but it was the pain of coming back together. The pressure came off Molly's jaw, then her cheek. She felt Byrne writhe beneath her aching wrists. She pulled back, brought her hands up over his head, and nearly fainted at the jolt of agony as her shoulder popped back into place. Her arm went numb past her elbow, down to her wrist. She stood, despite the fear she might pass out if she did, and saw the Wadi tunneling through the side of Byrne's head. Its little tail spun madly, its hind legs clawing at the air, its head fully inside Byrne's.

The powerful, armless, robot went berserk. He straightened his legs, attempting to jump out of his seat, but caught his knees on the dash and ripped a panel clean off. He tried throwing his head to the side to bash the Wadi against something, but his shoulder hit the dead pilot, who was slick with blood.

Molly tried to steady Byrne in order to protect the Wadi. She found herself transfixed by the sight of the animal, clawing through steel and twisted rods. She held Byrne's shoulders, her own arm screaming with shining pain, when something popped. There was a loud, cracking sound followed by a brief flash of light, and then a sizzle from Byrne's head just before his body went limp, slumping down into his seat.

The Wadi's hind legs emerged, its tail wiggling. It pushed against the side of the ruined head, trying to extract itself from the hole it had dug. Molly reached up to help and then recoiled at the zap of electricity and heat. The rear half of her Wadi shivered and fell still.

Molly ignored the pain and grabbed the animal quickly. She wrapped her hands around its waist and pulled it out. She heard herself cry out when its front limbs, then neck, came out limp. Molly pulled the animal against her chest. She adjusted her grip, using the sides of her arm to distribute the searing heat and keep it from ruining her hands.

Before her lay two lifeless Bern. Her every joint was in agony. Her Wadi was deathly still. It had all happened in an instant. Not even a minute.

Walter.

Molly turned around, searching for him, wondering where he had run off to, and saw that he had closed the cockpit door behind him.

She rushed to the door and slapped the controls to its side.

Nothing happened.

She peered through the door's round observation port. In the cargo bay beyond, she could see Walter standing off to one side, just on the other side of the door. Molly pounded the glass and yelled for him.

Walter glanced back, just for a moment, and then returned his attention to the open control panel by his side. He had a colorful tangle of wires out, the door's controls dangling from the wall. Past him, Molly could see movement—one of the Bern guards emerging from a room aft of the cargo bay. As soon as the guard saw Walter, he called out, his lips moving but his alarm muffled by the cockpit door.

"Get inside!" Molly yelled to Walter.

She cradled the Wadi in the crook of her elbows and slapped the glass with both hands, the metal rope between them restricting her movement. "Walter!"

He didn't turn. She could see the back of his head glowing as he fumbled through the wiring, looking for a particular one. He finally yanked one free, bit through it, and then clamped his teeth down over the insulation and drew the wire out slowly, leaving a coppery bit exposed.

"Walter! Get inside!" Molly banged her wrist restraints against the glass, wondering if she could somehow use them to break through.

Walter turned at the sound of that. He had just stripped another wire with his teeth. Two Bern guards were now running for him across the cargo bay.

Walter shook his head. His lips were curled down, tears streaking across his cheeks. He mouthed something to Molly and then brought the two wires up.

I'm ssorry.

He mouthed the words again as he pressed the coppery bits together, twisting them tight.

In an instant, the cargo bay filled with a white haze of condensed air. Wisps of it stirred, like speeding clouds racing for some unseen horizon.

The Bern guard farther away from the cockpit turned to his side, his eyes wide and white in horror. He slipped and fell and then was pulled after the swirling, escaping air—sliding out of view.

The other guard dove across the last meters of the cargo bay and crashed into Walter. His face was twisted up in fury and fear. He pawed at Walter's hands, trying to wrestle the wires away from him, but then the sucking of what must've been an open cargo bay and the vacuum of space beyond tugged at his feet, lifting him and Walter into the air.

Walter held the edge of the open control panel, his fingers wrapped around the square hole in the hull. He dangled there, stretched out sideways, the Bern guard hanging from his feet.

Molly's nose touched the glass in front of her, the Wadi pinned to her chest. She cupped her hands on either side of her face and peered through the porthole. Walter's eyes locked on to hers. She watched, horrified, as the vacuum of space tore the tears from his cheeks, sending them like twinkling bullets back through the bay.

The Bern guard lost his grip on Walter and went tumbling out of sight, bouncing off a bulkhead as he went. Walter started to mouth one last thing, but then the shine on him faded away, dulling into some state of calm. A wan smile broke across the Palan's face. His eyes twinkled as if some beautiful thing had appeared in his vision, and then he let go.

His arms waved in the air once.

His eyes locked on Molly's.

And then Walter was gone forever.

49

EARTH

As Lieutenant Robinson approached the offices of the GU president, the old Bern agent couldn't believe his good fortune. The invasion of the Milky Way Galaxy had played out in a strange mixture of stops and starts for him, almost like a perfect microcosm of his entire career. For two decades, he had toiled as a member of the human navy, trying his damnedest to push the war through the pesky Drenard front in order to secure the rift from their side. At the very least, he had meant his efforts to weaken their defenses while more Bern agents slipped through the rift, dodging the blockade. And just when he was starting to see some successes along those lines, the High Command got involved in some *prophecy* nonsense.

Robinson was one of the many older agents who frowned on Byrne's exploits, the crazy simulacrum obviously having gotten a wire crossed during his construction. But then, reversing a reversal, the daft bot had come through. A new rift had been opened, and the Bern fleet had begun pouring into the pesky galaxy in a manner unheard of, *undreamed* of, when considering the older, Drenardian rift.

That high elation had been followed by the awesome destruction of his Zebra fleet, which had gone well enough, if not ending up the absolute success Robinson had hoped for.

That brought a high, which was followed by another low as Saunders survived the attack, a failure that would reflect poorly on Robinson in future reports. Then the lows became even lower as Robinson was forced to watch a desperate herd of humans huddle together in that wooded clearing, plotting audacious miracles, aligning themselves with even more grotesque aliens.

But lows could be highs in disguise, he had learned. The arrival of the Drenardian girl had seemed to spell trouble, bringing the threat of peace between their race and the humans, but just when things seemed to be dipping, they soared again.

Here he was, walking alongside that cursed piece of paper, that *peace* treaty, and escorting his fat admiral through the antechamber of the GU president himself. He was strolling with them on the eve of a successful invasion of their galaxy, and all mere moments away from their personal destruction.

What better way, Robinson thought, *to sow discord through this mutant empire than by lopping off its head right as the fight begins? What better way to usher the rest of the body toward its violent demise?*

Robinson watched Saunders go through the security gauntlet first, once again waving his pass and vouching for the rest. That gesture was coming for the third time, and the nicety was pissing off Robinson. He *wanted* to be scanned. He *wanted* his credentials registered. He *wanted* his people and higher-ups to know he had been there, that it was *he* who did this. Let Byrne, that blasted agent, take credit for opening some trifling door, *he* would be the agent to go down in Bern lore, passed from one universe to the next, remembered forever as the man who began the war, the one who assassinated the president of a race grown notorious for their insolence, for their inability to just *go away.*

Saunders waved Sharee through the scanner next, her flanking gender somehow more important to protocol than Robinson's rank.

Robinson smiled. Soon, it wouldn't matter. Nothing on the entire residential wing of that building would survive the blast he was about to unleash. Not that piece of paper, that treaty promising peace. It would burn no less righteously than all else.

The secretary of galaxy waved him through the security screen next, and Robinson stepped forward between the scanning walls, smiling at the officials on the other side of the viewing ports. The barred gates ahead of him remained closed as he stood still, letting their futile scanners have their fun. His augmented innards were designed to pass the most detailed of scans. Security agents would see cybernetic lungs, rather than bombs and chemical agents mixing together.

"Credentials, please," a voice said through the security corridor's speakers.

Robinson smiled. *Finally*, he thought.

He reached for his pass, using the movement to hide the complex motions necessary to arm himself. His fingers became a blur, twitching in just the right pattern and at just the precise timing to activate the once-inert gels, now hardened into furious potential. His hand came away from his damp, mud-speckled flight suit bearing his badge, his body now little more than a potent bomb.

Robinson held the badge up in front of the viewing port, turned to the side, and smiled at the secretary of galaxy, who nodded back.

"Pass it in front of the scanner, please."

"Gladly," Robinson said. He looked the other way toward Saunders, that fat fool, only to see Saunders flashing a smile. The admiral was grinning like something delicious had just passed through his flabby gullet. Joy on that man's face brought a frown to Robinson's. He could see the GU president beyond the admiral and Sharee, coming out of his suite with his arm extended. Robinson thought about doing it right then, scanning his pass and blowing the serpent's head clear off, taking that nest of vipers with him—

But then the scanner beeped as his badge was registered. And it beeped again, the beep echoing louder. And louder. The initial acknowledgment seemed to morph into an alarm.

Robinson froze, but every other mechanical thing around him whirred into action. Ports slammed shut. Blast walls thundered down from the ceiling. The acoustics of his surrounding space altered as the dull press of thick steel shrouded him on all sides, swallowing even the now-distant sirens.

Looking down, Robinson saw the scanner's laser array hashed across his credentials, reading the black squiggles of information. He looked at his badge, the apparent trigger for the sudden lock-down.

He saw his face. His name.

But not his ID number.

Not, he could even tell at a glance, his *barcode*.

Something in Robinson's internal database, his perfect memory of navy secrets, signaled a match. Relays sent that information from one module of his computer-like being to another. It registered in his consciousness, accompanied by red blips and the alarm of his navy persona. It was the warning flashes of a C-15 Object of Interest.

According to his badge, Robinson was the most wanted man in the galaxy. But how could that—?

No, he realized, as the rest of the file came just nanoseconds later: he was the most wanted *female* in the galaxy.

The name belonging to the barcode flashed through his mind, remaining there as his fury and confusion tripped the hair-triggered bomb he'd just concocted. Robinson looked up, searching for Saunders and that infernal smile on his flabby face. But everything around him was gone, sealed off by thick blast walls that had long waited for just such a contingency. The barriers left Robinson alone with that name, the one that went with the barcode. It existed for a brief eternity, a fleeting thought amid a contained cloud of explosive and expanding debris, much like a star in the center of a fiery nebula:

Molly Fyde.

50

REUNIONS

Byrne's sleek command ship touched down on Lok, its cargo door already hanging open. With a matching atmosphere outside, Molly was finally able to open the cockpit door manually, the safety overrides having become disengaged. With her wrists still bound and her lifeless Wadi nestled in the crook of her arms, she stumbled out of the death-filled cockpit, past the tangle of wires hanging from the bulkhead, through the cargo bay, and out into the bright day and dry grasses. She had landed a stone's throw from the downed ship from hyperspace, but only a handful of faces turned her way—everyone was too busy or in too much shock to care about her arrival.

"Cole?" Molly stumbled toward the horrific scene.

The large Bern ship lay in a bent heap. Survivors staggered around it, walking among and carrying the bodies of those less fortunate. Still mounds were laid out in a neat line across the trampled prairie. Some were being tended to; a hand with life still in it clutched to someone's shirt. Scant covering hid another's face, knelt over by someone sobbing. Molly passed through the outer edge of the dead and wounded, so many alien races present, as she looked for recognizable features, dreading finding them in case those she loved were among the still.

"Cole?"

A girl with hair like fire caught Molly's attention, her bright green eyes tracking her. Molly didn't see Cole at first, not until the girl grabbed someone's arm, directing a man's attention—

Cole.

Molly ran to him. She clutched her Wadi and weaved her way through the crowd. Cole moved to stand, winced as if in pain, and then sank back down. Molly threw herself into his arms.

"Cole!"

He didn't respond.

His arms went limply across her back and felt heavy with fatigue. Molly kissed his shoulder, his neck, his skin scented like smoke and grease. She sat back, placed the Wadi on the grass like so many other dead, and went to throw her manacled hands over his neck.

Cole grabbed her wrists and stopped her. He still hadn't smiled or said a word. He shook his head, and Molly noticed the tear tracks cutting through the soot on his cheeks.

"I'm so sorry," he whispered.

She wanted to ask what he could mean, and then Cole's gaze drifted to the girl with the fiery hair. Molly turned to her. She noticed for the first time that the girl cradled a man's head in her lap.

A cold vacuum filled Molly's lungs.

She tried to breathe, to call out, but could do neither.

Her father was lying in the bent grass, his head turned to the side. Molly could see his lips, barely parted, amid the tangle of his beard. A beard much grayer than she remembered.

"Dad?"

Molly placed her bound hands on Cole's shoulder and shuffled closer on her knees. Her vision blurred as she groped for her father's hand. A distant part of her registered the wide stain of blood seeping through his white flight suit.

"Dad?"

She looked to Cole, and then the girl. This couldn't be happening. She dropped her father's limp hand and felt his neck. There was nothing there, but his body was still warm. Molly arranged herself beside him. She placed her palms on top of his chest.

"Molly . . ."

Cole started to say something, to pull her back, but seemed unable.

Molly performed a series of thrusts.

The girl cradling her father's head held out a hand. "We've tried . . ."

"So try again!" Molly yelled. She bent forward and blew into her father's mouth, his lips not cold and lifeless yet. It was those around her that seemed frozen, the dead and the alive alike. They all ground to a halt as Molly began another round of thrusts.

She pushed down and counted, looking at her father's face as she did so, which rocked eerily with her compressions. He looked as if he were merely asleep. He looked so much like Molly remembered him. She wanted him to wake up, to say something, to make sense of the hurricane her life had become. Molly moved to give him more air, but the other girl stopped her. She slid out from under his head, rested it gingerly on the grass, and then bent to do the breaths herself.

As Molly waited, she spotted more crimson by her father's collar. She undid his flight suit's zipper and found, rather than a wound and more blood, a Drenardian headband tucked down by his neck.

Molly ignored it, went to perform another series of thrusts, and then felt her mind spin with wild notions.

She grabbed the band and reached for her father's forehead. The girl seemed to understand; she moved out of the way while Molly arranged the band, working as well as she could with the short length of steel rope between her shackled wrists.

Molly patted her own chest, feeling for the band she'd taken off Byrne's body. She pulled it out as the girl bent for another round of breaths. Molly checked the fabric for any damage from the Wadi's burrowing. She felt Cole's hand on her back as she slipped the band on and spun the seam to the back. The icy hollow in her lungs was matched by a stab through her chest. To have Cole so near after so long—the thought of losing her father—not knowing whether the galaxy was doomed or saved—she forced it all out of her mind and concentrated on a single thought, bringing it to the surface, bright and loud:

"Dad? Dad!"

The universe was a dull thumping. Her own pulse filled her ears, the same pounding she felt in her chest, muffled wails and shouts a background around her, dim awareness of the bright flashes high above as ships bloomed into fire and then faded to nothingness, the last of the melting snow as the great rift closed up in the hazy Lokian sky, even the flutter of the parched grasses, their beady tips waving in a breeze, brushing against one another—

"Mollie?"

She turned to Cole, but her love's cheeks were pulsing as he clenched and unclenched his jaw.

He hadn't spoken.

"Dad?"

"Mollie, is that you?"

She fought the urge to throw herself across his chest.

"Dad, I need you to breathe."

Arms straight, Molly leaned her shoulders over her hands and gave his chest five more sharp thrusts.

"Dad, I need you to wake up!"

"Where are you? Your voice—It's my voice—Is it the bands?"

"Dad, I need you to try to wake up. I need you to breathe, damnit."

Molly fought to keep her words calm. Intelligible. She had to remind herself to breathe as well.

"Oh my sweetest girl, I don't think that's possible. I'm—I'm dying. I can feel it—"

"No you're not!" Molly gave his sternum five more thrusts. The girl with the red hair bent low and gave him more air; her father's cheeks puffed out in a mimicry of life.

"You're not gonna die," Molly thought. She tried to will it true, just like forming loud words out of mere thoughts.

"I already am dead, I think."

"Don't say that—" More thrusts. More air, cheeks billowing lifeless.

"Squeeze my hand, baby girl."

Molly shook her head, and tears leaped off her nose.

She kept her palms on his great chest and heaved down. She watched herself move as if a spectator from some great height. She saw her hands splayed wide, knuckles white from exertion and shock. She saw that the red stain across her father's chest had spread. She felt a wall of rapt eyes arranged around her. The other girl forced his cheeks wide with more air pushed down into his lungs.

"Squeeze my hand."

"Dad—"

"Please. Before it's too late."

Molly stopped her thrusts and checked for a pulse. She ran her fingers along the edge of her father's graying beard, probing his neck for any feeble hint of life. The girl with the fiery hair bent over and turned to the side, hovering her cheek above Mortimor's lips, waiting for a puff of breath. She looked up and met Molly's questioning gaze out of the corner of her eyes.

Set lips said enough.

"My hand—"

Her father's words leaked into Molly's mind, pleading her in her own voice. Reluctantly, she allowed her bound hands to fall from his sternum and her hopeful fingers to retreat from his neck. She clasped her father's hand with both of her own and held it tight. Some distant sense, some numb awareness, told her that Cole was holding her shoulders and crying, whispering her name, his body shaking with sobs.

"There," her father thought. "I can feel it. I can feel you. Oh, how I've longed for this."

Molly squeezed his hand harder. "Come back to me," she pleaded.

"Oh, my sweetheart, I'm so sorry I ever left you—"

Molly shuddered with trapped sobs. Her tears were welling up so thick and fast, the world around her had become a shiny, bulging blur. The only things clear were the words in her head, her father's and her own.

"How long do we have?" she thought.

642

"I don't—Are you still holding my hand?"

Molly looked down where her cream-white hands were wrapped around her father's. She squeezed as hard as she could, holding him as if she could trap what remained of his life and keep it forever.

"I'm holding it, Dad."

"Then I suspect our time is short. I—I can't feel anything."

Molly shook her head. She dropped his hand and went back to his sternum. This time, she didn't bother counting her thrusts. She just pressed and pleaded, shaking her head, tears falling down on him.

"Please don't—" she begged.

"Mollie—"

"Dad, please don't—"

"I love you—"

"Oh, gods, Dad!"

" . . . "

"Dad!"

" . . . "

"Say something!"

" . . . "

"Please—"

" . . . "

Molly stopped pushing on his chest and clapped her hands over her face. She searched the pounding silence in her head for some lingering thought, for some connection, for a single word from her father.

But he was gone. All that remained were the numb echoes of his quiet thoughts, the fading sense of a connection to another mind, and then the narrow rift between the two of them closed up and sealed itself with silence.

Molly cried out. She screamed. She sobbed into her hands and fumbled in vain for that retreating connection. She clawed after it in the harsh and lonely darkness of her own mind. She filled the vacuum of her loneliness with a rage for all that had been taken. And then she shuddered, her hands balled up in front of her, her fists empty of all else, as Cole wrapped her up in gentle and loving restraint. She felt his tears fall on her neck, heard his sobs of anguish and whispered, muted sorrow, all of it mixing with her own.

51

HYPERSPACE

The Bern Seer watched events unfold from her saddle, her eyes pressed tightly against the seeing cups, her lashes flicking across the glass lenses. An annoying rivulet of water snaked through her flight suit, having wormed its way in through her visor. The thin stream wrapped down the edge of a rib and slid out the holes cut in the feet of her suit. Normally, such a stream would tickle like mad, forcing her to squirm in place as she itched herself against the insides of her uniform, but she was too captivated by the sights ahead of her to bother.

Layer upon layer of happenings loomed in her vision, and the bumps in time came fast and furious, swaying her shack, making it difficult to stay on her saddle. She rode the flurries out and concentrated on *seeing*, on allowing her focus to drift near and wide, settling now and then on events in between and watching those play out as well.

Each thread of happenings was like a layer of cellophane with a small vid displayed on it. She had but to shift her focus mentally to tease out one from the other. She could blur a near happening and hone in on a deeper one, or ignore those and look at something more recent. So much to see. The days of long boredom, of unblinking ennui, had been shattered. Now she had so much before her all at once and not enough eyes or time to take it in.

Not enough time, she thought. *In hyperspace.*

A thin smile formed, but then her focus switched to the ships fighting over Lok, to the ferocious charge by the small but powerful fighters from Darrin. They tore through the larger Bern craft, their shields and exotic weapons more than making up for their diminutive size. They buzzed like hornets, but with a controlled and well-timed grace, as one large shape after another exploded into mist.

The small fleet from Darrin suffered its own casualties, though. Every now and then, one of them disappeared in a much smaller pop of debris. The Seer watched as two of the Bern craft turned on their own kind, and she knew these to be the ones with her friends from hyperspace. The shock from this treachery threw the Bern fleet into chaos. Formations splintered. Doubts coursed. More and more craft joined those that had perished down in the prairie, but now the lands of Lok were littered with far more foe than friend.

Looking deeper, the Seer saw the president of the Galactic Union back on Earth. She saw him confused and sleepy-eyed. She could see Saunders waving his arms in explanation, producing sheaves of paper as smoke leaked from a crack in thick blast doors and GU guards moved in to investigate a contained explosion.

Nearer, now, she saw three friends hugging in the ruin of an old building. A crack of light, emitting photons that had streamed past her just moments ago, drifted around them. But high above, the Lokian sky kept moving up like a great zipper to swallow the whiteness. The closing of the rift sliced a Bern ship in half just as it was coming out from hyperspace. The severed end of the craft leaked small figures, their arms waving in the snow-filled atmosphere as they and their craft fell toward the prairie.

And then there was Cole, emerging from the ruin of a downed ship. Cole the brave. Cole, her father. He was carrying a figure the Seer knew would be there, but didn't want to know. It was Mortimor, her grandfather. Cole was crying, and the Seer felt the need to look away. She wanted to, but she couldn't. Some things, some sights, she had avoided for too long. Avoided because such things shouldn't be seen until they had already happened. So she forced herself to watch, taking solace in the opportunity she'd had to tell them both good-bye.

And Molly, flying. Her brave mother, not yet half the woman the Seer would know her to be. Tears were streaming down her mother's young face, even though she did not yet know the full tally of her losses.

Her mother flew with bound hands, with a lifeless pet curled in her lap, with eyes sad and determined. She soared down toward the surface of Lok and all the horror and heartbreak that awaited her there.

And sitting silent at the locus of it all was *Parsona*. Her old ship. Her mom's old ship and her grandfather's old ship. It housed the one person—or *thing*—the Bern Seer had never gotten to pay her dues to. And now she never would.

The Seer suddenly realized she had seen enough. With a glance at the planet of Palan, that blue orb shimmering on its own film of cellophane-like vision, she saw that the time had come. The time had come to put a beginning to all things. She pulled her eyes away from the seeing lenses and returned to her world of utter blindness. Pushing up from the saddle, she slid back along its wet length to the small porch behind, the pounding of the rain on a tin roof loud and near.

With a shudder, the cabin heralded the passing of another event. Old hands gripped the rails, keeping the rest of her steady. With a weariness that can only come from seeing so much, the Bern Seer shuffled her way toward the back of her cabin, the patter of rain on her helmet urging her along.

She stopped by the two trunks on the back porch and sat on the one she never opened. She lifted the lid of the other one and set her helmet inside. As she nestled it in place, she rubbed her hands over the bumps and scrapes, feeling each indention.

Some of the marks were hers, and she remembered them well, her mind and recollection made keen from all the day's activity. Other dents and dings belonged to her mother, and she only had stories to go with some of them. A scratch here from her crash into Glemot. A dent there where she said she'd once gone through a carboglass canopy after some cadet named Jakobs. One deep gash her mom would never talk about, always looking away with tears in her eyes.

In her normal, daily routine, the Seer would next take off the flight suit. She would go to the galloping Theyrls, thank them for their hard work, and then dry off inside and crawl between her sheets. But in a land where there were no days . . . *this* day was different.

She closed the lid before her and rotated around to sit on it. Leaning forward, she opened the trunk she never opened, grasping the lid tightly as the cabin shimmied yet again. Once the tremor passed, she lifted the lid all the way and locked it into place, having to grope for the unfamiliar clasp.

Inside the trunk lay the last hyperdrive Doctor Ryke would ever build. His "masterpiece," he would one day call it. He had rigged it for the Seer's blind eyes: Three simple buttons that could be pressed only in one particular order. She ran her hands along all three, familiarizing herself with them, recalling instructions given so long ago.

First, she said a silent word to her Theryl friends, who had held her and her cabin in place for so many endless hours. Nothing fancy—gods knew she wasn't a poet—just a final thanks and a message of love. She then pressed the first button, setting loose half a liter of special fusion fuel.

There was a series of pops beyond the porch as the animals disappeared, whisked back to Phenos, hopefully for a long and lazy life of idle grazing on warm, dry fields.

As soon as they departed, the incessant creaking of the shack stopped. The vibrations halted. Like a ship turning out of the wind and moving to a broad reach, the Seer's world fell silent while her tiny shack ceased its long fight against a slide into the past. Now it drifted along, moving *with* events rather than be bucked by them, coasting along on the surface of hyperspace.

The Seer pressed the second button, freeing most of the remaining fusion fuel. At first, nothing seemed to happen. There was a delay as the low, flat rift began to open above Palan's solitary continent. Ryke had programmed the rift to iris out for seven hours, gobbling the rains before snapping shut forever. If the hyperdrive was his masterpiece, then *this* was Ryke's crowning achievement, a breakthrough he wouldn't have for many more years. The Seer tried to recall his explanation of how it would work, how hyperspace, by its very nature, multiplied the two keys of life: light and water. She never could appreciate how all the persistent rain and snow of her home came from mere molecules of water and a handful of photons, but she had seen enough strangeness there to take some things for granted. If Ryke said a single Palan rain, falling through a rift opened over its lone continent and multiplied a trillion trillion times would be enough to destroy hyperspace, the Seer was inclined to believe him.

Now that she had pressed the second button—that button she had long agonized over—the Seer could allow herself to feel sorry for the billions of innocents she had just doomed. They would become stranded as hyperspace closed to them forever. There were ships between work and home, fleets along lines of battle, families separated from one another by work or happenstance, people injured in need of a hospital. Soon, hyperspace would be unavailable to them. Jolts of electricity might shock fusion critters in their fuel tanks, but they would no longer respond. The days of cheap, instantaneous travel for most people were over, including for the spreading Empire of the Bern.

The Seer could no longer see their massive invasion fleet arranged throughout hyperspace, but she could *feel* their violating presence. She took solace in knowing that the billions of lives of blood on her hands would also be the undoing of the Bern, the rulers of tens of thousands of universes. She pictured her land, a giant cone, as it filled to bursting with Palan's water. She thought about all the slits, the little tears each of those invading Bern warships had left behind from their jumps into hyperspace. Each one would soon burst open, freeing a shower of frozen water, all of it laced with the Bern's microscopic undoing, the creatures known as fusion fuel. Soon, they would conquer all attempts by the Bern to hem in life and control it. They would free countless *other* galaxies, just as they had ensured the Milky Way and its local cluster would remain too wild to tame.

A sharp pain in the Seer's knuckle disturbed her lapse into dreaming. She was still holding down the second button, her finger trembling under the furious strain. She let go. She reminded herself to breathe.

She wasn't sure how much more time she had. It was a novel sensation after years of not being able to be late, of never having time run out on anything, but now she had so little of it left.

The floods were going to come and take her away.

So the Bern Seer pressed the third button, the one she had begged Ryke to include, the one they had argued over, as neither of them understood its consequences. Not even Ryke and his powerful mind, not the Seer with her all-seeing vision, could tell what might become of it. Still, they saw no other way to protect the past and warn the future, so the remaining fusion fuel disappeared, moving through time and space, taking along what they chose to, or were told to.

In this case, they grabbed a simple silver canister, beat up and dented, but containing a strange and dangerous letter. It was a letter addressed to the very person who had written it, kept safe in a cylinder once used to send messages of peace through hyperspace to the planet Drenard.

The Seer knew Doctor Ryke would find the letter and use his own imparted knowledge to best purposes. He would learn about the end of hyperspace and the need for a handful of rifts stationed throughout the Milky Way, rifts to link major planets like Earth, Drenard, and now Lok. He would also learn not to build too many, about the danger in weakening the fabric of space. He would even learn hints of a *new* type of hyperdrive that would aid travel in strange ways. He would receive the barest tease of formulas his older brain glimpsed brilliance in, that perhaps his youthful mind could fully sort out.

Three buttons pressed, three satisfying clicks, and the Seer's work was done. She was done and tired and ready to go. She stood, legs creaking audibly now that her home had fallen silent, and she considered crawling back into bed to wait for the floods.

But no, she decided, she would go to the front of the cabin instead, back to her wall of tin and her skinny porch. And she wouldn't get in the saddle or take her helmet with her. She would go and stand there, stand in the rain with no protection at all. She would raise her arms and wait for the floods to wash away the wicked.

And she would go gladly.

PART XXIV

THE CIRCLE CLOSING

"We are born into this universe.
We live, we play, we war in it.
And over time, it changes us."

~The Bern Seer~

52

FREE

"This is it?"

"Yeah."

Cole peered out his porthole at the maze of canyons below, at the web of black traces and the tan marble like the latticed skin of a Callite.

"How can you be sure?" he asked. "They all look the same to me."

"Trust me," Molly said. "This is the one."

She lowered *Parsona* into the dead-end canyon, aiming for a bank of shade long enough to reach the cargo bay and keep them out of the sun. The ship's struts met the hard rock and settled under the pull of Drenard's gravity.

"Be careful," Parsona said through the radio.

Molly didn't reply. She unbuckled her harness and left the cockpit without bothering to wait on Cole.

"I'm coming too," Cole yelled after her. He shrugged his harness off and hurried to catch up.

"Here." Molly handed him a set of egg graspers as he entered the cargo bay. She kept a set for herself. Neither of them wore any of the rest of the Wadi gear, their flight suits comfortable enough in the shade. Molly stomped down the cargo ramp and into the eerie howling of the windswept canyons. Cole watched her click the graspers nervously as she went.

"You've gotta talk to me about what's going on," Cole said, running up beside her. "How do you even know these eggs need rescuing?"

Molly pointed toward one of the Wadi tunnels at the base of the high cliff and started off toward it. The sight of the large tube, big enough to crawl inside, sent a powerful numbness through Cole's knees. He remembered his ordeal in just that sort of cave not so long ago. He hurried after Molly, his fears about her deep depression taking a new and more severe turn.

"Molly—"

She ducked her head inside the cave, one hand resting on the upper lip of the smooth hole in the marble. She turned and looked back, her face veiled by a shadow on top of a shadow.

"The Wadi told me," Molly said flatly. "I saw this place in her mind as if I were here. I saw the eggs, what the other Wadi did to her, and what we need to do right now."

With that, she turned to the darkness and stepped inside.

Cole fumbled in one of his pockets for a glow-stick. He cracked it back and forth and then hurried in after her, shuffling along on his knees and knuckles, his egg graspers in one hand and the feeble glow-stick in the other. Molly moved ahead of him as if she would've slid through the pitch black even had he not joined her.

They crawled for dozens of meters, past holes in the floor and drips from the ceiling. The green light from the stick would fade, Cole would work it back and forth, and a bit more soft glow would keep the cave barely discernable. When Molly stopped, Cole bumped into her, his knuckles scraping on the rough rock.

"Oh my gods—" Molly breathed.

Cole held the glowstick aloft.

"I didn't realize they would be this big," Molly said. She moved to the side to allow more of the light to pass, and Cole felt goose bumps surge up his arms when he saw the objects on the other side of her. There were at least three of them that he could see, nestled against one another and halfway reaching the roof of the cave. The colors and patterns were remarkable, even muted by the awful green cast of his glowstick. The shells of the eggs seemed to dance and waver like the skies outside. They were big enough that a fully grown human could pop out, which had him worrying about what was inside of them, and how safe this "egg canyon" really was.

"Hey, Molly, I think we need to reconsider this."

She looked back at him and brushed some loose strands of hair off her face. She bit her lower lip and nodded.

"I think you're right," she said. "I think we're gonna have to free them right here."

"No," Cole said, shaking his head. "That is most definitely *not* what I meant."

"Give me your knife," Molly said. She leaned on one palm and stretched her other hand out to him. Cole's lightstick ebbed a little, dimming the light in the tunnel.

"Molly, we need to pause for a sec and talk about this—"

"Give me your knife," she said again. Her voice had not risen nor modulated, but Cole felt himself succumbing. The past weeks had been full of one attempt after another to soothe Molly's hurts. He knew there was no denying her this, not after what they'd gone through to get permission to fly out there unescorted.

He reached back, pulled his knife from his ankle holster, and placed it hilt-first into her palm.

Molly situated herself in the tight confines, wedging her back against the side of the tunnel, her legs folded up beneath her. She gripped the knife with both hands and slammed its point down into the shell of the massive egg. There was a solid thwack, like an axe on wood, but nothing more. She looked over at Cole as she reared the knife back once more.

"In my vision, I saw a Wadi claw doing this." Molly struck the egg again, harder this time. It left a mark, and she pulled the knife up for another blow. "I don't think the moms sit on them. I think they guard them, and then they do something like this right before they die."

She hit the same spot, and a series of cracks appeared, fanning out from the impact. Molly ran her finger over one of the cracks, feeling it. Cole held the glowstick closer, but he was searching Molly's face. There was a grim determination, a profound sadness there that he wanted desperately to break through. He had high hopes that this day, this mission she had spoken of for weeks, would do her some good. He was suddenly worried that nothing ever could.

"I think it's trying to help," Molly said.

Cole moved the light and redirected his attention. Something seemed to stir beneath the colorful shell. Molly scrambled to the next one, the knife attacking with vigor.

"We need to hurry," she grunted between blows.

Cole extended the glowstick over the first egg to help light up the next two. He watched the creature inside the egg move like an amorphous shadow. Between Molly's blows, he could feel something striking the egg beneath him, but from the *inside*.

Molly moved to the last egg. "We don't have much more light," Cole warned her. He worked the plastic back and forth, but his efforts did little. Molly struck the egg's shell, her palm flat on the back of the knife's hilt, both arms driving as hard as they could. She rubbed the cracks in the shell and whipped her head around to face Cole.

"Go," she said.

Cole turned and went. He left the graspers behind and threw the glowstick ahead of him, crawling toward it on his palms and knees. When he reached the stick—barely glowing now—he scooped it up and tossed it farther ahead, repeating the process until the light of the tunnel's mouth came into view.

Behind him, something shrieked, a high and piercing wail that surfed down the skin of solid rock all around him. Cole looked over his shoulder for Molly. He stumbled forward, away from the blackness and toward the growing light. The peals of something newborn and powerful shot out again, the voices overlapping and resonating now that there was more than one of them. Cole scrambled the last few meters, dove for the edge of the tunnel, fell out to the shaded rock beyond, and rolled to an aching, sore stop. He looked back to the hole in the cliff. The screams came in triplicate now. Molly tumbled out after him.

"C'mon," Cole yelled.

The shrieks from the tunnel mixed with moans from the canyon walls, the combination causing Cole's heart to race. He reached for Molly and tried to pull her toward *Parsona's* open bay, but she darted out of his reach and moved up against the cliff face to one side of the cave. She waved Cole over to her side, her arm wheeling in fast and tight circles, beckoning haste.

Cole dashed over, obeying. He took up a spot between Molly and the mouth of the cave, shielding her with his body. He felt her hands on his shoulder, on the side of his ribs. Her arms were trembling, but not with fear. He looked back to see the barest of smiles on his love's lips, a sight that nearly erased the terror of the approaching screams and the harsh clack of claw on solid rock.

Cole put his arms around Molly and held her close while the awful sound grew and grew.

The first Wadi shot out of the cave in a shimmery blur. It shot out and kept moving, its feet not touching the rock, its body not falling toward the floor of the canyon. There was the leathery pop of fabric flapping straight in the air, and then a graceful curve up into the canyon winds.

"What the flank—?"

Cole traced the soaring flight of the Wadi as the next blur whizzed by to join its mate. The wings popped straight, the breadth of them several lengths of a man, and up the creature went, its colorful scales bursting with brilliance as it left the shade and met the light of the twin stars above.

Cole turned to Molly, wondering if she knew about any of this. He felt his own mouth agape as her hands clutched his flight suit with a renewed vitality. He turned and saw her looking up at the two circling Wadi, a wide smile on her face, tears welling up in her eyes.

"So beautiful," she whispered.

Cole wrapped his arms around her waist, his hands resting on her hips. They watched in silence as the two animals spiraled up on great, unflapping wings, catching the strong Winds of Drenard. They forgot about the third Wadi until its head emerged beside them, its claws gripping the edge of the cave.

The sudden presence startled Cole, but Molly remained calm. She moved around him and stepped closer to the animal as it extricated itself from the tunnel and unfolded its wide wings.

Molly reached out, her palm down, her fingers extended as if to touch the Wadi, but she didn't move any closer. Cole watched as she stood there, arm outstretched, eyes closed. It was like watching someone communicate with a red band on. Her face flashed with emotions, and tears that seemed not for sadness rolled down her cheeks.

Cole waited, transfixed, while the two seemed to share something between them.

After a moment, the Wadi strode forward, two large wings extending from where most Wadi bore ancient nubs. It bent low to the stone, flexed its spindly legs, and then threw itself up in the air with a shuddering leap.

The wings did the rest, catching the perpetual winds of Drenard, powering the animal up and into the bright light, soaring high to circle mightily with its newborn brethren.

53

UNIONS

Anlyn Hooo stood before the clockwise gate of the great Pinnacle. If she imagined Drenard's thin habitable band as a ring, this was the jewel on top, the meeting place for the Great Circle, walled off from the winds and filled to bursting with the flora and fauna of the Milky Way's lusher worlds. A haven for life, the Pinnacle forever stood as a reminder to the Circle of what they fought for.

Two ornate gates led through those high stone walls, one entrance on each side of the ring. Anlyn surveyed one of those gates, collecting herself. She could feel her heart fluttering with some unknown alloy of nerves and excitement. She could hear the trill of cloudswifts from beyond the walls, their high-pitched laughter seeming to beckon her inside. She was only dimly aware of the guards to either side of the gate, standing at attention and awaiting her signal to open them.

Anlyn considered the unthinkable event she was about to step into, the forbidden joy hidden deep within those tall walls. As she pondered the occasion, she became mutely aware of her escorts standing to either side of her. The significance of the moment washed over her for quite some time, and when the sensations ebbed, she remembered that people were waiting on her. So she rallied her nerves, stretched herself to her full height, and nodded to the gatesmen.

Oiled hinges and perfectly balanced steel swung silently open. Anlyn grasped her outer tunics, held their edges off the stone walk, and stepped through the arch of the clockwise gate and into the great and gorgeous Pinnacle.

The colors and vibrant hues immediately assaulted her senses.

Anlyn saw that the Pinnacle had been draped in its finest celebratory regalia. The predominant shades were orange and blue, customary wedding hues symbolizing the union of hot and cold and serving as a temporary celebration of each. But there were other colors mixed in: the bright yellows of hope, the black of peace, even the purple of empire. It seemed every banner, bunting, and flag from a hundred settled worlds had been gathered on Drenard and raised for the occasion, even though Anlyn doubted Ryke's rifts would be abused for such a trifle as her.

As she wandered into the full splendor of the bountiful decorations, Anlyn felt herself purple in embarrassment at the ostentatious show. It was a lot more than she had expected for such a simple affair, especially since her union remained controversial for so many; she knew it was still whispered among her people with sideways glances. Anlyn turned to Molly and her Aunt Ralei—her two chosen bridal escorts—to gauge their reactions to the festive gardens.

Molly was smiling from ear to ear, a welcome sight to Anlyn's eyes. Her dear friend had done her best to feign happiness the past weeks, trying not to chill Anlyn's warmth, but Anlyn could forever sense that a deep ice had taken hold of Molly's heart. Watching part of that coolness melt, seeing her friend's eyes flit about, her cheeks blush as Molly struggled to take it all in—it was enough for Anlyn to justify the ludicrous lengths the decorators and gardeners had gone to.

Anlyn looked next to her Aunt Ralei and saw that the elder statesman was ignoring their surroundings.

669

Her eyes were fixed solely on Anlyn, her face beaming with pride.

"It's a bit much for a wedding," Anlyn said.

"Nonsense," her aunt replied. "And it's more than just a wedding. Two empires celebrate this day. Think of it as a *galactic* union."

Anlyn smiled and nodded. She loved the analogy. She turned, and the trio of women set off down the adorned walkway, heading counterclockwise around Drenard and toward the Pinnacle.

As they entered the path of reflection, the three women had to fall into a single file, the blooming bushes and bursting flowers pressing in on either side. The walk was measured out to take four hundred and eighty steps, and they were to be walked in silence. It was a time for meditation and for dwelling on the upcoming promises to be made.

Anlyn lost herself in the path of flowers, her bare feet trampling the thick petals sprinkled over the stone walk. She reveled in the garden's lush elegance, the feeling of the Horis' reflected light warming her skin. She closed her eyes for a few steps and felt as if floating in a dream-like state of perfect contentment.

When she opened them, she noticed for the first time the crowds of women lining the path ahead of her beyond the four-eighty mark. So many! A dozen deep, they crowded the bushes to either side, pressing together and clutching bouquets or holding aloft video recorders. Anlyn felt her cheeks tighten, her lips quiver. The silence of the reflection walk became unbearable, the looming crowd positively vibrating with stifled energy. When Anlyn reached the end of the sprinkled petals and walked her last step of silence, the crowd of women erupted, cheering and waving and throwing flowers and paper-thin Wadi shells painted all sorts of bright colors.

Anlyn felt a stream of tears course down her face. She was awed at the sight of so many eyes directed her way and twinkling with their shared joy. The roar from their throats rang in her ears and lifted her up, making her feel light enough to soar up to the Horis. She wanted to take them all with her, wanted to run to each of the women, throw her arms around them, and celebrate together.

The Drenardian women kept up their cheers all the way to the grand steps leading up to the balcony. Wave after wave of renewed jubilation soared all around the Pinnacle, sustaining itself on the infectious quality of an excited crowd as confetti, petals, eggshells, and birds vied for airborne supremacy.

At the steps, a contingent of the royal guard stood at arms, saluting her. Anlyn scanned their faces and saw a few she recognized, including the young captain who so briefly had barred her and Edison from the Circle all those sleeps ago. She gave him the barest of nods, and he smiled, exuding obvious relief at the kind acknowledgment.

At the top of the steps, Anlyn had to pause and catch her breath. The sight of what awaited her stole the air from her lungs: All along the Great Balcony, stretching off in both directions around the low circular Pinnacle, stood a dense collection of the empire's mightiest. Circle members, planetary regents, entire lines of the royal lineage—they were all gathered and dressed in their heaviest and most colorful tunics.

So much status gathered in a single place caused Anlyn to reflexively bend her knees and bow her waist. Without even thinking, she found herself scooping up her outer tunics and lowering herself to the ground, her eyes falling to her lap. Out of the corner of her eye, she saw Molly repeating the gesture. No sooner had she succumbed to the weight of so much power and authority, Anlyn became self-conscious of her humble position and stood.

When she looked back to the crowd packing the Great Balcony, she found every one of its occupants had fallen to *their* knees.

Anlyn dropped her tunics and fought back the tears. To receive the blessings of so many—and for such an unorthodox union—her cheeks hurt from trying to hold it together. It was too much. A military

672

victory had bled over to her personal ceremony, carrying with it the exultation of an end to war. It was too much and also too wonderful to bear.

Anlyn suddenly felt herself glow in anticipation, positively radiating purple as the trio made their way through the circle of shade cast down from orbit. The ensuing coolness was symbolic for something—something about having left the heat behind—but her brain was too overwhelmed to seize upon the ritualistic meaning. She stepped through the great old doors of the Pinnacle and another crowd erupted, and again she was overcome with emotion. There he was, across the building, walking through the counterwise door on the far side of the pinnacle:

Her Edison.

Large and handsome and bedecked in the finest honeycloth tunics. Even across the great distance of the bowl-shaped building, Anlyn could see his broad teeth spread across his face. She fought the temptation to run to him. She concentrated instead on each step as she descended toward the Circle below.

Behind her, Anlyn heard the high-ranking guests from the Great Balcony file down after, all of them eager to become part of her retinue. She looked up from her careful steps and glanced to either side at the thick crowds standing among the benches. Thousands of blue faces were turned in her direction, silent and expectant. Anlyn had anticipated a fraction of their number; she had been embarrassed to even hold the ceremony at the Pinnacle. She looked up and saw that the balcony was packed as well, and again she found it difficult to breathe.

Across from her, she could see Edison struggling to match her slow pace. He took each plodding step one at a time, his foot extended and hovering over the next tread as he waited for her to catch up. Anlyn nearly burst out laughing, and she silently thanked her love for again keeping her grounded. For the rest of the descent, she kept her eyes on him and remembered just why they were there—and how lucky she truly was.

As they reached the end of the long flight of steps, Anlyn and Edison stopped at the circular table while the most honored guests filed down from behind and took their seats. Anlyn noticed the ambassador bridge had been set up on Edison's side. It was sometimes referred to as the treaty or peace bridge, reserved for the signing of great documents, royal affairs, and the occasional wedding. Ahead of Anlyn stood the original bridge, its ancient wood still speckled with blackened spots from the day, not too long ago, when Edison's lance had erupted, and her speech had paved the way for all else that had occurred since.

Anlyn began dwelling on the significance of that day, but her drifting thoughts were startled back into focus as the Pinnacle bells tolled. She glanced back at Molly, who stood dutifully to her side and behind her a pace. Anlyn's aunt reached out and squeezed her shoulder. The members of the Circle bowed and took their seats, their dozens of tunics rustling like distant thunder.

Anlyn looked across to Edison and nodded. They both began to ascend the steps of their respective bridges, which reached over the unbroken circle of the great table. At the top, they turned and bowed to the gathered. They next faced each other and bowed again. And then they descended into the center of the circle, each of them walking out to occupy one of the two spots of light shining down from above.

For Anlyn, it was the Light of Speak from Hori I, the same light that had bathed her during her great speech. Edison took his place a few meters away in the Light of Turn from Hori II, the same light he had given to her in order to conduct the speech. Anlyn smiled up at Edison and received an even bigger grin in return. She sighed at the sight of her love's fur, neatly groomed, as it shimmered in the concentrated starlight. The two of them stood alone in the great circle for a few breaths. Past Edison, Anlyn could see Cole and her uncle, the Empire's King, standing on the far side of the counterwise bridge. She knew without looking that Molly and her Aunt Ralei would be doing the same behind her.

She paused a moment, gathered in a deep breath, and attempted to take it all in: the rapt throng of spectators, the warmth of the light of Hori, the seated circle members. She scanned the great table and saw that Edison's chair and her own were draped with honor cloths. She saw Bodi's empty chair, and a brief pang of undeserved sorrow fluttered through her. His disappearance was still a mystery, and the trial that had exiled him had thus been mostly symbolic. She noticed there was no mourning cloth draped over his seat, so she assumed she was alone in her pity. She continued around the circle and came to Dani, Tryl, and even Bishar from the Great Rift. She saw Ryke, Ryn, and Scottie, and the girl with the burn-red hair. They were all smiling at her, and she felt her cheeks cramping with joy.

As the ringing of the bells subsided, the minister of ceremonies rose from his seat and ascended the bridge behind Anlyn. She turned to watch.

"Current and future Drenards," he bellowed. "Welcome!"

The crowd erupted, cheering for the sheer joy of cheering—cooing and clapping and stomping their feet. The minister waved them down, taking quite some time to do so.

"Today we celebrate much, including the union between two of our Circle members, two of our finest Drenards, and two heroes of the Bern War: Lady Anlyn Hooo and Lord Edison Campton!"

He paused and scanned the crowd while he waited on another round of cheering to subside. Finally, raising his hands, he chanted: "Gifts presented, promises made, lights divided, two become one." He dropped his hands and nodded down to Molly and then looked across in Cole's direction and nodded to him as well.

The minister made his way down the steps and into the circle. Anlyn watched with pride as Molly rose up the steps behind him. She admired her friend's choice of all-white tunics draped in modest layers. The two friends smiled at each other—both seeming on the verge of laughing as Molly approached. Anlyn glanced back over her shoulder to get a look at Cole, who was wearing dark green tunics, and wearing them nobly. Cole bore Edison's lance in both hands. He handed the large device to Edison, who received it with a slight bow. Anlyn turned back to Molly, who held out a small cloth bag for her to take. Breaking decorum, Anlyn accepted the bag and then pulled her friend into an embrace, pressing her head against Molly's shoulder.

The cooing and sniffles from the crowd assured Anlyn she wouldn't be thought of poorly for the slight break with tradition. She pulled away and turned to face Edison as their two witnesses, Cole and Molly, took their places to one side. High above, a chain began rattling down from the domed ceiling, signifying the start of the wedding ceremony.

Edison spoke first: "My gift to you is this lance," he said in Drenard, his voice booming and filling the Pinnacle. He held it out level, his palms flat. "Power turned to peace, harm transformed into harmony, electricity made electrifying. I give it as a symbol of what your own tinkering has transformed within me."

Anlyn smiled, flushing with pride. Edison stepped out of his light and walked over toward hers. He bowed low and gingerly laid the lance at her feet. After he returned to his circle, she held up the bag Molly had given her with one hand and opened her other palm beneath it. Slowly, she tipped the bag on its side. The crowd bristled with anticipation at what her gift might be.

Out of the bag fell a dull, normal, alloy of metal. She held it up between her fingers and showed it to Edison. "My gift to you is this broken circle," she said.

The crowd stirred, the strangeness of the gift sending waves of taboo through a people that idolized the perfect and the round, the harmonious and the unbroken, the shape of their great, ringed world.

Anlyn ignored them and continued: "This is the link you weakened to set me free."

She watched as tears spilled out of Edison's eyes and rolled down his furry cheeks. She fought back her own tears and struggled with the rest: "It was my bondage, and you broke it. It was my slavery, and you slayed it. You took out a piece, and then you made me whole."

She walked forward, set the dull, gapped hoop of her slave chain in his light, and then returned to her own illuminated disc.

"I promise to love no other for all the cycles," Anlyn said as the loose end of the shivering chain descended between them.

"And I promise to earn that love each moment," Edison replied.

The chain stopped a meter from the ground, and the minister stepped forward with the prism. He ceremoniously attached it to the end of the chain, bowed to Edison and Anlyn, and then exited the circle. Anlyn watched him go and caught a glimpse of Molly, who was standing behind her. Tracks of tears were on her friend's cheeks, a smile on her lips.

High above, the chain rattled as it began to spool back up. Anlyn looked at her feet, waiting for the pool of light to move. As the prism ascended over Edison's head, the two lights quivered and then began to come together. Anlyn and Edison walked with them, shuffling forward, urging the process along. The moment the edges of the two circles of light touched, the crowd erupted yet again. Anlyn and Edison stepped into each other's arms as the discs became one. They embraced while the prism above was hauled into the overlapping illumination of the two stars, spreading the rays in a glory of hues that made even the residents of that planet, with its eternal sunrise, shiver.

Outside, bells began to ring.

They were followed by the thunder of peaceful explosions.

0 0 0 0

When Anlyn pulled free, she noticed everyone around the circle was standing and stomping their feet, the boom of their approval mixing with the distant cannons. To her side, Molly and Cole were embracing as well and smiling at each other. Anlyn reached for Edison's lance. She was tempted to set it off one more time, showering the celebration in sparks, when her uncle's voice, the voice of the king of Drenard, interrupted her over the Pinnacle's amplified speakers:

"My people! Attention, please!"

It seemed to take several minutes for those gathered to heed their king. He rose to the top of the clockwise bridge and waved the crowd silent. "My people, we have more to celebrate this day than a marriage between two mere individuals. We also celebrate a union between two empires long at war." He turned to face the crowd behind him. "We celebrate the stability along both our boundaries that keeps us safe from our true threats. We have learned to distinguish friend from enemy, not letting appearances guide our hearts."

The king bowed and descended into the circle. The crowd applauded politely, but they were obviously annoyed at having the joyous occasion interrupted by talk of politics. Anlyn smiled at her uncle as he walked toward them, the shiny fabric of his royal tunics shimmering in the colors cast by the hanging prism. He rested a hand on each of the newlyweds' shoulders and beamed.

"Relationships are like alloys," he said. "The perfect mixture is stronger than either alone, but they are weak while being hammered hot, and are fragile if overly cooled." He turned to the audience. "The alloy of human and Drenard will forge the sharpest of

Wadi hooks, but we will need guidance on how best to wield them. That's why I want envoys to travel to Earth and foster this new relationship."

The king smiled at Anlyn, who was having a hard time processing what he meant through all the metaphor. Was she being exiled to Earth?

"My wife and I are to be those envoys," her uncle said. "We know better than any the cost of our wars and the price to be paid." The king reached down and lifted the hem of his outermost layer, his royal cloak, and pulled it over his head. The crowd reacted with coos and whispers. The king turned to Anlyn. He held the cloak open and nodded to her.

Anlyn found herself swimming in a dream. The lights danced through myriad colors as the crowd sucked all the air of the Pinnacle deep into their lungs. Her uncle nodded again, and Anlyn lowered her head, her mind fluttering and dazed. She felt the heavy honeycloth sink to her shoulders, wrapping her with its weight. She looked up to see her uncle holding the front edge of the garment off the ground for her, the back of the tunic dragging behind.

"It has been too many cycles since the peaceful sex ruled the land," her uncle said quietly to her. Louder, he said: "The empire is yours."

Whatever the crowd had left, they let it out. The entire Pinnacle shook from the foot stomping and shouts. Anlyn felt the vibrations from all that noise fluttering against the heavy cloak. She could feel it thrumming in her heart. Edison grabbed her hand and led her forward. He escorted her on a slow stroll around the interior of the great table, a stroll through a dancing rainbow, while he presented to a people his new wife and their new queen.

Anlyn's uncle, the former king, watched them from the center. After a pause, he bent down and scooped something off the ground. It took him a moment to figure out the modified trigger, but once he did, he set one end of the old weapon on the ground and activated it.

Edison's lance erupted in the Pinnacle for the second time, throwing up a glory of sparks and a ringing hum that would one day become legend.

54

PROMISES

Cole weaved through the raucous crowd of the reception party and tried his best not to spill the two overly full drinks. He looked around for Molly, but it was hard to locate any one person in the wedding celebration. Anlyn and Edison were being seen off on the Drenardian version of a honeymoon, and it seemed that everyone on three planets had to take a turn dancing with each of them before they left.

He bumped into Dani, and rather than practice his rough Drenard with the old interrogator, Cole simply yelled Molly's name over the din. Dani squeezed Cole's shoulder and steered him around. He pointed through the glass and out toward the balcony.

Cole felt relieved to see her away from the crowd and hurried out to join her, admiring as he walked the spectacle of the Drenard sunset in the distance.

"Hey, sweetheart."

Molly turned and smiled—a welcome sight he was gradually getting used to seeing once again. But he also saw something stirring beneath the guise, some lingering pain that needed addressing.

"You okay?" he asked.

"Huh? Yeah. Just thinking."

"I know that look. You're doing more than just thinking. Here." He handed her a glass.

"Thanks," she said.

He took a sip from his own. "Do you want to talk about it?"

Molly shrugged. "I don't know."

"Just missing him?"

He held his glass to his lips, waiting on her reply, knowing by now how best to discuss her loss.

Molly shook her head, no longer trying to conceal her dour mood.

"Walter?" Cole asked, still fishing.

Tears fell across Molly's cheeks, but she shook her head again. "No. Not until you brought them up." She forced a laugh, wiped at her cheeks, and then took a sip from her glass and looked out to the horizon.

Cole stepped by her side and Molly leaned against him, allowing him to wrap an arm around her shoulders.

"I'm prying, aren't I?" Cole asked. "Am I trying too hard? Last time you said I wasn't trying hard enough."

Molly pressed her temple against his shoulder. "You're fine, I promise. I—I just haven't gotten a handle on this new feeling."

They stood together and sipped the watered-down Wadi juice for a moment.

"How about that parade?" Cole asked, trying to change the subject.

Molly laughed softly and rested her glass on the wide, flat railing before them. She looked into the distance. "Do you remember dreaming of something like that back at the Academy?" she asked him.

Cole laughed. "Yeah, but we always talked about *licking* the Drenards, not joining them." He took a sip of the gingery, lemony drink, the foreign taste adding to his ironic sentiment. "And the parade was always in New York," he said. He lifted his glass to the perpetual sunset before them. "Not anywhere like this."

"Oh, I'm sure they're having parades there as well," Molly said. "I bet Saunders is standing on top of some float as we speak."

Cole studied Molly's face while his love peered into the sunrise. The wavering and colorful lights did magnificent things to her eyes.

"Is that what's got you down?" he joked. "Has seeing one of your Academy fantasies come true ruined your cheerful mood?"

Molly pinched his side as he went to take a sip, causing him to spill Wadi juice down his new tunics.

"Hey!"

"Sorry," she said, smiling.

"I know what it is," Cole said, dabbing at the juice with his napkin. He looked up and gave her his most evil grin.

Molly shook her head.

"Yeah, I do. You want a wedding like Anlyn's, dontcha? You do! You totally want me to sweep you off your feet and give you a sappy gift and cry and go on a vacation!" He taunted her while absorbing her playful blows.

"Not anymore, I don't!"

Cole looked through the transparent barrier around the balcony and raised his glass. "That's what it was," he said.

"No," Molly said, her voice suddenly serious. "I think it was the confetti. It was all the joy in the crowd."

"All the *joy's* got you down?" Cole scrunched up his face.

Molly turned to face him. "It's the idea that the war is over and everyone's safe. How can everyone feel that when the Bern are still out there and some of them are probably still among us? How long before people grow suspicious of one another, or they find some other way through to our galaxy?"

"Drenards, you sure know how to wreck a party."

"I'm serious, Cole."

"I know. I wish you wouldn't be. Look, you're right, but we've lived with those things lurking for years and years. And besides, Ryke seems pretty sure the Bern won't be a problem in the next universe."

"That's a long time from now," Molly said. "What about until then? How many people, how many alien races we've never heard of will suffer until then?"

Cole looked out at the shimmering colors beyond the horizon. He imagined he saw a black silhouette flying out there somewhere. "Gods, Molly, I don't know. What do you expect you can do for them?"

"Nothing," Molly said. She leaned her head against Cole's shoulder. "I think that's where this new funk is coming from."

Cole kissed the side of her head. "And that's what I love about you," he said. "Always demanding the impossibly good out of everything, especially yourself."

Molly lifted her shoulders. "But what if we could *do* something?"

"Like what? I mean, think of the scale of what you're suggesting. You're talking like we could march on Mount Olympus and knock the gods on their butts. Everyone else seems to think we've done enough to wall off our corner of creation, and I happen to agree. We have entire galaxies to safely explore. We have billions of years to foster peace. And when the universe wraps around on itself and starts off again, life is gonna spread in a way even the Bern won't be able to control." Cole laughed. "I mean seriously, we totally kicked their asses, right?"

He stopped laughing as Molly refused to join in.

"You're serious about doing something," he said.

"Of course I am," Molly told him. "I don't want to live in fear of them. I want to throw that door open and shine a light in the darkness. I want to spook them before they spook me."

"And I love you for that, but what's wrong with living our lives out and being happy and just letting things take their course? What long-term impact are you hoping to have that will justify risking the completely nebular next century we could have together?"

"I give you two weeks, mister, before *you're* the one itching to cause trouble."

"Fine, but I'll be convincing you to surf the Palan floods or to basejump through Ganji or something like that. I won't be hankering to take on some pan-galactic empire that sounds as if they're eventually doomed anyway."

Molly looked up at him. With that look. The same one she'd given him on Drenard over a month ago. The look that back then let him know they were going to escape the alien planet, eschewing a comfortable existence to try to end a war that was too big to contemplate denting. She gave him that look once again, and he found himself wilting.

"All right," he said.

Molly smiled and threw her arms around him, sending Wadi juice down his back. "I love you," she said. "More than you'll ever know!"

"On three conditions," Cole said.

Molly pulled away. "Which are?"

"We won't leave this galaxy until we're thirty, so you have to give me a dozen years of awesome bliss just living together and not trying to start any trouble with alien races."

Molly smiled and nodded. "Twelve years," she said. "I can handle that. What else?"

"You have to let me take you someplace special for our honeymoon."

"Okay," Molly said. She continued to nod, and then her head snapped up to gaze at Cole, her eyes wide, her brow wrinkled in confusion. "Wait. Our *what?*"

"Third condition," Cole said, sinking down to one knee . . .

Made in the USA
San Bernardino, CA
20 May 2019